The

Island

Harp

The
Island
Harp

Jeanne
Williams

AN AUTHORS GUILD BACKINPRINT.COM EDITION

AN AUTHORS GUILD BACKINPRINT.COM EDITION

Published by iUniverse.com, Inc.

For information address:
iUniverse.com, Inc.
620 North 48th Street, Suite 201
Lincoln, NE 68504-3467
www.iuniverse.com

Originally published by St. Martins Press

Design by Dawn Niles

ISBN: 0-595-09582-8

Printed in the United States of America

For Gary McCarthy
and his clan

Foreword

The first man who, having enclosed a piece of ground, bethought himself of saying 'This is mine', and found people simple enough to believe him, was the real founder of civil society. From how many crimes, wars, and murders, from how many horrors and misfortunes might not any one have saved mankind, by pulling up the stakes, or filling up the ditch, and crying to his fellows: 'Beware of listening to this imposter; you are undone if you once forget that the fruits of the earth belong to all, and the earth itself to nobody'.

—J. J. Rousseau, A Discourse on the Origin of Inequality

I went to the Western Isles or Hebrides in search of Brighde, ancient goddess of fire who metamorphosed into Saint Brigid. I found her ancient hearths at Skara Brae and saw her follower, the red-billed oyster catcher, on rocky beaches from South Uist to the Orkneys. Magic as all the islands were, the one that touched me most was the Long Isle, Lewis and Harris. With a small group led by Sandy Mitchell of Strathpeffer, I walked moors and mountains, rested in flowery hollows out of the driving wind, smelled the peat smoke in an old black house of the kind Mairi and her folk lived in, gazed in wonder at the Callanish stones which looked like hooded ancients, sailed out to the Shiant Isles where we were greeted by seals and clouds of sea birds, and visited weavers, including the only one still carding her own wool and using native dyes.

On South Uist, we stayed at the farmhouse of Ewan and

Kirsty MacDriskoll, which adjoins the fragrant machair that runs down to the sandy beach strewn with egg-shaped white stones which I thought were surely Brighde's. The MacDriskolls are crofters of a far more prosperous sort than their ancestors, but they still lift peats and burn them for fuel. On our last night, there was a grand ceilidh with neighbors and harvest workers in to dance and sing till dawning.

It was at some small shop on Uist that I discovered the book that begot my own, John Prebble's powerful *The Highland Clearances* (Penguin, Middlesex, England, 1969). After that, I looked at the black-faced sheep with different eyes, and wondered what stories were hidden in the crumbling walls of abandoned black houses, so called because they were laid up without mortar.

Most of us know of the Irish potato famine but few realize the potato blight had just as cruel an effect in the Highlands and Islands of Scotland. Even fewer have heard of the brutal Clearances that scoured thousands of crofters from lands held by their families for centuries. Perhaps because these uprootings went on for a hundred years and were carried out at different times by different landlords, there's no accurate count of how many were forced to the slums of Glasgow and other Lowland cities or compelled to emigrate to Canada, the colonies that became the United States, and Australia. Three hundred here, two or three thousand there, these wretched folk were driven out of their homes to make room for sheep and for huge deer forests which could be very profitably leased. Certainly, many Islanders chose to seek new lives over the ocean, but hundreds of others had their roofs burned and their walls leveled.

Many islands remain unpopulated to this day. But Gaelic is still spoken and there are many island families that survived the evil days, fought for their ancient rights, and are proud of their heritage. Many times, I've written of emigrants to the American West, but this time, I longed to tell the story of those who stayed, who lived on seaweed and shellfish between the rocks and the sea, and who finally triumphed.

A good many of the books I needed aren't available in the States and were ordered through Tam MacPhail, who has an excellent bookshop in Stromness, Orkney. Mr. MacPhail was very helpful in tracking down and recommending useful works.

I owe a great deal to Moris Farhi of London, who diligently searched for out-of-print books and also sent me volumes I wouldn't otherwise have had.

All published by John Donald Publishers, Edinburgh are: *The Making of the Crofting Community* by James Hunter, 1976; *The Scottish Gael* by James Logan, Volumes I and II, 1976 reprint of 1876 volumes. *The History of the Highland Clearances* by Alexander MacKenzie, first published in 1883 and reprinted in 1986 by Melven Press, London, was written by a man who watched the horror and tried to move the government and lairds to help the people. *The Western Islands of Scotland* by W. H. Murray (Eyre Methuen, London, 1973) is an excellent overview containing much natural history which was supplemented by many specialized small publications bought locally in the Islands, and by F. Fraser Darling's classic *Natural History in the Highlands and Islands* (Collins, London, 1943). *The Clans of the Scottish Highlands*, with wonderful paintings by R. R. McIan and text by James Logan, was first published in 1845 and 1847 and is now available in a 1980 edition from Pan Books, London. Byron Farwell's *Queen Victoria's Little Wars* (Harper, New York, 1972) tells how Highland regiments fought all over the world to expand Great Britain's empire. *Folklore and Folksongs of South Uist* by Margaret Fay Shaw (Aberdeen University Press, 1986) is a treasurehouse of waulking songs, other songs, proverbs, and customs. I. F. Grant's *Highland Folkways* (Routledge and Kegan Paul, London, 1961) is a trove of lore and facts, delightfully told. *Living the Fishing* by Paul Thompson (Routledge and Kegan Paul, London, 1983) provides a humanized picture of the industry. *Tales and Tradition of the Lews* collected by Dr. MacDonald of Gisla (published by Mrs. MacDonald, Stornoway, Lewis, The Hebrides, 1967) is a treasury of history, economics, folklore, and memoirs.

I wish I knew the names of the gentleman and ladies who joined our ceilidh one night at the Harris Hotel. He played the Northumbrian pipes. One lady played her Celtic harp and the other sang "Over the Sea to Skye" and tried to teach us some Gaelic songs. Wherever they are, and to all the folk of the Western Isles, *Slainte!*

—JEANNE WILLIAMS
Cave Creek Canyon
The Chiricahua Mountains

The

Island

Harp

1

The lochs on the Black Moor of Lewis flashed blue sky, sun and scudding fluffs of cloud on this bright August afternoon as Mairi MacLeod and Catriona Nicolson came from the shieling, the beehive-shaped stone hut where the cousins had made cheese and butter while the township's cattle and sheep grazed in the summer pastures. Now it was nearing autumn, time to reap oats and barley, time to bring the animals home.

Formidable as it was on somber days that deepened the brooding expanses of peat bogs, the moor was far from wasteland. As well as providing grazing land in grassy hillocks and hollows, early in summer it swarmed with families cutting peats that now dried beside cuts patterning the moor with squares, circles and lines, some grown over with grasses, yellow bog asphodel, bog myrtle and spongy sphagnum moss. Deep purple bell heather and hummocks of ling were courted by humming bees and drifting magpie moths and butterflies, dark green, white, peacock and tortoiseshell. Downy white fluffs of cotton grass were not only pretty but made soft pillows and mattresses and fairly good wicks for the fish oil lamps.

The peat almost everywhere was at least as deep as a tall man's height and often thrice that. Beneath it was clay, "skinned earth," where, with seaweed, sand and hard work, arable soil could gradually be formed. When food was scarce, Mairi's grandmother would nod and say, "There's the fine peats whatever else we're lacking, and God be thanked for that." Then grandfather, in his voice that roared like the sea, might retort, "We cannot be eating peats, woman!"

"Fearchar," Gran would soothe. That was what she called grandfather, dear man, and so did the children. "The fire shines warm and lovely. If you'd give us a song—"

And he would then, the white-maned man, Michael MacLeod, tough and weathered as his blackthorn staff, gentled by Rosanna's voice and smile as he had been all the years since a pretty young widow had persuaded him to give up an exciting life of smuggling whiskey to farm her croft. He would sing and play on the *clarsach*, the small harp brought long ago from Ireland, where the black or red willows grew large enough to make the best sounding boards.

The *clarsach* had belonged to an ancestor bard who'd played at the court of Conn of the Hundred Battles but in spite of its legendary past, the children regarded the harp almost like another grandparent and indeed it had a name, Cridhe, which meant Heart. Young ones were never scolded away from it where it stood draped in the MacLeod plaid, green and black with narrow lines of red and blue. The tightly woven wool protected the harp from smoke and dampness though the children knew they must never touch it without first scrubbing their hands.

"There's oil even in your wee fingers," Fearchar said, "and that's bad for Cridhe's strings." He taught them all to play but only Mairi found that music could express feelings she could not put in words. She would never be able to play like Fearchar, though. When his hands wooed Cridhe, she answered his touch with mellow tones that filled the house with magic, songs of love and battle, songs of the sea and birds.

The neighbors, hearing, would come in, the other two households of the dwindled township of Aosda, gathering around the hearthstone in the middle of the single long room. Red-haired Andrew Nicolson, Fearchar's cousin and Catriona's father, would tell stories in spite of the perpetual frown of his scrawny dark wife, Morag. She had reason now to worry, poor woman, for her youngest sons, Lucas and Paul, had gone to the army of Victoria, the English queen, as had Mairi's brother, Calum. The eldest Nicolson lad, blue-eyed fair-haired Barry, was still at home with his gentle, golden Sheila. He would contest with Adam MacNeill, thin and graying, to see whose jokes won the most laughter. Adam and his wife, Kirsty, with their three-year-old twins, flame-haired Brigid and Rory, were the only folk in Aosda who weren't related. Mairi, with her younger brother Tam, and little sister, Eileen, had lived with their grandparents since their father drowned and their mother died in childbed a few months later.

At these gatherings or ceilidhs, Mairi and Gran served round a brew flavored more from the peat in the water than from a few precious leaves of tea, but it was steaming and warmed the insides. From their byre at the lower end of the house, the cows listened as if the tunes made their sparse cuds juicier, and though Mairi's belly often cramped with hunger when she crept into the box-bed she shared with Eileen, she had seldom gone to sleep without music, some laughter, and Gran's blessing of the banked fire on the stone.

This hearth-stone, originally called a heart-stone, had been the center of their family's home from time out of mind, before the harp left Ireland, maybe even before the peerie or Pictish folk or those who raised the stones where Gran took Mairi for Midsummer sunrise in spite of what the minister said. They were all Christians but the old faith lived within the new one just as Brighde, the ancient Celtic goddess of fire and poetry, had merged with Saint Brigid, revered as the nurse of Jesus and hence very powerful.

Getting the peats that year hadn't been easy. Fearchar's back pained him too much for the digging and Calum was off with his regiment. Calum hadn't been recruited with a guinea and a kiss from the laird's lady in the fashion of some landlords raising levies for the Queen's wars. Once clan chieftains had counted the swords of their clansmen as wealth and rent, but since the breaking of the clans after Bonnie Prince Charlie's defeat at Culloden in 1746, even chiefs who hadn't lost their lands seldom lived on them but preferred the excitement of Edinburgh, Glasgow or London. That kind of high living took money.

Some lairds sold their estates outright to men who had no ties to their tenants. All over the Highlands and Islands, landlords saw that sheep were more profitable than farmers and refused to go on renting to families that had lived in the same place for hundreds and hundreds of years. Some tenants were driven out even though their rents were paid, others were evicted the next time rents were due. The island of Lewis was owned by Mrs. Stewart MacKenzie, daughter of Lord Seaforth, but her husband was Governor of Ceylon and they had spent little time on Lewis. Mr. MacKenzie had died last year, in 1843, and it was rumored that his widow wished to sell the island. Meanwhile her agent dealt with her factor on Lewis, Hugh Sinclair, who carried out the agent's instructions.

So Calum had taken the Queen's shilling for the promise of Mrs. MacKenzie's factor that his family could stay on their croft so long as the rent was paid—and paid it was, with tweed Mairi and Gran wove on the loom, with fish smoked by the peats and butter and cheese. It was time to pay it again, this autumn of 1844, but Hugh Sinclair had given his promise so surely the township of Aosda was safe.

Some of that fine butter and cheese that paid the rent was in the creel Mairi carried effortlessly though it was piled high with bedding, utensils and other gear needed for the six weeks while the cousins lived in the beehive-shaped stone hut and tended the township's twelve sheep and nine cows. Mairi thought her family's cows the sleekest and prettiest: Sholma, red with a white face, followed by her brown-spotted calf, and Rigga, dun with a broad black stripe running from nose to tail. This was the fattest they would be till they grazed the shieling next summer, and they exuded contentment as they ambled along, switching their tails.

4

Mairi, too, was full of well-being, rapt in the beauty of the moor, proud of the cheese and butter she was taking to her family. It was a sort of holiday at the shieling. After tending to their dairy chores, the girls could wander the heath in search of crowberries, nap among nodding blue harebells, and laugh and talk with the freedom of the young far out of earshot of their elders. Of course they had knitted and braided heather twine— at least Mairi had—but much as she loved her family, time at the shieling was delightsome, a change from the usual round of work. It must have been even more so in the days Gran remembered, when instead of three households, the township numbered a dozen, and whole families went together to the summer pastures, driving sheep and cows and horses. There were no horses in the township now and the empty homes of those gone to America or Canada or Australia were used as byres or barns. But when Calum got home from the army, and Catriona's brothers Lucas and Paul returned, oh then Aosda would surely flourish again.

Catriona, as she often did, was staring toward the sea. His Viking, Fearchar teasingly called her, driven to hanker after distant places and new things; Mairi was his Gael, loving her home island. "I wish I could have gone with Calum," Catriona said, almost scowling.

The long thick braid of her hair was the gold-brown of ripe barley and her slanting eyes were tawny. Though she was only a few months older than Mairi, who had turned seventeen in May, Catriona was curved and beautiful while Mairi knew that people called her pretty only because her red-brown hair was waving and lustrous, her skin smooth and fresh, and her smile ready. From the brass-framed mirror Fearchar had given Gran in his smuggling days, Mairi ruefully learned that her nose was too long, eyebrows too dark and heavy, her mouth too large, and her jaw too strong.

A *too* kind of face altogether it was! Her eyes, at least, were acceptable, a gray so deep they looked green, thick-lashed and wide-set. As for her figure, a childish boniness was starting to round and before long she should be passable—so long as she didn't stand too close to Catriona.

Mairi sighed. No wonder Calum had begged Catriona to wait for him till he had served his time. Since they were third cousins, there was no bar to their marriage but Catriona was so impatient that Mairi sometimes wondered if this cradle friend of hers would manage to wait for her betrothed.

"Do you suppose Calum's found another sweetheart?" Catriona asked now. "A year he's been gone! What do you suppose those Afghan women are like? Do you think they're pretty?"

"I hope he never finds out," said Mairi. "From his letter, the Afghan women carve up any wounded soldiers they come across."

Catriona shuddered. "How can you joke about his being wounded?"

"I'm not joking, Caty. But when you dream up such silly things—" Mairi broke off, shielding her eyes as she stared at a dark haze in the distance. "That's smoke!"

The girls exchanged frightened glances. Maybe a roof had caught. If that were so, by the time they got there the fire should be out or spread past remedy, but they put off their burdens, propping the creels against each other, and made all the speed they could, leaving the cattle and sheep to come at their own pace. For ease in walking the moorlands, their skirts were already gathered up by woven bands passing between their legs and attached to a belt, and they raised them higher yet, splashing through the bogs in their desperate hurry instead of seeking a drier way.

Breath sobbing as she flew up a slope, Mairi froze at the black-edged flames devouring the peat-smoked thatch of the houses. Even thatch remaining on the abandoned huts was ablaze. A keening reached her, wails and screaming.

Disbelieving her eyes, Mairi saw a man thrust a brand to the last dwelling, her grandparents', while other men forced back women whom she recognized by their clothing. There was Morag Nicolson, Andrew's wife, holding to her daughter-in-law, Barry's golden-haired Sheila, whose first baby should come any day. Kirsty MacNeill's Rory and Brigid clung to her skirts, and tiny Gran struggled to keep Fearchar away from their house. The two Nicolson men and Adam MacNeill were still away at the summer's fishing.

Gripped by the nightmare, unable to move, Mairi gasped, "Fearchar!" as he wrenched free of Gran and ran into the house. What could be left in there precious enough to risk his life? Cridhe, the harp! That must be it. Her grandfather's danger broke Mairi's paralysis. She sped down the slope, frantically, uselessly, calling his name.

How could they be driven out when the rent was paid and they had assurance from Hugh Sinclair, the factor, that they were secure in their tenancy because Calum had gone for a soldier, and Lucas and Paul also? How could it be?

Fearchar staggered out, clothes and white hair blazing, rested Cridhe on the ground, and fell beside the clarsach. Gran and the others beat out the flames with their skirts. Sheila caught fire. Morag forced her down to roll on the earth. Blood engorged Mairi's eyes and ears as her legs pumped wildly yet seemed not to move.

At last, she fell on her knees beside her grandfather. One hand, scorched black and bleeding, fell to the turf, slowly going limp. Gran held his head, imploring. "Dear man! Michael! Oh, dear man!"

He didn't look like Fearchar at all, snowy hair frizzled to the seared skull, mouth crookedly agape. The burners gathered to stare down at him. "Must be it was his heart stopped," said a burly young one defensively. "He's not burned bad enough for mischief."

Mairi sprang to her feet. Choked with rage and grief, she hurled herself on the man, gripping his throat, clawing at his jugular. When the others finally dragged her off, his neck was streaked with bloody grooves and he was gasping. He retreated, arms up before him, cursing. Mairi's teeth met the bone of another man's arm.

A buffet stunned her. There was blackness. Then, as strong arms raised her, she thought dazedly that Calum was home, Calum was here. Somehow he'd set things right . . .

But it wasn't Calum's voice, or any voice she'd heard before, that came deeply from the chest against which she lay. "What are you about, Mr. Sinclair?" the voice demanded in Gaelic, a better Gaelic than the minister spoke though the accent was different from that Mairi heard daily. "Has war been declared on women and children and old men?"

Wincing at the throb in her head as she opened her eyes, Mairi recognized the factor standing above her, black-bearded Hugh Sinclair with his beefy red face and thin lips. His hard black eyes slid away from the man holding Mairi.

"It's their own blame, Captain MacDonald, sir. I gave them writs of eviction last month. A fortnight ago, I warned them again. They wouldn't go peaceably so I had to fetch the constables."

"The rents are paid!" Mairi cried, sitting up. For the first time, she saw the face of her rescuer. Lean it was, and long, with sun-darkened skin taut over cheekbones and cleft chin. Lines at the corners of his eyes, straight nose, and firm, down-curved mouth showed that he wasn't young but there was no thread of gray in the black hair that fell in an unruly wing across his forehead.

Swept out of herself by grief and fury, Mairi seized his arm. Distraught though she was, her weaver's sensitive fingertips noted that the wool of his coat was soft and fine. Captain, Sinclair had called him, but he wore no uniform, only gray trousers and coat with a shirt of white linen.

A short distance away a blond youth held a gun and a brace of red grouse. She understood then. The stranger was from one of several hunting lodges the MacKenzies leased to gentry who came here for deer-stalking and salmon fishing.

What would this gentleman care about the troubles of tenant folk? Yet there was no one else so she did not let go of his handsome coat. He would hear her though others of his class

8

would not, and though he would soon forget, for wasn't it gentlemen like him who'd cleared off tenants in their thousands to make room for sheep?

"Our rents are paid," she said again, determined that at least one of the gentry should hear though she yearned to run to Fearchar, fall across his body, and howl like a beast. *Fearchar, Fearchar, we'll hear your songs no more! But Cridhe will remember them and so will I!*

Looking into the gray eyes of the stranger, even in that extremity, Mairi thought he had to be a man who laughed more than he frowned. She fought to control herself and speak coherently. "When Mr. Sinclair here did come to enlist our young men for the regiment, he promised that their folk could bide on their crofts. And 'twas plain enough what he meant otherwise— that if they stayed as they would rather have done, we'd be served the writs. Without that promise, never would my brother and cousins have gone." Her voice cracked. She swallowed and spat out her accusation. "Now Mr. Sinclair comes with constables and torches and clubs while even the few men left to us are off at the fishing!"

Letting go of the stranger, she got to her feet, swimmy-headed yet advancing on the factor in a manner that made him fall back. "God's curse on you, Hugh Sinclair." The voice did not seem to be hers. The words came of themselves, acrid as peat ash in her mouth. "And the devil's, too, and that of the Old Ones of the Stones. May you sleep sound no more and eat no more with relish and may what you have done this day come on your own head."

Paling, he fell back. "Curse all you've breath for, girl," he said gruffly. "I only took back Mrs. MacKenzie's land which is hers as Lord Seaforth's daughter."

"By right, as you well know, the land belongs to the clan, the seed of Torquil the Viking which we all are," Mairi cried. "To begin, we chose each new chief for wisdom and valor. He was our father, the *ceann-cinnidh*, and he lived among his *clanna*, his children and kin. Even after the chieftainship began to pass from

9

father to son, the land was still the clan's. By right, it should be so still.''

"Daft talk makes naught," scoffed the factor. "Lord Seaforth bought Lewis in 1825 for £160,000. It was his while he lived and when he died years ago, it passed to his daughter, Mrs. MacKenzie. Before the rents fell due this month for the next year, I served the writs as her agent instructed me. This land would be more profitable for sheep. Flit you must."

"We have lived here always!"

"Always is finished."

Mairi's wrath ebbed into overpowering grief for Fearchar and dread for those lamenting around him, despair at the smoking, flaming roofs. The burners had tossed belongings outside, chests, stools, clothing, webs slashed from looms, a broken spinning wheel jutting from a heap of bedding. Scant and worn from use, but things that had made a home.

"You burned the box beds," she said, aghast at such waste on a treeless island. "And the roof timbers!" These were driftwood and strong sound ones were hard to come by.

Sinclair shrugged. "You could have had them if yon old man hadn't been stubborn. In spite of that and your cursing, I'm a merciful man. I'll buy the cows and sheep at the going price."

"We need them ourselves." Mairi answered instinctively for her whirling mind could not take in the immensity of what had happened. She glanced at the weeping women and young ones crouching beside Fearchar.

Gran, huddled with his head in her lap, knew only that her dear man was dead. Morag was praying. Catriona wept. Kirsty huddled with her twins and Sheila, heavy with child, pressed Fearchar's limp hands to her streaming face. He was the chief of this small clan. Perhaps he would rather be dead than see this ruin. The township—it was no longer a township, of course, since it had no land—had lost so much that it seemed sure to Mairi that they must hold to what remained.

"We will keep our beasts," she said.

"Where will you graze them?" Sinclair demanded. "You have no land, nor can have."

"Then what are we to do? Throw ourselves into the sea? Swim to America or Australia?"

"Swim or fly, it's leave the island or bide on the rocks of the coast and live by fishing." Sinclair spread his thick hands and Mairi had a glimmering that he did not like this task and liked it less now that a man had died. "Lass, it's not the grand life you've led here, half-starving sometimes, scraping to meet the rents. Best beg or borrow the £3 a head it'll take to get you to Canada and start fresh. Or go to America where they do say rich good land's to be had just for the living on it."

"Since my grandparents were bairns, they have watched family and friends go away forever," said Mairi. "Of our township, three households were left of twelve."

"You are still too many," said the factor doggedly. "It's not your pitiful rents a proprietor needs, but pasture for sheep."

"Then we will live on the rocks."

Captain MacDonald spoke suddenly. "Mr. Sinclair, having dispossessed these people, you will now see that their goods are conveyed to the lodge. They will shelter there till their men return and they can decide what to do."

Sinclair's jaw dropped. "But sir, captain, the MacKenzie agent would not allow that, and a bad example you're setting—"

"I pay enough for my lease to have such guests as I choose." The captain's tone allowed no argument. He turned to the abashed constables. "Rig a litter and carry the old man to the lodge."

"No," said Gran, rousing to look up though she still held Fearchar's head in her lap. "He would rather be buried in sight and sound of the sea. This night we'll watch with him, one night only instead of two as it should be, and tomorrow we'll take him to the graveyard. The minister must be told and surely the men of the next township will come to bear the coffin."

"They will not," said the factor. "They had the sense, when

I brought their writs, to take themselves off in orderly fashion. From the sale of their beasts and goods and money sent from a relief society in Canada, they last week paid their passage and sailed for there." He added more gently, "But I will tell the minister. He'll find men to carry your man to the kirk."

"Not strangers." Gran moved her head back and forth but her voice was surprisingly vigorous. "We'll carry him ourselves if must be. And a coffin he'll have if it takes every stick left me."

"There will be a coffin," Captain MacDonald assured her. "But, good woman, it helps nothing to stay the night by these ruins. Let your husband be brought to the lodge."

"I thank you, sir, but this has been his home since I nagged him into giving up the sea. It would be pure kind of you surely to give the rest shelter, especially Sheila."

"I'll stay with you," said Morag, "for indeed a proud, haughty man like Michael MacLeod needs more than a night's praying."

Gran's blue eyes flashed. "Go on with you, Morag Nicolson. Whine your prayers where I can't hear them! 'Tis the harp my Fearchar will have this night, if you will play it, Mairi."

"I will play." Mairi looked at Cridhe for the first time since the horror. The plaid that had protected it trailed on the grass but the strings, though smoked, seemed intact. She moaned, though, at seeing a crack in the soundboard. Perhaps she could daub it with wax; besides, Gran's ears were no longer keen. Maybe she wouldn't hear a difference in the music.

Helping Sheila to her feet, Mairi embraced her. "Go with the captain, dear." Past Sheila's smirched white cap, Mairi sought the MacDonald's eyes. "What of our animals, sir?"

"If there's a problem about their forage, I will settle with the agent," the captain said, cutting off Sinclair's protest. "But, lass, can't you persuade your grandmother to hold the wake at the lodge? It's a grim night and grim place for you two to be alone."

Gran said nothing but held Fearchar as if he were all the world. Mairi controlled a shudder at the smoldering wreck of what had been Aosda. There was not even a roofed byre where they could shelter.

"We aren't alone, but with my grandfather," she said though she couldn't keep a tremor from her voice. "Only Captain Mac-Donald, if tomorrow you will send a coffin—"

"I will, and men to bear it."

"We will do that ourselves."

"Three miles to the kirk and two more to the graveyard?" he asked with a significant glance at Sheila, who could scarcely support herself. When Mairi stared at him, he sighed. "I will help and you cannot refuse, for I'm in your brother's regiment and you must let me take his place." He nodded at the fair young man who held his gun. "Jamie, too, serves in the 78th Highlanders, so he also has a right."

Mairi didn't want Fearchar's burying to be the death of Gran. After a hesitation, she nodded. "We will thank you then for taking my brother's and cousins' places."

Hugging Eileen, she bid her help herd the cattle and sheep. The women, the constables, even Sinclair, the captain, and his *gille*, began gathering up the jumbled heaps, stuffing smaller things into creels and baskets, bundling clothing and bedding into rolls.

"I'll send for the rest," said the captain. Catriona and Morag went back to fetch the creels left on the moor and soon only two women, a dead man, and a harp remained in the smoking debris of what had been a homeplace since time out of mind.

2

Mairi and her grandmother washed Fearchar in water from the spring before they dressed him in his best linen shirt and the kilt and MacLeod shoulder plaid. He'd inherited these from his grandfather who'd worn them in the terrible battle of Culloden.

That had been in 1746, almost a hundred years ago. The Highlanders were defeated with Bonnie Prince Charlie, slaughtered on the field, jailed, executed, or sold to American plantations. The heel of the Sassenach, the Saxon, ground the clans into the dust. Bagpipes and arms were outlawed, the power of chieftains shorn away, and for thirty-six years it was a crime to wear kilt or plaid. When the hated "Unclothing Act" was repealed in 1782, hidden garments appeared again but by the turn of the century Highland dress was seldom seen except on lairds who wished to look romantic at Edinburgh balls or London gatherings. Fearchar, though, vowed a kilt was the best garment ever designed for wading brooks and tramping through wet heather. He always wore it when he was walking far because if night overtook him, he had only to unfold the six pleated yards of the kilt and wrap himself in it. In cold weather, he dipped it in water and wrung it out, swelling the threads to better turn the wind.

He would feel no wind that night nor ever again at all. "Let us save the plaid for Calum," Gran said. "The kilt is ample for a shroud. And we'll make your bed of blooming heather, dear man, dear man."

Mairi cut armfuls of bell and cross-leaved heather, raising a sweet-smelling bier on which they laid Fearchar, wrapped in his tartan with his face uncovered. Gran tied up his jaw and crossed his hands on his breast. This time of year, days were still long but it was dusk when as carefully as if handling a baby or a person frail with age, Mairi cleaned Cridhe's strings and sound board. As soon as she could, she'd smooth the crack and try to fill it but for tonight she prayed it would not greatly affect the music. After she had washed her hands, she sat on a rock beside Fearchar, tuning the harp by turning the pins with the ancient silver key that still glowed with a sapphire though Cridhe's original precious stones had long ago been sold and replaced with crystals.

Gran took a place in the heather, holding her husband in her arms. A scent of clover and a hundred other blooms came with the sea breeze from the small stretch of *machair,* earth rich with shell sand that lay between the beach dunes and the township's croplands. Oats, barley and potatoes were thriving, fruit of much toil with the *cas-chrom* or "crooked foot" and copious dressings of seaweed.

Who, now, would harvest them? And without them, what would the folk of Aosda have for their food that winter? For that matter, where would they be?

If Mairi lived, she would be on the island. To keep from weeping, she began to sing from Ian MacCodrum, a bard of Uist, who lamented his people's ruin seventy years before.

> Look around you and see the gentry
> With no pity for the poor creatures,
> with no kindness to their kin . . .

She played on, recounting their life together, telling her love and loss. Sometimes she choked and could only speak through Cridhe. Sometimes her voice rang wild with anger and sorrow, but then she remembered how he'd loved the merry tunes that set feet tapping as Cridhe seemed to laugh, and she slipped into these, playing till the cushions of her fingers were raw and ended with her grandfather's favorite drinking song.

> Up with it, up with it, up with it!
> Down it, down it!
> From me, from me, from me,
> To me, to me, to me!
> May all your days be fine, my friend.
> Drink it down!

Gran was so still that Mairi thought her asleep. They had not eaten, Mairi not since morning, and though it seemed unfitting to be aware of such things, her belly cramped. Morag had left them some bannocks and meal and a kettle for boiling water. Did peats still smolder on one of the hearthstones?

Draping Cridhe with the scorched plaid, moving quietly so as not to disturb Gran till their scant meal was ready, Mairi made her way to the house.

With massive walls and heavy thatch, the houses were warm and snug and the fiercest winds couldn't be heard inside. *But, oh Fearchar, this cruel storm rose and we did not hear it. The hearth is open to the sky and will no more warm humans or beasts. The thatch smolders on floor and walls and the bed is burned where you and your Rosanna made with your loving my father who died at sea and his three brothers who fell in the English war against Napoleon. The grace was that they weren't forced, like some Highlander regiments, to drive out their own folk to "improve" the lands for sheep.*

Embracing the stones of the entrance as much as leaning against them, Mairi wept till her eyes felt hard and dry. The roof still smoldered where it had fallen on the box beds and in small, fitful blazes fanned by the wind. By this tainted light, she saw the grinding quern and, with a rush of thankfulness, saw that peats still smoldered on the hearth.

16

Their glow was like a promise, a covenant made when her forebears raised the Stones to mark the waxings and wanings of the moon, the ebb and flow of the fruitfulness of Nature. Even on barren rocks above the sea, the hearthstone would make a center for a new home.

And there, Fearchar, she promised, *Cridhe will sing your songs. Folk of your blood will live on this island after the lairds are gone, the sheep flocks and the hunting gentry. We were here before they came; with your songs, we'll outlast them, win back our land.*

Heartened by the resolve though she had no idea of how to carry it out and refused to place hope in Captain MacDonald— was he not gentry, too?—she built up the fire and set the kettle on. There was not even a leaf of tea but peat gave the water a flavor and its heat should comfort Gran.

As Mairi located the bannocks in a basket left outside, her fingers closed on an unfamiliar object, smooth and metallic. A flask. And beside it were several packets. The captain had left them. She uncorked the flask, sniffed, and took a wee nip to confirm that the pungent fragrance was indeed that of mellow whiskey.

That, now, would ease Gran's bones, she thought with relief. A distiller herself in the old days when the Crown's taxes had made the legal drink prohibitive in price, Gran knew and appreciated *uisge-beatha,* the "water of life" that came from malted barley. One of the packets contained raisins which Mairi knew because Calum had once brought her some from Stornoway. Her brother may have treated his mates to a drink or two after the fishing season ended, but like the other fishermen of Aosda, he'd spent most of his shillings on his family's needs after he'd paid the curer who furnished boats and supplies at a cost that more often than not left them in debt to him. Calum brought tea for Gran when he could, treacle toffee or sour plum sweeties for Eileen and Tam, a ribbon or trinket for Catriona and a treat for Mairi. Once this had been raisins.

These of the captain's were sweeter, plumper and chewier, but Mairi stopped with a mouthful which she chewed slowly, relishing the taste. Boiled, they would plump out and make the hard bannock tastier for Gran. The other packet contained some kind of strange dried fish. A restorative gift altogether and for herself, Mairi was too famished and for Gran, too concerned, to disdain the captain's leavings.

The water reached a boil. Mairi filled the cups Morag had left in the basket and added good dashes of whiskey, the most in Gran's. The raisins went into the remaining water and almost immediately sent up a tantalizing smell.

Shivering in a wind grown stronger and colder, Mairi shielded Gran's cup with her hand and carried it to the bier. Rosanna MacLeod hadn't moved, bowed over Fearchar whose head still rested in her lap.

"Gran, love." Mairi spoke in her softest voice so as not to startle her grandmother. "Here's a drop to warm you and there's a tasty bite simmering in the kettle. Take the cup, do, love, and I'll fetch the bannock and goodies."

Gran didn't stir. Mairi briefly considered urging her inside the walls which gave some protection from the blast, but she doubted Gran would leave Fearchar and also dreaded the effect on the older woman of seeing her home destroyed, its familiar coziness turned to smoldering desolation.

Kneeling, Mairi coaxed Gran to lift her head and set the cup to her lips. Gran coughed, then took a deeper sip, savored it a moment and took the cup in tremulous hands. "Ah, the velvet of the *uisge-beatha,*" she crooned. "The finest I've ever made. Smooth as a kitten's paw with the claws tucked in, Michael will call it and it's a brave price he'll get for it when he makes the run to Glasgow town, flaunting his arse at the excise-men, poor gormless Lowland creatures! Mayhap after this run he'll bide content at the croft."

Why, she talked as if it were forty years ago! Mairi's scalp prickled. Then she remembered that Calum had once been stunned in a fall and it had been a good fortnight before he remembered who he was or where. Small wonder if Gran's mind rebelled at Fearchar's death and slipped back to when they were courting and life promised brightly. Even without the smuggling, there'd been good money paid for gathering and burning the kelp needed to fertilize the fields of England during the almost seventy years when that the embattled country had no other supply. Kelp once brought the owner of Lewis £8,000 annually and a kelper could earn £8 a year compared to a laborer's £1 and 40 pence or a skilled dairywoman's 75 pence.

Folk had been valuable then. Those pushed to poor land by the sea to make room for black cattle suddenly earned good wages and multiplied. But after the wars with France when that country again supplied fertilizer and great deposits of potash were found in Germany, a ton of kelp that had brought £22 during the war with the American colonies dropped to £2 and by 1825, the trade all but ended. The mischief was that except for growing potatoes, people had almost given up farming and fishing to work in the kelp and there were now many, many more mouths to feed.

Herring failed around 1830. Three years later, when Mairi was six, her father was lost at sea as he searched to fill his casks. A strong, blue-eyed, auburn-haired man he had been, always with a kiss and a joke for his daughter. His body never washed ashore. A few months later, his wife died giving birth to Eileen, who was now ten. Tam, who'd gone to the fishing this year for the first time, was twelve.

Neither Eileen nor Tam remembered how potatoes rotted in the fields in 1835. In that year of starving, eight-year-old Mairi had gleaned shellfish from the beach and collected the kinds of seaweed that could be used for nourishment. It was then that nine households mourningly left Aosda.

So if Gran's bruised spirit fled back to the happy days, why try to recall her to this time of woe? Gran said briskly, "I'd fancy another dram, Mairi love, and this time spare it the water." She stared down at Fearchar and slowly shook her head. "And is it my poor father's wake we're having? Belike I've already drunk

19

too much yet my throat is awful dry. Where is Eamonn, child? My father loved him best of all his grandchildren. Eamonn should be here, showing respect."

Mairi's heart stopped and the chill fingering her bones was more than the sea wind. Eamonn was her father's name and Mairi, her mother's. It was eerie for Gran to speak to and of those long-dead parents whom Mairi remembered with a rush of longing and bitter loss. She was glad she could remember them, though, as her younger brother and sister could not. Still, if believing she mourned her father was easier for Gran than accepting Fearchar's death, the delusion was merciful.

"Eamonn's at the fishing," Mairi said, taking the cup. "I'll bring your whiskey, dear, and a bite to eat."

While Mairi devoured a bannock, Gran ate hers with the plumped raisins and shared a bit of the fish before she sipped the whiskey. Sighing deeply, she said, "Aye, but my eyes are heavy, lass. Will you watch with father for a while?"

"Be sure I will, beloved. I'll fetch you a cover."

"Why are we out here?" Gran asked with sudden sharpness. "Why are we not in the house and father laid out decent on the table?"

"There's been a fire. The thatch burned."

"So a new roof's to be made along of father's burying," Gran said, shaking her head. "But we must smoor the hearth fire anyway for 'tis bad luck for it not to last till morning." She tried to rise and fell back. "Give me your arm, child. That whiskey goes down smooth as honey but it's 'mazed my poor head."

Mairi helped Gran up, praying that the ruins wouldn't jar her into the present. Gran winced and mumbled about her rheumatism but when she gazed around at the embers that winked from the thatch, she only muttered, "Well, thatch do burn sometimes, and it's a pity, but my Michael's a good hand at the thatching. He and Eamonn will soon have us snug again."

The ordeal of getting another roof over their heads, or even a place to raise it was something Mairi couldn't think of yet though she must before long. It could be weeks before the men came in from the fishing. Kirsty, thank goodness, was reliable but Morag's back ailed her so that Catriona and Sheila always carried Morag's creels of peats, seaweed, oats and barley.

Catriona, how would she take this? She had often hoped aloud that when Calum returned, he'd take her to Stornoway or Inverness or Glasgow, even America. Mairi couldn't imagine Catriona being willing to undergo worse privations to cling to the rocks of the island.

Too overwhelming to worry about now. Kneeling beside Gran, Mairi tried to concentrate on Gran's nightly blessing of the fire. Thriftily putting aside the larger peats, Gran raked the embers into a circle in the middle of the ancient stone with a small raised heap in the center.

"In the Name of the God of Life," Gran said as she set the first peat touching the raised center. "In the Name of the God of Peace," she blessed the second. Placing the third, which finished dividing the embers into three parts, she said, "In the Name of the God of Grace." Then, covering the coals with ash, she stretched out her hand and as she and Mairi bowed their heads, Rosanna MacLeod blessed the hearth of her ruined home.

> Thou holy Three, Mary, Christ and Brigid,
> Save, shield, surround this hearth,
> this house, this household, this night,
> and every night. Each single night. Amen.

Her voice failed at the ending. Like a small child, she permitted Mairi to wash her face, brush and plait her white hair and wrap her in a blanket on the turf beside her husband with heather for a pillow.

Mairi didn't know whether to hope she would wake in the bleak present or in the past, where, though death came, life still held hope. But at least for now Gran slept.

Exhaustion suddenly, completely overtook Mairi. Wrapping in her shawl, she curled against Gran to warm them both, meaning to rest for just a little while. Strange, but she felt as if the captain were near, watching over them, and though that was foolish, it was comforting.

Gentry or not, he was a strengthening man. He had known just what to leave for Gran. Even the small amount of whiskey Mairi had sipped now curled warmly in her, and she soon slept sound.

3

"Drink this."

Mairi blinked and sat up, at first not knowing the thin dark face and then feeling as if it had always been in the back of her consciousness like one seen in a haunting dream. Something warm and vibrant passed between them as if lightning had left the sky to pulse here in lovely golden waves.

Gran muttered and stirred. Shamed that she could respond to a man while Fearchar lay close by, Mairi took the cup reluctantly but strength revived in her as she drank the steaming, fragrant tea. The captain turned and went to where the yellow-haired gille was busy over a fire.

Gran was waking. Would she still think they were burying her father? Mairi dreaded Gran's return to reality but it seemed wrong that Fearchar should be robbed of her mourning. Even so, he would be mourned enough.

Straightening her garments as best she could, Mairi pushed back her hair and went to the fire. "May I have a cup for my grandmother?"

"It's for the both of you," said the captain. His eyes swept her keenly. "It's good you slept but I think you haven't slept enough. Your grandmother, how is she?"

Mairi explained and he nodded. "I've seen it when someone's badly wounded. A soldier may deny for weeks that he's lost an arm or leg though he can see and feel the stump. In your place, I wouldn't try yet to make her understand."

"Gran's lost more than her arm or leg. She's lost her heart."

The angles of his face sharpened. After a moment, he said, "If they were that fond, they had more luck than many a lord and lady."

Mairi cried fiercely, "Will you say because they were loving it doesn't matter that they were oppressed?"

"No. Only that they were blessed if their hearts cleaved together as well as their bodies. But you're too young a maid to understand."

Even with her world destroyed around her, it stung that he thought her a child. Hadn't he felt what she did, that radiating flame? It sprang from their closeness, she was sure of that. But perhaps that happened for him with many women? Perhaps, to him, it was nothing special. "I know what's between men and women," she said, lifting her chin to face him for he was tall though sparely built. " 'Tis naught for shame be there loving and all decent."

"Loving and decent," he repeated, chuckling irrepressibly, though the mirth didn't reach his eyes. "You *are* young, lass. As an aging man of thirty-one, let me warn you that the two don't always march together."

She turned her back on him and carried a cup to Gran who was trying to sit up. Cradling her, Mairi coaxed her to drink but Gran insisted on putting her hair up under her ruffled white cap before she'd come to the fire. " 'Tis wrong to speak ill of the dead," she whispered to Mairi, "but I do hope these kind gentlemen aren't knowing what a rascal father aye was. Loved his dram he did and his 'baccy and he had them when we lacked for food. I'll see him proper buried right enough, but that's from duty. Now where are the men to bear his coffin? And for that matter, where bides the coffin?"

"It'll be here soon." The captain spread a blanket on a stone outcropping near the fire and led her to it, kind as if she'd been his own kin. "As to pallbearers, Mrs. MacLeod, since your men are fishing, Jamie and I will help if you agree."

"That's good of you, sir." She studied him timidly, obviously wondering why gentry was concerned with the troubles of poor folk.

The gille spread a white cloth on the stone and quickly put out a plate of hot bannocks, another of sausages, bowls of oatmeal porridge with butter, and jars of honey and preserves. "Jamie makes a fine bannock." Captain MacDonald, with a gesture, invited his guests to help themselves. "He's made them all over India and Egypt, and porridge, too. I didn't like it when my mother set it before me, but now I don't think the day's started without it." He took a bowl and added salt, pepper, and a generous lashing of butter. "Would you believe that in the Lowlands some have milk with their porridge, and even sugar?"

"A woeful thought, sir." Gran shook her head at such perversity and lavished honey preserves on a bannock.

Mairi watched to see how the captain ate and followed his example, cutting sausage with a knife and eating it with a tined utensil she had never seen before. The only knife on the family table had been Fearchar's, used for cutting bread, or dividing the potatoes and fish in the single large trencher. There were bowls for porridge and soup, spoons carved of horn, and cups, but that was all their tableware.

At first, she wasn't hungry but ate because it was unthinkable to refuse food which was usually scarce and never served, even at weddings, with such luxurious abundance. The tasty sausage whetted her appetite; she had both porridge and a bannock and felt much better.

A creaking rumble sounded from the north. "That'll be the carts," said the captain. "One brings the coffin and it and the other can take your township's furnishings to the lodge till it's decided where you will go."

"Where but the rocks?" said Mairi, the honey in her mouth all at once so cloying that she sickened. She gazed at Fearchar, and furious grief made her hate the captain for a moment—not as himself, for he had been kind—but as one of the class that wrung all they could from their tenants to support their wining and dicing—who, as regimental officers, made decisions that got lads like her uncles, brother and cousins killed, or who leased hunting lodges set on lands where crofters, even if starving, were forbidden to take a salmon or a deer.

The MacDonald must have sensed her mood for he said quietly, "We'll talk of that later."

Fearchar's mourners and the coffin arrived in two carts drawn by small, sturdy horses. While the women and children, furbished as well as they could be, got down, the drivers lifted out the coffin and then, at a word from the captain, drove beside the remaining goods and furniture and began to load them. The captain himself picked up Cridhe and positioned her between two cupboards, padded with bedding.

Mairi hurried over to warn Morag and the others about Gran's confusion. Sheila, her slender form heavy with child, drooped like a wilted lily, dark circles under her blue eyes. Eileen caught hold of Mairi and buried her face against her waist. "Oh Mairi, we were in a grand bed, Sheila and me, but I did miss you! I helped Catriona herd the cattle and sheep the way you told me and they're penned safe in a meadow." She added hopefully, "There's plenty of houses at the lodge. The people were grand to us. Will we be staying there forever?"

It was clear that she hoped to. Mairi almost rued the captain's charity for where they must go would seem the more bleak and dreary after the comforts of the lodge estate. She hugged Eileen close, smoothing the silvery blond hair. "We can't bide there, sweeting. 'Tis leased for hunting, not for making a living on. Folk there are servants at the lodge or gamekeepers and such."

Eileen's mouth quivered. "Can't we be servants then?"

"We'll not, Eileen Doireann MacLeod! Don't you remember how Fearchar said, 'Better seaweed and mussels at one's own hearth than fatted meat in the servant's hall'?"

"Oh, Mairi, have done!" Catriona had on her good black skirt and her shawl was caught at a graceful angle with a gilt pin Calum had brought her from his enlistment pay. "Blood money it is," Fearchar had growled. "Bribin' our lads into red coats that won't show gore when they die like our two eldest fighting English wars." If Catriona remembered who'd given her the pretty it didn't keep her from smiling at Jamie who colored to the roots of his fair hair but gave her a look of shy admiration. "The cook at the lodge needs a helper," she said with a toss of her head. "I'm taking the place."

Astonished, Mairi turned to Morag who sullenly spread her hands. "Pride makes thin porridge, girl. It's one less mouth to worry about and a mouth beside that has no liking for your shellfish and seaware. I cannot blame her."

It was unseemly to wrangle by Fearchar's corpse but Mairi couldn't restrain herself from saying, "You'll please yourself, Catriona, but you won't be pleasing my brother when he comes from soldiering to find you in the lodge's kitchen."

Catriona flushed. "Who named you Great Lady and Mother of the Clan?" she demanded. "Is Calum here, to raise a roof to our heads? I'll have my keep and a new dress and £2 each year, and as soon as I save my passage, I'm going to America or Canada!"

"But Calum—"

"I've told him I've no mind to starve on a croft. Get a little sense, Mairi MacLeod! We come from folk who left their homeland when it got too crowded. The Vikings did, the Celts did—it's always been that way, and a good thing. What if all Adam's and Eve's descendants had tried to stay huddled up close to the garden of Eden?"

It was such a comical thought that Mairi had to laugh. The anger faded in her, though she was still shaken at the thought of losing her cradle friend, and possibly her brother, too. "I'm sorry, Cat," she said.

"You'll wish me well?"

"Ever and forever." Mairi gave a faint grin, using their childhood's strongest vowing and gave her cousin's hand an affec-

27

tionate squeeze as they moved toward the bier. The captain and Jamie raised Fearchar gently and placed him in the coffin which was made not of driftwood but solid lumber.

Women and children dropped in heather and wildflowers as they knelt to kiss the chill gray face. "You don't ken the auld creature as I do," Gran muttered, "or you'd not be wailin'. But it's not fit to grudge any poor body some tears to wash it with."

The captain and Jamie secured the lid and took places at the middle handle on either side. Carrying a coffin was men's work and the women came to it uncertainly, Catriona and Mairi at the head, Morag and Kirsty at the foot.

By custom, all the men of a township took turns carrying the dead. This day, had the captain and his gille not put their strength to it, the women could never have borne the coffin three long miles across the moor to the kirk where the minister came once in the month to rain down brimstone on those hardy and devout enough to tramp the distance.

Only a few families were left in the tiny village. They were waiting, and when they saw the little procession, the soberly dressed men came to take the women's places although they were not much acquainted with the Aosda folk. They spoke awkward condolences and said they would help carry the coffin to the graveyard and dig the grave.

Gran thanked them with dignity, performing her part as chief mourner though she believed she was burying her reprobate father. The minister, Reverend Campbell, didn't come to meet them, but scowled from the door of the kirk, lips tight as his pursestring, lank black hair slanting across his forehead. His living face was more pallid than Fearchar's dead one which at least had the coloring of wind and sun. The reverend called to mind some light-hating creature turned out from beneath a mucky stone. His eyes were dull and dark as damp peat.

As if he grudged them entrance, he stood in the door till the bearers had to pause. "It's close on self-murder," he said. "When a man throws away his life for a heathenish harp, I cannot think God will shew him mercy."

"I would suggest, sir, that you leave that to God." Captain MacDonald looked at the minister in a way that caused him to move aside and let the coffin pass. The captain added in a tone low enough to escape Gran's ears, "The widow is confused and thinks this is her father. It would seem best not to shock her with the truth."

"There must be truth, whatever follows."

MacDonald let the other bearers proceed to the front of the kirk while he stopped beside the cleric. "Reverend Campbell, if you can't conduct a service that will not add to the mourners' grief, have the propriety to withdraw."

Campbell's cheeks stained red. "I will remind you, captain, that we are Free Kirk here. I serve at the will of the congregation, not the proprietor. It's my duty to warn the living against the sinful pride that brought Michael MacLeod to his end. He never came to service, jesting that he liked his harp's tones better than mine. Now he shall have his due."

Mairi smothered a groan. The wicked, wicked man! But what could be done? The captain hesitated for only a breath. Then, smiling, he slipped his arm through the minister's and drew him outside. After a startled attempt to draw back, Campbell had to willy-nilly march along or engage in an undignified scuffle. Mairi hovered close enough to hear as the others filed in and took seats, men on one side, women on the other.

"You'll give a fitting service, Reverend Campbell," said the captain, still in that soft but implacable voice, "or I'll introduce to your congregation a woman from Stornoway who can tell them about some of your interesting habits."

The minister's flushed cheeks blanched white again. "She's a liar! She—" He broke off, touching his dry lips with a surprisingly red and fleshy tongue. "Have you no fear of God, sir, to threaten his servant, and in the door of the kirk?"

"What I fear is death and disease and the twisting of minds that comes from your canting hypocrisy." The captain released his prisoner.

Campbell's lusterless eyes fleered against the captain's, fell like scuttling claws unable to find purchase. Shoulders sagging, the minister went down the aisle, giving Mairi a look so venomous that she recoiled.

"Thank you," she whispered to Captain MacDonald.

"A lucky guess." His smile flashed, teeth very white in his sunburned visage. "I hope I haven't robbed some poor harbor trull of her best customer."

He stood aside to let Mairi precede him. She stood beside Gran, one arm around an exhausted Sheila, the other hand nestling Eileen against her, through the scriptures and a sermon full of Calvin's dark gloom: all human beings deserved eternal hell; only through God's mercy would a chosen few escape. There was no solace in the words. They were the sort folk heard with the mute stoicism of dogs thrashed for unwitting trespass.

Fearchar's real funeral was last night with the sea wind and Cridhe, Mairi consoled herself. Right then, as if Fearchar's buoyant, life-loving spirit entered her, she resolved that though she mourned now and would surely mourn again, all her days she would be as happy as she could, laugh all she could, do any kindness or possible grace, and above all, she would sing and play on Cridhe to put heart into people cast out by their lairds and uncomforted by the kirk.

The graveyard's sandy earth was protected in some measure from the ocean by stone cliffs that jutted into the waves at high tide and rose, when the waters ebbed, like a palisade above them. A deep, narrow grave was dug within the hour while the women and children gathered sky-blue harebells, snowy sea campion and meadow buttercups that grew in the dunes and rippling dark green marram grass.

Most of the grave markers were Celtic crosses, many ancient and crumbling, the lettering scrubbed off long since by storms and blowing sand. Of names that could be read, half at least were MacLeods but Fearchar's immediate family had lived at the Butt of Lewis, the northernmost rocky point of the island. Atlantic winds hadn't scoured them away, but famine and poverty had. Half a century ago, Fearchar's surviving close kin had indentured themselves for their passage and sailed for the Carolinas. It was strange to Mairi that she had folk in America for whom she had no names, would never meet. More in Canada, some in Australia, scattered like seabirds in a furious storm. If she did not succeed, she and her brothers and sister, in holding to the island, their whole line would be swept away from the land won by their clan a thousand years before Lord Seaforth bought it.

Bought? The very word was sacrilege. Earth belonged to those who defended it with their blood, lived on its breast, and gave it their bodies in death as Fearchar did now, lowered into the grave. Mairi and the others covered him with flowers. The handful of turf that Gran tossed in resounded on the coffin. When the soil was mounded, Mairi and the rest smoothed it with their hands. She wished she had Cridhe, to sing her grandfather a last song, but the gulls would do that, the ever-changing charge and retreat of the waves.

"It's proper done," muttered Gran in her ear. "Let's be going, lass. My bones ache so I can scarcely drag them."

For a wild moment, Mairi wanted to seize the frail shoulders, shake Gran into the present. Wrong it seemed, terribly wrong, for Michael MacLeod's funeral to have no tear from his wife. Still, Mairi knew she couldn't deal with those tears, the ones Rosanna would shed when she remembered. With a sense of cowardice mingled with relief, Mairi gave her arm to Gran.

As they reached the level, she blinked in surprise. Carts waited, by their look the same that had transported Aosda's goods to the lodge, now cushioned with pallets spread on heather. Two saddled horses were tied to the backs of the wagons.

"You'll ride to the lodge," said the captain.

He lifted Gran onto a pallet and gently assisted Sheila while the drivers and Jamie helped the others. Mairi was starting to scramble up when she was lifted by strong hands and deposited in the cart.

No one had picked her up since she was a bairn. It was

discomfiting to be handled like one though there was something dangerously pleasant about it, realization of his strength coupled with an instinctive desire to rest in it and trust it. He had a clean, good smell as if he'd dipped in a stream and dried himself in the heather and sun.

His fingers were long and tanned, graceful though squared at the nails. She loved the feel of them but no honest thing could come of being touched by any of his kind. In rebuke to her treacherous feelings, she stiffened her back and got Eileen between them. His eyes, on a level with hers now, crinkled at the edges.

Such eyes they were, deep gray with a light to them like sun on the ocean. Drawn into them, Mairi was caught in the vortex of the fathomless black pupils. He stepped back a pace as if he, too, found their closeness unsettling.

With a flare of triumph, Mairi said, "Thank you, sir, for helping me up. It was kind of you to have the carts brought."

Dark eyebrows raised quizzically. "You don't allow much helping, Mistress Mairi. Take a word of advice. If you don't let people help you now and then you'll waste a lot of energy and wear out early." He smiled and that softened the wry edge to his voice. "You have a flower face, child. Don't make it wither sooner than it must."

"I could wither the more waiting for help," she retorted and instantly bit her tongue. He *had* helped where it was none of his concern. It wasn't fair to vent her wrathful despair on him. Swallowing hard, she forced herself to meet his gaze, this time raising her will like a shield against that frightening yet unspeakably sweet sensation of being encompassed by his eyes, drained of strength. "I cry your pardon, sir," she said under her breath. "I—I do thank you with all my heart. Without you, we would be in much worse case."

Indeed, without his succor, they'd be huddling on the moors, not that they could bide long at the lodge even if he were willing. They must find land somewhere, get something of a start to hearten the men who'd find such a cruel welcome when they

32

came from the fishing. But where? With Gran demented and Sheila near childbirth, how would they manage all that must be done before the winter?

"I have some proposals to set before you," the captain said. "Of course, you'll need to wait till your men return to make a final decision. But," he added with a mocking twist of his mouth, "I've no doubt that what you women decide is what will be done."

Before Mairi could respond, he set boot to stirrup and vaulted into the saddle of the mettlesome iron-gray horse. The carts rumbled off. Eileen fell asleep at once, flaxen head in Mairi's lap. Poor little chick, who could wonder that she was dazzled by the plenty at the lodge? How could she understand what happened when you lost your land, how then you drifted from place to place like flotsam seized by the tide and at its whim cast ashore again?

With great tenderness, Mairi cradled her little sister and thought yearningly of Tam only a few years older, trying to do a man's full work at the fishing so Aosda would have its crew and could get financing from the curer. Tam idolized Fearchar and would be wild at the loss of him, at not even being there to carry the coffin.

Thinking of her brother and that grave down by the sea, Mairi bowed her head and wept. She cried for a long time, but gradually the creak of the wheels and motion of the wagon lulled her to sleep. She didn't awaken till the cart came to a halt.

4

Turrets and round towers reared in profusion from the gray stone walls of a rambling two-story building so immense that Mairi wondered if the English Queen's castle could possibly be larger. What amazed her the most, though, was the glass, panes and panes and panes of it, glinting from a multitude of windows. Black houses might have a small window in the bedroom, set deep in the double wall and made of oiled skin like the two small roof lights set in the thatch, but the only glass windows Mairi had ever seen were in the kirk, narrow and small at that. And there were trees, real ones, some already higher than the first floor of the lodge. The roof was of what looked to be thin, flat slabs of dark gray rock, not a friendly bit of thatch anywhere to be seen.

A man was working in a star-shaped bed of flowers and another trimmed blooming shrubs around a sun dial. Think of that! Men paid to putter with flowers that couldn't serve for food! The carts had stopped in a court behind what appeared to be the back of the lodge. At one end was a wall against which fruit bushes grew, heavy with ripening berries, and a grilled gate opened into what must be a kitchen garden, for Mairi could see a lad inside, pulling weeds in a leisurely fashion.

One end of the court was open, the way they must have driven in. A block of buildings formed one side of the courtyard. Boys ran out to take the captain's and Jamie's mounts and lead them inside a stable. Through one entrance, Mairi glimpsed what had to be a carriage, though where it could travel here was a puzzle. Perhaps there was a road to Stornoway. Facing this block were eight white houses made with mortar, of the sort once inhabited by chieftains and their close kin. Each had several glass windows and chimneys rose from the sides. Mairi almost cried out at the waste of good peat smoke curling off into the air instead of smoking fish or permeating the thatch so it would make rich fertilizer, but it was clear that all things here were different from Aosda.

The others must have felt the same uneasy awe. No one moved in the carts till Captain MacDonald came over in his loose, long stride. "You may use the same cottage where you stayed last night," he told the other women. "I've bade that it be provisioned but if you need anything, come to the kitchen of the lodge and you'll be supplied."

He hoisted down the twins who readily tumbled into his arms, and Mairi saw why; as he set them on the ground, he tucked into each small fist a black strippit ball, peppermint candies she recognized with a watering of the mouth, for Calum had sometimes brought home these plump striped sweeties. The captain also helped Sheila down. "You had better rest," he advised in a surprisingly gentle tone. "If you should need a midwife, the head gardener's mother, old Marjorie, is reputedly most skilful."

Blushing with distress at having her condition spoken of by a strange man, gentry at that, Sheila murmured her thanks and moved slowly off with Kirsty and Morag, the twins racing ahead to a cottage on the end.

Gran, rousing, looked around in bewilderment. "What is this town?" she asked. "Is that a cathedral yon, one of those papish kirks full of idols and incense?"

"That's no cathedral, Mrs. MacLeod," chuckled the captain, extending his hands to her. " 'Tis an ugly abomination meant to resemble a castle, but it keeps out the rain."

While he lifted her down, Mairi made haste to jump to the turf and swing Eileen after. The MacDonald gave her a half-grin and lifted eyebrow but read her no more lectures on accepting help. "You three should be comfortable in the butler's quarters," he said. "There's a small kitchen so you can be quite to yourselves."

"But the—whatever he is—the butler—"

"I don't have one. I much prefer living without the complication of a household with all its layers of authority. The cook and housekeeper have their helpers but I'm not overrun by chambermaids and footmen."

He proffered his arm to Gran but she held back, still glancing around in bemusement. "I do not ken this place at all, at all. And how will my dear man be finding me when he comes from the fishing?"

"Your roof burned," said the captain matter-of-factly. "I'll send a message to Stornoway so when the fleet returns your men will come here straightaway."

Intimidated by the vast heap of stone, Mairi hung back. "Sir, we would liefer stay with the others."

"That cottage is crowded enough with three women and two children," he said. "There are no more empty houses." His smile flashed and she marveled at how it changed the grim lines of his face, made him seem almost a lad. "Besides, your harp is waiting by the fire in the parlor, and your other belongings are there. That seems a fine clarsach, and very old."

"It is that." Mairi couldn't keep pride from her voice. "It's sung through many strings and many, many lives since one of Conn's descendants brought it from Ireland."

"I hope you'll let me hear it."

In answer, she held up her swollen, abraded fingertips. He made a choking angry sound. It was a moment before he spoke. "The young heal swiftly. And I think you are one, Mistress Mairi, to tell your harp what you'll tell no mortal."

"You would not like the songs I feel like playing now."

"My favorite harp piece is the Laird of Coll's 'Royal Keening' that he composed when King Charles lost his head. The harp is for dirges and battle songs, not just for dance and love tunes."

"Fearchar taught me the 'Keening,' " said Mairi proudly. "He had it from his grandfather who learned it from Rory Dall himself. Rory was born on Lewis, you know, and came back to spend his last years when the new chief of MacLeod decided he needed a piper but no harpist."

"I'd forgot Blind Rory was a Lewis man."

"That he was. His father was a tacksman, a 'gentleman of the clan.' " That meant he held lands from the chief and collected rents from small tenants as well as raising and leading fighting men at the chief's need, and generally serving as the chief's lieutenant.

The captain nodded. "My great-grandfather was tacksman to his chief, but when the clans were broken after Culloden, there was small need for tacksmen. Many like him went to Canada or the Carolinas, often with dozens of their followers. Great-grand-father stayed in his glen but he would not squeeze his tenants to meet the higher rents levied by the chief and he died impover-ished. Two of his sons emigrated, three went to the army, and so it's been with us."

"Yet once the MacDonalds were Lords of the Isles."

Iain MacDonald laughed. "True enough, till James IV took for the Crown the lands of the Lordship. That was long ago, lass. The year after that Genoan, Columbus, stumbled onto America while seeking India."

"If it hadn't been for America—and Canada and Australia, I wonder where the Highlanders and Islanders would have gone since the chiefs lost all care for their people?"

"Thousands have gone to the army. Truth is, Mistress Mairi, that we Gaels are much like the red Indians of America. We lived as tribes. Raiding, fighting and glory were our main pur-suits while canny Lowlanders and English were becoming mer-chants and manufacturers. The courage and loyalty that should have served our clans was spent far away against folk who never harmed us—the French on the Plains of Abraham outside Quebec and again in the Napoleonic wars in every battle from Walcheren to Waterlooo. Battle airs played by the pipes at Culloden urged our young men against the American colonists, Kaffirs and Afghans and Egyptians, Indians rebelling against the British Raj, Chinese who dispute British merchants' rights to sell opium in China. The list is long and can only grow longer as the Empire takes with arms what it can't gain by trading enterprise."

"You talk so, yet you're an officer! If you believe what you're saying, why do you lead lads like my brother into battle?"

His eyes hardened. "I do *lead* them and I'll fall first."

"Much good that is when they shouldn't be there in the first place."

"I'm a soldier," he shrugged, "and the son of soldiers. It's the only faith that I have left, though indeed an uncle who made his fortune in India has tried to get me to leave the service. Not that he loves me overmuch but he wishes to protect his heir."

"Then you're no different, sir, than our poor tykes who shout clan slogans while they fight for the Crown that broke those clans."

His mouth tightened. They had reached the lodge and he opened the door, nodding for her to pass through before he said with a wry smile, "I've been called worse than 'poor tyke' but it doesn't do much to support my pride. A clever woman, lass, will strive to burnish a man's opinion of himself."

"With our men brought low, we crofter women know little of such tricks."

"You, at the least, have pride enough for a whole township."

"That's all we have, except our songs and stories."

"Perhaps they are the same." They had entered at the side, through a plain passageway, but now they stood in a great hall with a massive fireplace and antlers forking from the walls in numbers that made Mairi gasp.

"There must be more antlers here than there are stags on the island!"

"Oh, there are plenty left, though who knows what will happen with young Prince Albert so keen on deer-stalking and the able-bodied aristocracy imitating him?"

"You're not one of those, sir?"

He laughed outright, taking on that young look which incongruously tugged at Mairi's heart for wasn't he a man of the great world, gentry, and not needing any softness from the likes of her? "Bless you," he said, "I was feeding my family with deer off the mountain while Albert of Saxe-Coburg-Gotha was still with his tutors. My father died fighting Ashantis in one of those wars that still go on and he left my mother with debts and a hungry brood. I was the eldest. It's a pleasure to me now to see a stag and not have to shoot it."

Bewildered, she glanced around at the elegant furniture, soft jewel-toned rugs, and ornately framed paintings of hunting scenes, leaping salmon, and slaughtered grouse, otters, and hares. Reading her thought, he laughed again, but this time there was no mirth in it.

"No, Mistress Mairi, my captain's pay doesn't stretch to luxuries like this. My uncle's money does. He insisted on taking the lease for me when I wouldn't spend my leave in his Edinburgh house. A sore disappointment I am to Uncle Roderick but I'm his nearest kin. He does what he can to make me fashionable."

The captain pulled on a woven rope attached to a bell. Almost instantly, as if she'd been listening outside, a thin woman in black dress and white apron and cap appeared, a ring of keys at her belt jingling with every step, moving fast as a bird after a bug and cocking her head while bright dark eyes took in every smudge and wrinkle in Gran's and Mairi's clothes.

"Mrs. Munro," he said, "kindly take Mistress Mairi, Mrs. MacLeod and the child to their quarters and see that they have whatever they require."

"As you say, captain." Her expressionless tone was in itself eloquent.

"I have business in Stornoway tomorrow," said Iain Mac-
Donald to Mairi. "I'll leave a message for your men. Rest and
when I return we'll talk about what you should do."

"Say the word, sir," put in Mrs. Munro, "and I'll put the
young ones to work in the laundry."

"Thank you, Mrs. Munro, but I have not said that word."

The woman ducked her head and, back poker-stiff, led the
way down a passage that wound past countless doors till it
stopped at the last one. She unlocked it with one of the keys and
grudgingly opened it.

Mairi's glance flew straight to Cridhe, draped in the plaid like
a welcoming *seannachaidh*' or story-teller. She started to run
forward and embrace Fearchar's harp, but Mr. Munro's voice
checked her.

"You'll soon be brought a meal," she said. "If you need
aught, tell the lass." Her nose wrinkled. "You'll take baths
before getting into those clean beds. I'll send a tub and water and
soap. You *do* ken soap?"

Mairi's cheeks burned but Gran rounded on the housekeeper
and blew through pursed lips in a sound like breaking wind.
"Wheesht, woman, with your mouth screwed tight as a rooster's
arse! Ken soap? I've made enough of it from kelp ash and fish oil
to wash all the sheets you've ever seen and take the skin off your
pointy bones beside!"

"Why, you old—"

Gran chuckled. "You may clank your keys and walk like
you've swallowed a dirk, but 'tis the captain lays silver in your
claw and don't think I won't tell him if you spew your bile at
us!"

Mrs. Munro chokèd, went crimson, caught in her breath with
a hiss, and whirled toward the door. "Last week the captain
hauled home an orphan otter cub," she said. "It bit his finger to
the bone. He's learned naught!"

Gran made her suggestive noise again and as the door
slammed, turned to Mairi with blue eyes sparkling. "Off she is
with a flea in her ear. I doubt we'll see our lady again."

"Oh, Gran—"

"I could never bide that sort," said Gran, looking almost her old self. "And now I'm old enough and poor enough that I don't have to! Look at the brave fire, lass, and a steaming kettle and teapot ready!" She lifted a white cloth from a basket and sniffed rapturously. "Scones! These do be scones, and there's heather honey and cream so thick that look! it scoops like butter!" She took Eileen's eager and grubby little hand, marching her to the open door of the kitchen. "Let's wash our hands to spite that witchy-wife and then we'll have our feast!"

In spite of Gran's feisty words, they took the cushions off the chairs before they dared sit down and then were very careful not to drop crumbs as they savored the golden-crusted currant-filled scones and sipped hot tea which smelled and tasted deliciously of spice.

"Yon great hall with all those antlers was a grue place," said Gran. "This is homier though it seems o'er grand for a but— but—whatever kind of high-nosed servant it is that the captain won't have. And that's honest peats in the fireplace even if that chimney wastes all the good smoke."

"There's no thatch to smoke, Granny," said Eileen, closing her eyes to relish the last of her scone. "And they no be smoking fish, either." Though red and swollen from tears, the fair-haired girl's eyes shone with excitement. She actually left the toothsome scones to move around the room, examining the dishes in an open cupboard set atop a chest close to a table with more chairs, the pictures on the wall, several lamps with patterned globes that did not smell of fish oil, a settle plumped with cushions, and a shelf displaying china animals.

"This nice room and all these things and no one even lives here," she sighed. Vanishing into the kitchen, she proclaimed that the many cupboards were filled with all manner of pans and cooking supplies as well as tins of food and covered crocks of shortbread and small cakes. "And here's a tin of sweeties!" she cried. "Toffees and pan drops and sour plums and oddfellows— oh, there be kinds you never saw!"

41

"Well, leave them till after we have what they'll send from the main kitchen," Gran ordered. "Whilst you're dancing about, peek through that other door, do, and see if there's a bed. I declare I could lay me down though it's only the middle of the afternoon."

Disappearing, Eileen was quiet so that Gran called impatiently, "What's there, henny? Be you fallen down a well?"

"There's a brave big bed all with tall posts and a cover over," Eileen marveled. "There's a narrow bed along t'other wall. And at the foot's a sweet little bed that must be for me! You never saw such coverlets and pillows soft as clouds! Our clothes be in a big chest and our bedding's piled in the corner."

Shabby and sad it must look there, more fit for a byre than a house. Warning chilled Mairi. This comfort, these luxuries, would give her small sister a taste for what she couldn't have. And for that matter, she herself winced at comparing these quarters with their home at Aosda, ruined now and deserted.

In a room like this, though, the fire wasn't the center, it didn't gather folk around it, or bless the beasts at the lower end. Sholma and Rigga were either well-stalled or in good pasture, no doubt. In summer that was well enough, but in the long months of winter, they'd long for the fire surely, the sight and sound of folk going and coming.

For all its ease, this abode lacked a heart, the heartstone with the fire. You couldn't smoor this one at night, make the holy circle, invoke the Sacred Three. The family's heartstone was under the burned thatch, but Mairi would loose it from the hard-packed earth and it would make any shelter home. But would Eileen, having tasted the sweets and comfort of the lodge, be cheerful over the diet Mairi foresaw that winter, seaweed and shellfish?

Catriona had jumped at going into service here. Would that be the captain's solution for the rest of them? There was no shame in working for someone else. The ill lay in giving up your own roof, your own bit of land, and with it your pride and independence. Though for the poor to talk of pride and independence buttered no bannocks and boiled no porridge.

"Pour me a drop more tea, Mairi love," said Gran. "I vow there be in it cinnamon and ginger and such good things to warm the cockles."

Mairi obliged but did not pour more for herself. She mustn't let herself wallow in pleasures or it would be harder to keep her pledge to Fearchar and all their folk who'd blessed fires on that hearthstone long before Torquil's Vikings brought Celt women to bed by soft words or ruthless hands.

There was a tap and the door opened to a sonsie bright-cheeked young woman with yellow hair curling from beneath her frilled cap. She set a big tray on a small table between the arm chairs. "May you eat in health," she said with a lilt. "When you're finished or if you need aught, pull that cord by the mantle. It'll ring your bell in the servant's hall. Cook asks if you'd fancy roast grouse or lamb for supper, and of course there'll be salmon and white fish."

Breathing in the tempting odors wafting from several covered bowls and platters, Mairi said quickly, "There's plenty here for days, lass! Don't fash yourself about us."

The young woman's smooth brow puckered. "Captain told cook you're to sup well," she said. "What's in the kitchen here's just should you crave a bite between meals."

"We'll have the grouse then, lass." Gran spoke with aplomb that made Mairi's jaw drop, cool and gracious as a lady used to phrasing wishes that were treated as commands. "And happen it's fresh, a bit of white fish."

"Wouldn't be in the captain's kitchen else," the young woman twinkled. She smiled at Eileen. "Cook's baking you a raspberry tart, poppet, and that pretty crystal bowl there holds crannachan."

"What's that?" wondered Eileen.

"Toasted oatmeal and nuts mixed with honey, slathers of

whipped cream, and just a blessing of good whiskey." With a bob of her head, the young woman withdrew.

At the tray in a flash, Eileen pleaded, "Granny, Granny, let's see what's under the lids!"

A mouth-watering broth thick with leeks, peas and barley; potatoes roasted in drippings; crisp oatcakes; eggs poached in a spicy red sauce, and besides the big bowl of crannachan there were plump glazed buns studded with ginger and three beautiful rosy-yellow pears in a silver dish.

Watching Eileen' eyes widen at the sumptuous repast, Mairi felt a pang at knowing that never again in her life, not even at wakes and weddings, would her little sister enjoy such food. Deciding that pride and independence could survive a few plentiful meals, Mairi began to ladle up the broth.

The end of the day was so different from its start beside Fearchar's bier that Mairi felt like one rapt away for a peerie banquet to wake and find one night was a mortal's lifetime. They had bathed in a copper tub with scented soap, and she had washed Eileen's and Gran's hair and her own before Gran climbed into the high bed and, looking almost as little as Eileen, cuddled into the pillows.

"If my dear man were by me, I'd know I was in heaven," she said, and grinned. "I doubt me that there's crannachan in heaven, nor barley broth nor pears. God Himself can't have a bed so fine as this."

Mairi closed the door so Gran would sleep sound, relieved that her delusion was lasting though when the men returned, if not before, she'd surely fret about Fearchar. When her memory came back, that would be a time so terrible that Mairi quailed at the thought and couldn't keep from hoping, even it were cowardly, that Gran would never have to remember that cruel day, or know her Michael would never again come home to her.

After bathing, the three of them had put on their good dresses, Gran's the black she'd been wed in, and Mairi's, also black, was her mother's bridal gown. Eileen had the heather-dyed brownish-purple dress that had been Mairi's till she out-grew it past any altering. Peggy, the yellow-haired friendly lass who'd brought the tray and later helped another woman bring in the tub and pails of water, had gathered up their other clothes for washing.

"They're no busy enough in the laundry," she said over Mairi's objections. "The head laundress' father was driven off his croft when she was a bairn but she's not forgot it. We all be sorry for you, lass, and want to do what we can—excepting Lady Hen's Arse." She doubled with laughter at Mairi's shocked look. "Aye, your Gran was o'erheard, and for that fittin' name we thank her for we'll laugh behind our faces when Madam comes scolding and bemeanin' us."

Smiling at the thought, Mairi granted Eileen's wish to go visit the twins and Sheila and turned to Cridhe, slipping off the plaid to examine the strings and the crack in the soundboard. Filling it with beeswax still seemed to her the best remedy. As she knelt by the harp for which Fearchar had died, Mairi was seized by a tide of grief and shame.

She wasn't out of her wits like Gran or a child like Eileen. How could she have gorged, reveled in being clean? She had laughed! Light-minded she was, feckless as Catriona. Fearchar, dear man! She buried her face in her arms, racked with sobbing, and wept till her eyes had no more tears. *Fearchar, I won't forget you. Your Rosanna will bless the fire again on our hearthstone, Cridhe will sing your songs, and I'll find someone to play them after I am gone. You won't have died for nothing, dear man, Fearchar.*

A rap at the door brought her stumbling to her feet. Scrubbing her wet face with her sleeve, she called, "Come in, Peggy, do!" for the young woman had said she'd bring thread and needle to replace those lost in the burning.

It wasn't Peggy that stepped inside, but Iain MacDonald, fresh-shaved and garbed, his dark face made even browner by the white frills of his shirt.

As if he didn't note her blotched face, he stepped over to Cridhe and gazed at the old harp with unfeigned admiration.

"There are few *clarsachs* left," he said. "Perhaps none as old as yours. I've a great mind to hear her." Reaching into his pocket, he brought out a small box of some sort of veined and polished stone. He smiled and said, "Out with your hands, Mistress Mairi."

She hesitated, not wanting him to see her broken nails, ragged cuticles, and work-roughened skin. Gently, inexorably, he took the fists clenched at her sides and laid them open in his palm. She trembled as if he had bared her body,

"Here," he said. His voice sounded through her with the pulsing of her blood. "I have balm for your fingers."

Feeling as if she had just drunk deep of Gran's heather ale, she scarcely felt the stinging that slowly eased to assuagement. Inwardly shaken as if seized by an imperious wind, she yearned to bow her head to his hands, feel them warm and strong and vital beneath her lips.

This man, this stranger, had entered her heart. There would never be, her whole life long, a way to cast him out. But he was of the gentry. There could be nothing honorable between them. So there must be nothing at all.

5

In spite of exhaustion and having barely slept the night before, Mairi turned and tossed more than she rested. Perhaps the bed was too soft, the feather-stuffed pillow too plump. More likely it was the bliss that swept through her when she remembered Iain's deft fingers applying the sweet-scented ointment, his touch as healing as the balm, yet as wounding in a fatal, irrevocable way as if he had grasped her heart and held it naked in his hand.

Rare daft that was! She might better have loved a selkie man who once in the year changed seal-shape for mortal. Not once in a twelvemonth, once in a lifetime, could Iain MacDonald assume a guise that would let them love. Oh, a gentleman might lie in the heather with a girl who took his fancy. If Iain wished that and laid siege, she doubted that she'd be strong enough to refuse him. But there could be nothing honest, nothing lasting like the love between Gran and Fearchar.

So long as Mairi's grandfather had rested on his heather bed, stayed on top of the earth, he hadn't seemed really dead. Now that he was beneath the ground, he was gone indeed. This finality crushed in on her as if she, too, were weighted down by dense black soil that pressed more heavily with each spadeful.

Where was his soul now, whatever didn't die? Fearchar hadn't admired the kirk's heaven but she couldn't believe he was in hell. Perhaps he moved in the sea wind or swirled on the waves in the sparkling clouds of spindrift that he'd once told Mairi must hold the spirit of God as it had been in the first days of Creation when it moved upon the face of the waters.

As if he spoke to her, Mairi remembered then something he'd said. "When Cridhe sings, it's not just soundboard and strings that make the music, lass. It's that bard who brought her from Ireland centuries ago, and all those of our blood who've played her since. Something of them lives in the harp just as the rub of their hands polished and mellowed the wood. Don't forget, ever, that you hold here not only Cridhe but the spirits of our folk."

Comforted by imagining the deep, rough voice, Mairi slipped out of bed and hurried to the parlor where she sank down by Cridhe, resting her face against the tartan drapery, embracing the swaddled harp.

Fearchar, she prayed, Fearchar, bless me. Give me the passion and the pain, give me the love and hope of our people. Let me sing your songs.

The wool against her cheek felt like his plaid, and the odor of course was his, peat smoke and heather. Mairi could almost hear him rumble, *"There, lass, don't weep for me. Take care of our folk. Find food for their bellies but don't forget their hearts. Tell them the land is ours and still is though we're torn from it. It will surely be ours again if even a few remain. Give them a song and I will hear you and be glad.*

I will, she promised. I will, dear man. After a while, feeling oddly light but almost happy, she got to her feet and returned to her bed, glad that the soft breathing of Gran and Eileen meant they were sleeping sound. She drifted off herself and as she sank from consciousness, the captain's hands held hers again and she joyed in it, for the stern judge in her who condemned that melting sweetness, that intoxication as if she'd drunk deep and deliciously, that judge was sleeping. And soon, smiling into a dark face bent tenderly above her, Mairi slept, too.

* * *

Catriona brought their breakfast, special bannocks dipped in egg and baked crisply golden, porridge with fresh butter, and thick slices of what she said was ham, a food Mairi had never tasted for pigs didn't thrive well on the island. "If beasts or folk would live here," Gran sometimes said, "they must be seaweed eaters."

But there was no dulse or carrageen, the best-tasting sea-weeds, on their plates that morning. Catriona, in a ruffled white apron, sat down to have a cup of tea with them, eyes shining as she described the room she had to herself, "with a real glass window! And even a little rug!"

Eileen shivered. "I wouldn't like having that *gruamach* Mrs. Munro over me!"

"She's a terror," nodded Catriona. "But she stays out of the kitchen and cook, Mrs. Fraser, is nice and so is Peggy. When Mrs. Munro tried to come the high-mighty with cook, the captain called in Madam Hen's-Arse—she'll never lose that name, Gran! He told her he could put up with cobwebs and dust but a good table he was bound to have and would she kindly see to it that Mrs. Fraser was not interfered with? So we have good times in the kitchen." She added thoughtfully, "Besides, even the maids Mrs. Munro chivvies around have snug lodging and plenty to eat. Not so ill a life."

Mairi lost her appetite for the delicious bannock and ham. "They may sleep soft and eat fat," she said, "but they have no bit of land nor their own hearthstone."

"No more do you."

"I will."

Catriona shrugged graceful shoulders. "Good luck to you, I'm sure, though I think you're cracked in the head." When Mairi said nothing, her cousin set down her cup and got to her feet with a flounce of the skirts of her best black dress. "Use your wits, love. The men won't be back in time to build new houses before winter, even if they've heart for it. I talked with Morag and Kirsty this morning. They're of a mind to go to America if a way can be found."

No one could blame them, especially Kirsty, whose roof had burned before, yet Mairi felt a stabbing sense of loss and almost betrayal. "What of Sheila?"

"What of her?" Catriona replied. "She'll do what Barry says, and Barry, great blond laddie that he is, will do as father bids."

Bluff, good-natured Andrew, now that Fearchar wasn't here to bolster him, would probably give in to Morag for the sake of peace. Mairi's heart sank. Aosda had already been depleted to the fewest men who could take out a boat and work the croplands. If the others gave up, how could one household manage, and what was the good of it if they did somehow cleave to the barren rocks? For a moment, she almost bowed her head in despair but then she remembered Tam. He was growing; in a few years he'd have a man's growth. And surely next summer Calum would put by his red coat and come home to them.

To find Catriona in the lodge kitchen? Mairi refused to think of it, seized only on the hope that her brothers would share her resolve to stay on the island.

"We'll manage," she said doggedly.

Catriona sighed. "Oh, Mairi love! Why will you make a cruel matter worse?" When Mairi didn't answer, Catriona picked up the tray. "The captain's already left for Stornoway. An early-rising gentleman he is though Jamie was still yawning and rubbing his eyes when their horses were brought."

Her cheeks pinkened at the thought of the gille and Mairi spoke more derisively than the young man warranted. "I'm bound he's a feckless sort, all grins and yellow hair but no backbone."

Catriona's eyes widened. "Why, what has he done to you?"

"The question is what has he done to *you*?"

Flushing deeper, Catriona retorted, "Jamie's done naught but be pleasant and kind—which you are not, surely!" With that, she hoisted the tray and went out with her nose in the air.

Fussing at Caty would only provoke her and wouldn't in the least advance Calum's interests. Besides, if Caty was fickle enough to succumb to a new suitor, what kind of wife would she make, especially in these bad times?

After another cup of tea, Mairi went with Gran and Eileen to see Morag, Kirsty, Sheila and the twins. Rory and Brigid were shouting and running with several other children. It hadn't taken them a day to feel at home. How long would their three-year-old minds retain any memories at all of Aosda and Fearchar?

One thing was sure, if they left the island soon, they'd have no ties to it. They'd belong to Canada or America or wherever they went. That was best, surely, but Mairi ached as they dashed towards her on thin little legs that hadn't been chubby since Kirsty weaned them. Mairi hugged them with special fervor, smoothing back their tight red curls. They squirmed free and grabbed Eileen's skirts, proud to have a "big girl" to bring to their games. Resident children of her age were at work, of course, and so would she have been if Mrs. Munro had been left a free hand.

Inside the cottage, the women sat knitting by the hearth with a pot of tea and dish of scones. Sheila had dark circles under her eyes but insisted in her soft voice that she felt all right.

"Well?" demanded Morag. "What does Captain MacDonald intend for us? Has he told you?"

"He said when the men are back he'll make some suggestions."

"He means to help us?" Kirsty asked, hazel eyes brightening. "Maybe even loan us passage across the ocean?"

"I think he will offer, but—"

"Three bairns we've lost to starving," Kirsty said with a snap of her jaw. She looked out the window at her twins. "Twice we've been driven out and our roof burned, the land we tilled and planted taken for sheep. If there's a way to leave, we'll go."

"So will we," said Morag. "Our exile is God's punishment."

"For what?" Mairi flashed. "For working hard, paying our rent, asking only to stay on the land our folk claimed long ago?"

"You arch your neck against God's will," the dark, rawboned woman chided. "Just like your grandfather, you're full of pride and those heathen songs and tales that entice others to bootless vainglory. 'Tis a great pity yon plaided harp didn't burn with the thatch. Without its beglamouring, we might have all by now been settled in good homes in America." She gave a nod of bitter satisfaction. "Andrew wouldn't listen before but he will now."

Hot words burned on Mairi's lips but she forced them back. No use to wrangle. With a look of warning and a slight motion of her head toward Gran, Mairi said, "You'll do what you decide is best, certainly." Turning to Gran, she said. "I'm going to walk down to the cliffs for a breath of sea air. Don't worry if I'm gone till supper time."

While Iain was gone, she hoped to find a place where a shelter could be made before winter. That would arm her against his proposals which would surely be for emigration or hired labor uprooted from the land. Morag cast her a dour smile.

"Whilst you're by the coast, better eat some seaweed and mussels so you'll know your fare if you're daft enough to try to burrow away in the rocks."

"Dulse's fine if it's simmered long enough," retorted Mairi. "Carrageen makes nice pudding, and laver's good with oats."

"Don't prate of it!" Kirsty burst out. "If you'd eaten only those with shellfish as long as Adam and I did, you'd never want to touch them to your lips again!"

After the sorrows Kirsty had endured, Mairi didn't want to argue. As she left the cottage, even the marvel of the trees couldn't lift her heart. Maybe the others were right. Maybe it would be impossible to stay.

If only Calum were here! As she left the walled estate, wind, unbroken now by anything, overbore her as if a hundred invisible hands pressed against her. It was all she could do to keep her feet. Lewis winds were famous, even on this comparatively sheltered eastern coast blowing at gale force one day in eight and more in winter. She wrapped her shawl tightly to keep it from flapping like a sail, and walked obliquely against the wind, bearing toward the distant glint of the waves.

A mixed day it was, clouds roiling gray and purple-shadowed with spiraling masses of purest white, and just sun enough slanting through now and then to transfigure the moor rent by deep fiords cutting sharply into the land. Wind drove white spume before it, lashing cliffs serried with unnumbered rifts and corridors. Along some of these dark walls, in crevices above the reach of the tides, nested green-black shags, white kittiwakes with gray wings, and guillemots whose white breasts and dark backs gave them the look of fine gentlemen. The shrill call of birds filled the air as their wings dazzled the eye with wheeling and diving among the gulls and terns. A beam of sun bronzed the wide-spread wings of a cormorant that was drying off after swallowing its catch. Waves hurled themselves on the cliffs with thundering crashes that for a moment muted the cry of the birds, surging through channels till they collapsed and eddied back, leaving pure white sand studded with glistening stones and shells in clefts and grottoes among the rocks.

Beautiful it was, God's glory and the sea's, but an awesome world of wind and rocks and sea where only powerful wings could capture a living. Mairi looked behind her and before. Was it this way all along the coast? Should it be, then indeed she'd have to give up the dream of a refuge. But before she did, she'd search the whole coast! Surely, somewhere, there had to be a tiny haven, a foothold, however precarious.

The fiords, stretching far as the eye could see, compelled her to go around, but finally, after tramping for miles, she caught in a breath and stared, giving a choked little laugh of delighted relief.

A building, or part of one! Like a tower tumbled away on one side. Why, that must be the *broch!* She had heard of it though she had never been near it. Built long ago, Gran said, maybe by the Pictish folk though no one knew for sure.

Walls! Already built! In spite of her weariness, Mairi's step

53

quickened. She could hardly wait to get there and see if the Old Ones had left her an abode. What cheered her even more was a shimmer of grass. The tower was situated on a small inlet and though cliffs reared from the sea they didn't seem as formidable as those she had skirted.

She ran the last distance but her eager feet slowed as she approached and was seized by a kind of fear. One wall rose to a point thirty feet high but from this apex, the sides were worn down though a tall man could hide behind their lowest level except for one wide gap on the east where the stones had crumbled.

So big it was, so fallen away and ancient. Coldness fingered her spine. Still, the wind blew much less fiercely here, a stream danced nearby, and best of all, there was grass growing tall for a small stretch between the bogs and the cliffs. Not much. Not enough to pasture herds of Cheviots, or even Rigga and Sholma, the calf, and their few sheep. But it would help, and it showed there was at least a scrap of soil.

She was still afraid to enter the *broch*, but it seemed almost like a gift from those vanished folk whose blood surely mixed in her veins along with that of Celts and Vikings. *We need shelter*, she told the spirits, if any lingered in the tower. *Help us for we are your children.*

Silverweed, like a welcome with its cheery yellow flowers, grew high around the walls. It was good to eat as well as pretty and she took its profusion for a good omen. Bees and butterflies visited the harebells and purple-blooming wild thyme, and tiny white flowers of eyebright sparkled from the grass outside the stone lintel.

Bending, she had to walk doubled over through the entrance that cut through the thickness of the double wall with space between. The passage was dim and smelled of moss and mold. She was glad to be able to see light at either end, and gladder to stand up. No matter how many attackers tried to storm the broch, only one at a time could come in, and he'd enter stooped, a handy target for some defender's club.

What builders these unknown ancestors had been! How had they cut and laid the stones of the main walls so closely that they presented not even a toehold? Peering into a low entrance in the side, she saw that galleries ascended the space between the heavy walls, linked by stone stairs. These were too small for living quarters, but when, climbing up a way, she looked out the window into the court, she saw that any foe penetrating that far could be easily killed by missiles or arrows from the galleries.

Wouldn't the children love to play here? Mairi clambered to the top and looked slowly all around, from purple moor to cliffs to the magical sea with its muted rhythm like a lullaby. A fine place they had chosen, the builders of this tower.

From her vantage point, Mairi saw that the walls enclosed an area about forty feet across. There were tumbled stones aplenty to divide it into sections and a shelter for the cattle and sheep could be built on the side eroded to the ground. Divots of heather turf would make a good roof and heather rope could secure the thatch. The problem on this treeless island was to find wood for supports and rafters. Wicked it had been of Hugh Sinclair to burn the treasured roof timbers! She wasn't sorry she had cursed him, not a bit.

But these walls were here, wonderful strong walls, and though the roof couldn't be as securely nested as on a house wall, the worst of the winds would strike the tower wall rising above like a shield. Gratefully, Mairi pressed her face against the ancient stones.

A shield indeed it would be to them, from the winter and a landlord's cruelty. *Fearchar, we have a place!* She could almost hear him laughing as she hurried down the stairs.

Feet light with joy in spite of the miles she had walked, she ran till she was breathless, walked till she stopped gasping, and ran some more, not only because she burned to tell her good news to the others but because even though these were long summer days dusk was falling and she didn't want to get lost.

Twilight thickened on the moor ahead of her, concentrated into a shape. At first she was afraid, but then the vague shadow became horse and rider and Iain's voice reached her, half-laughing, half-exasperated. "By all that's wonderful, Mistress Mairi, what are you doing out here so late? They said you'd gone to walk by the sea and I feared you'd slipped from the cliffs."

"I'm sorry, captain." After his trip to Stornoway, fancy his riding out to look for her! He reined his big bay horse to a stop and she stroked the animal's sleekly muscular neck, looking up with such triumph that she felt as if her face must shine with it. "I've found a place where we can stay!"

"You've what?"

She explained, ending happily, "It only needs a roof and we'll be snug for winter!"

Even in the dimness, she could see his eyebrows rush together. "Did you also find pasture for your beasts and tillable land?"

"There's some grass." It was clear he didn't approve. She met his gaze defiantly. "We can heap up seaweed and sand to make new soil."

"My God! I hope the others have better sense than you, girl."

"It's the only place I found along the coast—"

"There are other coasts, most a deal more hospitable than this one."

"This one is ours."

He stifled something profane. "Put your foot on mine and get up behind me. I'm tired and want my dinner even if you do not."

"No one asked you to miss it."

He fairly swung her in place behind him. "Don't fret about your skirts," he growled as she tried to tug them down. "I'm not looking. Besides, it's almost dark."

She'd never been on a horse before. It was a little frightening to be so far from the ground, but exhilarating, too. "You'll have to hold on to me," he said, and laughter was back in his voice. "There, get a good tight grasp and lock your hands in front."

Strange it was and wonderful to be pressed against him, face buried against his back, hearing and feeling the deep, steady beat

56

of his heart. Her arms moved with his breathing and her own heart pounded till she was sure he felt it. She had to swallow hard before she could speak.

"Thank you, sir, for coming after me."

"I came solely because I couldn't relish my dinner while imagining you smashed somewhere on the rocks."

"I grew up near the sea. I'm careful on the cliffs."

"Then it must be the only place you are."

She didn't want to argue, not while it was so sweet to be closer to him than she would ever be again. Closing her eyes to savor the delight, the sensations of his breath and heartbeat, she asked, "Did you leave word for our men in Stornoway?"

"I did, at the curers where they'll bring their catch. They should come along tomorrow."

Scalding grief rose in Mairi. She could only bob her head and blink at stinging tears. How could she laugh and joy in Iain's company with Fearchar's mound not yet settled firm above him? Then she remembered what she'd decided at his bier, to be as happy as she could and spread that gladness as he had always done.

"It will be cruel hearing for them all," she said. "Especially for Tam, my brother. He and grandfather were rare fond of each other."

"Tam's older than you?"

"No, he's scarce twelve. It's his first year at the fishing. He's small for it, but with Calum and my cousins gone, Tam was needed to make up the crew."

"So your grandmother, younger brother and sister and you, have no man at home?"

She didn't like this line of questioning. "Calum should be back in a year."

"You could starve long before that."

"That's not your worry, sir."

His rough laughter vibrated through her. "A 'poor tyke' you must think me indeed if you believe I can go off and leave you in this condition."

"Sir, there be folk in our condition all through the Highlands and Islands."

"True. But what happened to you was right under my nose. I couldn't pass you by."

"Ah, then, 'tis shame you're not the MacKenzie agent."

"When three or four families try to exist where only one can scrape a living, it's clear some must go."

"And that's your word to us?"

"It will be when the men come." She was silent, choked with bitterness. He spoke more gently. "Lass, there are too many people. As you know yourself, in some places for every croft, there'll be three or more families, or folk on no land at all. Thousands, in these last seventy years, have left the Islands because they saw the hopelessness of staying."

"I say 'Good luck' to them, and God's blessing."

He shook his head in exasperation. "How can you be so young and yet so stubborn?"

"Is it stubborn to love one's home place?"

"Let's not wrangle. Wait till your men are at the lodge."

"When you'll convince them to emigrate!"

"I hope so. For all your sakes."

She said in a taut cold voice, each word clipped off between her teeth, "They can go. All of them. But I will not. I'll bide on the island. I will be here, Iain MacDonald, when the lairds are gone, and you, too."

To her surprise and outrage, his shoulders heaved and after a moment he howled with laughter. "If you think I'm prating—" she began furiously.

Shaking his head, still chuckling, he raised her hands and stroked the fingers to the tips. "What? No claws? I would have sworn I had a cat behind me. No more of this for the nonce, Mistress Mairi. It's not healthy to dine on a riled stomach. See, there's the lights from the lodge. We'll soon be at our dinners."

Regret surged over her wrath. Why hadn't she kept quiet and stored up every moment of this ride? Pressing her cheek as close to him as she could, she closed her eyes again and didn't stir till he reined in the horse.

6

The men of Aosda trudged in next evening, carrying their nets which would now need thorough mending. Tam's eyes were swollen in his thin, narrow face, and he didn't tug free of Mairi when she threw her arms around him and held him close.

"I—I wasn't there when Fearchar needed me," he muttered. "I didn't help carry him to his grave. Och, Mairi! I didn't get to say good-bye—"

His voice broke off and he shuddered with trying to repress his sobs. She stroked the back of his neck beneath curling hair bleached till it was almost white, the hidden place still fragile and childish though he was tall as she. "You can tell him good-bye," she comforted. "He'll hear you, Tam, I know he will. He was proud of you taking a man's part, off with the fishing."

"We caught a brave lot of herring," rumbled Andrew Nicolson. His thick red hair showed much more gray than it had two months ago and his brawny shoulders bowed as if too much had been heaped on them. His very largeness made him seem all the more lost and vulnerable. His cousin, Fearchar, had been so much older that Andrew had respected him as head of the family, relied on his judgment. It apparently hadn't yet dawned on Andrew that now he was the eldest man. "The gentleman who left word at the curer's for us said to buy naught till we'd talked to him." He rubbed his hand across his broad weather-burned forehead. "Ever since we heard, my head's been fair spinnin', Mairi lass. Fearchar dead, the houses burned—it's too much to take in."

Adam MacNeill, Kirsty's husband, gave a harsh laugh. Wiry and quick, he had green eyes and black hair streaked with white that fell across his left eye so stubbornly that he was forever shaking it back which added to the impression he gave of being high-strung and impatient. "Don't strain yourself, lad. It'll still be true when you get used to it. Twice before, we've been driven out. 'Tisn't hard for me to credit. That bloody Hugh Sinclair! Servin' writs on our women and an old man whilst we were away!"

Barry Nicolson crimsoned. The veins in his forehead and massive neck stood out. Big and deliberate like his father, he was slow to wrath but fiery when aroused. Arm close around Sheila whose face was transfigured now he was safely back, his free hand knotted into a powerful fist.

"Aye, and Hugh Sinclair's thatch can burn, too!"

"I'll help!" cried Tam, green eyes blazing as he knuckled away a tear.

Mairi caught his shoulder and covered Barry's fist with her hand. "The factor only did as he was bid," she reminded them. "Sheila and the rest of us need you here, not on the end of a rope or transported to Australia."

Nodding, Sheila stroked his cheek, eyes brimming with tears. "Och, lass," he groaned in bewilderment. "What can we do, then?"

"I've come to talk about that," said a voice from the open door of the cottage Sheila, Morag and Kirsty were using. Tall as the Nicolson men, the captain wasn't dwarfed by their bulk but simply made them look ungainly. An impression heightened by the contrast of his well-cut gray coat, trousers and handsome boots to their thick jerseys, homespun pants, and rough home-made footwear made of hides sewed with thongs.

As they stared at him, abashed and suspicious, the captain gave his name and offered his hand to Andrew who identified himself and the others. Iain shook hands all around. When he got to Tam, the boy held back but something in the man's smile won him. He slipped his chapped fingers into the captain's.

"I won't intrude long," said Iain. "You have much to talk about. But I have a proposal you should hear before deciding what to do." His deep gray eyes rested on Mairi a long moment before going to the rest. "The eviction was heartless but quite legal. You cannot return to your crofts. Leaving your homeland is a sad thing but it offers chances undreamed of here."

Andrew and Barry seemed not to understand but Adam, a twin hugged tight in either arm, shook his hair out of his eyes and stared at Iain with guarded hope. "God knows you speak truth, sir. We'd have been gone the first time we were burned out but we had no money for our passage. This third time—" His eyes smoldered. Kirsty tugged at his sleeve as if to keep him from blurting out rash thoughts.

"I'll pay your way wherever you choose to go," said the captain. "There's a ship in Stornoway right now that sails for America next week, but if you prefer Canada or Australia—"

"I've a bellyful of the English," Adam burst out, looking years younger in an instant. "Do you mean it, sir? All of us?"

"All who wish to go."

Excited murmuring. Morag gripped Andrew's arm; Sheila and Barry gazed at each other in puzzlement; Kirsty and Adam embraced each other with the twins in between them squealing delight at their parents' joy.

No doubt what they would do. Mairi couldn't blame them but her heart contracted with pain that deepened as she glanced at Catriona. Blue eyes alight, Catriona took off the maid's cap and clapped her hands. "I don't have to think about it, Captain MacDonald. I'm for America, thank you very kindly!" She gave a rich, joyful laugh and couldn't refrain from a few quick dance steps. "I'll pay you back, sir, be sure I will."

"It's not necessary."

"Oh, but I will," she cried airily. "I'll never miss it from that fortune I'll make in America!"

"There can only be one answer, to be sure!" Morag almost shook her bemused husband. "Thank the captain, man, and then let us thank God who has been more merciful than we deserve!"

As Iain's gaze swung to her, Mairi read pity in it. That turned her pain into cold resolve. Even if they all left—and yes, it would only be fair to let Tam and Eileen go if they wanted to—she would stay, she and Gran. Gran was in the lodge, napping in her fine bed. The trip to America would probably kill her, and if it didn't she'd be lost in a strange world.

I wouldn't be, Mairi thought. Part of her understood Catriona, admitted the truth of Adam's and Kirsty's disillusionment. The courage, work and energy it would take to survive here would win a place anywhere in the world. But she would stay. Fearchar had entrusted her with the harp and his songs. They belonged on the island with folk who somehow, anyhow, managed to hold on.

"Captain MacDonald is generous," she said, cheeks burning though she controlled her voice. "But before you accept his offer, I want to tell you what I've found."

"Unless 'twas a pot of gold with more buried, nothing will keep me here," shrugged Catriona but she smiled sympathetically. "Well then, Mairi love, go ahead and tell us."

"Let me know when you've considered." Iain paused in the door. "The couple next door have agreed to move in with their daughter and son-in-law in the end house so that some of you can stay there." He grinned at Tam. "I daresay your sisters and grandmother will find room for you."

He must have still been in earshot when Morag rasped, "Gormless this be, Mairi, even talking about anything else if we've a way to leave! Let's hope your wicked nonsense won't put the captain off or anger God."

Andrew tugged ruminatively at his thick curly beard. "Let's not be hasty, Morag lass—"

"You're never that!" she snapped. "Get your wits about you,

man. If it opens a way to America, getting burned out may have been our good luck!"

"You'll say that when Fearchar died of it?" His look was so fierce that she shrank away. Most of the time, Andrew bore her chidings like a great bull twitching his ears at flies, but he, like Barry, had the slow-kindling but fervent wrath of the Nicolsons, the clan that had been on the island even before the MacLeods. "Now, Mairi darlin', what have you to say?"

"I won't beg you to stay," she said painfully, trying to keep her voice steady. "But I will never leave. Fearchar told me to mind his harp. Where shall Cridhe sing but on this island?"

Eyes blurred with tears, she looked from face to face of these people who had been her world, who had shared the hearth and songs her whole life long. If they all departed in the white-sailed ships, wouldn't she and Gran be like two stalks of grass left to wither when the tussock was rent away? But it was the others' right to choose. Without making it sound better than it was, she told them about the broch.

Adam flung the hair from his eyes and said regretfully, "Mairi, was this our home place, we'd think on it, but lass, we have twice had our roof burned over us. Our bairns sleep near the sea where they died of ills they could have thrown off had they been half-nourished. Were it only us, Kirsty and I might stay, but we don't want these young ones to live as we have, at the laird's whim with never a sure footing. We will go."

Mairi bowed her head. "Come with us, child," pleaded Kirsty. "You can sing the old songs in a new country. Had Fearchar lived, I think even he would say we must flit."

Unable to speak, Mairi could only shake her head. Tam came to her and gave her a hug. "I'll stay, Mairi, and take care of you and Gran and Eileen." He gave his fair head a toss and his eyes glittered. "When I grow up, I'll have my own boat. The lairds don't own the sea yet, or the herring in it."

Andrew brooded. At last, glancing at Barry and Sheila, he said apologetically, "You'll not take it ill, Mairi, if we think the night on it? 'Tis heavy, however we decide."

"Father!" Catriona entreated. "You'll never say I can't go!"

He gave her thick braid a teasing fillip. "Would it grind much barley if I did? Wheesht, lassie! You're the age for journeyin' and can travel with Adam and Kirsty. Decide for yourself."

Throwing her arms around him and even including her dour mother, Catriona gave them each a kiss. "Och, then, I'm good as away!" She sobered as her eyes met Mairi's. Coming close, she spoke so softly that no one else could hear. "Look you, Mairi! Think what fun we'd have together in America! We'd see the red Indians and those great beasts called buffalo. And when Calum comes—"

"Don't make sure he will," Mairi warned. "Calum, for all your fuss about moving to a town, never meant to live anywhere but in Aosda."

"Well, now he can't and if he wants to live with me, he'll have to follow." Catriona's eyes flashed. "If he stays, I'll find a man over there."

"No doubt you will! If you can change countries, why not a man?"

Catriona went crimson. "You're a hateful cat, Mairi Mac-Leod!"

"Cat yourself, Mistress Nicolson. You seem ready to rub up against any legs you come across."

"Lassies, don't wrangle," commanded Andrew. "Is that broth I smell? We're nigh famished after our tramp."

"There's broth," smiled Sheila, always relieved when harsh words stopped. "There's sausage and currant scones and I was just making bannocks."

"Cook's made a tub of Athole brose especially for you," Catriona said. "I'll go fetch it." For a moment, she gave Mairi a hard stare before, in a breath, each said, "I'm sorry, love!" They went into each other's arms and set off to the lodge together.

"I'll bring Gran down," said Mairi. "Ask Mrs. Fraser if we can't all eat in the cottage tonight."

"Bring the harp," urged her cousin. "Oh Mairi, I will miss it! I'll miss you."

But you'll go. Mairi forced away the spurt of bitterness. "I'll miss you. But you can take the songs with you, Cat, sing them to your bairns."

"It won't be the same."

How could it be? Songs grew out of the air and sun and soil of a place. In an effort at cheer, Mairi said, "There'll be songs there. Learn them, Caty. If you're going, don't hark back more than you must."

"You preach a good sermon for one who won't come in the kirk," laughed Catriona and turned to the kitchen while Mairi went down the hall.

Rounding a corner, she almost bumped into Iain. Each stepped back. His eyes searched her face. "Have they decided?"

Was he, for her sake, rueful about the choice he must be sure the others would make? "Adam and Kirsty want to leave." The lump swelling in Mairi's throat stopped her words. "So does Catriona. Tam will stay. The others want to think."

"It's the most important decision they'll ever make." He hesitated. "Forgive me, Mistress Mairi, but I hope you won't try to persuade them to stay against their better judgment."

"I know 'tis their lives they're choosing. I'll say naught."

He smiled a little. "Fair enough. But I could wish *they'd* persuade *you*. You're certainly deaf to my arguments."

"I hear them, sir."

"Then why? Why in God's name persist in this folly?"

"Can't you see?" she cried in ringing passion. "Folk of mine have lived on this island from the dawn of time. I will not abandon it to lairds who buy with money what belongs to the people. I will not take our songs away to leave only the bleating of Cheviots and the sound of hunting guns."

"By God, girl, what a soldier you'd have made!"

She shook her head, fire dying. "I'd only have fought well defending my home. I could never go into other lands and kill folk I'd no quarrel with." His face tightened and she flushed. "I meant no slap at you, captain, but that seems to be what soldiers do."

He shrugged. "Your views are disconcerting, lass, but let's cry truce. Are you taking your grandmother to see the men?"

"Aye. We'll sup together and have some songs."

"Your fingertips are healed enough?"

" 'Twas good balm you gave me."

"I haven't heard you play. Would you allow me to trade tunes on my Northumbrian pipe for some of yours?"

"You play the bagpipe?"

"I can do a grace-note or two. Of course, these are small pipes and I'm far from being a MacCrimmon." The MacCrimmons had been hereditary pipers to the MacLeods of Skye till late in the last century after most chieftains had given up maintaining their own musicians. Fearchar used to snort that the pipes replaced the harp for battle music only after the armies grew too large to hear the harp or the bard's voice calling out "The Incitement to Battle."

"A-shriekin' and a-skirlin' like lost souls, those pipes," he scorned. "How the poor tykes can make out the music from the wailin' of the dying is more than I ken. When there's too many to heed the harp, the battle's got too big. Fighting turns to butchery, not men showing courage."

That thought of Fearchar brought a smile along with the hot sting of tears. "Why," she said, "we'll have a regular ceilidh! Do come, and bring Jamie, too, if he likes."

He stepped out of her way with a small bow. Odd of gentry to bow to the likes of her but the bemused expression on his face said that he didn't mock her.

As if by common consent not to mar this reunion, no one talked of the captain's offer. Gran, with that peculiarly divided awareness of hers, welcomed the returned fishermen while accepting that her Michael must have extended his trip. She had three helpings of Athole brose, declaring there was just the right amount of whiskey and honey to flavor the oats and was already merry by the time Iain appeared. He and Jamie brought a jug of whiskey, another of ale, and a flagon of wine which Iain offered to the women.

"To the devil with wine when there's whiskey," Gran said, holding out her cup to Jamie.

"Be sure," croaked Morag, "the devil will find those who drink his brew."

She was the only abstainer. The captain poured a little wine in a goblet of water for Eileen, filled another for Sheila who timidly asked to taste it, and foamed ale into a glass for Kirsty before he filled one of the beautiful crystal goblets he'd brought and carried it to Mairi where she was tuning Cridhe.

"I think you'll like this." He handed her the wine which sparkled like liquid sunlight and poured some for himself, lifting his goblet in salute. "Here's to music and friends, lass. May you ever have them."

She took a sip. It was cool and delicious with an edge of velvet fire that curved through her so that she wondered if it came from wine or his deep gray eyes. Almost desperately, she said, "Will you play first, sir?"

"I can give you 'The MacLeod Salute', but my little pipes are meant for *ceol beag*, the small or light music, rather than *ceol mor*, the great."

Under his arm, he tucked the bag, covered with the tartan of MacDonald of the Isles, green, black and purple crossed with thin lines of white and red, and worked the bellows under his right arm which filled the bag through a wind-pipe that lay across his chest, moving the drone slides to make them harmonize with the ebony chanter, the flute-like part which the piper fingered. When he was satisfied with the sound, Iain played the opening, the *Urlar* or Ground, of the old clan melody and quickened into variations that transformed the basic tune with doublings, treblings and grace notes to the *Crunluath* or crowning movement which flowed back into the Ground.

Applause filled the cottage. "You're a brave piper, sir," cried

Andrew, lifting his cup. "I ne'er heard 'The Salute' played better."

"I love the pipes," said Iain, handing them to Tam who had come close, wide-eyed, to gaze longingly at the silver and ivory embellished instrument. "I wouldn't ask better than Walter Kennedy.

> 'I will nae priests for me sall sing,
> Nor yet nae bells for me to ring;
> But ae bag-pype to play a spring.'

But you know what they say—to make a real piper takes seven years' training on top of descent from seven generations of pipers. So I must be content to entertain my friends."

Tam looked stricken at that, but Iain said, "If you'll come over tomorrow afternoon, lad, I'll give you a lesson. An odd-looking thing, isn't it, for music to come out of? But they skirled in Egypt and Assyria, China, India and Greece. Some say Roman legions brought them to Scotland though the Celts may have done so first. It's even said that instead of fiddling while Rome burned, Nero played the pipes."

Who were all those people, where were all those countries? Mairi wondered, feeling ignorant. Hers was not the only bewildered look, and Iain said quickly, "Anyway, ever since Clan MacDonald used pipes to scare the enemy at Bannockburn when Robert the Bruce beat the English over five hundred years ago, they've been part of the Highland arsenal. Even when the pipes were forbidden after Culloden, they were still used in the army. The lairds no longer have pipers but The Black Watch does, and all the Highlander regiments."

He played a march that had even Morag tapping her foot and then "The Red-Speckled Bull," singing the words in a deep, resonant voice. He finished with the song of a piper who went down into a cave and died in a struggle with a monster. "Oh," cried the doomed man. "Would I had three hands, two for my pipes and one for the sword!"

It was the way Fearchar must have felt when he snatched Cridhe from the blazing house. Cridhe was eager to sing. The strings pulsated under Mairi's fingers, almost as if they would sound of themselves to play Fearchar's favorite, "Seagull of the Land Under Waves."

> "Little gulls and white wave crests,
> Gulls of the ocean, hide not your song . . ."

She could imagine Fearchar was there, humming softly, nodding to the melody. She sang of summer at the shielings, and played the best-loved milking song of the Highlands and Islands, "Crodh Chailein," but after that she played songs Fearchar had composed: a love lilt for Rosanna; a tune of prideful joy on the birth of Eamonn, Mairi's father; a lament for the sons killed fighting Napoleon; a rollicking smuggler's taunt to the excise men; his thoughts on leaving the sea for the croft.

> "I lose my soul in the sea, lass,
> The wind bears it ever along,
> But I find it in peace at your hearth, love,
> And you are my loveliest song."

"Aye, Michael made that song when he gave up smuggling," Gran sighed, graciously allowing the captain to refill her cup. "But he still yearns after the sea. Look at the man, still away with all the others home! I vow I'll put my foot down this time no matter how he smiles at me!" Rising briskly, she said, "Andrew, lad, if you'll make some mouth-music, I'll dance a fling for my part at this ceilidh. Captain MacDonald, will you stand up with me?"

He swept a low bow. "Honored, Mrs. MacLeod."

Andrew had a rare gift with the mouth-music, developed to accompany dancers when there was no pipe, fiddle, or harp. Its repetitive tongue-twisting cadence had a passionate human intensity no instrument could rival. Everyone clapped the rhythm as the two danced, Gran with skirts gathered, the captain with toes pointed in a way that showed him no stranger to flings and reels.

They stopped with a flourish amid great applause. Then Barry told how the warrior maiden, Fair Lilliard, helped defeat the English at the Battle of Ancrum Muir nigh three hundred years ago. Adam gave the tangled marriages and genealogy of a woman who'd became her own niece and her own aunt. It was late when Mairi noticed that Gran had dozed off with her head on Sheila's shoulder.

Iain saw it, too, and got to his feet. "I've never been to a better ceilidh." Perhaps, being gentry, he hadn't been to any, though he had joined in lustily. His hand rested on Tam's shoulder. "Come tomorrow, lad, and we'll let you try the pipes." His gaze swept the circle of faces. "When you've had time to think over what you want to do, let me know."

He tossed the pipes to Jamie in a way that made Mairi grin to remember the tradition that the famed pipers heaved away their instrument in just such a manner, often over a shoulder, to show that the music lay in their skill, not in the bag of pipes. It was with care, though, that motioning back Barry, he lightly lifted Gran and carried her out the door. As Mairi followed with a sleepy Eileen and Tam, the boy caught her hand.

"We still have Fearchar's songs, don't we, Mairi?"

"We always will."

"I—I'm glad you played them tonight." Tam's voice broke. "It—it seemed he was there. Happy with us."

"Maybe he was."

"What if the others go to America? All of them?"

"We'll wish them well."

"Wheesht, Mairi! Aren't you ever scared?"

"Lots of times. Aren't you?"

"Well—yes, but men can't let on."

Her twelve-year-old brother-man. Between tears and laugh-

71

ter, Mairi said, "You can tell me, lad. That's what sisters are for, and mothers and wives. To tell things men can't tell other men, great bairns that they all be."

He said plaintively, "I'm too sleepy to worry that one out."

"Never mind. There's a bed ready, so soft you'll think you've fallen in a feather mountain, and you can sleep late as you want."

"Where's our cows, Sholma and Rigga?"

"A milk-maid's seeing to them. She sings them the same song I do. They're fine." Mairi gave him a quick hug. "Don't fash yourself, Tam, there'll be plenty to do and very quickly! Rest while you can."

The captain put Gran down on the big, postered bed, told Tam and Eileen good-night, and turned in the door. "You have a rare gift with the harp, Mistress Mairi. Were you in Edinburgh or Aberdeen, I think you could make a living. For my part, I'd far rather hear you than Jenny Lind or even Franz Liszt."

More names she'd never heard of, but his sincere admiration made her glow. "Yourself, you're grand with the warblers, sir." These grace notes, devised to suggest repetition of a note, had become perhaps the greatest beauty of pipe music.

"You know what they say about pipers." In the lamplight, his eyes were very dark, but a smile softened the firm line of his mouth. "The time comes when they demand their pay."

Something leaped between them like those dancing fires that sometimes darted over the moor at night. "Indeed, sir, we all are in your debt and must remain so, I fear, for what could we give you?"

He took a step forward. She stood transfixed, trembling within, knees feeling as if they were giving way. There was a humming in her blood, a yearning for his touch. His hand raised, brushed her cheek, but then he caught in his breath, swung violently away.

"I'm paid with your song. Sleep well, Mistress Mairi."

The door closed after him, but Mairi knew, shuddering as if

released from the grasp of towering, crashing waves, that if he had taken her hand and led her down the hall, she would have gone with him, and gladly, even though it was wrong, even though it could only bring her heartbreak.

7

That night, when Mairi roused between fitful dreams, she wondered if Iain, in some chamber above, was restless, too; if he
thought of her. Not likely. He must know many fascinating
ladies who belonged in his world. Give him credit, at least, for
not seducing her for a few days' diversion. From what she'd
heard of gentlemen, most wouldn't look beyond their night's
pleasure.

How many of that sort would have interfered at the burning?
How many would give shelter and comfort to evicted folk? How
many could come to a crofter ceilidh and fit right in? No, Iain
wasn't like most of his class, but there could be nothing honest
between them.

Well, yes, there was. The feeling she had was honest, true as
blood and breath for that was where it stemmed from. No matter
what the minister said, she couldn't believe anything so natural
and inevitable was a sin; but it would be if the pure fire of
unspoken love changed into a joining of bodies forbade by God
and man. And well she knew that hadn't happened last night
because of Iain's scruples, not because of her virtuousness. If
he'd stretched out his hand . . .

Flame coursed through her, sweet and wild, reckless. She
scourged herself by remembering how Fearchar had died, how
Aosda lay in ruins. And what would happen now? Would An-

drew yield to Morag? Did Sheila dream of a different world for her unborn baby? Long before dawning, Mairi knew she couldn't stay around the lodge that day while the fateful decision was being made. She must not plead or argue. Those who stayed must truly want to, for hard as a crofter's life had always been, harder times lay ahead.

Mairi sighed and tried to be very quiet as she turned over for the dozenth time. She would rise at first light and go to fetch the hearthstone. More than walls or roof or furnishings, that made a home.

As soon as she could see without lighting a lamp, she built up the fire and had tea and a leftover bannock before she waked Eileen just enough to whisper that she was going over the moor and would be very late getting back. Selecting their broadest creel, for the stone, though flat, was two feet across, Mairi dropped in several bannocks and some cheese. It was so early that no one was about. Mists still brooded on the purple-brown moor as she followed tracks made by the carts sent to Aosda for the township's belongings.

At first, it was a hushed world, no hum of bees or hover of butterflies, but as she passed a brook, a disturbed dipper flew fast downstream, with a "Cli-i-ink!" It lit on a stone where it bobbed jerkily, dark brown plumage a shadow except for its white breast.

"Good morning to you," Mairi called. "Did you raise two broods this year or is one all you managed?"

A skylark winged almost straight up, warbling, and hovered before it plummeted on its insect breakfast. From a tussock came the nervous cough of a cuckoo. Those big gray birds would soon be going south, having long ago deposited their eggs in the nests of other birds, especially those of meadow pipits, who would exhaust themselves in rearing these ravenous changelings while the parent cuckoos loafed through an idle summer.

Some birds, like curlews and greenshanks, had already gone south, but a gray wagtail darted along the gravel bordering the stream, showing bright yellow at the base of his long, ever quivering tail as he caught a grub. Rays of diffused light beamed through rose and gold clouds. The moor suddenly glowed, every loch, lochan and pool luminous, bees pillaging ling and heather which gave out a sweet odor that permeated the senses like slow nectar. Butterflies, appearing with the light, clung like new blossoms to harebells and wild thyme. A kestrel hovered above, alert for some unwary vole.

Surely nowhere else in all the world was the air like wine or the land so magical, transmuted by every shift of light, responding to sun like a woman to a lover, revealing gladly all that was hidden. *Now how would you know about that?* Mairi derided herself with a throaty chuckle. All the same, wouldn't it be lovely in fine weather to spread a plaid on the heather and love beneath the broad sky rather than shut up in a house?

She started as a laughing voice hailed her. "Mistress Mairi! Tell me where you're going with that creel so I can decide whether we need horses or a wagon."

Blushing as if Iain had read her thoughts, she decided it would do him good to be mystified. "I'm fetching our home."

"What?" Dark eyebrows rose to the fall of black hair that curved over his forehead. "Lass, not even you would try to carry those tumbled stones across the island."

"The walls aren't our home. They're like the pipes you toss over your shoulder—nothing without folk to use them."

"What is your home then?"

"It'll fit in my creel."

He shook his head, smiling. "This sounds like a riddle."

"I suppose it is."

"Do you plan to live in a tent like the bedouins?"

"One of tartan would be handsome," she allowed, casting him a merry glance. How wonderful it was to walk along with him on such a beautiful morning! But any walk with him would enchant the darkest day. "However, sir, I doubt if a tent could stand up to our famous gales."

The harsh planes of his face softened to boyishness. "If you won't tell me, I'll have to march along and see."

"It's a long tramp to Aosda, sir."

"Shall I go back for horses?"

"Not for me."

"Then we'll walk." He jerked his chin at the pack slung over his shoulder. "When I saw you striking out, I raided the kitchen so we've provisions."

"You won't be at the lodge if Tam comes about the bagpipes."

"Jamie skirls a rousing march and swinging reel. I told him to show the lad some of the first things and I'll give him a lesson tonight if he hasn't decided pipes are a thing of the devil."

"He was mightily taken with them." *And you.*

"Does he play the harp?"

"A little. But he thinks it's old-fashioned."

"You don't."

"There's no fashion about it. It belongs to all times."

"I've heard there aren't many pipers on Lewis."

"That may be so. I've only heard them a few times. Cridhe is the only harp I know of. Mostly now it's fiddles and trumps and maybe the Box—the accordion. Of course if the ministers get their way, we'll have no music at all."

"Music has a way of outlasting laws."

"Can it outlast the kirk?"

"It's in the heart before kirk or law. It comes with the beat of the mother's heart before a babe is born."

She stopped to stare at him. "Fearchar once said that!"

"More than one man can speak the truth. Music is in us like blood and breathing and whoever, whatever, stifles that, stifles some of the person, too." He laughed softly. "Don't look so sad, Mistress Mairi. Music always wins."

"Can it?" she asked wistfully.

"For years after Bonnie Prince Charlie was defeated at Culloden, it was a crime to own pipes unless one was in the army, because the English feared the music would encourage rebellion." He smiled at her. "Now the pipes are played all over Scotland. They will always be. Cridhe may sing alone now but in your lifetime I'll wager you see the harp come back to the islands."

"I pray that may be so, captain. There are songs that don't sound right except from the harp."

"And some need the bagpipe."

They laughed together. That was a kind of music, the lilt of her laughter sparkling against the deep vibrance of his. He reached over and lifted the creel from her, slipping the woven heather band across his chest so that the basket hung against his back.

"Och, sir!" She was horrified. He—*he* was not made for bearing such a workaday burden. "Give it back, do! I'm used to it. You'll spoil your clothes!"

"I can't see you lugging that great basket, lass."

"There's naught in it but bannocks and a bit of cheese."

He shook his head. "You'll not get it from me, Mistress Mairi. A girl like you should walk light and free, dance a few turns just from being young and alive."

"I walk light with the creel, and can knit at the same time."

"Sing, too, I daresay!"

"Of course. There's always singing. You can come in from sea with the men's rowing songs and meet the reaping songs of the women as you step ashore. There's songs for the quern and loom and fulling the cloth. Even," she laughed, "for spreading manure."

"It's like marching," Iain nodded. "Folk move better to a tune. Would you sing me some of the work songs, Mistress Mairi?" As she sang, he'd listen till he caught the melody and then would whistle. And what a whistler he was! He trilled and warbled like a chorus of birds, weaving his notes around her voice.

It was like dancing with their voices, meeting, retreating,

soaring with flourishes. "I'd like to try that with the harp," she said, breathless and smiling as they finished a lively churning song. "Sir, I think we do sound well together."

"We do. For sure we must have another ceilidh so we can show off."

"Captain!"

"Why not say it?" he bantered. "We all like to do what we're best at."

"But it sounds so vain!"

He wagged his finger at her. "To know what you can do is the basis for self-respect, lass. No boot in being mealy-mouthed about it."

Again, he sounded much like Fearchar. She wished they had known each other. As she caught her first glimpse of Aosda, a rush of grief and loss flooded through her. Had she been alone, she would have wailed aloud, lamented the roofless houses, the trampled gardens, and most of all, Fearchar. Her throat ached and her eyes filled with bitter tears. It was a graveyard as sure as the one by the sea, the grave of a little community that had existed for countless centuries.

She couldn't move the walls and fields but she could take the ancient heart-stone. Wherever it was fixed and a fire lit on it to warm and feed her family, that was home.

"What have you come for, lass?" Iain's voice was strange. "What can be left?"

She answered by going through the entrance with its charred remnant of a door. Better not look at the blackened bits of box-beds and roof timbers. These were limned forever in her mind. She knelt by the stone in the center of the main room. The peats were as Gran had left them that last night with the mounded center of ashes.

Now that it was time to move the stone, the deed seemed awesome, close to sacrilegious. But leave it to be dunged by sheep, possibly torn up for use in some building made by strangers? Still, it seemed an undertaking that required a ceremony.

Closing her eyes, she stretched out her hand and thanked the Sacred Three, Mary, Christ, and Brigid, for blessing the hearth these many years.

"Come with the stone," she prayed beneath her breath. "To save, to shield, surround our hearth, each night and every night. Amen."

Feeling that the guardians gave consent, Mairi opened her eyes and caught a breath of dismay. Why hadn't she remembered to bring a tool for prying stone from the hard-packed clay of the floor?

"So it's the stone," Iain said. "Before you started scowling at the discovery that you need more than your hands to get it loose, you looked like a priestess." He produced a stout claspknife. "Let's see what this will do."

"You'll dull the blade."

"It can be sharpened."

He began to dig around the rock. Mairi found a piece of wood strong enough to dig with, dig through the years, through many lifetimes. Almost perfectly flat, the stone was about two inches thick. As she worked, it seemed to Mairi that the spirits of those who had smoored the fire through generations and centuries gathered about her, outstretching their hands in benediction. Celt and Viking, Pict they were. Among a cloud of small dark women, one smiled and, without words, conveyed to Mairi that she had found and placed the stone, cooked there and warmed her people. Beyond this throng shone a bright and beautiful being. *I am Brigid, Brighde, once mortal, who tamed the lightning for my people's sake and brought it to the hearth. Saint or goddess matters not. I am the soul of the home-fire. When you light it, I am with you.*

It was to Mairi both a brief and endless time till Iain tested the stone and it moved. A few minutes more of delving and he lifted it.

"Since this makes home," he said softly, "You could take it to America."

"No!"

"Why not?"

She couldn't tell this Edinburgh-educated gentleman that the spirits wouldn't cross the ocean, that they belonged here. "It wouldn't be the same," she said tersely. "If—if I ever went over the ocean, I'd leave the stone on the island."

"Very Gaelic," he said between a smile and a frown. "And though I'm a Gael myself, I do not understand you."

"Ah well, you're a man." She laughed to take away the sting and added truthfully, "To be fair, captain, of our township only Gran and perhaps Sheila would feel the same. You may be sure Catriona won't carry a hearthstone to America and I doubt if the others will fetch theirs even if they stay on the island."

She put the half-burned peats from the hearth into the creel with it. Before she could bend to slip it on her back, Iain took it. "Let's find a place where we can see all the way to the Harris hills," he said. "And then let's have our luncheon."

He *did* understand that she wouldn't want to eat among the devastated houses and he went ahead of her, not looking back. This left her to glance around what had been her dwelling. *You sheltered us well from wind and weather,* she told the walls. *Thank you and be peaceful.* As she stepped outside, a current of warmth flowed with her. She knew she was taking with her all that had made a home.

They found a hillock tufted with blue moor grass above a lochan rimmed all around with yellow irises. The little lake shimmered with sun and fleeting clouds that flashed from every trace of water as if from a thousand odd-shaped diamond mirrors. Blue in the distance rose the hills dividing the Long Island, Lewis from Harris. Above the sparkling swells of the sea, she could just make out the Stones of Callanish.

"Have you been to the Stones?" asked Iain, following her gaze.

"Now and again." *Each Midsummer Morn since I bled for the*

first time. "The Stones are buried deep in peat except where people cleared the aisle of it, but the pillars still stand tall. In mist or rain they look like hooded giants."

"There must be stories about them."

She didn't want him to laugh at the ones she believed, so she told him a harmless fancy. "When cuckoos come to Lewis in the spring, each is supposed to fly to the Stones and give its first call from there."

"About the time of Beltane?" He laughed at her expression. "I'm Gaelic, too, my lass. Here, try this truffled woodcock and have a bit of pâté. The figs are nice, and I made off with a whole raspberry tart."

"Greedy!"

"It'll taste much better here than at that dismal long table in that dismal dark dining room. Jamie and I huddle at one end but even so, it doesn't spur one's appetite."

Now there was gentry for you, needing spurs for tucking into their food! "All food's good when you're hungry," she said.

"I'm very hungry now." He handed her a silver flask and smiled at her dubious expression. "Only ale, lass. It won't make you tipsy. Would I risk what your Gran would say if we came staggering in from the moor?"

The ale was mild but she felt as if her blood filled with sunlight and danced gay and exuberant as the brilliance of the lochs.

Iain set the creel just inside their door. "Now hear what I say," he warned Mairi. "Don't set off to the broch with that stone on your back. If you must and will take it there, we'll go on horses."

"I must and I will."

He gave her a grim look before looking past her to Tam who had jumped up and hurried forward eagerly. "There you are, lad. Will you drink tea with me and have a go at the pipes?"

"Och, sir, may I?"

"If your sister agrees."

There was nothing to do but consent, though Mairi felt a pang as Tam trotted off down the hall with Iain, struggling to match his long, easy stride. He beguiled them all, did Iain. Because he had no guile. But he was not their kind. She had to remember that.

That night they gathered again at the cottage. Almost afraid to look at the Nicolsons for fear of what she might read in their faces, Mairi got Gran comfortably seated and brought her a cup of tea. Lines seemed to have smoothed from Kirsty's face and her step was light as she scolded fondly at the twins to keep out from underfoot, the twins who would grow up Americans, probably with only the dimmest memories of the island. Well, that was best, to have an undivided heart.

If Catriona had qualms, they didn't show. Her eyes danced and her laughter bubbled, especially after Iain and Jamie came in. She offered them a plate of shortbread and poured out tea. After glancing around and uneasily realizing that he was the eldest man, Andrew cleared his throat.

"Mairi lass, we've chased it up and chased it down, whether to stay or go. I have a question which I charge you to answer as if you were in court before a judge. Barry and I went to the broch today. If we find roof timbers, we could last the winter there, but then what?" His hazel eyes, usually gentle, fixed on her insistently. "Do you believe that we'll have proper crofts again? With croplands and pasture? Where we can make a living, not just starve along?"

"Andrew! Only God could promise that!"

"I'm not askin' for a promise," he said with a shake of his massive head. "I just want to make sure you've thought hard and long past this one winter. You've much of Fearchar in you, lass. I always trusted him."

"And see where it's got you!" Morag snapped.

Andrew steadily regarded Mairi. "All you need say, lass, is what you believe."

She straightened. *Oh Fearchar! It's not easy, is it, to take on your shoulders what others decide?* She searched her heart. Like

83

rock beneath blowing sea sand, she found a faith so strong, a hope powered with such will and purpose, that it was more certainty than she had about anything else; except her love for Iain.

"We can build soil on skinned earth, build it on the rocks," she said. "For the cows, we can cut grass wherever we find it, and eke it out with seaweed. We have a lot of spun wool and can weave it this winter to trade for what we need. Next summer, we can build houses." She looked from Morag's sneer to Sheila's flower face and Barry's hopeful one before meeting Andrew's adjuring eyes. "I believe we'll have crofts again, in time better than at Aosda."

Catriona shook her head at such solemnity. "Mairi, Mairi! Is it second sight you've got then?"

"No." Though what had it been, those presences she had seen and felt at the hearthstone? "But I believe, sure as I live, that if we can hold on—and it may take years, it may take our lifetimes—we'll have our rights again, we'll have our land."

Andrew moved his head in ponderous affirmation. "Then we will bide."

"Fools!" burst out Morag. "It's not only beasts will eat seaweed but us as well, and lucky we'll be if it's for this winter only! Why, *why*, hang on by our fingernails when the same work would get us farms in America—real farms with plenty of land that we'd own free of landlords?"

"You may go and you will, woman," thundered Andrew, flushing scarlet beneath his weathered skin. "But if you stay, let's hear no more of your sour carping!"

She shrank in amazement before she gave a wild laugh. "Och, man, you ken well I've no choice as a God-fearing woman but to cleave to my wedded husband, be he ne'er so daft! But what's this of what does Mairi think and what does she believe as if she were aught but a carnaptious lass with that stiff proud MacLeod neck that was her Grandfather's undoing?"

"Hold your noise, woman!"

"I'll have my say first, for isn't it my son, too, you've brought to this folly?" Hands on gaunt hips, Morag glared from husband to son. "You stay for a song, that's the truth of it! I knew last night, knew in my innards, that the harp 'tranced you. You, too, Sheila, that should know better for the sake of the bairn you carry! It's not for any reason or sensible hope that you trust your fate to this green lassie! 'Tis all for a song . . ."

"Mother," began Barry.

Slumping to her chair, she buried her face in her hands. "Aw, lass!" Andrew gathered her to his broad chest, rocking her. "It'll work out. You'll see."

"I'll carry things for you when your back hurts, mother," Sheila promised, and Barry said, "I'll make you a fine wicker chair, and you'll sit in our new house like a queen. Besides, when Lucas and Paul and Calum get home from the army—"

"I hope they'll have the wit of Catriona and be off this Black Moor as fast as they can." Morag wiped her eyes on her apron. "I must have greatly sinned to be condemned to the rocks, but I will bear it since it's God's will."

"Chirk up, mother." Catriona patted her mother's hand. "If it goes ill, you can come to me. I'm bound it won't be long till I can send money home."

"You're a good lass," sniffed Morag. She shot a withering glance at Mairi. "What's more, you've a head on your shoulders."

"Don't we all?" jabbed Gran. "Captain, dear, be that a jug of the uisge-beatha you set in the corner when you came in?"

"Let's try it and see." Rising, he got the jug and filled cups and glasses before lifting his own. "Here's to Celts and Vikings, those who stay and those who go! May they flourish both!" Turning to Mairi, he smiled into her eyes. "Most of all, here's to songs and those who sing them."

He downed his drink while Mairi sipped at hers, warmed more by Iain's gaze than by the mellow whiskey. She couldn't long enjoy that pleasure for as she looked at her kinfolk who had chosen to stay, she had to confront the truth.

Youngest of them all except for Tam and Eileen, it was she

who had swayed them, she who would have to lead, hearten and plan. Along with relieved joy that they were staying came the heavy weight of responsibility.

Could she take Fearchar's place, in grimmer times than he had ever known? If only he were here! Then, as if he spoke to her, she knew he was. He was in the harp; he was in the songs. And they had the hearthstone.

Reassured, she looked up, met Iain's watchful eyes. Smiling, head high, she raised her glass to him—and to the future, even though it would have to be lived through without him. She would rather have these sweet-painful times with him than everything there could be between man and woman with anybody else.

The next days flew in readying Catriona and the MacNeills for their journey. Gran finished a warm shawl for Catriona, dyed from heather, a rich plum color. Eileen said with a quivering lip that she was too old for poppets and gave her beloved only doll to little Brigid, while Tam solemnly bequeathed to Rory a Viking ship handsomely carved by Fearchar from a piece of driftwood. Kirsty and Adam had little enough but they left large, heavy things like their quern, a wicker cupboard, the twins' cradle for Sheila's baby, and most of their implements.

Shaking his head over the peat-cutting iron, Adam said, "The captain says we won't be needing this. There's no peat in America. They do be burning wood or coal. Wood! Can you believe that? But he says there are many forests." He hefted the caschrom, the crooked foot, with which he'd dug up many an acre, and gave it to Tam. "Here you are, lad, It turns beautiful clods if you press your foot down hard and give it a proper jerk. The captain says it's all plows in America, with fields a sight too big for diggin' the way we do here."

Mairi had no treasure to give Catriona but her red flannel underskirt was almost new so she made her take that and tucked into it a small bag of dried heather blooms. "So you won't forget the moor," she said, blinking back tears as they embraced and clung in the realization that after all their life together, they probably would never meet again. That ocean between! Oh, so far!

"I won't forget anything," Catriona promised, eyes moist. "I love you, Mairi. You'll always be my sister, even if Calum—" She broke off. "I *have* to go, though. You do see that?"

Mairi nodded. "Yes, love. I see that. I—I wish you luck and joy and a fine life—ever and forever."

On their last night, they shared a festive meal in the cottage and held a farewell ceilidh. Mairi brought the harp, Gran a jug of heather ale for the travelers to take with them, and Iain came with bagpipes, whiskey, ale and sparkling wine.

Gran saluted him with a grin. "Here's meat and music both, as the fox said when he stole the bagpipes. That's right, lad, pour me a dram of the good whiskey and I'll tell you about heather ale." She handed the jug to Kirsty. "When you drink it in America, lass, let it remind you of the Peerie folk that some call Picts. Aye, they were grand fighters! Thrashed the Romans time and again, and when the Scots came over from Ireland, they had at each other till the Scot king wed into the Pictish royal line. After that the Picts sort of melted into the Scots and we've the blood of both along with that of Vikings."

She took a slow, appreciative sip and picked up her knitting. "Now the Picts were main fond of heather ale and only the king and his eldest son could know the trick of brewing it. When they were defeated by the King of Scots, that king was bound to know the secret. 'I'd have shame to tell you while my son's alive to know it,' said the Peerie chief. 'Slay the lad and then I'll tell you.' So the Scots king had the boy killed. 'Now,' says he, 'What of the ale?' 'What of it?' says the Peerie. 'You said you'd tell,' said the King of Scots. 'Devil I will,' says the Peerie. 'And my laddie, he can't now. You may lord it in my hall and you may steal my kingdom, but you'll no brew ale from the heather flower.' Well, wouldn't you know the Scot was so wrathy he cleaved the Peerie's head with his battle-ax, and that was the end of the secret."

"But Gran, you brew the ale!" cried Eileen, diverted from looking wistfully at the doll Brigid now cuddled close.

"I do, henny," said Gran with a twinkle. "I tested and tried and by now I think my ale's as full of the spirit of the heather as was ever that Peerie king's."

"His couldn't have been better," Andrew said. "Though maybe there were other things to put in it. My grandfather, who had it from his grandfather, who heard it from his grandfather, did say that when Norway claimed these islands and the Highlands, that it was warm for the span of three long lives. Magnus Barelegs—he got that name from beltin' on the kilt which shows he had some sense—brought a great fleet to put fear into the Islanders, and he burned the fig trees that grew then on Lewis. Think of that! Figs! He burned the other trees, too, while he laid waste to Skye and Uist." Sadly, Andrew shook his head. "Before the trees could grow back in strong plenty, the warm years ended and there were more folk to use what trees there were. So it was that in a summer nigh onto eight hundred years agone, that barelegged chiel from Norway lost us our trees forever."

Fearchar had taught Mairi the song of Magnus' skald and she quoted from it. "'Fire played in the fig trees of Lewis . . . Fire gushed out of the houses . . . Greenland's king caused maids to weep south in the islands.' "

Barry screwed up his eyes and after a moment delivered a rhyme. That was a favorite pastime, making up verse on the spot. It sometimes went back and forth for hours in a sort of contest.

> " 'Stead of bringing fire and plunder
> Like his heathen god of thunder,
> That barelegged bright-haired laddie
> Should have eaten Finnan haddie!"

Grinning, Adam tossed back his wayward strand of hair and added his doggerel.

"The Picts wore paint, the Scots wore plaids;
Now ladies paint but not the lads."

Tam picked up Cridhe's tartan and swathed it around him, parading as he chanted from "The Whig's Supplication" by Samuel Colvill, a rhymer who'd poked fun at a dour Glasgow minister, Zachary Boyd, the translator of the Bible into excruciatingly bad verse.

"And Jacob made for his wee Josie,
A tartan coat to keep him cozy!"

Applauding louder than anyone, Iain chuckled. "I never thought of it before, but of course a coat of many colors should be a plaid."

"To be sure," nodded Gran in her freshly goffered cap. She had spent the afternoon heating the tiny poker that then fitted into a holder so that the frills of her caps could be bent over and under to flute them. Gran had a special box in which, when she went anywhere, she carried a clean cap, edging shaped to crisp perfection. In her youth, she said, some married women still wore *curtches*, a white linen triangle tied beneath the chin with one point hanging down the back, but Mairi had never seen them, only caps or *mutches* that tied in a bow under the chin. Gran wore her best cap tonight, snowy ruffles of lace and eyelet work making a delightful frame for her fine-boned face and vivid blue eyes. "Now, captain, dear, won't we hear your pipes?"

It was very late when Mairi played "Loch Lomond," about how the spirit of one dying in a foreign land returns to the homeland by The Low Road, an underground path, and traveling faster than the living, reaches the beloved loch before the surviving friend. Did The Low Road stretch over the ocean? There were tears in most eyes when Cridhe's music faded. Mairi was glad when Iain tucked the pipes under his arm, pumped the bellows, and skirled into "MacLeod's Rousing Tune."

90

It was so rousing that Catriona challenged Jamie to join her in a reel with Kirsty and Adam. When it was over and they said their good-nights for the last time, there was laughter with the tears, a feeling of hope beneath the sadness of parting. Iain was a soldier. He knew how to hearten folk for what they had to do.

Farewells were said in the dim light of morning. Adam handed the twins to Kirsty and climbed up himself, giving Catriona a hand. Barry was driving the wagon, piled high with belongings, so at least one person of Aosda would wave the travelers out of sight from Stornoway Harbor.

"I'll write," Catriona promised, weeping as she bent down to kiss her parents a last time and clasp the hands of Mairi and Sheila so tightly that it pained.

Mairi nodded. Swallowing hard, she managed a smile. "Good fortune, darling. Ever and forever."

"And to you. I can't help but hope you'll change your mind— that by this time next year, we'll be together in America."

Mairi didn't reply to that but stood back with the others to watch till the wagon was out of sight on the track leading north. With them vanished more of the safe, familiar life. Mairi shivered. One arm around Eileen and Tam and the other around Gran, she went into the cottage to have another cup of tea with all that were left of her folk. Iain had stayed away, feeling this was a private time, but she would have given much for the sight of him.

"My only daughter gone!" Morag wailed against Andrew's shoulder.

Awkwardly, he patted her back. "For sure, lass, Sheila's our daughter. When Lucas and Paul come back, they'll marry, too. We'll have a host of daughters! Besides, Catriona was not one to bide quiet in a little township. I doubt me Stornoway would have been far enough for her."

It must have hurt Sheila to have her mother-in-law make such a difference between her and Catriona, especially when she was never rebellious or pert, which Catriona often was, but the gold-haired young woman said comfortingly, "If Barry and I have a wee girl, mother, we'll name her for Catriona."

That only set Morag off anew. "I'll never see her children! And she won't be here to lighten my old age! What can you, Sheila, and you, Mairi, know about mothers and daughters when you're both orphans?"

"Stop your rant, woman," cut in Andrew. "Devil the care you'd get from our Caty any road with you spittin' at each other like two wet cats! You have all your children living. Few women do. And I hand over any coin I earn and put up with your clatterin.' "

"What we need to do," said Mairi, "is get ready for winter."

Morag pulled back from Andrew's clumsy attempts to daub her eyes. "That we must, since we're doomed to stay. Have you found our roof timbers, Ceann-cinnidh?" She mocked Mairi by calling her Head of the Clan.

"The captain's giving us the timbers meant for a new stable roof," said Andrew. "He said the MacKenzies owe them to us for those Hugh Sinclair burned."

"Fine for the captain," cried Morag, bony fingers rising to her throat. "But what if the factor is on us for thieving?"

"Captain MacDonald says he'll see to it," said Andrew confidently. "And he's fixed it with Sinclair for us to harvest our crops."

"What's gentry making such a fuss over crofters for?" demanded Morag with a suspicious glance at Mairi.

"He's a good man before he's gentry," retorted Andrew.

Cheeks hot, Mairi ignored Morag's stare. "I think we'd best tell the captain we're ready to go to the broch."

"Good." Iain spoke from the open door. "The other wagon's loaded with timbers. All the men who work at the lodge want to lend a hand. They either lost crofts themselves or remember their parents being evicted."

Tears prickled Mairi's eyes. "That's mightily kind of them.

But captain, will you have to join your regiment while we're gone?"

"I must do that soon." His tone was so regretful she felt a stab of pain to know these blessed days of being near him were coming to an end. "But Jamie and I are working, too. It's been a long time since I helped thatch. I want to see if I've lost my knack." As she gazed at him in wonder, he smiled in the way that lightened his features as sunlight did the moor. "Will you come with us, Mistress Mairi? There's food and bedding in the wagon. We'll stay there till we're finished so as not to lose hours of going back and forth."

"I make better bannocks than any of these lassies," Gran boasted. "So I'll come along. Eileen, child, you can make yourself useful. Sheila must stay in shelter, Morag, so you'd best wait here with her."

"If I ne'er see that broch, it'll be too soon," Morag lamented. "Full of heathen spirits and Lord knows what else! That my first grandchild should be born in such a place—"

To everyone's astonishment, Andrew took his wife by the shoulders, greenish-brown eyes burning till she hung her head. "It's not too late to send you on the ship, woman! I've let you clack whilst it fell on my own ears but we'll all live close this winter. A tongue like yours we do not need!"

"Aye." Gran stepped forward and gazed hard at Morag. "Go if you will and God bless you, but if you stay, it's smiles we need, not frowns, and happy tunes, not dirges."

"That my husband and cousin should bespeak me so!"

"Not a patch on what Caty'd tell you, or Paul and Lucas," retorted Gran. "What is it, Morag? Stay or go?"

"As a God-fearing woman with a wedded husband, you know well I must bide."

"Bide then," said Andrew. "But 'tis time you feared me as well as God." It was not in him to take leave of his wife on such a note, though, and he tweaked the frill of her cap. "Give us a smile, lass, as you did that fine summer day when we met at the shielings. 'Twas the start of our life. Now we're starting again."

His voice was so masculine and coaxing, tenderness blended with exasperation, that Morag gave a wavering smile, and weak as it was, it changed her face. Mairi hurried to the lodge for things she, Gran and Eileen would need. Iain overtook her. "Let me put the harp in the wagon," he urged. "I'll cover it with oilskins. If it rains at the broch, the harp can stay dry in the tunnel."

"Can we take the hearthstone now?"

He gave her a whimsical look. "Won't we need it for cooking, and even more, to sit around?"

"You'll bring your bagpipes?"

"Certainly. I've never had a more flattering audience." He called to Jamie as they entered the lodge. He took the harp, Jamie the stone, and they went out while Mairi hastened to throw necessaries in the creel.

This day, this very day, they'd start their new roof! With Iain helping. If he helped set the hearth stone, secure the roof, if he mingled his music with hers, then the place would be filled with him, even when he was gone. She would be able to picture him there, rejoice in memories till he came back.

Would he come back? What if he didn't renew his lease? And soldiers died, not only from enemy fire but from diseases of camp and barracks. Warding off such thoughts, she had to face another question. Even if he came back, what could there be between them?

If I can see him, I'll be grateful, she vowed as she slipped out the door and hurried toward the courtyard. *If we can talk and be together sometimes, have a bit of music, I won't ask for more. Thank the good God I will and say I was lucky.* Iain took the creel from her, wedging it in the wagon, and as his hands brushed hers, she knew she lied. It wouldn't be enough.

The Aosda men set off across the moor with the lodge workers, but there was a gentle bay mare for Mairi, with Eileen riding pillion and Gran, mounted behind Iain, hugged him with a right good will, smiling beatifically as she rested her cheek against his broad shoulders. Gran had always been roguish and outspoken but with Fearchar gone, she seemed disconcertingly girlish. Would she go on, all her life, believing her Michael was at sea? It would be merciful if she did yet it was eerie to hear her speak of him as if he still lived.

By now it was bright morning. Skylarks had been caroling for hours, their swift upward flights and sudden falls outdone by golden plovers and lapwings in mixed flocks. Tumbling, gliding and joying in their wings, the lapwings cried, "P-weet, peewit, peewit!" as they plummeted from the sky or caroused above the moor.

"Don't they have a grand time?" laughed Eileen. "Mairi, could you make a song of theirs?"

"I'll try. I'm glad they stay all winter. See their crests and the way sun turns their backs bright green? In a flock with plovers, you can tell lapwings by their broad rounded wings. The plover's are pointed. Hear that mournful trill of theirs?"

"Tlui!" laughed Iain in a creditable imitation. "You'll have to make the tune on the harp, Mistress Mairi. The pipes can't do it."

A golden eagle wheeled toward the sun, disdaining a huge mass of starlings that swarmed at a headland. Though skirting the fiords, the party rode near enough the sea to watch gulls and terns soaring and dropping while shags, kittiwakes and guillemots amiably shared the cliffsides. And that water, gleaming emerald and molten silver, diademed with crystalline froth, would carry away Adam, Kirsty, the red-haired, playful twins—and Catriona.

Unable to believe she'd never see again her companion from the cradle, Mairi felt a great lump swelling in her throat. God bless them all, she prayed. Keep them safe on the water and bring them to a good place. Would Calum follow Catriona? Mairi couldn't bear to think of it.

"Look, love," she said to Eileen. "See that shape that comes to a point—there, against the bay? That's the broch. Just wait till you climb up in the galleries and look all around like a sentinel. You'll spy the seals on their skerries—see way out to the Bird Islands and south to the hills of Harris. On a fine bright day, you might see the ocean on the east."

Eileen's grip tightened. "You—you don't think there be ghosts?"

"No, sweeting. Though there may be a sort of kindliness in the air. After all, the folk who built it were kin of ours." Mairi lowered her voice so no one else would hear. "Anyway, we're going to do a magic. When we put down the hearthstone, that brings the guardians, that makes it home."

"Will it, Mairi?"

"Of course! That's where we'll cook and eat and work and sing and tell stories. That's where we'll be together."

Eileen shivered. "It won't be the same without Fearchar."

"No." Mairi blinked and swallowed. "But we have his songs and Cridhe."

"I'd rather have him!"

"So would I, *m'eudail.*" Brushing away her tears, Mairi reached back awkwardly to stroke her little sister's fine, silvery hair that clung to her hand like grain silks. She searched for true words that would comfort them both. "Fearchar would tell us, surely, that men must die but a harp like Cridhe holds their memory and all the songs they made."

Eileen didn't argue but her next plaint showed that she was feeling more bewildered and bereft than she had right after the burning. The lodge and its luxuries had been a potent diversion. Now she, and all of them, must come to grips with a life that would be very different, a life without Fearchar and the loved ones who'd gone away. "I miss Brigid and Rory," Eileen mourned. "I always looked after them. Brigid wouldn't let anyone else comb her hair and she snuggled up tight to me when folk told ghost stories. I don't think Kirsty can take care of her anything as well I did."

"She'll manage. And it wouldn't hurt for you to pay more mind to Tam."

96

"Tam! He's a big boy. He even went to the fishing."

"He loved the twins, too, and you're the only young ones now. Besides, he and Fearchar were special for each other."

Eileen nodded. "Yes, Fearchar loved Tam best, except maybe for you," she said without jealousy. "I'm Gran's girl, though."

"Mine, too, love, and now you're the only girl for all of us."

Peering around Mairi's shoulder at the crumbling tower rearing before them, Eileen squeezed her mightily. "It's like a castle! A place a king's daughter might live! Oh Mairi, can I run up and look out those windows?"

"You should do that first thing," Mairi laughed. "And take Tam with you."

The wagon rumbled up behind them and the men bringing the cattle and sheep followed close. Before Mairi could dismount, Iain sprang down from Chieftain, set Gran on the turf, and swung down Eileen before, almost as easily but much more slowly, he lifted Mairi from the saddle. At his touch, a tremulous thrill ran through her.

He stared at the broch, then turned toward her, a muscle jerking in his thin brown cheek. "Mairi!" It was the first time he'd used her name by itself. "This is madness. Come back to the lodge. I'll work out something with the agent for you to shelter there."

Mairi gazed along the bay to the sea, around the surrounding moors and back to the walls, drawing courage from each tuft of grass, each hint of fertile soil. "The agent won't give us land," she said, meeting Iain's angry, troubled eyes. "We must make our own." Closing one arm around Eileen, she circled Gran with the other. "Please, captain, first of all, let's place the hearthstone."

9

One hearthstone could serve for the three households which after all numbered only eight souls. "I'll make the bannocks," Gran said decisively. "And the rest of you lasses can share the other cooking."

"That much less peat we'll have to carry down from the cuttings." Andrew stood in the middle of the court, scanning the walls. Grinning, he waved back at Eileen and Tam who leaned out a window twenty feet above. "We'll divide the space into three parts, all opening to a big main room with the hearth, and we'll build the byre at the fallen side so the beasts can see the fire, too."

"I suppose it's the sensible thing," grudged Morag. "But next spring, husband, you must build me a proper house—if we're still living."

"With the grace of God, we'll be that," he said cheerily, and called to the smith, stocky bull-chested Lachlann MacKenzie who had somehow fathered the two tall blond muscular young men, Simon and Fergus, who had charge of the stables. "Lachlann, man, think you if we pitch the roof from high at the walls and slanting to run out over the byre that it'll drain away water so it won't seep down on us? What would you say to that, Ewan?"

Ewan Fraser, the gamekeeper and cook's husband, was rangy

and freckled, with crisp brown-red hair and warm brown eyes. He joined the others in assessing the problem. His golden-haired son, Liam, was loose-limbed, and probably near Mairi's age. He dropped his tawny eyes, blushing, when their glances crossed. Mairi thought him very young, indeed, but from her perch in the window above, Eileen watched him with obvious adoration. Of course, to him, she was a little girl. Mairi made a face at the perversity of life.

"We've got naturally curved couples, strong ones, to bear the weight of the roof," said Iain, to Mairi's great surprise. In spite of his talk of an impoverished youth, it was hard for her to believe he was no stranger to this kind of toil. "We can bury them deeper at the byre end to make the pitch right for shedding rain. To help that, we can dig trenches outside the byre and barn walls to carry away water that pours off the main roof."

The other men gave him a startled look. After a moment, Lachlann said, "The trenches are a good idea, captain. We'll dig one anyway to drain the byre."

"Then let's begin," said Andrew. "Rosanna, darlin', show us where to put the hearthstone."

Though the lodge men and those of Aosda had never worked together and no one was in official command, the work went smoothly. Tam, Jamie and Liam raised walls for barn and byre. Iain, Lachlann, Simon and Fergus set up the timbers. Andrew and Ewan expertly cut divots, some plain for the lower layer of the roof, others, for the top layer, scallop-edged. Since every bit of grass and every inch of soil that would grow it was sorely needed, the divots were cut from heathery turf. It would outlast barley straw, the favored thatching, but was quite heavy.

Eileen and Mairi cut creel after creel of heather. As she piled her loads by the wall, Mairi always stole a glance at Iain, full of pride that he knew how to peg the timbers and set the couples. Gran had bannocks and crowdie, soft white cheese, for those who needed a bite but it was nearly dark when the company washed in the little burn that ran below the broch and gathered around the hearth to enjoy crispy golden-brown potato scones, fish stew thickened with barley, mealie pudding or sausage, and a large container of *crannachan,* the whipped cream and toasted oatmeal treat that was Mrs. Fraser's specialty.

It would be a long time, if ever, before such feasts were common. The food was relished to the last slather of crannachan scooped up by Eileen's finger. "We've not done so ill." Ewan Fraser sighed with proud contentment as he looked up at the rafters secured together by tie-beams resting on the main beams. "Tomorrow Barry will be along with lumber for the box-beds, doors and partition—and his strong back."

The first divots were already laid over the highest rafters. Between the three households, frames for shoulder-high wooden walls were in place. Barn and byre would share one common wall. A passage between living quarters would connect byre and hearth room. As if they knew a home was being prepared for them, the cattle and sheep grazed near the broch. When Mairi had found tufts of grass amongst the heather, she'd plucked them for Sholma, Rigga and the other animals. It was a good feeling to once again be caring for the gentle beasts.

"A fine start," said Iain. "At this rate, we should finish in three or four days."

And then you'll go? Mairi thought with a pang. It seemed so right, so natural, to be with him. As if answering her unspoken question, his eyes touched hers as he said, "I sail Monday from Stornoway and must be back at the lodge Sunday at latest."

"No fear, captain," grinned Ewan, stretching his long arms. "We'll finish Friday. Saturday for sure. And now, sir, do you suppose we could hear harp and bagpipe together?"

Iain smiled at Mairi as he rose to get his pipes. "Shall we try 'Over the Sea to Skye'?" That was the tender, beautiful song about Bonnie Prince Charlie who, after Culloden, had been hidden for months by the Islanders, at the risk of their lives and despite the price on his head.

"Let's do it," Mairi nodded, taking the plaid from Cridhe.

She couldn't help noticing that Liam got as close to her as he could and Eileen's moonbeam hair was soon close to him.

As the peats on the hearthstone winked and smoldered, she and Iain joined in melody after melody, notes slipping in and out like the weaving of an intricate pattern on a loom. Mairi had never played with anyone before. It was a musical conversation, a language between them—twice the pleasure of playing alone.

Something to remember with thankful joy every time she touched the strings. Always now, she'd hear Iain's pipes, sometimes supporting, sometimes luring her into wild flourishes as if they improvised a dance, a dance she'd never want to do now with any other man. He'd bewitched her sure enough, but she'd rather have had these days with him than a lifetime with someone else. She would call this time her luck and bless it as such.

Late Friday afternoon, the dwelling was finished, the thatch fastened down with old fishing nets secured all around with rocks. Andrew secured the heavy iron crook and links from the main roof beam, positioning them above the hearth where they'd hold cooking pots and the kettle. The hearth was to one side of the air vent in the roof so that heavy rain wouldn't drown the fire. Flagstones paved the floor. Box-beds formed part of the wall between each household, and over heather mattresses were linen sheets, blankets and coverlets, woven on looms now reassembled in the hearthroom.

"You made this?" Iain asked incredulously of Mairi as he admired the coverlet on Gran's bed, muted tones of brown and gray in a tiny check, and the one in a bird's-eye pattern in hues of rose-purple that dressed the nook Mairi would share with Eileen.

"Of course I did. We learn our weaving early, sir. Eileen, with a little help, made that wide-bordered red blanket on Tam's bed." One side of the MacLeod space opened into the entrance tunnel through a roofed side passage and this Tam had claimed for his own, rocking up the way to the tunnel and lining it all with heather and rushes to make a snug niche for his bedding.

"Could you make me a coverlet like this?" Iain asked, touching the heather-hued one. "It would cheer my tent and keep me warm when General Napier starts campaigning against the northern hill tribes in India and Afghanistan as he's sure to do now that he's conquered Sind and been made governor."

Mairi didn't want to think about that, or of Calum, Lucas and Paul fighting in those far lands. What were the English queen's armies doing there any road? Especially when that meant Highland and Island lads would die, who had more against Lowlanders and the English than ever they did against Mahrattas, Afghans and suchlike. She could do nothing about that, but she could gift this man she loved. What a comfort it would be to know he slept warm in wool she had carded, spun, dyed, waulked, and woven. She pulled it off the bed and began to fold it.

"Take it with you," she said. "I got the colors from the root of lady's bedstraw and a certain kind of lichen. The wool's not combed so it's especially soft."

"You'll need it," he protested.

"I've others in the chest, one made by Gran's granny. They're long in the making but they last forever." Mairi smiled, pressing the coverlet into his arms. "Take it, do, captain! 'Tis little enough when you've done so much for us." He hesitated and she pleaded softly, "It would be my pleasure, sir, to think of it keeping you warm."

Eileen chimed in, "Please take it, captain. I'll help Mairi do another just as nice."

That swift smile melted years from his face, brought dancing lights to his gray eyes. "It's the best present I ever had, kind ladies both! When I draw it over me at night, it'll whisk me away from whatever forsaken camp I'm in and bring me to your fire, and your music."

"I'll remember your pipes," she said, grieved at his leaving but grateful that this dwelling held so much of him. The sweet liquid fire that his closeness always sent glowing through her throbbed now in her veins with special poignancy. "Will you come back to the Island, sir?"

"I've already leased the lodge for next year though I can't be sure my duties will permit me to come."

Oh, if he were coming back, that would speed the winter! She wouldn't allow herself to think beyond that or dwell overmuch on his saying it was to this hearth, the one he had helped her place, that he would come in his dreaming. She wasn't the only one at this hearth, after all. There was Tam, who followed the captain like a shadow, the men with whom he'd established a camaraderie, Sheila, who merited his consideration, Gran, with whom he loved to banter, and Eileen, petted like a young sister.

Compelled, Mairi said to him, "You have become our chief, you know."

He shook his head. "Head of the clan? You're that now, Mairi, God help your young shoulders."

"Supper's ready," called Gran, and they went into the hearth-room. Gran tried to make Iain take Fearchar's chair which now was Andrew's but the captain made Sheila sit there and pulled up one of the stools as did the others, except for Gran who also had a chair.

There was crab stew in one pot and pease porridge in the other, Gran's tasty bannocks and butter and crowdie. Everyone helped themselves.

"Real glass!" laughed Gran as she sat down with her bowl and looked up at the panes of the skylights through which a luminous blue twilight shone. "Isn't it a marvel to see the blessed sky? Why, it'll be so bright in here we won't need the cruisies except in deepest winter when days speed fast." Cruisies were lamps with twisted linen wicks that burned fish oil.

The glass, Iain's thought and gift, was a wonderful improvement on the oiled skins of the Aosda crofts. Even the windows opening to the roofless space between the double walls of the broch were covered with glass, and these panes could be used, like the good lumber and timbers, when permanent houses were made. Glancing around, though, Mairi delighted in how comfortable and home-like their shelter was.

Except for chests that held clothing and bedding which were in the bedrooms, the families' other furnishings were in the main room, tall cupboards arranged to partition off private quarters. To save room, only Gran's quern or grinding stone was out but three churns lined up neatly, along with handled wooden milk buckets and other milk vessels on a bench at the side of the byre passage. Two more benches were occupied by the men from the lodge. There were tight chests for storing meal. The cupboards had three open top shelves for dishes, and closed lower shelves with a top where food could be prepared and served since there was no table.

In the byre was a stall for each cow with a post where she could be tied, and the barn had room for the sheep in foul weather though most of the time they could range outside. The potato corner was ready, barrels for salt food awaited filling, and the winnowing floor was clayed. Thank goodness—and Iain— they'd have barley and oats to thresh there.

There was music late that night, with stories and riddles and rhyming contests. Mairi stored up Iain's every word, every smile, the proud set of his head on his muscular neck, the grace of his movements. Most of all, as they played together, she tried to absorb the pipe's melodies so she would, with her inner ear, hear them when she played those tunes alone.

As Gran smoored the fire that night, she asked a special blessing on Iain and those who had helped raise the roof protecting the hearth. "Let them sup with us again," she prayed. "And till then, Holy Three, have them in your care."

"Amen," said Mairi.

Iain and the lodge workers were off at dawning. Mairi's heart was too full and her throat too aching for saying much. After shaking hands with the men, including Tam, bowing to Morag and Sheila, and kissing Gran and Eileen, Iain came to Mairi. "If you come into trouble," he said, handing her a paper, "write my solicitor in Edinburgh. I'll instruct him to send money or assist however he can."

"Thank you, sir." Mairi folded the paper carefully, because he had written on it, not because she expected it to be of any use. Edinburgh seemed as far as Sind. If a sudden disaster occurred, it would be over one way or the other before a message could go to the city and get a response. "You've said you'll seek out Calum and my cousins and tell them what's happened," she reminded Iain. "Please tell them you left us well and in good shelter so they won't worry."

He nodded. "I will, and I'll give them your letters." Taking both her hands, he held them between his long tanned ones, so warm, so vital, that she felt as if they held her life. "Thank you for the covering, Mairi. Thank you for your music and your hearth."

"They—" Her voice failed. "They'll always be here for you." And so will I.

Bending his head to her hands, he kissed them. "Oh, sir!" she cried in protest, for her fingers were rough and work-stained. His eyes traced her face, lingering, before he gazed full into her eyes. She felt as if her soul rushed out of them to join with his.

"Oh, sweet Mairi!" he breathed. Releasing her abruptly, he swung into Chieftain's saddle. At the crest of the slope, he turned to wave, and then he was gone.

As when Catriona and the MacNeills departed, Mairi found her best solace in work. There was much of it, the most pressing to return to Aosda for harvest, for it was now early September. Only Sheila, Eileen and Gran stayed at the broch, Eileen downcast because Liam was gone and hadn't paid her any attention anyway. The others put oatmeal and smoked fish, blankets and scythes in the wagon Iain had loaned them for transporting their harvest and peats, and set off across the moor.

Andrew, Barry and Tam were so stricken at the sight of the blackened walls of their burned homes that tears ran down their

105

cheeks. Barry swore, Andrew muttered beneath his breath, but Tam was worst of all, for he stood in front of the MacLeod house, face contorted, and Mairi knew he was seeing Fearchar, all ablaze, stumble from the door.

"Tam," she said, touching his arm. "Come away, laddie. Fetch some water so I can make the bannocks."

His raw-knuckled hands clenched into fists. "I won't forget! Never and never! If there's ever a chance to burn Hugh Sinclair's thatch—"

"Tam!" She shook him hard, then gathered him to her breast, stroking the back of his neck, downy and vulnerable as a child's. "Much good that would do Fearchar, for you to hang or be transported! You're the man of our house now. Act like one."

He jerked away, eyes glistening. "Eileen says you your own-self cursed the factor."

"I did." Though it hadn't been she alone but something ancient and implacable speaking through her. "But I wouldn't lift a finger to him and I pray you will not. We need you, Tam. We need every hand, if we're to last the winter."

He gave her a rebellious stare, then hung his head. "The captain said I was to mind you. He made me promise. I said you were only a girl and for that, wasn't it two whole days he wouldn't let me touch the pipes?"

Taking the pail, he flung off to the spring. She blessed Iain through a wrench of pain and wondered if by now he was on the road to Stornoway.

After their meal, they began to reap the barley. Ordinarily, three worked together, the scyther followed by one worker who laid the grain in bundles and twisted bands for the other who bound the sheaves and stooked them in conical stacks. Today, though, Tam and Mairi both bundled and bound and left the sheaves to be piled in the wagon.

They all sang to the rhythmic swing of the scythes as Barry and Andrew swept their blades in a skilled, flowing motion that sheared the stalks as close as possible to the ground since their beasts couldn't feed on the stubble. Keeping time as best they could with their double tasks, Mairi and Tam took two handfuls of the cut grain and knotted the ends together, laid this band on the ground and placed the bundle on it, crossing the ends of the band and tucking them beneath each other. Instead of making them into stooks of eight sheaves, they piled them in the wagon. The wagon was heaped high by evening, so Barry, eating his bannocks and fish as he drove, hitched up the horses and set off for the broch while Mairi and Tam both worked behind Andrew till dark.

None of them wanted to sleep in the burned houses but the wind blew so fierce that at last they cut heather, spread it on the floor of the MacNeill cottage, and rolled up in their blankets, feeling snug though the wind soughed hungrily outside the thick walls.

They weren't long in the field next morning when Barry drove up and took his scythe while Tam unhitched the horses and rubbed them down, giving each some barley before hobbling them so they could graze without wandering off.

"You gran's making heather ale," Barry said when they stopped at noon for a bannock. "And Sheila's at her loom, weaving a soft blanket for our baby."

"Eileen, I hope, is fetching seaweed for lazybeds," said Mairi, straightening and working her shoulders to ease the cramp in them. Lazybeds were an invention to create more planting soil on this island of bog, peat and rock. Alternating layers of sand and seaweed were heaped up inside rock barriers that sometimes ran at precarious angles down a hillside.

"She is that," said Barry with a twinkle. "But sort of staring off in the direction of the lodge and Liam." Twinkling even more, Barry added, "And that laddie, no doubt, is mooning in this direction."

"He's just a boy," Mairi shrugged.

"A bit older than you," Barry agreed, and laughing, dodged the clod she threw at him.

* * *

The oats and barley filled half the barn, stacked on plank flooring to protect it from damp. Because they were almost out of grain, the men threshed some, spreading loosened sheaves on the clayed floor and beating them with a flail which was two pieces of wood joined by a leather thong. Gripping the staff, the thresher whirled it to snap the striker into the sheaves. Then, with barn and byre doors open to create a draft, the grain was tossed up from a hide secured over a circular wooden frame. Wind blew away the chaff and by St. Michael's Day, September 29th, the grain was ready for the quern.

Gran made bannocks of the first ground oats and barley. Though there was no egg to dip them in, they were sweet with currants and treacle brought from the lodge. The household feasted on these bannocks on St. Michael's Eve, but Gran made more next morning when the broch was hailed by a St. Michael's cavalcade Liam, Simon, Fergus and some of their friends all mounted bareback and racing in the ancient way.

Eileen handed Liam his bannock. When he smiled his careless thanks, her face let up like a candle that faded when he called to Mairi, "Will you ride behind me, lass? 'Tis a fine day for a canter!"

"Thank you," said Mairi in her primmest tone. "I have too much to do."

Eileen screwed up her courage. "You—you have a lovely horse, Liam," she murmured, stroking the smooth shoulder.

"Well then," he smiled indulgently, "Would you like a ride?" Eileen almost flew up, he barely had to lift her, and though he only swept her around the bay and back, the child glowed for days.

With grain harvest safely in, the men and Tam fished in the burn and from rocks along the shore. Some of the fish were stuck on wooden hooks for drying in the hearth room and others were salted down in the barrels. Mairi and Eileen were out every possible moment gathering seaweed and sand to spread in alternate layers along the craggy slope that stretched toward the sea from the precious bit of arable land close to the broch. As a change from this, they wandered the moor with sickles, seeking out tussocks of grass to cut and dry for hay. One day Andrew brought in the carcass of one of the MacNeills' old ewes that had fallen from a cliff.

Animals were too precious to be killed for food though if a mother beast lacked milk for a calf or lamb, the little creature might have to be killed before it starved. When sheep or cattle died, though, every part was used: fried liver for supper, heart and lungs chopped fine and cooked with barley into a thick stew on the next day, head singed and made into soup, the meat salted in a keg, blood made into black puddings formed in casings made from washed intestines.

"Let's leave the fleece on the hide," said Gran, when Sheila started to clip it. "It'll make a warm soft rug for your baby to play on."

The peat cuttings were miles away, but it was worlds easier to bring them home by wagon instead of in creels on the back. As she helped stack peats outside the entrance, Mairi thought of Iain with worshipful gratitude. He was far away by now but when she looked at the rafters, she saw him setting them in place. The light streaming through the panes above made the hearth room lighter than any house she'd ever been in, illumining the webs on the looms, making it easier to do every task. And now the wagon and team he'd loaned had one more expedition to make, to fetch the potatoes.

The hills were turned out carefully with delving spades and the potatoes shaken free of roots and sod. When these were piled in the bin near the salt barrels, it was All Souls Day which also was the eve of All Saints Day and the ancient festival of Samhain that marked the change from summer's long days to the shortening ones of winter.

This was a time for divination and peering into the future. Mairi was tempted to winnow with an empty hide or set two straws up in the ashes, but that Iain was beyond her reach made her feel it was wrong to seek an answer. Perhaps even more, she didn't want to be warned that her love was hopeless though she knew that all too well. In the end, as Gran blessed the hearth that night, Mairi prayed for Iain, that he slept warm and safe in her coverlet, and that he would return.

10

Tam went with Andrew and Barry to return the wagon. About sundown, as she and Morag finished with the milking, Mairi heard a faint distant sound, not music, exactly, but on the way to it. "Can that be a pipe?" she wondered.

"It's not the fairy bagpipes—sounds more like a pig with its tail caught in a crack." Morag shielded her eyes. "Look, isn't that our lads long-legging over the moor? But what's on their backs besides creels?"

"Let's go see!" Eileen bounded off like a blue hare. The women put the milk coggs on the bench and hurried out, joined by Gran and Sheila.

Tam piped zestfully, heedless of the creel on his back, striking many a sour note so that Morag clapped her hand to her head and muttered, "Lord save us, where did the chiel get that?" before her tone brightened. "Och, can that be a spinning wheel astraddle Andrew's shoulders? And another on Barry?"

Spinning wheels they were, and in wicker cages, the men carried four red hens. In Andrew' creel was a carved stone cross for Fearchar, engraved with his name and the dates of his birth and death. Barry's creel held a jug of whiskey for Gran and tins of tea and sweeties. Mrs. Fraser had loaded Tam with preserved fruit, honey, and a large ham.

"It's all from the captain!" Tam cried. "He had the pipes sent from Inverness! Look, the base of the chanter's silver, just like his!"

"Ewan Fraser just brought the spinning wheels from Stornoway where the captain had them made," Andrew said. "It's too much. I said we could not take them, but Ewan had his orders and they need no more wheels at the lodge."

Gran furrowed her brow. "I think I'll stay with my spindle."

"Then the more fool you!" said Morag, caressing the scalloped wheel as Andrew set it down in the hearth room. "There was a Saxony wheel like this at the farmer's where I worked before I married. It'll spin in a day as much as you can in a week with the spindle, and see, there's a treadle. Your foot does a lot of the work."

"And the yarn may look it, too," Gran retorted.

"Wait and see." Morag was actually smiling.

"There's a note with this wheel," Barry said, and handed it to Mairi.

Iain's bold, slashing scrawl fitted him. *"Mistress Mairi, To ease my guilt at bearing away the covering that took you so much time and work, I'm sending something to speed your labor. The most, perhaps the only peace I've had in my life was at your hearth. Bless you and fare well."*

His writing, words he had penned to her! Blinded by happy tears, Mairi carefully refolded the paper and Mairi tucked it in a niche of the box-bed where she could touch it before she went to sleep. In all the world, there was no one like him. But as Tam gave a great screech of the pipes, she winced and thought it would be only fair if Iain were here to share the racket of Tam's apprenticeship.

Fortunately, there was also a practice chanter without a bag, and on this Tam could play with much less harrowing effects. It was this he carried with him when all of them except Sheila and Gran journeyed to the little graveyard by the sea with Fearchar's stone. Barry carried the harp, and when they had set the cross with the sun circle at the head of the sunken rectangle which the men mounded up again, and Tam and Eileen had scattered the pure white round and oval pebbles they'd collected from the shore, Andrew and Barry spoke their memories of Michael MacLeod and then Tam played the chanter and Mairi the harp. We're still on the island, dear man, she told him silently. And so is your music.

This was his real funeral. Mairi wept but she felt more at peace when they started back across the moorlands. It couldn't be many years till Gran joined Fearchar; meanwhile she was happier believing he would return. *As I would be*, thought Mairi, *if I thought in spite of Iain's being gentry there was the slightest chance we might be together for a time, any time at all.*

When they reached home, Gran was brewing a pungent tea while Morag walked up and down with Sheila who had been in labor since midday. Sheila's fair skin was dewed with sweat and there were bloody tracks where she'd bitten her lips, but she went into Barry's arms with a glad cry. "I was afraid, *m'eudail*, that the babe would come before you did! Oh, I'm glad you're here!"

Barry stroked her golden hair for she had taken off her filled cap and the shining mass was braided into a single plait. "I'm here, lass, and soon so will be our bairn. Does it help to walk or should you lie in the bed?"

"She's better to walk for now," said Gran. "Here, love, let me pour you another cup of this marsh trefoil tea."

Sheila dutifully sipped the brew though she made a comical face. As if Barry's arrival had told her body to get on with its task, her pains grew stronger and closer together. Soon she wanted to lie down.

"Scream when you need to, lassie," Gran urged. "Don't fash yourself about anything but borning this wee one."

"I—I don't want to frighten Barry."

"The devil with that," snapped Gran. "You'll no fright the lad into stopping what brings babies and for the rest, 'tis good for men to know what it costs a woman to birth a child. It's our battle, love! Why shouldn't we get honor for it? The Vikings had the right notion. They thought women who died in childbed went to the warriors' heaven." She added hastily, "But you won't die, henny. Don't fight the pains, breathe with them. They'll bring the wee one."

Sheila did scream before it was over. Barry was in such a state that Andrew had to take him outside for a calming walk. This was the first birth Mairi had attended; Gran had thought her too young to help at Kirsty's confinement with the twins though she well remembered those cries that had echoed through the township. Now, as she washed Sheila's face and took turns at giving the panting young woman her hands to grip, Mairi wanted to run away from her friend's travail and yet was awed at the ferocity with which gentle Sheila worked with the deepening contractions, the way she indeed did battle.

As the head pressed more and more against the orifice, Gran kept a light hand against it. "So the bairn won't come too fast and tear the opening," she told Mairi. After long hours, the head emerged, the shoulders with another scream and mighty push, and the rest of the tiny creature slipped out in a rush.

Almost at once, there was a protesting howl. Gran cleared the mouth and nostrils, wiped off bits of the sac that had enclosed the infant, and said loudly to Sheila who seemed unconscious now that her final pains had expelled a mass of glistening bloody matter, "You've a fine little lass, girl. With gold hair like yours. Och, won't she wrap us all around her wee finger, especially her Da?"

Morag, with surprising care, rubbed her daughter-in-law's belly. As soon as the bluish cord stopped pulsing, Gran tied it with two bands of old linen and then cut it six inches or so from the baby's navel, tying it below the knot. Gran then washed the baby, who screwed up tiny flattened features and sucked avidly at her fist. Wrapped in a soft towel, the baby was placed in Sheila's arms. "Now, dear," said Gran, eyes moist, "soon as we clean you up, you can show Barry what you've done this day!"

Though they were too far from church to attend regularly even had they wished, Sheila couldn't rest till the baby was christened. A more tolerant minister than Reverend Campbell looked to the spiritual needs of a parish that included the lodge. His nearest church was about five miles north of the lodge off the Stornoway road. Barry walked the long way to see him and arranged for the baptism as soon as Sheila could make the journey.

Leaving Eileen and Tam to look after the beasts, the others set out on Saturday and spent the night divided between the Frasers' and MacKenzies' homes. "A sonsie lass for sure," crooned Mrs. Fraser, though to Mairi the babe still looked mottled and crumpled. "When you come back, we'll have a christening feast, for of course you mustn't have that trudge home in one day, Sheila dear. The new tenant won't, I trust, have the men work on Sunday beating out the game for him, even though he be a Lowlander with more coin than manners. At least he's only here till Christmas and then I think there's no one till Captain MacDonald's lease begins in April. God keep him. We did hear from a tinker that a war's started up again in that heathenish country where he was bound."

Fear chilled Mairi and that night, between Eileen and Gran, she was more wakeful from worry over Iain than from Gran's hearty snoring or Eileen's thrashing about.

It was lucky to give a baby silver, so at the celebration of her baptism as Seana Catriona, the MacKenzies and Frasers pressed coins into the baby's hand. She promptly dropped them. "Och," chuckled Ewan, who had served as godfather. "A liberal lass she'll be! She'll need a rich husband, Barry man!"

Mairi had carried her godchild from broch to kirk and next day carried her home. By then Seana's looks had greatly improved. She had a sweetly curved mouth, impenetrable eyes of a misty hue that seemed to be watching a world no one else could see, silky gold hair that already curled, and her crying was a soft, melodious "Hlah!" until, if she felt her wants neglected, she fairly yelled, bringing the company to a halt while Sheila nursed her.

At those times, Mairi's breasts ached yearningly. What joy it would be to hold a child with Iain's black hair and gray eyes, see his face in one belonging to a mite she could cherish and fondle and care for. Shielding the baby from the wind, Mairi nuzzled the soft cheek and murmured, "Seana Catriona! You'll brighten the house as much as the skylights."

Becoming as much a center of the households as the hearth, Seana never got out more than a few wails when she was taken up by someone, most often by Gran or by Eileen who found her more bewitching than any poppet. The cradle, during the day, stood in the hearth room where the baby was lulled by the hum of the spinning wheels, songs for the grinding of grain and for churning. At night, she was soothed by the harp and Tam's efforts on the bagpipes.

The spinning wheel, once Mairi got the knack of it, never ceased to astonish her. A double band connected the wheel and the spindle on which a bobbin turned, taking the yarn evenly by means of a hake, a horseshoe-shaped device that fed the yarn as it came twisted from the eye of the spindle. All the spinner need do was hold the fleece and work the treadle. The big room was always busy and companionable, and though they sadly missed Fearchar, Catriona and the MacNeills, wee Seana did much to fill that void.

When it wasn't raining or too windy, Mairi spent part of most days carrying up seaweed for the lazybeds. In a smaller creel, she collected purplish fronds of laver that were good rolled in oatmeal and fried in butter; carrageen, which when washed, bleached white and dried, made a delicious pudding boiled in milk with a bit of treacle or dried fruit added; and dulse. The flat brownish leaves of this plant had to be simmered for about five hours, but then were quite tasty and supposed to be especially good for nursing mothers, as was carrageen, so these dishes appeared often. Just because they were resorted to in starving times, Mairi saw no reason to scorn nutritious food that was there for the finding.

Tam and Eileen used such expeditions as an excuse to wander far up or down the shore. They also had the task of digging tuberous roots of silverweed and earth-nut which could be cooked like potatoes or eaten raw. This gathered food was as important as the fish Andrew and Barry caught from the rocks. Using roots and seaweed would make the potatoes last longer. Gran made delicious stews of shellfish and fish. It was especially important this year to eke out the stored foods till the next harvest because the cows had no field stubble to fatten on before winter and would have to be fed more precious grain in the months they were in their stalls.

One late morning when the baby was a few weeks old, Mairi was fetching water from the burn when the wind brought her the snatch of a cry. Straightening, she scanned the curve of the bay and the line of the coast. The men had gone to the south fishing, and Eileen and Tam had been out since early morning, nothing unusual for them. They carried bannocks and chews of dried dulse and were often out all day.

A small figure was pelting up from the sea. That was Eileen's yellow shawl. For her to be alone, running like that, something must have happened to Tam. Gripped with dread, Mairi caught up her skirts and ran to meet her sister.

Had Tam fallen from the rocks? Been swept out to sea? Nothing prepared her for what Eileen gasped when she was near enough to be heard. "They've stolen Tam! Oh Mairi, they've taken him!"

Not believing her ears, Mairi froze. "Who?" She reached Eileen and caught her shoulders. "Who stole Tam?"

"A big ship!" Eileen wept. "We were gathering some fine dulse from the rocks when we saw the ship. They put a little boat over the side and four men rowed to shore. They—they asked Tam how he'd like to go on the ship and see the world. When he said he wouldn't, they took him anyway, tied him with rope and threw him in the boat. He—he fought hard, Mairi! So did I, but we couldn't stop them. Can we get him back? Can't we help him?''

Holding her young sister, Mairi forced her numbed brain to function. Oh, if only Iain were here! He'd know what to do. But even Andrew and Barry were away and wouldn't be home till late. If anything was done, Mairi would have to do it.

"Do you know the ship's name? Were the men foreigners?"

"They didn't talk like us but I could make out what they said. The ship's name was *The Cormorant*—and just like a cormorant, it swallowed our Tam!"

"Did they say anything about where they came from or where they were going?"

Eileen thought hard. "I couldn't hear all they said. One of them hit me so hard my head knocked against a rock. When I came to, they were throwing Tam in the boat. The biggest one was laughing about how when they got to Stornoway, the captain would give them extra money for whiskey since he'd turn a neat penny selling Tam for a cabin boy."

Selling Tam! Mairi felt the hair on her nape bristle. Years ago, boys and men, too, had often been abducted from fields and beaches, not by regular press gangs that seized men for the navy, but by unscrupulous captains who sold their victims to American plantations or forced them to be sailors. It still happened occasionally.

Stornoway! The ship would be in harbor long before she could get there, but the men looked forward to a night of carousing. If they took on cargo or replenished supplies, the vessel might be several days in port. No time to wait for Barry and Andrew. She must set off straightaway. Perhaps Ewan Fraser or Lachlann MacKenzie would go with her.

Whirling with Eileen, she ran for the broch. "Put some food in a basket for me, darling. I'll get Tam back someway!"

She ran till her side ached, walked till she had her breath, and ran some more, watching out for rabbit holes lest she snap an ankle. All the time, her mind worked furiously. She doubted that appealing to the constables would do any good. They could burn out crofters right enough but according to the men, had little stomach for confronting ship captains with their rough crews. It seemed to Mairi that her best hope lay in pleading with the captain, letting him know Tam had a family that loved and needed him. That, and offering the only valuables they had. Sheila had sent the silver coins given Seana at her christening, Morag produced a hoarded shilling. Gran gave up the silver Luckenbooth brooch Fearchar had given her when they were courting. Mairi wrapped up Cridhe's tuning key with its remaining precious stone. And into the creel had gone such weaving as had been fulled and was ready for sewing, yards of warm crotal-dyed rust brown, a tweed of the fashion come up from the Borders with natural colors of brown, white and black woven together, and a most beautiful length of misty blue got from roots of yellow flag.

Please let it be enough, Mairi prayed. She also prayed that one of the men at the lodge could go with her.

The men were all out beating game near another leased lodge, said Mrs. Fraser. It was likely the sportsmen would hunt together and stay the night at the other tenant's hall, shooting on his lease next day. "Gentry have ever liked to bang away at grouse and deer," sniffed the cook. "But now Prince Albert's taken to it, everyone who can afford it will do the same. 'Twill be a mercy if there's a creature left for those with honest hunger. Och, those wicked men, to take your brother! Ewan, I know, will try to help you, lass. Best wait for him."

"The ship could be gone if I don't hurry." Mairi blinked back tears and the lump in her throat made it hard to swallow the sweetened tea through it sent a grateful warmth through her. "I'll have to go on."

"It'll be dark when you get there." Mrs. Fraser shook her head worriedly. "A lass shouldn't be near the harbor alone in daylight, much less by night." When Mairi only looked at her, the woman pondered. "I'll take it on myself to loan you a horse,

Mairi. That'll get you there faster and spare your poor feet. Now have another cup of tea and some of this mealie pudding while I have Peggy saddle that gentle old mare you rode before."

The sun wrapped itself in thick gray haze before it set. Darkness came quickly on these shortening days. Still, it was just twilight when Mairi rode down the cobbled street of the only town in all the Western Isles. She had never been in Stornoway before but spent no time now in looking at the shops lining the high street, the dwellings behind, or the spired church. She made straight for the harbor where a dozen ships dwarfed smaller craft and where the Beasts of Holm crouched to the north, treacherous rocks which had claimed their tribute of seafarers from the first dim times when men dared the waves. Fearchar had been wrecked there but with great luck swam to shore.

If he were here, he'd know how to talk to the captain. If Iain were . . . She found a safe place to tether the mare behind some sheds, loosened the girth to ease her, gave her a few handfuls of oats Mrs. Fraser had sent along, and hesitated. She didn't want to board *The Cormorant* with her creel because if entreaties would free Tam, she wasn't going to offer their treasures. One of the sheds was empty. At this time of evening, it was unlikely anyone would be peering into it. Mairi unbound the creel from behind the saddle and hid it under some old nets in a corner.

Now. Drawing a long breath, thinking of Iain for courage, she walked along the quay, peering to make out the names on the ships. Lanterns glowed yellow from most of the vessels, and shone from the cabin of the next-to-last ship on which, as she was beginning to fear the ship hadn't anchored here, she made out in bold black letters *The Cormorant.*

Heart bounding, she scanned bow to stern though she realized that Tam wouldn't be on deck; locked or tied in the hold most likely. Poor lad, how frighted he must be! *I'll have you off there, laddie, or die trying.*

But how? No sounds came from the ship. The crew must be ashore. Was the captain? Was it possible there was no one on watch at all? Could she row out in one of the small boats and free Tam?

She had to quickly discard that hope. Without a ladder, rope or help from above, there was no way she could climb up the hull. There was nothing for it but to try to locate the captain. Cupping her hands, she shouted, "*Cormorant!* I need the captain!"

A guffaw sounded over the water. "Do ye, dearie? Much good he'll be to ye after drinkin' for hours. Try me instead."

Could she overpower the sailor? Trick or coax him into loosing Tam? She didn't see how, and knowing what the man wanted, after a moment's frantic quandary, she decided her best chance was with the captain.

"I have to see the captain," she called. "Where is he?"

"Well, dearie, if ye must, ye'll find the auld devil in that first tavern where the street opens to the quay. Cap'n Tarbert he be, a stingy, sour one to be sure. Best wait till it's my turn to go ashore, dearie."

Without answering, Mairi turned and sped toward the ramshackle huddle of taverns, inns and sailor's boardinghouses. The kirk's rule didn't reach here. A woman kissed a sailor on the mouth and drew him into a hovel. Accordions and fiddles competed with roaring laughter and boisterous merry-making. Two men spilled out of a tavern, struggling, biting and gouging. In the dusk, Mairi almost stepped on a man sprawled at the edge of the road. "What be you doing here, slut?" a woman shrilled from an upper window. "We be too many whores as it is."

Mairi felt as if she'd stepped into the edge of hell. She longed to run to the mare and get away but of course she could not. Gulping in a deep breath, she opened the door to the first tavern.

Smoky light from several cruisies flickered orange at the draft, smearing faces with patches of yellow and darkness. A fiddler perched on a high stool in one corner. Several couples capered wildly in the tiny space unoccupied by tables, and a fat, balding man with rolled-up sleeves moved among the roisterers, filling cups from a jug.

121

"Wurrah, lads, look what's here!" The man nearest her, hulking and red-bearded with a patch over one eye, caught at her skirt. "Fresh from the country, I'm bound! Sweet as honey and smooth as cream. Sit here on my knee, lovie, and let old Jacob buy you a drink."

Mairi wrested away from him, dodged other hands. Fighting sheer panic, she forced her way to the fat man. "Please, sir," she gasped. "Is Captain Tarbert here?"

A heavy-bodied man with graying hair and tangled beard squinted up at her from pale brown eyes. His mouth, buried in hair, looked wet and red. "I'm Cap'n Tarbert. Now who would you be, my pretty?" He winked at the men at his table. "I hope you're not here to say you've a bairn to me."

Hot blood washed to the roots of Mairi's hair. How she'd love to smash him in that ugly mouth! But she must hold her temper. "I have to talk to you, sir."

He winked again and weighted his arm around her hips. "What's your price, lassie? I've a tender lad i' the ship so I don't need a wench as much as I might."

He couldn't mean—Mairi had never heard of what he seemed to imply but the hint turned her sick. Had he—hurt Tam? If he had—She wished she had a pistol or a knife. If this awful man had done something vile to her brother, she'd find some way to do for him, if it meant luring him off someplace and biting through his throat!

Shivering with loathing and fear, she struggled to keep her voice even. "That's my brother you have on your ship. I want him back."

He stared in surprise, then burst out laughing. "Too bad you weren't on the shore instead of that little girl. We might have made a bargain. Still may. What'll you offer?"

Such cool rascality made her gasp before it turned her furious. "You stole him! You ought to be in gaol!"

"Can you put me there?" he taunted.

The biggest man she'd ever seen rose up from where he'd

been sitting. In that nightmare, he shone with the brightness of the North Star, young and fair-haired as a Viking prince.

"I can snap your neck and throw you to the fishes, Tarbert," he drawled in a voice of soft thunder. "And that I'll do with a right good will unless this minute you send for the lass's brother."

11

The fiddling ceased. "To me, lads!" shouted Tarbert, jumping up with surprising speed for such a hulk. Eight or nine men pushed their way to him, some drawing knives, others snatching up bottles or stools. "Now, how loud do you crow, my rooster?" grinned Tarbert.

"I've no quarrel with your men, only with you." The stranger looked from one sailor to another. "There you are, Geordie," he called to a tall dark man with hard eyes and a pock-marked face. "Been sportin' with more killer whales?"

"Not since the one snappin' at my heels when you dragged me out of the sea, Magnus." The man thrust his dirk back in the sheath hanging under his shirt and came to stand by the big stranger.

"I'll have you flogged till you can't crawl!" bellowed Tarbert, face purpling as he crashed down his fist on the table and set the cups jangling. "Harris, Brown, MacTavish! Haul this bastard to the ship and put him in irons!"

The three started forward but in no great hurry. Geordie slipped out his knife again and they halted. "Mac," Geordie said to a wiry older man whose red hair had faded to dull orange and who was missing an ear and finger, "weren't you dragged off the shore near Stromness? When you finally got back, hadn't your poor widowed mother died of grieving?"

"Aye," muttered MacTavish. And he stepped back.

"I'll have the lot of you hung for mutiny!" yelled Tarbert.

"You flogged my mate to death," rasped a brawny yellow-haired seaman.

"Rats won't eat the grub you lay in for us," charged another.

The men of *The Cormorant* looked at each other. By the harsh code of the sea, they had earned brutal floggings or even death. They had nothing to lose. They sauntered out of the tavern.

The captain stumbled after them. "You sons of whores! I'll swing you high!"

Magnus felled him with a chop to the side of the head. He said to the sweating tavern-keeper, "Not that it'd be a loss but if he goes out anytime soon, he may fetch up anchored to the bottom of the harbor." His smile broke like sun coming out from behind a cloud as he took Mairi's arm. "Come along, lass. We'll get your brother."

While Magnus and Mairi watched from the shore, Geordie and several of the others rowed to the ship. There was no sound of a struggle with the watch, only muffled voices. Shuddering with anxiety and the bite of the wind, Mairi didn't resist when her rescuer drew her into the shelter of his broad arm. "Where do you come from, lass? Don't you have menfolk?"

His arms tightened as she explained. "Yes, I see you couldn't bide for the men," he said, shaking his head. "But to walk into a den like this of a night—lassie, lassie, it makes my hair stand up!"

"Mine, too," she admitted, and veered to the terrible thing Tarbert had joked about. "Do you think—is there—is there aught the captain might do to Tam? Something nasty?"

"Aye, and he has the name, but Geordie was sure naught had happened yet. Seems there was a lot of commotion in the cabin and Tarbert came out limping. Told the cook to give the lad nothing but water till he'd learned some manners."

"Won't the men get in trouble for helping us?"

"They can hide on my boat till Tarbert fills out his crew and sails. Then they'll find other berths or I'll take them to a main-land port where they can find a ship. Tarbert won't make much of it since he kidnapped your brother and won't want the law looking into that." Above the lapping of the waves came a rhythmic plashing. Magnus's arm tightened. "Here they come, lass. And soon as we have your brother, we'll go to an inn I know of—a decent one—have a good supper and settle you two for a sound night's sleep."

"Oh, we can wrap up in our plaids a little way out of town, sir. I have some food." She didn't want to spend Seana's silver or Morag's shilling. "I can't thank you enough for all you've done, but once Tam's ashore, you needn't trouble more for us."

"You can thank me by your company," he said. "I'll pay the reckoning at the inn." When she started to protest, he chuckled. "Save your breath, lass. I won't hear to your sleeping by the road with naught to warm your stomach but a cold bannock. I still don't know your name."

When she told him, he repeated it softly. "I'm Magnus Eric-son of Rousay in the Orkneys putting in here on my way to Barra Head." His breath stirred the ringlets that had escaped her shawl and she felt the strong, steady pound of his heart. Amused laughter rumbled in his chest. "There's no big hurry, though. I'm thinking I should get better acquainted with this island."

The grate of wood on sand put everything but Tam out of Mairi's head. She ran toward the boat, calling his name. In a moment, laughing and sobbing, they were in each other's arms.

A short time later, Mairi's creel resting against the wall, they sat in a much cleaner, quieter inn at a table near the fire. One of Tam's eyes was swollen shut and his face was bruised but he devoured buttered oatcakes and hot chowder with ravenous ap-petite and seemed amazingly unmarked by his experience.

"I had it figured out that the next time the captain tried to put his arm around me—he said I reminded him of his son—I'd let him and then kick him hard as I could where it hurts most, knock him out with something, and get away. But this way was lots better."

Mairi gave a heartfelt nod. "I just wish Gran and Eileen and the others knew you were safe. Most likely, Andrew and Barry started here when they got home from fishing. I expect we'll meet them along the way tomorrow."

"It's sorry I am to be such a trouble." The combative light in Tam's green eyes faded. Awkwardly, he touched Mairi's hand. "Och, if that one had hurt you!" The straight look he gave Magnus held a man's responsibility for his womenfolk. "I'm in your debt, Captain Ericsson, sir. I hope the winds blow me a way to pay you."

"I was paid by your sister's eyes," said Magnus. "But if the winds place us so you can aid me, Tam lad, I'll be right glad of your hand."

Going to the creel, Mairi piled the woolens on a bench. "You must at least have your choice of these," she said, thinking the hazy blue was just the color of his eyes. "It was all for the captain, with the little silver we had, to get our Tam back."

Tam's eyes rounded. "You'd trade all that for me? After you clipped the fleece and washed and carded and dyed and spun and wove it?"

"Daftie! We can do that again but where could we get another like you?" Overwhelmed by what might have happened, Mairi brushed her eyes with her sleeve before she held up folds of fine rust, tweed and blue. "Please have one, sir."

" 'Tis grand work, lass." He touched the fabrics admiringly. "If you must give me something, though, what I'd give a tooth for is a jersey like your brother's—that would fit me, to be sure." He showed the fraying cuffs and darned snags on his heavy sweater. "My mother made this before she was carried away by ague five years ago. There's no one else to knit for me and I don't want the kind got in the shops."

"Sheila's begun a blue-gray one for her husband. I'm sure she'd let me finish it for you. If you'll tell me where to send it—"

"My men won't mind some time in Stornoway. I want to make sure you're safe home. If there's room for me in your barn, maybe I could stay till the jersey's ready." He lifted his hands pathetically waving the unraveled bits. "You seem too kind a lassie, Mairi MacLeod, to send me out in winter like this."

"He can have my bed in the wall," Tam said eagerly.

Mairi flushed. "We're not living in a proper house, sir. Three families we be, sharing an old broch."

At the seaman's stunned look, Tam cried, "But it's snug and fine inside! We've a barn and byre, and you can go up the stairs in the galleries and look out over the sea. I like it better than a real house!"

Magnus grinned. "Now I'm bound to see it! When I was a lad my friends and I used to play at Midhowe Broch, some defending, some attacking. I thought it would be a splendid place to live but my mother did not."

"It's serving us well." Remembering Iain who had much to do with that, Mairi felt a stab of guilt for responding to Magnus's cheerful vitality. "Next spring, we'll build houses. There—there wasn't time this year."

She looked away. Any sudden reminder of Fearchar still brought tears. Tam quit chewing his currant scone and watched the floor. "Belike my big foot's again in my bigger mouth," their new friend said ruefully.

In the fewest possible words, Mairi told of the burning. "But we're still on the island," she said. "If you don't mind a pallet by the fire, you're very welcome."

"Don't fear I'll lout about underfoot," he assured her. "I grew up on a croft. But you must be wearied to the bone. Tam, there's an extra bunk in my room. Lass, you're next to us, so don't fash yourself about anyone bothering you." His grin broadened. "If you're nervous of a strange place, though, I'd be glad to hold your hand till you get to sleep."

Improper as the suggestion was, it was made in such a droll way that she couldn't be angry. After all, earlier that night, she had sheltered in his arms, drawn warmth and comfort from him.

Avoiding his merry gaze, she felt a bit hypocritical as she said in a prim tone, "That won't be needful, sir, thank you very much."

He grimaced. "Call me by my name, at least."

"Thank you—Magnus."

The innkeeper's wife lit them to their rooms. Mairi slipped off her clothes and was instantly asleep, but she woke in the night, thinking. If Magnus had no one to knit his jerseys, there must be others like him. While she was in Stornoway, she should find a shop that would buy the woolens in her creel—perhaps the owner could be persuaded to sell the knitted and woven goods made by the women at the broch. Now they had spinning wheels, they could produce more than they needed. Such an income would let them feed the animals and themselves even on the small amount of arable land they'd have till they gradually reclaimed enough to grow all the grain and potatoes they needed.

Exciting as the prospect was, Mairi was too sleepy to ponder on it long. She called up Iain's face to obscure Magnus's, and drifted happily into slumber.

As they breakfasted early next morning, she explained what she wanted to do. "I think I know the right merchant," Magnus said. "Seafaring men buy from Annie Gordon, not only because her husband had a fishing boat that was lost in the Minch some years back, but because she has always a smile and jest and won't sell anything that isn't good quality at a fair price. You'll like Annie."

Mairi did. The brown-haired, full-figured young woman whose warm brown eyes rested often and somewhat wistfully on Magnus, admired the weaving, the skillful dyeing, and Tam's jersey. "I knit while I tend the shop," she said, "and buy work from several women, but I'm bound I can sell all the jerseys you can make. Caps, too, and stockings." She then named what seemed an astounding figure for the woven goods. "The colors are seldom this clear," she said. "I'll wager I sell all three lengths before the week's out. Bring more when it's wove, lass. If you run out of fleece, I'll advance what you need and save out the cost when I pay you."

"That's wonderful!" Mairi gave Tam's hand a squeeze. "Pick out some sweeties, lad, enough for everyone. Gran loves those Jeddart snails. And Mrs. Gordon, I'll have a pound of your best tea, some raisins, treacle, and some good tobacco." Barry and Andrew rarely got any for their pipes. She was being extravagant but the cloth might have gone to Tarbert along with their few treasures, and it had brought a fine price. Besides, they had the assurance of selling more.

Tam, thrilled at having more than a penny to spend, chose some of every sort of toffee and a generous lot of black strippit balls and fudge tablets. After a moment's inner debate, Mairi also bought some indigo. Gran could coax some lovely blues from roots of white water lily and yellow flag, but the rest of them only got undistinguished shades of gray. It would be nice to have a dependable blue dye. Besides, mixed with yellows from bog myrtle or heather blooms, indigo gave a lovely green.

The creel was much lighter now than when it had held the woolens but Magnus took it from Mairi and swung to his own back. That reminded her that Iain had done the same. Island men were used to seeing their women bearing creels. The kindest of them never gave it a thought though Barry hadn't let Sheila carry anything heavy during the last months of her pregnancy.

Getting spoiled you are, Mairi thought, enjoying the extra lift in her step, which might have been there even had she carried the creel, for wasn't Tam safe, hadn't she found a grand market for their work, and not least, wasn't it fun to pace along with a handsome young man and bask in his manifest admiration? She loved Iain, couldn't imagine making love with any other man, but this one brought her singingly alive, deliciously aware of herself as woman. Since he was clearly fond of women and probably had sweethearts in every port, she didn't have to worry about hurting him.

"You've been to France?" Tam was asking him. "And even

130

to Spain? Oh, it must be main glorious to own your own ship—sail far away, not just out to the fishing grounds."

"The *Selchie*'s not glorious," said Magnus. "More contrary than any woman, and costly. Long ago 'tis said one of my family's women called a selchie, a seal, from the waves to love her and ever since, though we've been farmers, too, our men have followed the sea."

Such tales were common in the Islands. The MacCodrums, for example, a line of famous pipers, descended from a seal woman who'd returned to the sea when she found the hide her mortal husband had hidden from her. "So when you sit or lie down," teased Mairi, "is there a damp spot left when you rise up?"

"Not unless I've been in rain or water." He looked at her straight. "Nor do I lose my man's body. I can love a woman not just one magicked day in the year but all the days and nights."

Feeling on boggy ground where a misstep could plunge her knee-deep, Mairi sparred. "Little good that'd do your wife with you always at sea."

With a look of feigned ecstasy, he cast his eyes upward. "Oh, but lass! Think of the homecomings!"

"And the bairns to rock while you sail away!"

He raised startled eyebrows bleached silvery as the streaks in his pale blond hair. "Women *need* to rock and cuddle bairns."

"They *have* to," Mairi retorted. This highly improper exchange made her feel guilty as she thought of Seana's sweet warmth and what a joy she was to all of them. "For the men are off sailing or fishing or, should they be at home, they think it's none of their concern to change a baby's clouts."

Magnus roared at that, throwing back his strong neck. Mairi blushed and snapped, " 'Tis not so funny! We've good men at our hearth but neither would dream of changing the babe if a woman was within five miles."

"Will that be part of your marriage lines? That your man must change the wee ones' clouts?"

" 'Tis no task for a man," said Tam who'd been watching his

sister with scandalized shock. "Give over, Mairi, for look, here come Andrew and Barry and," he added severely, "I don't want them to think you've gone daft!"

Tam was embraced and made over as one snatched from the grave, first by the Nicolson men, then by Mrs. Fraser, who gave them a tasty meal, and then, when they trudged in at twilight, by those waiting at the broch. Eileen, watching from the highest gallery in the walls, gave a glad cry that sent the others hurrying out, and though she reached Tam last, she was his shadow and willing servant the rest of the evening. When Mairi told what Magnus had done, he got a hero's welcome and she herself was praised and fussed over till she begged them to stop. During supper, she gave the news of what good prices Annie Gordon had paid for the weaving and the chance of earning a very handy sum. Even Morag looked impressed.

"She wants jerseys? The kind we make for our men?"

"That very kind," assured Magnus, and again exhibited the sorry state of his.

"Why, you must have the one I'm making," Sheila said quickly.

"Bless you!" Mairi hugged her friend. "I knew you'd feel that way. I'll help you knit because Magnus will have to get back to his ship."

"I'll help, too," put in Gran. She studied Magnus. "The image of Michael you are, lad, though a mite bigger. You won't have seen him in your voyaging?"

"I haven't, Mrs. Macleod." Magnus knew of Gran's delusion and his tone was gentle. "But he sounds like a man I'd like to know."

Mairi got nervous when Gran talked so, fearing that something would shred the merciful veiling in her mind. "Tam," she suggested, "Fetch the sweeties to share around, but give Gran her Jeddart snails." These were a chewy candy Gran especially loved. "And please give the tobacco to Andrew and Barry. Will you fill a pipe, Magnus?"

132

"Thank you kindly but no. I threw away my pipe when the skipper of the ship I was on set fire to it and himself by falling asleep while he was smoking. 'Tis no habit for sailors."

"Praise be I'm not a sailor," Barry laughed as he fetched the pipes.

For a while longer, they sat around the fire, unspeakably grateful that none of their small group was missing. Eileen rocked Seana's cradle, but it was Tam to whom her eyes clung. That night they all said silent thanks while Gran blessed the hearth.

As he had promised, Magnus wasn't underfoot. The weather was favorable for several days and he fished with the men till violent rain and wind kept them in and he joined in braiding heather rope and mending nets. At night, Sheila or Gran knitted on his jersey so Mairi could play the harp.

"And to think I never heard one before." He shook his massive head. " 'Tis a sin to lose such music." Glancing from Mairi to Tam who could now play several tunes, Magnus added softly, "You two look like the spirit of the Islands."

Flustered, Mairi said, "I heard you crooning to Seana this afternoon. Something about a selchie. Would you sing it now?"

"If you'll find some chords for me."

He had a rougher, deeper voice than Iain but in its way, it was equally pleasing. Telling them that Sule Skerry was a seal rock in the Atlantic about fifty miles southwest of Orkney, he hummed till Mairi caught the tune.

> "Oh, I am a man upon the land
> And I am a selchie in the sea,
> And when I'm far frae every strand
> My dwelling is in Sule Skerry."

When he had finished the long, haunting ballad, Eileen had tears in her eyes. "That's awful, Magnus! Why didn't the

133

woman tell the gunner not to kill the selchie and his son that was hers, too?"

"Why, lassie," he said, clumsily stroking her hair. " 'Tis but a song. Now I'll tell you a true story. When my grandfather was a bairn just toddling, he fell from a cliff to the rocks. His mother ran down frantic. Searched and searched but she couldn't find him. Then she heard a selchie crying and she hurried along to where she sees this selchie on a crevice of the rocks standing guard over the child who was stunned by the fall. After that, grandfather's father left fish for that selchie on those rocks. Since that time, none of my family has ever killed one. And when my grandfather was carried to his grave by the sea, out in the waves the selchies followed and lamented as for one of their own." He smiled at the little girl who moved closer to him though she continued to rock the cradle. "Shall I teach you a song the seals have?"

"Och, yes!" cried Eileen and Tam at once.

> "Ho i ho i hi o ho i,
> Ho i hi o ho i . . ."

Soon the children were chant-singing with him to a wildly sweet and eerie tune. Mairi plucked out the melody and that was their last song for the night.

On the fifth day of Magnus' sojourn, the jersey was almost finished. He would leave next morning. Mairi felt sad, for he had become dear to her. Indeed they would all miss him, but she felt a certain relief.

She didn't love him. She couldn't! Not when she loved Iain. But if it hadn't been for Iain, she'd have fancied herself in love with Magnus, for his gaze could make her blood leap, then slow to the lazy warmth of heather honey in summer sun. She pleasured in his company, the caress of his deep male voice; she loved to laugh with him. He was twenty-six, five years younger than Iain but there was a somberness in Iain that she didn't think age would ever bring to Magnus. He breathed in life, fully and naturally as his lungs filled with air, found it good, and didn't trouble himself with reflecting on it. Since Fearchar's death, especially since Iain left, Mairi had fought a tendency to brood, but even Morag smiled when Magnus was around.

That evening, Mairi was down by the burn scrubbing out milk vessels with a heather brush when Magnus approached with the rolling gait that identified him from a long way off. It was the first time he'd sought her out alone. *Don't spoil things,* she implored silently. *Don't change the way we are . . .* She scrubbed harder, keeping her head ducked low as Magnus towered above her.

"Are you trying to wear a hole through the wood, lass?"

She straightened, shaking back her hair. "I—I'm finished." Why must she sound so breathless? "Maybe you'd help me fill the vessels with water and carry them inside?" Since there was no way to heat by kettle the amount of water required to scald the milk things and keep them sweet, they were filled at the burn and heated rocks were dropped into them till the water boiled.

"I'll help you in a minute."

He wasn't laughing. His mouth had as grim a tuck to it as on the night he confronted Tarbert. Tingling, voluptuous fear shot through her. The wind was rising, the sun was gone. They were alone, and she trembled.

12

"Let's get out of the wind." He took her hand and brought her to a small hollow grown with heather and bog myrtle, drew her down beside him. "There. Now we're cozy."

"I can't stay." She tried to conceal her panic. "I—I've got to help get supper."

"The others are managing finely," he said with dry amusement.

She tried to rise. He kept her where she was. A scramble would destroy her dignity, perhaps touch something off in him—and her—that couldn't be controlled. The beat of her pulse, trapped by his fingers, surged heavily, increased as if his blood, his powerful heart, now pumped with hers.

"Magnus! Please let me go!"

"As soon as I've told you a story."

"A story!"

"You like them, don't you?" In the hastening dusk, his eyes were luminous, unearthly blue. "It seems there was burning thatch, a good man dead, confusion and weeping. This gentleman happens along, an officer of the Queen. He shelters the families like a fairy-tale prince, sends those who would go to America and helps raise a roof over the others before he joins his regiment. Now how do you think the story ends?"

" 'Tis none of your concern," Mairi flashed, humiliated. He knew, then! Knew how she felt about Iain.

"It's my concern." Magnus's tone was equable but his jaw thrust forward. "Don't you see I'm crazy for you? The Mac-Donald aided you and your folk. I credit him that, and might make shift to keep myself to myself but for a thing that's bound to ruin the happy ending of your fairy tale. He's gentry." Magnus clasped both her hands between his. "Och, darlin'!" His tone was soft, compassionate. "Your prince can't carry you off where you'll live happily ever after. Up that road there's only grief for you. Maybe a bastard."

She flinched and stiffened. "How dare you drag me out here— make me hear such things?"

"Someone's got to." He grasped her shoulders so hard that her head snapped back. "I dare because I love you, girl."

His honesty forced honesty from her. "I wish I loved you, Magnus. I do, as a friend. But Iain—" Her voice broke.

He swallowed. She knew he was struggling to keep himself in check. "I can be real for you, Mairi. Your Iain can only be a dream." Magnus's voice harshened. "Unless he makes it a nightmare, puts a bairn in you."

"He wouldn't! Always we were with the others. He never dragged me away like this. He never—"

Magnus's mouth closed hers. Catching her close, he held her so her hands were trapped against the sledging of his heart. She tightened her lips but his demanded till with blurring, overwhelmed senses, she resisted no more. It was as if he drank or fed from her, drawing her essence into him, filling her with his. Flame leaped through her, melting her bones.

It was Magnus, not she, who drew back with a groan. "There's fire between us, lass, but it's Brigid's lightning that can tame to warm a hearth. I want to marry you."

"I can't."

"Will you wither, grow old, and never even bloom?" Warm fingers on her throat, he laughed in male triumph at the violent leap of her pulse. "Not you, Mairi! I could have taken you just

137

now and well you know it, but I want your heart along with your body." Rising, he drew her to her feet. "I'll be back. Till then, think on what I've said."

She dared chafe him a little. "You don't need a wife when you have your ship."

"I'd fix up the cabin and keep you with me."

She shook her head. "I'd pine for the Black Moor."

"Aye, the Black Moor, and black lairds, and mouldy black religion! I should think you'd be blithe to get your feet out of the peat bogs, especially now you're pushed to the rocks. With me, you could fly with the waves and wind."

"I'd like it for a day. Even a week. But I belong to the island."

"Only if you set your mind that way. Why stay where there's no hope?"

"There's hope because we stay."

He swore under his breath. Turning abruptly, he picked up two of the filled milk vessels. She got the others and, moving cautiously in the dark, they started for the broch.

That night, Gran did the final stitch on Magnus's jersey. He knelt by her while she pulled it over his ears and snugged it down, dark gray with broad red bands at throat, cuffs and bottom. It became him well.

"May it warm you in any blast," Gran said, kissing him. "May it keep you safe till you come again."

"Thank you, Rosanna MacLeod. But to finish the wish, I'd like a kiss from the others who helped with the knitting." He bent for Sheila's shy kiss, returned it on her forehead, but Mairi he kissed full on the lips and said to her startled kinfolk, "I've asked Mairi to be my wife. I want you to know that, because though the gormless lass refuses for now, I'm hoping she'll see what a bargain she's missing." He gave Mairi a devilish grin that set her blushing even more. Sobering, he looked around at those gathered by the hearth. "Mostly I want you to know that if there's aught I can do for you, leave word with Annie Gordon.

138

It may be a while before I'm in Stornoway but if *Selchie* stays on top of the waves, soon or late I'll anchor there."

"Can't you anchor closer and come see us?" Eileen demanded, hugging his arm.

"I won't bring my crew down on you, but it may be I could come to shore in a small boat and stay an hour or two." He patted the child's fair hair. "You know, m'eudail, if your cruel-hearted sister won't have me, I may wait for you to grow up."

Her face blazed and she threw her thin arms around his neck. "Och, Magnus, will you?"

"If your sister won't wed me," he stipulated.

Eileen was not to be damped. "If she does, you'll be my brother. That's almost as good. Just so we have you."

"You have me," he laughed but his eyes were grave when they met Mairi's above her little sister's head.

He left next morning, striding off across the moor in his new sweater, heedless of a fine mist. With the going of that bright head, winter came upon them. All that day the wind blew colder. Before nightfall, it seemed wise to bring the cows into their byre where they'd remain till spring. Sholma lowed till her heifer calf was beside her, Rigga stood next, and from behind the waist-high wall, the animals could see the fire and people, some solace for their long confinement. As the fragrant heather on the byre floor was soiled, it would be covered with fresh heather, dry seaweed and sand. As needed, these layers would be scooped behind a wall at the far end of the byre and covered with seaweed to make a rich dressing for the earth come spring. A drain carried off the urine. The chickens had a roost and nests in the barn. In the foulest weather, or when they lambed, the sheep could shelter there.

Eggs were used like money on the island and had they lived nearer town, the broch families could have traded eggs for salt, tea and other things they couldn't produce. As it was, they often had bannocks rolled in egg and baked again, and on Sunday a boiled egg apiece. Because Sheila was nursing the baby, after morning and evening milking, Gran made "broken milk" for her, whisking it till it frothed before sprinkling in toasted oats.

Each cow had a favorite song. After Mairi had brushed Sholma and placed hay before her, she sat on one side of Sholma with the little heifer suckling on the other and sang to the tune of the spurting milk. *"Ruddy faced and smooth-cheeked, gentle lady, you are my dear one; whiter than crowdie is the milk of my cow . . ."*

Sholma swished her tail and chewed her cud, acknowledging the praise as her due. She gave twice the milk of any of the other cows even in winter when fodder had to be eked out by every means known. When water was drained off boiled potatoes through their wicker-bottomed serving dish, this nutritious liquid was soaked in a bundle of feed which was given to the cows along with cooked seaweed.

Much as the MacNeills and Catriona were missed, the oats and barley they would have eaten left considerably more for the rest of the household and made it possible to give the cattle a little grain. The next harvest from such small plots as could be scratched next summer would probably not even feed the people, but if weaving and knitting continued to pay well, grain could be bought. Mairi was resolved that the cows would have enough. Some crofters kept more beasts than they could feed. By February, the poor creatures couldn't stand. By the time they were turned out to pasture, some had starved and the rest were so weak they had to be carried out to grass.

Winter was the time for making and mending nets. This year, Barry, Andrew and Tam did that, made rope, repaired tools and crafted shoes. The women spent every possible moment spinning, at the looms, and preparing the cloth.

Dyeing the washed wool before it was spun into yarn was the most exacting task, one at which Gran excelled. On a fair day so the odorous task could be done outside, she filled the big dye pot with alternating layers of lichen or roots, wool, and just the right pinches of the staghorn moss she used for a mordant before filling the kettle with water and setting it on the fire to boil. Gran might let someone else stir it, but it was she who dipped up fleece from time to time and decided when the sopping mass was the right shade. She had used indigo before and knew how to soak it in ammonia for several days before adding the wool to be boiled.

"The easiest dye of all's crotal," she said one day as she examined a warm rust obtained from the lichen. "But we can't use it for any clothes a man may wear at sea for crotal comes from the rocks and will go back to them."

The women took turns singing at their work when they were doing different tasks so there wouldn't be what Gran called "a right Tower of Babbling" but it took them all to waulk or full the ammonia-soaked woven web and then they sang together, first one, then another, taking the solo as they passed the web backwards and forwards over a plank table the men set up. Beginning with slow songs, the women rubbed and thumped as the tempo increased, never singing the same song twice for that was believed to harm the cloth. Many of these were love songs. "Oh, golden-haired lad, it's your word that has wounded me . . ."

But there were songs of soldiers, too. *"A heavy sorrow lies over me for I am carrying a gun for King George,"* Gran lamented. But the song that held Mairi's feeling about Iain made her cheeks burn for she couldn't keep from imagining what the words expressed. *"It is with you I would lie without conscience troubling me; it is with you I would rise without regret . . ."*

Singing together lightened the tedious chore, but they were glad when Gran pronounced the web sufficiently shrunken. When the finished cloth was given its final stretching and tightly rolled, Gran blessed it, and it was ready for sale or use.

"It's a proper factory," Andrew sighed one night when Morag was combing dyed fleece to make a smooth, fine, almost water-proof fabric, Eileen and Sheila carded another lot, Gan sang at her loom, and Mairi readied carded yarn for knitting by twisting two strands together and running them backwards on the spinning wheel to give springiness. "Tam, lad, give us a skirl on your pipes and we'll let you out of twisting rope."

Either he or Mairi, and sometimes both, were coaxed from their work each evening to play for a time, but there was always diversion. Barry could perfectly imitate birds, Andrew had an inexhaustible store of riddles, tales and jokes, and all of them made mouth-music to rival the sound of fiddle or pipes, and sang together, alone, or in combinations.

At Christmas, Gran concocted Athole brose. The cows were given some of the first and last sheaves of harvest to keep them healthy. The broch was too isolated in this season for lads to visit for Hogmanay bannocks on New Year's Eve, or for anyone to come "first-footing" as the year's earliest guest, but the family had extra thick bannocks and drank each other's health with Gran's heather ale.

"Let's drink to those who're far away but deep in our hearts," Andrew refilled the cups, called out the names, and for each, everyone took a few sips. "Catriona. Calum. Lucas. Paul. Kirsty. Adam. Wee Brigid and Rory. Magnus Ericsson. And the captain, Iain MacDonald! *Slainte!* May they all have love, health, luck, and may the mouse never leave their meal chest with a tear in its eye!"

That night, as she always did, Mairi held Iain's note to her heart and said a prayer for his safety. He had been gone now almost four months. Would he come in the spring? In summer? She didn't think she could bear it if he didn't come before fall, but then hastily took back that fate-tempting impatience. If he's only well, I can wait, she affirmed. Let him be safe. And Calum, too, Lucas and Paul. With a pang she thought of Catriona, wondered how she and the MacNeills had passed the holiday so far away, wished them happy, and was soon asleep.

A storm with drizzling sleet howled over the moor in those first days of January, 1845. The men, Tam and Mairi went searching for the sheep, scarcely able to keep their feet against the gale, crouching and stumbling as they searched out animals huddled in clefts or rock, in hollows, and in washed-out banks. They took them to the barn as they found them for the beasts were soaked and miserable.

"Sheep are born wanting to die," grunted Andrew, pulling a half-dead ewe over his shoulder. "We can't give 'em an excuse."

Numb to the bone, ducking her head and blinking against the stinging ice-rain, Mairi found one of the last of their small flock collapsed under a bank and was urging it up when she heard a thin wail. Hauling the ewe into a sheltered hollow, she cupped her hands and shouted, "Who's there?"

The cry came again, sounding like Seana when she was too sleepy to give lusty howls. How could a baby be out here? But it didn't sound like any bird or animal Mairi knew. Calling, she worked her way along the bank. To her great relief, Barry answered. Soon she could dimly make him out through the storm as he hurried from the other direction.

"Are you hurt, lass?"

Before Mairi could answer, he stopped short where the bank had eroded to a shallow cave, dropped to his knees beside a motionless heap wrapped in sodden plaids. Mairi knelt, too. As they drew back the coverings, the wail sounded from between the young man and woman who lay clasped in each other's arms, so pallid and still that Mairi thought them dead. A dark-haired baby of perhaps five or six months tried to suckle an emaciated breast. Screwing up its face, it voiced its complaint. The parents had shielded the child with their bodies, but from the look of them, they had no warmth left to give.

Barry felt for the pulse at the side of the woman's throat. "Her soul's still in her but not by much." It took him longer to find the beat of the man's blood but in a moment, he gave a relieved sigh. "Alive. But we've got to get them warm, and something down their bellies, from the look of them. I've lifted creatures out of the byre in spring that looked better than they do. Take the babe, I'll fetch the lass, and da' will come back with me for the lad."

* * *

143

"Bring in three of the cows and make them lie down," Gran ordered as they stripped the young woman and wrapped her in a soft blanket, chafing her hands and feet. "Heat from a cow'll warm her quicker and better than anything, and her man, too, when they bring him. Poor, poor lass, no flesh to keep the cold off her bones!"

"The babe's better-nourished than you'd think," said Morag, cuddling the tiny boy as she warmed some milk. " 'Twas God's mercy that your heard him, Mairi."

"Where's God's mercy that they're starving?" Mairi demanded, helping tuck the black-haired mother between Rigga and Sholma. "Odds are they've been driven from their croft, as we were. Can't we give her some hot broth, Gran?"

"Not till she starts to come around. She might choke. Och, here's her poor young man!"

Andrew and Barry soon had him in another blanket, nestled between Rigga and Luch, so-named from her mouse color. Tall, with his bones showing, the young man had russet brown hair and thick brown lashes fringed his gaunt cheeks.

"I've brought in the last ewe." Tam came from the barn by way of the byre. "Now the sheep are out of the storm, they'll warm each other." Staring at the couple resting between the cows, he asked fearfully, "Will they be all right?"

"I've known drowned men brought back by getting warm amongst the cows." Steam rose from Andrew's garments as he stood near the fire. His rugged face softened as he watched Morag feed the baby with a cloth dipped in milk. "That one, he's just hungry." Extending a big finger, he chuckled at the grip of the tiny hand that closed on it.

Mairi half-knelt beside the young couple. They were about the age of Barry and Sheila. Without Iain's help, Barry and Sheila might well have been in the same state, with little Seana. All of them could have been. Mairi shuddered, not just from damp clothing.

Thank goodness, the young faces were gradually losing their pinched bloodlessness. The woman's eyelashes fluttered. She moaned, and her arm moved under the blanket as if to clasp something.

"M'eudail!" Black-fringed eyes the violet-blue of harebells flew open, huge in her thin face, skin pulled to translucence over the bones. Staring wildly, she tried to raise herself.

"Here's your wee laddie." Morag brought him over. "His tummy's full of milk. Now you must have some. Hold your baby and lean on Mairi."

"First tea," said Gran, ready with a cup. "And then some gruel. That'll soon have you feeding your baby again."

Folding the child to her, the woman looked at them dazedly before dread constricted her features. "Donald! Where—"

"Your husband's right beside you, love," said Gran. "We've got you between the cows to put heat into you."

Turning her head, the young woman's eyes found her husband. Her face lit up, turning beautiful in spite of its wastedness. Reaching across Rigga, she just managed to touch his face. "Donald, *a luaidh*, my darling."

He lay still, though his color was now more of the living than the dead. "Are you sure he's alive?" his wife cried. "He's alive," Andrew assured her. "Drink and eat, lass."

Grasping the blanket around her, the woman clambered over the patient Rigga, lifting her husband's head while still holding the baby to her. "Donald! Wake up, love! Look, here's our Alai wanting his da'!"

She kissed her husband's mouth, her damp black hair a curtain around them. It was as if she breathed life into him along with her love, for his hand wandered up to her. "Donald!" Laughing shakily, she drew back, stroking his face and curling hair. "Oh, my Donald! Are you waking?"

His eyes opened, glowing as he saw her. "Katie! Are they burning peats in heaven, then?" Trying to sit up, falling back against Luch with his wife and child in his arms, he frowned and blinked, moving his head as if to clear it as he looked from one strange face to the next. "You—you don't look like saints or angels though you are for sure the last!"

"Wheesht, lad! Tell your lassie she must have her tea or she can't nurse her babe," said Gran. "A drop of whiskey in it wouldn't hurt either of you."

His lips, like his wife's were cracked but he grinned broadly. "Now I do know you're an angel, mistress, but what's your mortal name? Where has the storm blown us?"

"Drink your tea and eat," said Gran. "We'll talk while you do that and then you must tell us about yourselves."

An hour later, the cows were back in their stalls and Katie and Donald Gunn, warmed with gruel, broth, and tea with whiskey, slept snug in Gran's bed with little Alasdair between them.

"It's a mercy none of them have frozen toes or fingers," said Gran. "If Donald loses the lobe of his ear, he can cover it with those ringlets. What they need is rest and food." She banged the spurtle against the edge of the pot in which she was stewing mutton with potatoes and barley. "May worms gnaw his rotten heart inside his body, that factor who drove them from their house in the heart of winter! Wandering all the way from Harris as they have, it's a marvel they've kept alive."

"A few more hours and they wouldn't have been," growled Barry, holding little Seana close. He and Sheila were so near in age to the destitute couple that he was especially shaken. "What men like us should do is kill a few factors and constables and landlords! Better get some satisfaction and hang for it than starve meek as lambs!"

"Barry!" Sheila pressed her hand across his mouth. "Dear love, don't say such wickedness!"

" 'Tis not as wicked saying as the lairds' doings!"

"What folk like us must do is help each other and hang on," said Mairi. No one said there would now be two more mouths to feed through the winter.

"Aye," nodded Andrew. "We need another man for the fishing and 'twill help with breaking soil and cutting peats." He sounded so relieved that Mairi knew he'd worried more than he'd let on about he and Barry being responsible for all the heavy

146

man's work of three households, for though Tam worked valiantly, he hadn't the strength and weight for many tasks.

By supper, the Gunns, clad in loaned garments, could sit by the hearth and eat, seeming as nourished by the fire and friendliness as they were by the flavorsome stew. Alai still had to be fed with the cloth but from the color in Katie's face, it wouldn't be long till her milk flowed again, especially with plenty of carrageen pudding and Gran whipping eggs into the broken milk she fixed for her.

"There were eight families in our township," Donald explained when he had eaten all he could and was sipping heather ale. "My sister-in-law's from North Uist so she and my brother and their two bairns went to her family. Two of my cousins sold their beasts and plenishings for enough to get them to Glasgow where they hoped to find work in factories. The rest scraped and borrowed to go to Canada." He shook his head as his eyes found Katie's. "I reckoned on finding work. I can build boats and carpenter. We traded our cow for a pony to carry our things but when I got no work, we had to trade our belongings for food and lodging. Then we had to sell the pony and carry what was left on our backs."

"And then there was nothing to carry," Katie finished when Donald could not, closing her slender pale hand over his brawny tanned one. "We lived on sea weed and shellfish as we made for Stornoway. We thought with the harbor and fishing there, Donald could find work. But the storm came." Shivering, she glanced from small Alasdair to her husband. "Never, never can we thank you enough."

"But we won't burden you." Donald held his head proudly. "It's hard to feed one's own folk. From the little you've said, you've had your own troubles. What I would ask is would you let Katie and Alai bide here whilst I find a place in Stornoway to fetch them to?"

Andrew closed his burly hand on the younger man's shoulder. "The favor would be to us if you'd stay," he rumbled. "We need another man and the women have plenty your lass can help with. Why, man, if you can build boats, maybe we could make our own and not be tied to that cheating curer!"

After a startled glance, Donald beamed. "If you can get the wood, we can build a fine, tight boat." He stared in amazement at his wife. "Now lass, will you be weeping when we've found a home?"

"That's why," she said, laughing through her tears.

Gran got out her jug. "Let's have a drink to that!" She poured brew into every cup and Andrew called out a toast, "Here's to the folk who've stayed on this island! Here's to our outlasting lairds and factors and troubles till we claim our lands again!"

13

That very night three more starving, near-frozen people from an
evicted west coast hamlet found shelter at the broch, Murdo
MacKinnon, pounding at the door with his last strength while
his son, Gavin, supported his grandmother, Murdo's mother-
in-law, Meggie Ross, who had unaccountably survived the privations that had killed her daughter.

They were fed and warmed. When the household finally got
to bed, tremulous, frail silver-haired Meggie was tucked between Gran and Mairi while Eileen, for that night, slept between
Sheila and the wall. The MacKinnons had pallets by the hearth.

Again it was a story of a small community rent asunder,
scattered to Australia, America, the Lowlands, while this family,
trying to remain near their ancestral home, lived in a byre till
they were driven from that a few days before the storm. It caught
them unprotected on the moor, but they struggled on, and
though Meggie, when she could no longer keep her feet in the
slashing wind, begged the men to leave her and try to save
themselves, they had taken turns carrying her.

"Hadn't have been for that glow cast up into the night, we'd
have given up," Murdo said when he could talk. He was a tough,
knotty little brown man with steel gray hair and eyes. "We'd fall
and think we could not go on but the light beckoned. Gavin'd
drag me up, or I'd pull him, and we'd go on."

Perhaps in his mid-thirties, Gavin was stocky with butter yellow hair, blue eyes and a round, ruddy face. "The light called us for so long we began to fear it a trick of the Peeries but when we sniffed peat smoke, we knew 'twas a real hearth with human folk."

"Glad we are to share it," said Andrew, though three more mouths would dangerously stretch their provisions.

The Gunns and MacKinnons understood this. By the time the storm blew itself out several days later, except for Meggie, they were out gathering laver, dulse, carrageen and shellfish. "We don't want to use up your grain and taties," Murdo said. "It's a grand thing to have a roof over our heads and a fire to warm by."

In answer, Gran handed him a bannock and filled Meggie's bowl with sowens, husks on which some grain was left which were soaked till the liquid thickened and soured. This was quite tasty, especially with milk, which was now saved for the nursing mothers, old Meggie and Eileen.

"We can all eat more seaweed and shellfish," Mairi said.

"And we'll fish more," Barry added.

"We can help with that," said Gavin. "Also, you say there's a hunting lodge within a half-day's walk. I'm a stone mason. Maybe I could work in return for food and a place in the stable."

Besides farming and fishing, some crofters were part-time shoemakers, tailors, masons, weavers, carpenters, millers or blacksmiths, though except for the last, these trades alone seldom earned a living. Andrew had made shoes for the Aosda folk and Barry was known for sturdy and attractive wicker work.

"You're welcome to share what we have," said Andrew. "We can use a good mason when we build houses in the spring. And Murdo, you're a canny fisherman. Donald here can build us a boat for a crew of six. Counting Tam, we'll have enough men for the first time since my lads and Calum went for soldiers."

Barry nodded. "Without the curer's charge for a boat, we'll win enough of our living from the sea to make up for what we can't grow."

"And," said Mairi, "Soon as we've waulked the webs that're on the looms, we'll see if Annie Gordon will pay what she did for the others!"

She did, and was eager for more, saying Gran's dyes were the truest and best she'd ever seen, and the weaving and knitting of the highest quality. It turned out that Meggie, though skewed in the head from her misfortunes, was a notable weaver and happiest at the loom. Humming softly, now and then crooning some ancient song, her fingers shaped intricate overchecks and tiny checks as if creating these patterns was a solace in the chaos of losing daughter, home and village.

The wool was almost used up so a new supply was brought with the barley and oats the men carried back from Stornoway. Their great triumph was in bringing sailcloth and cordage for the boat. They'd bespoke good timber from the mainland for its making and it was time to begin for this was St. Brigid's Day, February 1, when the sea warmed because the saint dipped her hand in it.

"Our own craft!" Andrew marveled. His eyes glistened and he touched the cream-white sails as if he couldn't believe they were real. "You're sure, Donald, we've coin enough for the timber?"

"Aye," said Donald, brown eyes shining. It was three weeks since the terrible storm that had in a day added six souls to the broch dwellers. The newcomers had lost the look of skeletons and gained back their strength though probably everyone save Sheila and Katie—and their babes—went to bed with what Gran called a "mite hungry corner." This happened more winters than not. The difference this time was that they stood to possess a boat in time for the rich herring fishing of May and June.

Pride for the skill he could use for his family and friends gave a jaunty lift to Donald's curly head as he took little Alai from his wife's arms and smiled into sleepy eyes that were the deep blue of Katie's. "For £25 we can make a good stout boat that would cost £40 if we had it built."

151

Twenty-five pounds! It was a fortune. Four men could hire out as laborers for a year and earn less than that. True, cordage and sails were paid for, but—

Barry glanced from his wife and mother to Gran, Mairi and Katie. Meggie, as usual, was at the loom, which she left only to eat, sleep, and dandle the babies. When she sang to them, her wispy voice took on strength and she even smiled. "If we make a loom for Aunt Meggie," he proposed, "can you weave as much plaiding and tweed as we carried up to Annie Gordon this time—maybe knit two more jerseys? If you can, Mistress Gordon's assured us the money for the timber."

The women stared at each other, awed and a bit apprehensive. It seemed too good to be true, that their work could be the means of winning a boat. "How long will it take to build the boat?" worried Morag, though eagerness lighted her usually somber eyes.

"We can do it in less than a week," Donald said confidently.

"Then you'll need the cloth by mid-April," Gran calculated. "And the wool's to be dyed and spun. Can we do it, lassies?"

Looking at the men, Mairi had a sudden thought. There was small use in the six of them, counting Tam, spending the rest of the winter making more heather rope than they'd soon need, or wickerware that was useful but not essential, while the women strained to cook, care for babies and beasts, attend to the dairying, and spin and weave far into the night.

Facing the men, she said with a smile, "We might just be able to do it, lads, if you'll take on some of our work."

"*Your* work?" Barry frowned in puzzlement.

She laughed into her cousin's bewildered eyes. "Aye, laddie. Fetch water from the burn, bring in the peats, feed and brush and milk the cows, grind the grain, do the cooking—"

"Wheesht!" Andrew grinned after his first shock. "Do you think we can't do it, lass? Why, we cook while we're at the fishing and I'm bound we can do it here if it means we can sail out of here in our own boat."

Barry gaped at his father and Morag's jaw dropped, but after a moment, the younger man shrugged and put an arm around his wife. "I never thought to do woman's work—but then it's a lot we're asking and all the way home I was wishing there was some way to help."

"But it never entered your curly head that you could do our chores," said Mairi a trifle acidly.

He flushed and squirmed. "Och, Mairi, give over! And promise, all of you, you'll never tell on us."

"We won't," said Mairi, chuckling. "But we'll remember! And when we're burdened we'll expect a hand from you." She had thought of something else and though reluctant to broach it, that seemed the only fair thing to do. Looking at the Gunns and MacKinnons, she said, "Fifteen pounds would take you all to America. If you want to go, I think we could agree to loan you the passage."

Donald turned to Katie. She shook her head so that black ringlets escaped from her cap and her violet eyes glowed. "Who'd cross the ocean if we can live in our own dear land and speak our mother tongue?"

Murdo, after a silent exchange with his son, grinned hardily. "We want to stay and crew the boat, build a house, and make a township. You're our *clanna* now."

"Clanna," mused Gran, tilting her head. "That would be a good name for our township."

"And for our boat," said Andrew and laughed. "Then there'll be no fash about which wife to name it after."

The muscles in Gavin's round face tightened. He had no wife. When he went out by night to walk in the wind, Murdo said he was grieving for his Honora who'd died of exposure within the week they were driven from their home. "A frail lass she was," her father-in-law had said. "Never birthed a living babe, but it was rare how she and Gavin set store in each other."

Going even redder at his misstep, Andrew tried to cover it. "For a boat, our own boat, I can make bannocks and porridge though you may all be the sorrier!"

As guests, Donald, Murdo and Gavin could scarcely object.

153

Gran, eyes agleam, clapped her hands. "That calls for a round of heather ale! Set down your creels, my boys, and let's drink to our boat—*The Clanna*—and to the looms!"

That night, holding Iain's note to her heart, Mairi summoned up his face. His blue-gray eyes seemed to dance as she told him fondly, *That's what comes of your carrying my creel, love. What will you think of it all when you come home? And when, when, are you coming?*

There was no way to partition off sleeping quarters for the newcomers. The Gunns continued to have Gran's bed, Meggie was snugged into a wall nook like Tam's in Andrew's and Morag's room, and heather and dried eel-grass heaped against the low byre wall made a springy mattress where Gavin and Murdo spread their blankets by night and which could be pushed out of the way while the hearth room was busy.

And busy it was with all of them caught up in having the cloth and jerseys ready in time. Strange as it was to see men grinding at the quern, patting out bannocks, scrubbing milk vessels and churning, they soon sorted out tasks to abilities, and though no Lewis man, alone, would have done woman's work, together the broch men made it a game. On favorable days, some went fishing or gathered seaweed and sand for lazybeds, while two attended to domestic tasks.

The only chore they couldn't do was the milking. The cows kicked at the coggs and refused to let down their milk till Sheila and Mairi and Morag sat down at their sides and sang their favored songs. While they had been at the lodge, the dry cows had been left with a bull and, with good luck, would calve in July when grass would be at its best. Mairi hoped for heifers that would increase the dairying to where it would provide for the little community and even produce some butter and cheese to sell or trade.

From before dawn to bedtime, webs grew on the three looms while yarn twined on the bobbins of the spinning wheels and from distaff and spindle. Gran presided over the dyeing, and as a change of occupation, knitting needles flashed. Eileen helped where she was needed and took charge of the babies. They would both fit in the cradle so rocking them was easy. Well-nourished again from Katie's breast, Alai was beginning to push up on his knees when the infants lay on the sheepskin, Seana so golden, Alai so dark except that he had Katie's beautiful eyes. He was teething and to soothe him, Gran, sighing, rubbed the last of her whiskey on his sore little gums.

Not only were the MacKinnons and Gunns hard workers but Katie had a sweet, rich voice, Donald had a store of sailors' jokes and ditties, Murdo could play tunes gay or plaintive on his trump or Jews'-harp, and Gavin could compete with Gran in telling stories. Cridhe spent some evenings plaided in the corner like a benignly dozing elder but usually Mairi was urged for "just a song or two, lass," and left her work to woo music from the strings. Every night was a ceilidh. This did much to make up for the monotony of their suppers.

Though the potatoes, except for those needed for seed, were gone by March when it was time to plant them again, and the salt mutton and fish were used up so that on days when the men didn't fish or had no luck, the main dishes would be some form of seaweed and stewed shellfish, there was still enough milk for the mothers, a little cheese and butter and whey, oats, barley, and enough eggs to now and then beat to dip bannocks in for browning. All remembered hungrier winters, and food they tasted was doubly good for the sharing with folk who would otherwise have perished. Even Morag ate her dulse and laver without pulling faces, but then she had her fine wicker armchair that Barry had made for her. To everyone's surprise, she shared this with Meggie.

All spots of arable soil had been dressed with seaweed, sand, and manure from the byre. To make sure the soil was warm enough to accept the seed, Andrew, bare-rumped, sat on it, and only when he judged it hospitable did the men break the earth with cas-chroms or foot plows and sow the oats. Where there was only a thin skin of earth on the rocks, alternating layers of decaying seaweed and sand formed lazybeds about five feet wide, covered with soil dug from between one bed and the next. This left a drainage ditch so rain wouldn't stand on the potatoes. Late that summer, a planticrue, a walled bed layered with seaweed and sand, would have to be prepared for kale seeds sent by Mrs. Fraser when the men stopped on their way back from Stornoway. The cabbage-like vegetable would be a wonderful addition to their food though plants sprouting from these seeds wouldn't be ready to eat for over a year.

By early April, the last potatoes were cut to leave an eye in each piece and buried in their hills. The sky filled with wedges of trumpeting whooper swans, kow-yowing white-fronted and hoarse-calling barnacle geese, their greylag cousins, and the whole tribe of ducks and other south-wintering birds. Some flew on to the Arctic, others like greenshanks and dotterels and wheatears dropped to summer breeding grounds. Along the cliffs, shags and cormorants that had braved the winter were joined by kittiwakes, puffins, guillemots and terns.

The sheep had ranged loose all winter except during bad storms and now the cows were led from the byre, lowing with joy at being under the sky and able to wander. Mairi was proud that the veins in their necks hadn't been opened, as was usually done, to get blood for puddings.

"They're weak enough as it is," she'd protested when Morag suggested it. "If we can't feed them all they need, at least we can leave them their own blood, poor creatures." That may have been why none of the beasts had to be carried from the byre and moved around till they regained their strength.

Soft green brightened the Black Moor, skylarks and lapwings exulted as they winged up, caracoled, and plummeted, rejoicing with humans in these brighter, lengthening days. The younger women and Eileen escaped the broch to gather tender nettles, wild mustard and spinach which tasted as wonderful as only fresh greens can after months without them. It was a trial to stay at loom and spinning wheel during this glad stirring of the earth, but right after Easter, when as Fearchar used to say, the rising sun danced for joy, webs were rolled tightly, jerseys folded, and the men set out for Stornoway.

In four days they were back with ash and larch from the mainland, iron fittings for the boat made by Lachlann MacKenzie at the lodge, fir pitch from Norway, grain, and wool, with a new order from Annie who had long since sold their winter's production for a good profit.

"Och, Clanna will be beautiful!" Donald sighed. "With a steep stem and stern like the old Viking galleys, and two fine sails like wings. The first thing we have to do is steam the ash to shape it for the frame."

For the next week, from first light to last, the men hammered away down by the inlet where the boat would be launched, overlapping the larch planks forming the sides and caulking between with pitch-soaked moss. The stern was deeper than the stem so the water would run to that end and could be easily bailed. Twenty feet long, the craft was partially decked. There were three planks to seat the oarsmen and strong thole pins of ash to hold the oars.

"No more trudging to Stornoway with creels to our backs!" exulted Barry after the boat was put in the water to test for any leaks and found to be watertight. "We'll take the high road of the waves. We can come home to help with the heavy work for a few days or a week and then go back to the fishing. And on good winter days we can seek the white fish rather than chill to the marrow along the rocks and still come home empty-handed."

"Aye, with our own boat, we're masters, not bound to the curer," said Andrew. "Aosda had a boat years ago but it splintered on the Beasts of Holm. We could never raise money to build another. Would that Fearchar had lived to—" He broke off, but Gran, caressing the gracefully curved stem, seemed not to hear, but smiled and said, "My Michael will think we've done grandly."

A boat was usually the pride of the men but since the women had earned the money for building *Clanna*, she belonged to them, too. Sheila carefully painted on the name and Gran blessed the boat. The nets were ready, treated with a bark solution that helped keep them from rotting, and with a supply of bannocks and a keg of water, the men were ready to start for Stornoway where they would shelter in an old hut near the harbor for the time they were away.

Everyone except Meggie helped drag and push *Clanna* down the beach to waves that on that day frolicked in like racing foam-maned ponies. All bowed their heads while Andrew prayed for good winds, good catches, and a safe return. Then, so that the men wouldn't start out soaked, they climbed in and took their places while the women, skirts kilted above the knee, waded and shoved till the boat was floating and the men could push out with their oars.

As *Clanna* lilted toward the open sea, the white sails were rigged to catch the wind and the boat moved like a great swan, suddenly alive. Beautiful! And as much as the looms, it held the hope of making a living without much land or pasture.

Watching the sails that swept their men away on depths that both blessed and murdered, that could, like a mistress, smile invitation or snarl in fury, each woman silently invoked the powers.

On May Day morning, Mairi woke to the song of skylarks who caroled from faintest light to darkness, intoxicated with lengthening days that told them it was time to make nests in safe tussocks or nooks on the breast of the moor.

"We must wash our faces in the dew for beauty and health," said Gran, winking broadly. "I've no hope for the first, but can try for the last."

Even Meggie trooped out with the others to wet her hands on yellow whin and spearwort, heath-spotted orchids, violet-pink blooms of butterwort and such grass as had escaped cows and sheep by growing where they couldn't reach. Eileen washed so enthusiastically that crystal droplets glinted on her hair and

Mairi teased, "For whom are you washing, m'eudail? Liam Fraser or is it Magnus?"

Eileen flushed. With a surprised qualm, Mairi noticed that her sister had grown inches taller that winter and the bony angles of collarbone and elbow were beginning to round. "It's not a joke, Mairi. Turned eleven, I have. Some wed at fourteen or less."

"An ill thing," said Mairi. "A child shouldn't be put in the way of bearing children. Make no hurry, love." She tried to slip an arm around Eileen but the child pulled away.

"You won't be taking Magnus?"

"I won't. But henny, he's old enough to be your father—"

"He's not!" cried Eileen fiercely. "He was twenty-six on the twelfth day of Yule. That's only fifteen years older." Her dark blue eyes glistened. "If you won't have him, didn't he say he'd wait for me?"

"Sweeting! That was a joke, to be sure."

"It won't be! You just wait!"

Eileen ran for the cliffs. She stood there, a small thin shadow facing boundless sea and sky as if willing them to bring Magnus to her. Meggie's cracked voice came from within. *"Fair-haired lad, you rest your head on a seaweed pillow, that head I would pillow on my lap . . ."*

Mairi said a prayer—not only for Magnus, so kind and strong and laughing, but for those on *Clanna* and for Iain, too, for it was possible that he was on the sea, homeward bound. *Let him come soon. Let him come safe.*

Suddenly as lonely as her little sister looked, Mairi turned to the others and said, "This might be a day as good as any for washing."

Gran gave her a knowing smile. "Aye, thumping sheets and clothes and treading blankets is a good way to ease your worries, lass. But first come in, all of you, and let's have our bannocks."

Great washings of sheets, towels, and bed curtains were done in spring and fall. These were strong, beautiful linen, some older

159

than Mairi, made of homegrown flax painstakingly retted or soaked to rot away stems and stalks and then combed fine with the iron combs used for sheerest woolens before the thread was spun. It was such a laborious process, and the retting such a smelly one, that Mairi was glad the present supply would last for years.

"Och," chuckled Gran. "When I was distilling the good uisge-beatha and the excise man came snooping, I hid the jugs in the retting pond. That long-nosed gawk didn't poke it there, you may be sure." She was in a blithe mood that day. While kneeling at the burn, they pounded the linens with wooden beetles or sticks, and Gran said, "Hard work, lassies, but we would not be wanting the Fairy Washerwoman's help. When she washes a man's shirt, that man will die. Before a battle, she often has a great pile. My gran saw her washing granda's shirt and didn't he drown that very day?"

May she never wash Iain's, Mairi thought. Eileen was treading blankets in a big wooden tub to free them of peat smoke. After Mairi and Sheila wrung out the bed curtains and spread them to dry on clumps of bog myrtle, Mairi fastened up her skirts and got in the tub with Eileen, laughing as she took her sister's hands and leaned slightly backwards. "Let's go around and around and around," she chanted. "Squish! goes the dirt! Weesh! goes the smoke!"

"Round and round and around," laughed Eileen, leaning far back and treading so fast and hard that she splashed Mairi thoroughly, but after all, it was wash day so why fret about keeping dry?

They spun faster and faster, the women at the burn cheering them on till Eileen stopped abruptly. Mairi tripped into her. They went down together. Giggling and spluttering, Mairi tried to wipe the water from her eyes, heard the creak of leather and the soft clump of hooves.

She scrambled out of the tub, hastily tumbling down her skirts, and stood there dripping. "It's the captain!" Gran cried and ran from the burn nimbly as a girl, hugging and patting him as he came off his horse. Eileen, wet as the blankets, wasn't far behind.

He opened his arms to them both, but over their heads, his eyes found Mairi's. The glad cry wedged in her throat. His face, his dear face, what had happened to it? Why did he move like an old man, or a sick one?

Whatever and whyever, he was home, her love was here. The joyful greeting broke from her then, and she ran forward.

14

A good thing his arms were full of Eileen and Gran or Mairi, in spite of soaked clothes and propriety, couldn't have kept from embracing him. His eyes, the intense blue-gray of seas mirroring a building storm, found hers in shock that stopped her blood and breath before her heart began to race. Air flooded her lungs as if she'd been running.

So often she had dreamed of this, pictured his return! But he was to find her on the beach or wandering on the moor, not with other folk about—especially not just when she'd fallen in a tub!

It didn't matter. He'd come back to her. But what had made the puckered seam from cheekbone to chin that gave a slight twist to the left side of his mouth? With a pang, she saw when he moved forward, Gran and Eileen clinging to either arm, that his stride, once confident and graceful, was now a limp.

Her dismay must have shown for he stopped dead. "Do I frighten you, Mairi MacLeod?"

She closed the space between them. Slowly, she traced the scar, sending love through her fingertips, and strength, for he was starving thin. The pallor beneath the weathered brown of his skin gave it an ashen cast. "You—you've been hurt." It sounded weak beside her joy at his return, her sorrow for his wounds. "Is Calum all right? My cousins?"

"When last I saw them. I got these mementoes only a few

weeks before the northern tribesmen that have been raiding Sind submitted to General Napier in March. We'd been after them since late last year, poor devils. They've raided Sind for centuries and couldn't see why they had to stop. Some sort of damned epidemic killed half the 78th, a lot more than the tribes did." His tight smile twisted the scar. "Having survived the sickness and the worst fighting, it's likely your men are in fine fettle and resting up after Napier's victory which should win them some of those medals the Queen is so fond of devising. I know Napier commended their valor in several dispatches. He's the first officer in the history of the British army to mention private soldiers, drummers, too. He even honors native troopers by name in his reports."

"Small comfort when our lads die in battles that are none of our concern," frowned Mairi. "But you will rest while I bring you milk. Would you have crowdie and bannocks?"

"I'll thank you for milk. For the rest, I can wait till the rest of you can share what I have in my saddlebag." For the first time, he noticed Katie. "Has your clan increased?"

"The Clanna has." Quickly, Mairi explained the coming of the Gunns and MacKinnons. "And we've got our own boat!" Eileen burst out. "The men are off to the fishing with naught to owe the curer but barrels and salt! We womenfolk made the cloth to build the boat while the men baked bannocks. And—"

"Wheesht!" chided Gran. "Go jump up and down in that tub, lass, instead of on the captain's toes! You, Mairi, fetch the milk and sit down and tell him all that's passed. We're nigh through with the washing."

Mairi hurried for a beaker of milk. When she returned, Iain had tossed Chieftain's saddle over a rock and the big bay nibbled somewhat disdainfully at such grass and herbage as had escaped cows and sheep. "No need to tether him," Iain said, thanking her for the milk. His fingers warmed hers a moment before he took the cup and sat down on a rock. "Chieftain limps, too. Caught arrows in the thigh and haunch in the same fight where I took one. Everyone thought I should have him destroyed but

163

I'd hobble out and get him to eat and he finally started to mend. No more wars for him, though. I'll leave him in the meadow when I join the regiment."

Mairi felt as if an unseen fist had knocked the wind out of her. Scarce here and already talking of going away! "When—when will you be going, sir?"

He frowned. "I'm not your commanding officer, Mairi. Call me by name. I have leave till mid-August and can request more if this stupid leg requires it." Turning the scarred side of his face to her, his eyes hardened and he watched her closely. "Does my scar distress you?"

"Only because you were hurt—"

He made an impatient gesture. "Tell truth, lass. Don't I revolt you?"

Scarred from the crown of your head to the soles of your feet, you wouldn't revolt me, she thought, longing to hold and comfort him. "A handsome man you are, captain," she said, trying to laugh. "I won't say more than that to puff up your head. If you'd lost an arm or leg, that would be a drawback but a mark on the face just shows you've lived through danger."

He laughed wryly but most of the wariness left his eyes. "Next you'll say I should wear it proud as a medal."

"Indeed, and so you should! But tell me about Calum and my cousins. Will they be home this year?"

"Calum will, but you mustn't count on his staying. When he heard of the eviction, he was for going to America, and when he learned his sweetheart was there, it settled his course."

"The devil fly off with Catriona!" Mairi cried. "We need Calum here!" After a moment's thought, she brightened. "When he sees we have our own boat maybe he'll stay."

"Don't count on that, lass. Lucas and Paul, though, mean to stay here if they can. In order to save more money, they'll soldier for another two years."

Her cousins were hardworking, lighthearted lads and she was fond of them, but it was Calum she'd grown up adoring, Calum she'd expected to take responsibility for the family, act as a father to Tam and Eileen. Bad enough to lose Catriona, but Calum, too! The ocean between and never to see them again on this earth . . . Mairi bit the inside of a trembling lip.

"Now, Mistress Mairi," Iain said briskly, "tell me how you've managed these wonders—a boat, taking in six people when you'd scarce provender for yourselves. I see you lost no cattle and lazybeds are hugging every place where there's an inch of soil on these bony rocks."

"Oh, Iain, we have done well, haven't we?" She flushed at his praise. "But if you hadn't helped us, we'd have been in as cruel a fix as the Gunns and MacKinnons. Truly, it's luck they're with us, though we supped often on seaweed and shellfish. Now we've a crew for the fishing—three more strong men for the heavy work instead of it all falling on Andrew and Barry with Tam straining at a man's share."

"But thirteen people and two babies in the broch! I thought you crowded before but reckoned it would do for a winter."

"We'll be glad to move into houses, right enough," she admitted. "But we had grand times in the hearthroom, everyone busy, snug from the winds, with the fire warming us and always a story or song. Oh, Iain, it was kind of you to send the pipes to Tam! Set him in the clouds though it was mightily thankful we were when he stopped sounding like a scalded pig. He'll be after you to teach him more." That was presumptuous and she added quickly, "That is, if you have time."

"I'll have time." After a pause, he said slowly, "This leg, Mairi, they wanted to cut it off but I said I'd die sooner. Jamie kept them off while I was out of my head with fever and opium. Do you know what I remember more than the fear and pain?"

She shook her head, grieved that she hadn't been there to nurse him. "I remember the softness and warmth of the coverlet you gave me." He smiled and though he didn't touch her, she was filled with awareness so sweetly piercing that it was near torment. "There was still a hint of peat smoke and heather in the wool. Jamie says most of the time I thought I was at your fire, and when it seemed you were playing your harp, that would quiet me into sleep."

"If only I could have been there—"

"I felt your hand on my forehead, felt you bathe away the sweat and corruption. You gave me to drink and made me eat. If you had not, I would have died."

"But, Iain, I wasn't there."

"You played the songs I asked for." His voice dropped till she could scarcely hear. "When I shivered with chills not even your coverlet could banish, you held me in your arms."

"Iain!" she almost begged. A wild pulsing drummed in her ears. She felt suffocated though she was breathing fast and hard.

He got to his feet. The washing was finished, even the tub emptied and blankets spread to dry. "I know it was a dream, but it was a dream that saved me. I wanted you to know." There was sadness in his eyes. "And know this, Mairi. I would rather die than harm you. Come now, and let me meet the new ones of your Clanna."

Katie was so awed by Iain that she wouldn't talk beyond answering his direct questions, but he won her heart by hoisting Alai to his shoulder and declaring him the strongest, handsomest baby boy he'd clapped eyes on. Seana, golden-haired and elfin, went to the other shoulder, gripping the silver cup he'd brought as a belated christening present. Mairi couldn't stifle the wish that the children were theirs, made from their love.

Meggie never glanced up from her loom when Katie told her a gentleman was visiting. She only continued, in her droning old voice, with a lament.

> "Oh, young and beautiful lad, for whom pipes played
> and standards waved,
> Alas, your fair body lies in rocks and seaweed
> And the Apostles have carried your soul to Paradise."

But when Seana crowed and reached for her, the old woman roused, secured the shuttle, and took the baby, crooning, *"Mo cubhrachan,* my little fragrant one, Meggie's no milk for ye but ye can warm your sweet cold toes under her arm. Let's go i' the yard and find you a flower."

Ignoring the rest of them, wrinkled old cheek pressed to the fresh one, Meggie scarcely had to bend to go out the low entrance. "She loves the wee ones," Gran commiserated. "A good thing we have them or the poor confused body might go daft entirely."

Mairi went cold. Gran pitied Meggie but what if her own mind ever admitted that Fearchar was dead? The delusion had lasted so long that Mairi dared hope Gran would die in it. Iain had brought so many delicacies that nothing else was needed but tea and bannocks. Cheeses, figs, dates, nuts, ham, smoked salmon, and Mrs. Fraser's excellent shortbread, black buns and crannachan soon made a brave show on the snowy cloth spread on the waulking table.

"It's like a wedding!" Katie's violet eyes were wide as she tried to choose. "Och, if only Donald and the others could share it!"

"We'll feast them when they return from the fishing," Iain promised. He himself ate with relish, as if it had been a long time since he'd enjoyed his food.

When Katie saw Sheila had no fear of Iain and heard Gran call him laddie, the young woman let him hold Alai while she worked at a loom. Mairi and Sheila ground meal for that evening's bannocks and Gran and Morag knitted, occupying their chairs with dignity. Iain was shocked to hear about Tam's abduction and gave Mairi a swift glance when Eileen praised Magnus as "just like a Viking chief—tall and strong and handsome!"

Mairi's cheeks burned. She was glad Iain couldn't see her face, bent as it was over the quern. He answered their questions and asked a few but for the most part, he seemed content to watch them at their tasks and hum along with the rhythmic grinding song.

"I must go or Jamie'll think I met a kelpie." Iain got reluctantly to his feet. "Will you be doing anything tomorrow that I could help with? I'm weak from lying about and need to try my muscles."

"Won't you be hunting?" Gran squinted shrewdly. "Banging away at grouse and deer and any hare misfortunate enough to run across your path?"

"I've seen too much death these last months to pleasure in killing."

"Och," said Gran, disbelieving. "Will a gentleman help with the shearing? Swing the *croman* to chop out weeds?"

"I want honest work, Rosanna. Work that puts food in people's bellies and clothes on their backs." He looked at Mairi. "I want to cut peats for the hearth and feel I've earned the right to sit by it."

"You want to lose yourself, laddie," said Gran.

"I want to rest from what I am."

"Aye," said Gran drily. "Your whim is our must. But it serves your health and our need. We'll keep you busy." She grinned at him. "If you'd sit at the hearth though, you must fetch your pipes."

He grinned back, for a moment seeming almost his old self. "Remember! I waited till you asked."

Mairi and Eileen went out with him to saddle Chieftain. He didn't spring up in the old way. With effort that hurt Mairi to watch, he got his wounded right leg over the saddle and into the stirrup. White creases showed at the sides of his mouth. *Love, my love, don't do things that pain you!* Mairi wanted to cry, but she knew he was driven to do exactly that as a person with an excruciating injury may strike or pinch elsewhere to diffuse the sensation. She was sure that it wasn't in his body or on his face, though, that Iain was most sorely wounded . . .

He helped shear the sheep, tying the forefeet before cutting off the fleece with a sharp knife. The four ewes that had lambed in

168

April wouldn't be shorn till July because a chill now would hinder their flow of milk for the small creatures that skipped and danced over the moor.

One of them, claimed by Eileen as her special pet and fondly named Cailin, young maiden, was a throwback to the ancient Highland sheep, a dainty particolored beastling with four weirdly curling horns, a short tail, very large, golden eyes, and a pink nose. Gran remembered when sheep with four or six horns were common but they had long since given way to the hardier black-faced sheep of the Borders. These, in turn, were being cross-bred with or superseded by Cheviots whose high yield of meat and fleece was the woe of men driven off their land to make room for vast sheepwalks.

Panting as he let up a belligerent old ewe who tried to horn him and succeeded in scoring a smart kick, Iain said, "This would go faster with shears."

"I doubt they'd like the click around their faces," Mairi said.

"They don't like anything about it anyway." He stared at the pile of fleece, exceedingly dirty because of the mixed tar and butter daubed on to keep off pests, especially the dreaded blow-flies. "How will you ever get this clean?"

" 'Twill need a good washing. But the wool in your coverlet once looked just like this."

He looked at her between respect and puzzlement. "You take it for granted, don't you, that everything takes work?"

"Och, no," she laughed. "Only look at those larks and pee-wits rollicking, and their songs pure joy! See Brigid's servant, *gille Brigdhe*, with the scarlet rim in his eyes that matches his legs and beak? Isn't he the handsome one with his white breast and wing edges with the rest shiny black? 'Tis said he hid Christ in the seaweed and for that was given a cross on his back. And the sea pinks solid beyond the marram grass that bows to the white shore and blue-green sea—not all the money in the world could make that, and yet it's free!"

He watched her so strangely that she faltered. "Perhaps you've seen such grand things that this is naught—"

169

"Don't say that." He caught her hands in a grip that hurt. "You see the bright first day of God's creation, and you're a part of it. No laird's gold can buy that."

She knew she was lucky—still on the island with winter gone, and instead of a dazed remnant, a Clanna knit together in common hopes and endeavor. Mairi was proud and glad of that, but though she gloried in the thousand marvels of the sea and moor, she longed for him as if he were a severed part of her.

Without him, she could never be whole. While he'd been gone and she took comfort in that scrap of his handwriting and the signs of him throughout the broch, she'd been able to believe she could be content if he simply returned, that seeing and being with him would be enough.

Wicked as it was, she couldn't be close to him without yearning to be closer; couldn't see his scarred face without yearning to caress it, or watch him limp without wanting to massage his leg, send her strength and energy into his ravaged flesh and muscle. She couldn't see his mouth without burning to feel it on hers, or look into his eyes without that rush of warmth that radiated through every nerve and melted the secret woman part of her that hungered for him in primeval savagery that knew nothing of man's law or God's—though surely the desire that created life was God's law whatever the ministers croaked.

True. Had she desired young Liam Fraser or Magnus, the kirk's law would bless their bed. But she loved Iain and though she couldn't stop, there was no good way for that love to flower, no way that wouldn't shame her and her folk.

Turning the subject to Iain's mention of lairds, Mairi said, "The Frasers at the lodge say Mrs. MacKenzie's sold the island to a Sir James Matheson. Do you know him?"

"I do. A canny Scot who's made his fortune in the Hong Kong opium trade. I met him at a friend's home in Edinburgh on my way here. Again, Mairi MacLeod, you're lucky."

"How?"

"Unlike most Highland lairds, he can live well without squeezing tenants. Instead of wringing money from the island, he intends to pump money into it. Build roads and quays, plant marram grass to hold the sand, encourage industries—"

"And the folk?"

"He says he won't force any hard-working crofters to leave though he'll pay fare to Canada for all who want to go. I told him about your people, Mairi. He was impressed with your determination to stay. He won't lease back crofting lands already cleared but I think if some of your men called on him, he'd consider letting your cattle and sheep range on the moor and might allot you enough arable land for sustenance."

"That would be no more than just." Mairi tossed back her head. "For he's bought with his new money earth that's mulched with flesh and bone of my ancestors."

Iain's eyes flashed amusement which they had rarely done since his return. "I don't believe I'd tell him that."

"I'm no daftie," Mairi shrugged with a reluctant smile. "I won't tell him, either." Together they cornered a ewe and brought her to the turf.

Three evenings later, Eileen spied *An Clanna* trying to make shore in a rough sea. Everyone except Meggie ran down to the inlet. Andrew, at the rudder, tacked back and forth, avoiding submerged rocks, watching for a chance to run for shore between the frothing waves.

"Good lads!" Gran approved, shouting to be heard by the other women. "They've packed away the sail, mast and gear to keep *An Clanna* even. The stern rides low with ballast. That's needful because if the rudder comes out of the sea, the boat'll go wild and be thrown on the beach. Our Lord and Brigid preserve them! Here they come!"

The oarsmen bent double. *An Clanna* dashed for the shore as the women ran forward, tying up their skirts as they reached the water. They splashed to meet Donald, the bowman, who, as the prow touched sand, leaped out with the painter cable and hauled till the women could take a hand. Andrew stayed in the boat to direct the effort, but the oarsmen, Tam, Murdo, Barry and Gavin, leaped into the sucking waves and helped shove *An*

Clanna out of the tugging reach of the sea. Clear of the worst breakers, they unloaded the gear and a keg of fish brought for eating and drying. Together, men and women pushed and pulled the boat safely above the draggled high-water mark of seaweed, shells and pebbles.

Sheila and Katie wept joyfully as they embraced their young husbands. Morag gripped Andrew's arm, her usually dour face softened as she whispered prayers. Mairi hugged Tam, supporting him without seeming to for his knees were ready to buckle under him.

Gran stared out to sea. "When Michael comes—" Her eyes struck on Gavin who walked by himself. His yellow head drooped from exhaustion and perhaps, too, because his wife would never greet him again. Gran slipped her arm through his. "Welcome home, lad. Water's on the boil for tea. There's fresh-churned butter for bannocks, a great pot of barley broth, and we'll top it all with some of these good fish. Dry clothes are ready and you'll soon be snug by the fire. How went the fishing?"

It had gone well and a nice credit was building up at the curer's. When the sail and nets were spread to dry on the outside walls, the men sat blissfully around the hearth in dry garments, savoring the fuss made of them as much as they did the steaming tea fortified with a generous splash of the whiskey Iain had brought for Gran.

"Och," sighed Andrew, ruddy face beaming. "Wasn't it grand to stroll into the curer's and tell him we had our own boat and all he need tally against us was salt and barrels? We were the envy of the fishing, let me tell you! Only a few crews own their boats and they were sorry hulks alongside *An Clanna*." Andrew clapped Donald on the back. "Why, lad, if we need another trade, we could go to boat-building."

Barry grunted, "We have more trades than we can juggle now, father. Didn't we have to leave the fishing to dig peats and start our houses? And before the houses are up, it'll be back to fishing. Even with the women stacking peats and helping with

172

harvest and lifting up potatoes, it'll be a close thing to have roofs over our heads before winter."

"Wheesht, lad," chuckled Murdo, whose steel gray hair seemed a vital color, not a fading one. "Wouldn't it be dull, the same task day after day? Nothing but fish or nothing but farm, or worse yet, spend your waking hours in a mine or factory? We make our living from land and sea all out beneath God's sky."

"The laird's factor said that's why we're poor," Gavin reminded them. "Because we do too many things. The fishing calls us off when we should be farming, or if we plow properly and harvest, we miss the best fishing."

Andrew thrust out his jaw so that his red beard jutted defiantly. "It's a life I'd trade for no other."

Into the chorus of agreement, Mairi said, "According to Captain MacDonald, our new laird, Sir James Matheson, will pay passage to Canada for any who wish to go."

Donald looked at Katie. Murdo and Gavin exchanged glances. "We burdened you in the winter," Murdo said. "Now we can help. And we make a township. We want to stay if we're welcome." Donald and Katie nodded agreement.

"Of course you'll stay!" said Gran indignantly. "Aren't we the Clanna now, with a boat for fishing and spinning wheels and looms so we can buy what we can't grow on our bits of land? Of course you'll stay!"

"The captain thinks that if he's asked, the laird might let our beasts feed on the moor," Mairi said. "He might even lease us some crop land."

That jerked the men's heads up. In the heart of each was bound to be an Islander's passionate wish to have his own small croft. A landless man was like driftwood, borne here and there by tides he could not control. They mulled over this news with hope bright on their faces.

"It's too late to plant this year," Andrew said. "And the beasts we have fare well enough along the coast. But after the harvest and fall fishing, we'll visit this Sir James. And Mairi, I trust we'll see the captain?''

"To be sure you will. He made a hand at shearing and wants to help with the peats." Laughing at their amazement, she said to Tam, "From the two of you, we'll expect some fancy skirling on the pipes!''

15

Through mutual restraint, good humor, and thankfulness that they had a roof over them at all, the broch dwellers had lived in surprising harmony but everyone looked forward to having more privacy, especially the young married couples. The good timber in the broch along with salvaged driftwood should suffice for building three houses. Till next summer when separate homes for them could be built, Barry and Sheila would share with his parents and Murdo and Gavin would have a small room in Donald's and Katie's place which would later serve as a kiln.

Elbow room had its costs. Three dwellings meant that many hearths, each requiring cutting, drying, and carrying home about fifteen thousand peats. Fortunately, the weather was kind during the week of cutting. Rain would have made the work impossible. As it was, the peats the women spread to dry were soft and damp and would take several weeks to dry enough to lean three upright against each other and place a fourth on top in what were called "little feet." This would finish drying the blocks so they could be burned.

Andrew located a good peat bank only a mile from the broch. The men cleared the surface with spades and ranged themselves along the bank in teams, one to cut with the *taraisgear* or peat-iron, long-flanged in the special style of Lewis, while the other caught and lifted the oblong chunks to the bank where the women spread them. Iain lifted for Andrew to start with, Jamie for Barry, Tam for Murdo, Donald for Gavin, but the cutting was hard work and they took turns at it. Tam lacked the weight to drive the iron into the bank but after some practice and much laughing advice, Jamie and Iain could make their cuts though the results were not the almost perfectly even blocks of the experienced workers.

Donald and Gavin were at first uncomfortable with Iain. Murdo cast him periodic glances of ironic questioning, but by the end of the first long day, Iain had earned their acceptance. In truth they were all so smeared with muck there was no way of telling one from the other except by build and way of moving.

"Well, Tam," Iain said as they started for the burn to wash. "Will we play a spring on the pipes tonight?"

Tam looked as if he wanted to do nothing but sup and collapse in his cozy wall-bed, but he braced at Iain's grin and said jauntily, "Aye, captain, let's do that thing."

After supper, Iain played the lament for Brown-haired Allan Morrison, a sea captain drowned between Stornoway and Scalpay on his way to make a marriage contract.

"I remember that," cried Gran. "Ten years old I was, and wept buckets for poor Annie Campbell. She died of grief and when her family crossed with her coffin to bury her in Rodel, there was such a storm that the coffin had to go overboard. Her body washed ashore at the Shiant Isles, just where her brown-haired Allan's had."

"Poor lass! Poor lad!" Katie glanced at her Donald, perhaps thinking they had almost shared a sadder fate only five months ago. "Have you no merry tunes, captain?"

With Jamie singing, he gave them a spirited song about a drake that had a fine time courting ducks on other crofts till some lads caught him on Hogmanay and had him for dinner. "Now," said Iain, into the applause, "It's your turn, Mistress Mairi."

The mood was not for hero tales and if she played a love song, she feared it would give her away. Morag already watched her and Iain as if suspecting wicked dalliance though they were never alone and seldom out of earshot of half-a-dozen people. So Mairi clowned through the trials of a man who went to the fair and was asked to pay his debts by everyone from the tailor and tea merchant to the midwife, imitating each creditor so drolly that even Gavin joined in the laughter.

Morag, when she could stop chortling, had to pull a disapproving face. "To be sure, if he wasn't making his own creels and shoes and was buying all those other things, he deserved his troubles!"

" 'Tis but a song, lass," said Andrew. As his part of the ceilidh, he gave a triad. " 'The three most beautiful things in the world: a full-rigged ship, a woman with child, and a full moon.' "

"The woman might not agree," sniffed his wife, but she began mouth-music. Murdo joined in, and the day's weariness slipped from them like an old coat and they sat up till Gran yawned and rose from her chair.

"To bed now or not at all," she warned. "Captain, you and Jamie will be staying what's left of the night, surely."

"We brought our blankets," Iain said. "And heather's a fine mattress." That was true. Since warmer weather, Murdo and Gavin slept out, moving into the barn if it rained.

That night, Mairi didn't hold Iain's note to her breast. Why dream over a bit of paper with the living man close by? He was her love. He'd been wounded, in spirit as much as body. He'd come here for comfort but the comfort Mairi longed to give him would be her disgrace—more, the shame of her family and friends.

Shivering, she remembered the pale face of a young woman made to stand outside the kirk while folk walked by and scorned her for bearing a bastard. Had that lass been as beautiful as Andrew's full rigged ship, his opulent moon? But in spite of that pinched sorrowful countenance, and sin, and the pride of the family, Mairi would have sought her man that night had he slept alone on the heather, not with three men nearby.

Seeing him without being able to do more drove her so frantic that she was almost glad when, after the peat cutting, he was called to the mainland for the wedding of one of his lieutenants. The relief quickly vanished in missing him and worrying about what sort of capers gentry cut at their weddings. Among common folk, in spite of the kirk's preachings and punishments, many a wedding was forced by what had chanced at a wedding celebration a few months earlier. Iain wouldn't seduce a woman but if there was a bold wicked one fancied him and he had a drop too much— Mairi ground her teeth as she carried rubble for the walls and called down maledictions on any hussy who'd take advantage of a tipsy man.

The only good thing about that would be if it made Iain less conscious of his scarred face. Mairi wanted desperately to kiss the livid weal, smooth it with her fingers till he let the mark be part of him.

When she grew too upset, Mairi forced herself to concentrate on the house that was starting, the Nicolsons'. All the men had skill in working with stone for on this treeless island, any building or wall was cleverly laid drystone except for houses of the well-to-do which were mortared. Still, Gavin, with his mason's knowledge, was in command and worked at the doors, the one window, and the rounded corners.

Built into a slope that protected it from gales blowing in from the sea, the earth was leveled for the hearthroom that would have a built-in box-bed dividing it from the small bedroom where there was another capacious box-bed. Actually, with their thick curtains, these made small private chambers, a good place to dress. Byre and barn followed the gentle downward slant that allowed drainage, and the whole was enclosed with walls six feet thick. As the men laid inner and outer layers of stone, the women carried creels of rubble from the broch and sand from the bay to fill the inside.

There was driftwood enough to make the roof of this house, including a stout roof tree, exactly that for it was a tree, branches

178

splintered from the trunk, that the sea had dashed onto the rocks. Wherever it had grown, in some mainland forest or on a Norwegian fiord, it would rest on the couples to support the roof, sheltering a family and very likely their children and children's children. The inner layer of thatch was removed each year, but the cherished roof tree and other timbers moved when the family did. Unless they were burned out by a ruthless factor like Hugh Sinclair.

Sometimes Mairi again saw Fearchar stumble from the house, Cridhe in his arms, hair and clothes afire. Her heart wailed *"Fearchar!"* Then she'd seem to hear Fearchar say, "You swore at my bier to be happy as you could, lass, to keep a high heart, and play our songs so that our folk remember who they are. That's the best service you can do for me." So, as tribute to her grandfather, Mairi joked to cheer the others and played Cridhe at night though her fingers were stiff from rough labor.

In eight days the house was finished. The timbers of the roof and the thatch, weighted down with stones at the edges, rested on the inner wall so that there were no protruding edges for the wind to catch and tear away. Rain would come off the thatch into the core, which with the outer wall made a convenient platform for repairing thatch and also formed a warm, sheltered place to sit. Women who stood on these walls to scold their husbands or argue with neighbors were called *Piobairean nan Tobhtaichean,* Pipers of the Four Walls. Morag had been the shrillest piper of them all but oddly enough, set as she'd been against remaining on the island, the months of the broch had mellowed her, or perhaps that was due to having Seana and Alai to dandle.

The Nicolsons slept one night in their new home before the men went back to the fishing. In a month or so they'd return to build the walls of the other houses, and when the fishing finished in September, it wouldn't take long to bring down the roofs of the broch and its byre and barn so those timbers could roof the MacLeod and Gunn cottages.

It was mid-June and though the cows couldn't go to the shielings, their breath was sweet from grazing flowers and the milk was scented with orchids and harebells. Iain had been gone two weeks. Why was he lingering at Inverness? At his leavetaking, casually and generally made the night they'd finished cutting peats, he'd sounded as if he meant to attend the wedding and cross back to the Long Isle on the next boat.

Had he met some high-born lady? Fallen ill? The dreadful and ever-present possibility of a shipwreck plagued Mairi. She was glad of outdoor work like hoeing potatoes that made her tired enough to fall into bed at night, hold her talisman as she breathed a prayer for Iain, and sink into exhausted slumber.

There was plenty to do. Fleece had to be cleansed of tar and dirt and the dye stuffs collected. Mairi waded into the loch to wrest out water lily roots which twined themselves in deep; gathered crotal and another lichen, beard of the rock, from boulders near the sea; found sorrel to make a lovely red, and the lady's bedstraw that had dyed Iain's coverlet.

As the ewes lambed, several needed helping, and when one lamb died, Mairi took off his hide and fastened it to the twin of another lamb who was sniffed and gladly adopted by the bereaved mother.

Round rock walls were made for planticrues and filled with sand and decayed seaweed mixed to a rich bedding for kale seeds. Nets were taken off the roofs of byre and barn and the clean part of the thatch saved to make the first layer for the new roofs while the peaty thatch was worked into lazybeds and planticrues. The women carried stones to the site of the Gunn house, and cut heather and rushes for thatching. Eelgrass and cotton grass had to be cut and dried to make mattresses for the Gunns and MacKinnons.

Of a night, though it never got really dark this time of year, wool was carded and spun and woven, or knitted into socks and jerseys. Before autumn, the women hoped to add to the two rolled webs that were ready to take to Annie Gordon so supplies could be got, and glass panes for the skylights and windows of two of the houses. The panes in the broch, those Iain had brought, would lighten the MacLeod home.

There was no dearth of things to do, but as the days passed with no sign of Iain, Mairi thought of going to the lodge and trying to learn what kept him, but she had no good excuse and it wouldn't be right to spend a day on such a selfish errand.

One day Ewan Fraser stopped by with Liam. They were making a survey of game on this side of the island for the new laird. "He's building a castle overlooking the inner harbor at Stornoway," the red-haired gamekeeper said. "Money to burn Sir James has, from the opium trade. At least he seems ready to spend it improving Lewis."

Katie's eyes grew big with fright. "God forbid that his 'improvements' are those of the other lairds—clearing people and bringing sheep!"

"No fear of that, Mistress Gunn," soothed Ewan. "Mind you, his factors don't ooze the milk of human kindness. The cleared land will stay so."

Here was a chance to mention Iain. "Will Sir James keep on leasing the lodge to the captain?" Mairi asked, trying to ignore Liam's wistful gaze. He was a nice boy—but just that, a boy. It was amusing and a bit alarming to see that Eileen, faithful to her dream of Magnus, rocked the babies in their cradle instead of hovering near the handsome golden-haired lad. "So far as I know, lass, the captain will keep his lease," Ewen gave Mairi a searching glance. It must be the talk of the lodge folk, how Iain had worked at the peats. "But why is beyond me. Two weeks he's back from that wedding and hasn't gone out of the house in daylight though he saddles his horse and roams dusk to dawn like some lost soul. He doesn't hunt. He's not taken a salmon from the burn. He seems stronger in his body than when he first came from the wars but there's something amiss with the captain in himself."

Two weeks returned and Iain hadn't come near her! What had happened at the wedding? Perhaps he'd decided he played the fool to company with common folk. Who could know? Except that he hadn't come. He hadn't wished to see her.

Stricken, Mairi somehow managed to offer the men a refreshing drink of oatmeal stirred into cool water, and inquire after Mrs. Fraser and the rest of the lodge people, but she was glad when the Frasers went their way and she could escape down to the sea to gather crotal and weep where no one could see.

Dolphins leaped against a white-feathered sky. A basking shark, a plankton eater, quite harmless for all his size, cruised among submerged rocks, but this day she could not be beguiled. Even in her bewildered distress, she was sure Iain was at least in part doing what he judged best for her. He knew no honest love could flower between them. Always, always, it must be squeezed back into the bud; how long could that go on? But she felt there was more than that behind his shunning her and the light of the sun. Something had hurt him on that trip to the mainland, something that made him hide away.

Her heart ached for that, but what could she do? It was almost Midsummer when she, Gran and Eileen would go to The Stones to greet the rising sun as their people had done since those stones were raised. If Mairi fasted and prayed, perhaps the ancient powers would guide her. The sea wind stung her face and the salt of her tears mixed with the salt of the spray.

The midnight sky glowed with enchanted twilight, a luminous, living blue as the three made their way across the moor. At first Gran disdained Mairi's arm, but after tripping into a rabbit burrow and plunging to her knees in a bog, Gran shrugged and said, "What's a granddaughter for if not to hang onto?" and gripped Mairi's arm as they bent before a blast that threatened to send them flat in the heather or peaty scum.

"I don't see why we have to do this," Eileen whimpered, sheltering as much as she could in Mairi's wake. "Not when Sheila and Katie and Morag don't."

"Their folk aren't of the Stones," muttered Gran. "But from the raising of those pillars, women of ours have been there for Midsummer."

"Morag says it's heathen."

Gran made a rude noise. "When you're older, you can choose

whether to come or not—choose with your conscience, not your laziness. Trot along now or we'll be late."

"And who'd care?" retorted Eileen under her breath. Mairi gave her sister's arm an admonishing squeeze. She had never questioned going to the Stones and intended to do so all her life, but she might be the last of their family to keep that tryst. The realization made her sad. Over the years, how many customs, how many songs, how many stories had been lost that held the spirit of their people? It was always tantalizing to Mairi to know only part of a song, only a snatch of a tune.

You couldn't look back so much that you didn't look ahead but surely true things were eternal, Past, Now, and Yet To Be. That was the feeling Mairi had at the Stones and when she played melodies older than Cridhe. *Things* decayed, fell away like the broch, but songs and legends glowed with new life each time they were sung or told.

This great wealth cost nothing but once lost, no riches could bring it back. Mairi faithfully visited the Stones but it was an act without knowledge, piety without a creed. All that remained of what must have been a potent ritual was a tradition that when the cuckoo welcomed the sun, The Shining One walked down the aisle and blessed the fullness of the year, high summer of the folk. Mairi had heard the cuckoo most Midsummer morns but she had never seen a vision, shining or dark, though sometimes heavy mist shrouded the stones so that more than ever they looked like cowled giants in long robes, rapt in postures of mourning or meditation.

Gran was so tired that though they were within a mile of the Stones, they stopped to rest in the cover of a ruined byre. Gran and Eileen shared a bannock but Mairi abstained. Her senses must be clean and clear if there was a sign for her at the Stones, "Best be getting on." Gran winced with the effort of rising. "Och, my dry old bones! On the way back, lassies, I must lie down a while and sleep."

"I'm sleepy now," Eileen yawned.

Mairi gave a lock of silvery hair an affectionate tweak. "Pretend Magnus is there," she teased. "Or would you rather see Liam?"

"Liam's only a boy," Eileen retorted loftily. "Magnus said he'd wait for me if you don't take him—and you won't, will you, Mairi?"

"Will I, won't I?" Mairi laughed before she sobered. "I won't, darling, but you mustn't set your heart too much on Magnus. He's old enough to marry now. It'll be years before you are."

In the dim light, Eileen's face looked older. She said positively, "He'll wait for me. If you don't have him."

"Poor tyke!" Gran wagged her head and gave a wry chuckle. "Not a word to say for himself and you two settling it all!"

If I hadn't met Iain, Mairi thought with a sore heart, I might have loved Magnus. We could be wedded by now with a bairn on the way. Iain she could never wed, nor, it seemed, could she even see him. Surely, surely, he wouldn't go back to his regiment without a farewell. But much good farewells were! Sorrow without joy, loss without having.

She almost wished he hadn't come to her at all that summer if now he meant to ignore her. Still, those days he'd worked with her, those nights by the hearth, were the best times of her whole life for unlike last year when he'd helped roof the broch, she was no longer distraught by Fearchar's death and the burning of Aosda.

No, she was glad of every hour, every word, every glance, every song. Each time she laid a peat on the fire, she'd remember him . . . Her head went up. Yes, and bless him, too! Nothing could change what he had been to her. She would pray for his happiness and place his well-being above her selfish longing.

Approaching dawn crimsoned the east with rose-red flame. The sky blanched gray, but vapors thinned, parted, and coalesced on the promontory of the Stones like diaphanous cloud beings. Only now and then did one of the pillars rear among constantly wreathing veils. This mystical sight was entirely different from the sun-warmed calm of Stones on the day Mairi and Iain had stopped to rest on their way from Aosda with the hearthstone. Suddenly cold, wrapping her plaid more closely around her, Mairi followed Gran into the mists.

16

The Stones formed a Celtic cross, a long aisle leading to a circle from which radiated three single rows. Peat cuttings had cleared deposits five feet deep from between the aisle stones. There, with the shrouding mist obscuring anything more than an arms-length away, the three of them, old woman, maiden and girl, awaited the dawn.

It came with a burst of rose-gold rays slanting through the mist. Like a glimpse of a fairy world, Mairi saw the hazy purple hills of Harris and Uig, the waters of Loch Roag, drenched with light jubilant as a shout of angels before sinuous vapors, still glowing like living forms, hid that vista with their own magic, and the cuckoo called.

Had she seen a Shining One pace through the golden clouds, Mairi could not have been more entranced or reverent. Suffused with splendor, part of the radiance, she wished for Cridhe in order to add her song to the joy of larks and lapwings. It was one of those rare moments when matter lost its density, dissolved into particles of dancing light that might solidify into weird and beautiful shapes, engendering a new creation.

"We can go now." Gran's voice jarred Mairi. She wasn't ready to leave.

"Why don't you and Eileen have your rest at the byre?" she suggested. "I'll come in a bit."

Gran sighed. "These long tramps draw the bones right out of my legs. Give me your arm, Eileen child, and don't streak along like a plover!"

The mist hid them before the whisper of their steps faded. Drawn toward the center and the great stone that reared twice Mairi's height from the peat, she felt as if the filmy opalescence was alive but not in a frightening way. Advancing between the stones, she entered the circle and approached the central megalith, a squared pillar with a graceful bend as if the island's eternal wind had gradually flared it.

How had the island looked when the enormous stone was set in place either by forgotten spells or ingenious, equally mysterious methods? No peat then, no Black Moor. And according to ancient songs, there were birch trees, hazel and rowan, vast forests of them. So different it was now, yet blood of Mairi's blood, flesh of her flesh, had built this place of worship.

In spite of their brief lives, her people were like the rock underlying peat and thin soil. Perhaps that was all the message the Stones need hold for anyone.

She started forward, and as she did, Iain loomed out of the mist. "Is it you, Mairi?"

Her heart stopped. "Yes."

Was he real or an apparition? No, the dark stubble on his face did not grow on the scar. His gaze probed her as no phantasm's could, scanned her as if to discover the tiniest wisp of reaction. What should she say? What could she do?

"You haven't been to us," she said into the weighted silence. "I—I was afraid some ill had befallen you."

"Is it ill to know the truth? That I am disgusting, even to a woman eager to wed my uncle's money?" The wound twisted his mouth. Through his slurring words, she smelled whiskey on his breath.

"Iain—"

He said judiciously, head tilted to one side, "You look substantial enough, Mairi, but if you're really standing there why don't you shrink as my uncle's choice did?"

"You've been drinking, Iain."

"I wouldn't have married the lady, in spite of my uncle's urging. He's hot for another heir in case I'm killed. But it was educational to watch her try to overcome her disgust. So I visited a whore. She kept her eyes closed, and not from ecstasy."

Mairi did then what she'd wanted to do ever since he returned that spring, took his face in her two hands and reached on tiptoe to sweep the scar with her lips, press her mouth against it as if the kiss could heal. His breath sucked in. His arms closed around her, crushing her to the hard length of his body. Their lips sought each other's.

Trembling, they sank to the earth but as his hands found her breasts, as she cried out in gladness, he tore his mouth away, shoved her from him as he started to rise. "My God, Mairi! Get up, girl. Get away from here!"

"I love you, Iain."

"And I love you." He buried his face in his hands. "Run away, child, before I do what your Clanna would rightly kill me for."

"Iain, I am no child." Rising on one arm, she drew him down to her. "Oh, Iain, love me, make me your woman!"

His kiss was flame and worship. His hands sent honey sweetness through her, a melting, rushing flood that swept her into a boundless sea. Then there was pain but he moved in her so gently that her sundered tissues cleaved to him, she herself, with a cry of triumph, thrust till he filled her in a wild throbbing that left them drained, light and floating.

"Mairi," he sighed at last against her hair. "Oh, my darling! I'd rather lose my battered soul than hurt you but see what I've done—"

She smiled at him, rich with the feel of him within her, his essence spilling all rose and gold and lovely as the mists. She caressed his seamed cheek, smoothed his black hair with her hands.

"See what I've done," she challenged tenderly. "My man, my laddie, you had no chance at all."

He stared at her in wonder, then traced the contours of her face and throat, said with a rueful, husky laugh, "If I didn't know better, Mairi MacLeod, I'd swear you seduced me."

"If I did, I'm not sorry." At his troubled look, she added fiercely, "Sorry I'll never be!"

He kissed her and it seemed she had always known the rough sweetness of his mouth, the clean male scent of him with its tinge of sea salt, the embrace that while it filled her with fresh hunger gave her an inexpressibly safe and protected feeling. Perfect peace. That's what it was with him after the loving. But that peace changed.

Could it happen again? In spite of the aching where he'd entered her, she ran her hands beneath his shirt and stroked the back of his neck, savored the joy of touching him, learning the muscles of his shoulders, following the bones.

With a shuddering sigh, he imprisoned her wrists and sat up, drawing her with him though he kept the length of his arms between them. "Sweet, sweet Mairi, this must not happen again."

"If you love me—"

"That's why. I won't make you my mistress."

She didn't understand the last word and she'd always known he couldn't marry her. But never to be with each other again? It seemed a death sentence till she read the need in his eyes. "Wheesht, lad," she said with fond confidence. "You won't be able to stay away. Not now."

He grinned at that, shaking his head. "Little witch! So fast you've learned! You tempt me to carry you off to Inverness or Edinburgh, keep you for myself for always."

"I wouldn't go. Not even for you, Iain."

"No. It wouldn't be life for you with loving me your only purpose and me off most of the time with my regiment. But you must see that we can't be lovers. It would disgrace you, keep you from wedding a good man like young Liam Fraser or that Magnus I've heard so much about."

"I won't wed anyone."

"Don't say that, Mairi. You were made to love a man—love him and bear his children." He fastened her blouse and got to his feet, bringing her with him though he held her at armslength.

"I love you. Because I do, I won't come back to your island."

"Never?"

He made a defeated gesture. "I wish I could. Working with your people, sharing your hearth, hearing your music, all these are happiness of a kind I've never had. I thought I was strong enough to delight in your company and not seek more." His hands moved to either side of her face, spanning from temples to chin. "I won't see you again, my darling, for your own sake. Because I've known you, I'll be a better man. The memory of you, kind and brave and beautiful, wise beyond your years, heartened me when I might have died. It's because I love you past all measure that I must take myself out of your life."

How could he condemn her with such beautiful, loving words? "I think I will die if I never see you!"

He gave a twisted smile. "No, Mairi. Beneath your sweetness, you're enduring as the stones of your island. You'll live to be an old, old woman, head of your Clanna and soul of your people."

"I can live without you. But I will never love."

"Love?" he mocked tenderly. "Oh, Mairi mine! You must love, you can't help yourself. Not only me and my ruined face; not only your family and friends. You have loved strangers, fed and sheltered and comforted them. You will stop breathing before you fail to love."

"You know well 'tis men I speak of."

"My sweetheart, you're so young! Young enough to say never."

He would think what he wished to and she would do what she did. Fighting tears, she said, "You'll surely come to the broch and take your leave?"

"Yes, but this is our good-bye, Mairi." He paused. "It's most unlikely that you'll be got with child this one time, but should that chance, write my solicitor. I'll instruct him to inform me at once and meanwhile aid you however he can."

"What good for you to know?" she flashed. "I don't want your money, Captain MacDonald! Should I have a bairn to you, I'll cradle it as warm when it leaves my body as when it lay under my heart."

His mouth was grim. "If you conceive my child, I'll marry you."

She gasped. Amazed joy filled her to be followed with hurt and anger. "You won't! I could never live among your kind, make you scorned and outcast. What would your uncle say?"

"Mairi! If I thought you could be happy in my world, I'd marry you and the devil with my uncle and everyone! But that would never be a life for you—away from your family and island with only me and me gone most of the time with my regiment." His jaw set. "But if you have a child, I won't have it doomed to bastardy on this kirk-ridden island."

He'd marry her out of duty—and what kind of life could be there for them? And the child? They'd hate each other soon. Too upset to speak, she huddled against her knees, wishing him gone, gone so she could weep.

"Mairi," he said in a voice that tore her heart. "Must I tell Andrew what I've done? Ask him to get word to me if it's necessary?"

No use wrangling. If she didn't soothe him, he might indeed confess to Andrew and then if a bairn did come of this, she'd have them all to fight. Much as she adored Iain, the thought of living away from her people, away from the island, surrounded by gentry who'd shun Iain because of her, made her cold to the heart.

She framed her words carefully in order not to lie. "If there's anything you should know, I'll write to your solicitor. No need to fret about me. I must go now. Gran will be rested."

He raised her hands to his lips. "Don't!" she cried. "If one last kiss is all I'll have from you, kiss me on my mouth."

191

He swept her against him, kissed her till the bones went soft in her body and he was shuddering. "Be well, be happy. Fare well, my only love."

"You cannot go so far away that my love won't follow. Thank you, Iain, for all that you have done." *And for today most of all though we must end like this.*

Moving away from him was like tearing away from part of her body, severing her heart. As she plunged through the stones and down the ridge, the rosy gold had left the mist. It was gray now, and cold.

At the end of the week, the men returned and were working on the MacLeod cottage when Iain rode up with Jamie. The two of them helped pass stones to the men laying up the walls. Mairi thought with a stab of pain and gratefulness that now Iain had set his hands to the stones of her dwelling, that much of him would always be with her. But could it be true? That she'd never see him again? She couldn't meet his gaze in front of the others but that evening she stored up images of him—the proud carriage of his head, the sudden breaking of a smile, his bantering with Tam and Eileen and joking gallantries with Gran.

He had his pipes and the farewell ceilidh lasted into the small hours. Mairi couldn't have endured it had she not been able to express some of her feelings in the songs she played on Cridhe. *"Oh, black-haired lad, it's your word that has wounded me. Neither fiddle nor harp nor pipes can lift my spirits . . ."*

Must they part forever? She couldn't believe that, not in her depths. A forlorn hope whispered that someday, after they were old and their passions mellowed, they might see each other now and again, share memories and music in this house he'd put his hand to, sit by the ancient hearthstone. She let herself cling to this distant hope; it was simply too painful otherwise.

"We must be riding," he said at last. "Our ship sails tomorrow."

Iain took leave of each of them in turn, shaking hands, kissing Eileen and Gran, touching the cheeks of the sleeping babies.

Mairi was so cold inside, so numb, that the warmth of his hand couldn't spread to her frozen core. She was the only one who knew he wasn't coming back.

Standing by the hearth, Gran caressed his face and rested her hand on his forehead. "May the Lord keep you safely and straighten your road. May you be seven times better a year from now than you are this hour. And when you come again, there will be as many welcomes for you as there are rushes in the thatch."

Except for Meggie, long abed, they all went out to call good-byes after the travelers. Under cover of the dim light, Iain brushed Mairi's lips with his. "Live happy, darling," he whispered. "I'll always love you."

Then he was up on Chieftain. The sound of hooves echoed in her heart as if the iron shoes trampled there.

Mairi couldn't show her grieving and was rescued by the round of work that tired her into sleeping sound most nights. She learned, too, that the best help for loss was to build something that would last. Raising the walls of her house gave her pride and a feeling of power that was the exact opposite of the helpless shame she'd felt when Aosda burned or when she knew she could never fit into Iain's world. When the men went back to the fishing, the women collected stones and paved the floors before claying the barn floors. With two more families, new lambs and calves, the little township would need more pasture and crop land though for this year they'd trade cloth to Annie Gordon for extra supplies.

When the men took in their last catch and settled with the curer, Andrew would lead a delegation to the new laird and ask that the folk of Clanna be leased pasture and arable soil. That wouldn't noticeably intrude on Sir James's game parks and sheepwalks. From all Iain had said, the island's new owner would be impressed that they'd progressed in less than a year from broken remnants to a community owning its own boat and producing fine woolens. Few long-established townships could claim as much. Of course, if it hadn't been for been for Iain—

Always, her thoughts came back to him. Would it always be that way? Would it always, always hurt? She wasn't sorry, though, that they had been together that dawning at the Stones. It was a magic to hold deep and secret as long as she lived. Forcibly, she turned her musings to Calum.

He should be home soon—her big brother, who'd carried her on his back, comforted her when she fell down or met with childish tragedy. Though he'd sadly miss Aosda and Fearchar, he'd *have* to see life on the island held fresh promise. Mairi wouldn't let her hopes get too high for his staying, but she prayed that he would and even day-dreamed in snatches about how lovely it would be if he could convince Catriona that she should come back. Katie and Sheila were good company but Mairi greatly missed her willful and spirited friend to whom she could confide anything, to whom she was just Mairi.

Though Andrew and Gran, as eldest man and woman, often spoke as leaders, it was Mairi to whom everyone turned. She was, without wishing it, the real center of Clanna, much as Fearchar had been. This was disturbing. She felt too young and inexperienced for such responsibility. And then there was something else.

As July slipped into August and she found the first pure white bloom of grass of Parnassus with its dainty golden anthers, as some of the yellow iris began to go to fruit, she could no longer hope that her monthly flow was only a few days late.

To know that she was nurturing the start of their bairn—oh, let it be a laddie, one who looked like Iain!—thrilled her with wonder at the same time that she shrank from the others knowing and dreaded the effect, especially on Eileen and Tam.

A fine example she was for them! And when the folk at the lodge knew—and Annie Gordon, and even people she didn't know at all but who'd savor the gossip about that lass at the broch who'd found a baby but not a husband—why then, what shame upon her family! The thought made her flinch from

Calum's return. As for Magnus, she could only hope he'd forgotten her.

Facing now what Iain had tried to provide for, she thought in her desperation of writing his solicitor, of going to the mainland and leaving the child in fosterage. The temptation was scarcely more than a flash. She could feel in her arms a baby sweet and warm as Seana or Alai, with Iain's eyes and hair. She couldn't give up his bairn.

What, then, should she do? She'd have to tell the Clanna. If they could accept and love her child, it wouldn't harm the bairn so greatly to be without a father, for there'd be no one in those early years to cry names and point fingers. Growing up with Seana and Alai for playmates, her child would have a family and whether lad or lass, would have a share in what the Clanna owned. But if the others recoiled? If Morag preached, if Katie and Sheila changed, if Andrew and Barry looked at her with reproach and the other men with scorn or speculation? Mairi writhed at the thought but faced it. If that happened, and it might, though she was sure that after the first shocked distress her kin at least would rally to her and make the best of it, she must leave. Annie Gordon might give her work or there might be a farm where she could earn her keep and the baby's.

This decision not to force herself on her people eased her worst misery though she was sick with apprehension. Gran wouldn't fault her too much, she was sure, and Tam would want to help her but he was close to making a man for the household he, Gran, and Eileen could form if Mairi went away. It would be wrong to let them go with her and lose the start they'd made.

One, possibly two more flows would pass before the men returned from fishing. That would make it certain. She'd tell them then. Pride wouldn't let her wait till someone noticed in the winter when they'd be forced to let her stay. She would rather perish, she with the bairn, than be grudged a place at the hearth.

Gran wanted to make heather ale that fall and the rose-purple blooms were at their best. The younger women were gathering blossoms one afternoon when a horseman appeared, mounted on a fine black.

Now what would a gentleman be doing out here? He rode up to them, a dark keen-eyed man, still vigorous looking though he was past youth. Unsmiling, though his tone was perfectly civil, he wished them a good day in an accent similar to Iain's and said, "I am looking for Mistress Mairi Mac-Leod."

Surely Iain wouldn't have sent his solicitor? "You've found me," said Mairi. "Won't you get down, sir, and have a cool drink or bite to eat?"

"I might at that," he said, eyeing the broch. "So you really live in the ruin?"

"It was grand good shelter through the winter, sir, but now as you see, we're building houses."

"I see. You have leases?"

Lord save them, was he Sir James Matheson's factor? Someone to make them trouble? Stomach knotting, Mairi said, "If you know my name, sir, you must know we were evicted a year ago from Aosda. This is wasteland, almost on the rocks of the sea."

He scanned the lush beds of potatoes, the oats and barley ripening, the cows with calves grazing in the distance, and sheep foraging along the bay. With a grim chuckle, he said, "You don't have much grain, but what there is promises well. And those look a rare crop of 'taties."

"We made the beds, sir. We carried sand and seaweed, creels of sand and seaweed, for every inch of soil."

"Yes, it's clear there's been some work here."

"May I ask, sir, who you might be?"

He grinned at her then and his dark eyes traveled over her with bold admiration. "I would be James Matheson. Do I still get my bannock and sip of milk?"

Mairi's heart skipped. When she recovered a bit, Mairi said,

"You're welcome indeed." If he wanted to put them out, at least he'd learn their manners were better than his. The byre stones had been moved away so she led him by that way into the broch.

17

Though his dark eyes probed every corner, Sir James Matheson, lately merchant-prince of Hong Kong and now owner of all Lewis, was very pretty-mannered to Gran and Meggie, praised his bannock and drank his milk as if it were French claret.

"That's a beautiful web you're weaving, Mistress Ross," he said to Meggie. "Those tiny checks and overchecks require great skill."

Meggie gave him a fleeting, vague smile and went on singing in her endless monotone but when Alai let out his usual tentative whimper on awakening, she left her loom and went at once to the cradle. Lifting the child to her shriveled breast, pressing her withered cheek to his bright one, she crooned, *"Mo cubhrachan,* my little fragrant one. Are you waking now from your play with the angels?"

Katie, a wee bit possessive of her baby, took him and said, "To be sure, he needs changing," and whisked him into the sleeping room.

Meggie, unruffled, returned to her web. She responded to the need of the babies but never seemed to mind if someone else assumed their care. Sir James drained his second cup of milk and straightened his elegant cravat.

"It's clear that Captain MacDonald exaggerated neither your efforts nor your results. I applaud enterprise and wish to encourage it. I'll instruct my factor to devise leases that will give your township cropland and the right to pasture your cattle and sheep on the neighboring moor. Discuss it with your men when they return. They can call on my factor and go through the formalities."

"The men will be pleased, sir," said Gran. "After the fishing, they meant to ask if we could rent some land."

"I'm sure it will be to our mutual advantage." Rising briskly, not as tall as Iain but broader, he smiled quite charmingly. "Thank you for your hospitality. I hope I'll be welcome to stop if I ride this way again."

"Indeed you will, sir," beamed Gran. "I believe you mean to behave as the chieftains of our clan once did."

He shrugged that away. "Those times are gone, Mrs. MacLeod, but I do aim at building up this island instead of draining it. We'll help each other, eh?"

"With all our hearts, be sure of that. Och, I can hardly wait to tell my dear man what luck we're in!"

Sir James looked startled, then evidently remembered something. Iain had probably told him about Gran's belief that her Michael was on a voyage. "Could I have a word with you?" the laird said to Mairi.

Might he have seen Iain, have some news of him? "Of course, sir." Heart thudding, she went out with him to where his horse was tethered.

He studied her a moment. "You're with child, aren't you, lass?"

How could he guess? A blush scalded her. She glanced involuntarily at her waist, confirming what she knew, that she was slender as ever, thinner even, for she lacked appetite.

"It's not yet apparent." Sympathy warmed his voice. "But there's that soft glow to your skin and your hands hover in front of you as if protecting something precious. Does the father know?"

Mairi's throat was dry. "He must not."

The laird's eyes narrowed. "Was it rape?"

"No! I—I love him, sir, and he loves me. But I'll never see him again."

"Is he dead?"

"I pray not."

"Then you shouldn't speak of 'never.' Is he in the army? Married, perhaps?"

"You've struck it, sir. My lad's in the army."

"I could write his commanding officer. Insist that you're sent a bit from his pay."

"I'll manage fine. My lad felt bad enough over it all." It was a peculiar but immense relief to speak of what she had wrestled with alone, even though the laird assumed her lover was of her station. "If he knew there was a bairn—" She shook her head. "Please believe me, sir. There's reasons we can't marry. It's best he never knows."

"He should help pay for the child's rearing."

"I can take care of my bairn," she said softly, then in sudden alarm gripped the laird's arm. "This—this won't make a difference with the lease?"

"Why should it? I'm a landlord, not a minister." He frowned. "Do your people know?"

It seemed indecent that a stranger knew before her family. "I—I'm going to tell them when the men come home."

"They'll stand by you?"

"They would, but if they can't do it freely—welcome my bairn, I'll take myself off and find work to keep me and the babe."

"What kind of work?"

"On a farm. Or perhaps I can weave for Annie Gordon in Stornoway."

His straight eyebrows lifted. "Captain MacDonald praised your skill with the harp."

It took her a moment to catch his meaning and then she laughed ruefully. "Bless us, you mean I might make a living at the harp? It's long and long since anyone's done that. Didn't

Rory Dall, last harper to the MacLeods of Dunvegan, die here on Lewis over a hundred years ago after his chief came to prefer pipers and fiddlers?"

"I prefer the harp." Matheson spoke lightly, but his eyes made her uncomfortable. "It would please me well to have a harpist at Lews Castle. I would see that your child had a good education, or if a lass, there'd be suitable employment."

She looked at him and he looked back. "Or if you'd rather be in your own house," he said, "I will give you one on the grounds or in the town."

That settled it, even for one of her inexperience, even though she could scarce credit that this man of the great world, wealthy beyond imagining, lord of the island, would fancy her. Nor did she think he was duping her, making promises he wouldn't keep. But she could no more be his than Liam's or Magnus's.

Grateful that the laird hadn't put his real offer into words, that she could pretend it hadn't been made, Mairi said courteously, "You're very kind, sir. But I want my bairn to grow up among our people. Then, you see, he'll have a family and not feel the lack of his father so much."

"I see." Sir James's tone was dry but amused. "I see you love the rascal father more than he deserves. But good luck to you, Mistress Mairi." His smile flashed as he mounted. "Should you, after all, need to find a living, I'm serious about employing a harper." He emphasized the word, raised a hand in salute, and sent the black off at a smart canter.

Bemused, Mairi went inside where the others were exulting over the assurance of the laird's good will and sufficient land for pasture and crops.

"A fine gentleman," Morag approved. "What did he ask you, Mairi?"

"He wondered if I knew of any harpers. It seems he wants one at the castle."

Gran chortled. "Did he want a bard and fool, too?" She winked at the others. "Why didn't you take the post, love?

Belike you could work Tam in as piper and the next thing we'd all be waulking webs at the great table and have the gentry singing with us!"

They all laughed gleefully at the nonsense. "And you could be his jester, Gran," teased Mairi with a hug.

The men returned in mid-September, jubilant that the township now had leases on their home sites and for each household, six acres of arable land and the right to pasture up to four cows with followers—calves of up to three years of age. There wasn't that much good land near the broch so the township had leave to build stone walls or dykes to enclose tracts of tillable land within several miles of the broch.

Almost as exciting was a letter from Catriona which included greetings from Kirsty and Adam. They had taken up land on the Medina River in the Republic of Texas, not far from a settlement of people from Alsace-Lorraine. "Can you believe that for fifty cents we bought land scrip entitling us to 640 acres, what Americans call a section?" wrote Catriona. "This part of Texas is not a prairie at all! It has good grass and huge oak and black walnut trees. The hills abound with deer and turkey. A little to the south roam countless wild cattle that belong to anyone who can catch them, and wild horses, too. Winter days are often warmer than summer on Lewis and the sun shines so much and so hotly that I'm glad when what they call a 'norther' blows in and it rains and turns cooler. We have a nice log cabin with two fireplaces where we burn *wood* in beautiful roaring fires though I confess I miss the peats. Just before we came, Comanches killed a whole family who lived a few miles up the river. The Republic won its independence from Mexico only seven years ago and lacks money to protect people living beyond the settlements." Catriona gave special messages to each of them, hungrily asked for news, and concluded: "Every night you are remembered in our prayers. Still, we are glad to be in a country so big and beautiful with almost everything free for the taking and hard work. Calum had better come swiftly! Men outnumber women a dozen to one and I've had five proposals of marriage. Tell him to come, Mairi, so we can start our own farm—and our family! Your Viking, Catriona."

In order to take it all in, Mairi read the letter aloud three times. A laird's estate, 640 acres! And trees, plenty for building and even burning. That shocked them, accustomed as they were to hoarding every stick of driftwood.

"Comanches!" Tam's eyes glowed. "When I'm older I might go over for a year or two. Just to see what it's like and catch some of those wild horses and cows to sell."

"We're mightily glad to get five acres a household." Andrew rubbed his burly neck before he brightened. "Still, we're at home, with land enough to live from along with what we win from the sea. Who needs more?"

"It's sure to harm the eyes, all that Texas sunlight," said Gran.

"But the trees must be grand," marveled Sheila.

"With so many of them, where would you get a proper look at the sky?" countered Gran.

"I couldn't live out of sight of the sea," admitted Andrew. "But Adam was more farmer than fisherman."

Mairi had nervously pondered how to tell about her baby. Confide in Gran? Or Sheila and Katie and ask them to tell their husbands who could inform the other men? That would have been easier, but Mairi burned at the thought of her friends perhaps having to beg for her. If she couldn't be accepted without pleading, she'd rather go away. She couldn't bring herself to confess that night, though. Let them all enjoy the reunion, Catriona's amazing news, and the pride of securing the land and grazing.

The fishing had gone well, too. After settling with the curer and buying supplies, each family had silver to tuck away. Grain stood tall and ripe, ready for harvest. If only Mairi didn't have to give her folk such news! More than what they'd think of her, she hated what they'd think of Iain. Well, she wouldn't let them blame him. Nor would she lie and say that she was sorry.

203

The heads of grain were full and heavy. It would be a fine yield though not enough for their needs. Fortunately, there should be plenty of potatoes, the men would bring in fish for drying and salting, and there'd be woolens to trade for grain.

Next year the township would have enough land to grow their whole supply of oats and barley. There'd be kale, and Mairi wanted to try planting turnips. Four young pullets would be laying eggs before spring, and the fresh cows, besides suckling their calves, would give milk, butter, whey and crowdie.

The men's and women's voices mingled as they sang to the rhythm of the reapers' scythes. Those bundling and stooking knelt and rose almost in unison. Harvest was the reward for carrying countless loads of seaweed and sand up from the shore, for the men's patient tilling with the cas-chrom, for cultivating and weeding. In spite of the itching discomfort of chaff that burrowed into her skin, and wrists and forearms scratched from binding, Mairi delighted in the work that meant winter food for the Clanna and the beasts.

On St. Michael's Day, the harvest was in. As everyone gathered about the hearth to eat special bannocks of new grain, Mairi resolved to tell her secret. With each breath she drew, she intended to speak, but her courage would fail or someone else would make a remark.

Iain! Iain! She closed her eyes a moment, drew in a long breath. It would never get any easier. Say it and be done!

"I've something to tell you." She didn't recognize her own voice, it was so cracked and thin. The familiar faces turned to her suddenly seemed those of strangers. "I am with child."

"Lassie!" cried Gran, starting up.

Shock in all those eyes. Disbelief. "I've been offered work by the laird so you needn't feel you're casting me out," Mairi said painfully, compelling herself to look at each person in turn. "If—if you cannot love the babe—be its family, I will go away."

Tam's face was white but he came to stand by her. "I'll take care of you, Mairi." Eileen ran over to throw her arms around her and cry, "Don't go, Mairi! If you do, take me!"

"There'll be no going," rumbled Andrew. "You're the living heart of us, Mairi lass."

"You saved us," said Katie simply. "How could we not love your bairn?"

"Aye," nodded Murdo.

Sheila slipped an arm around Mairi while Barry, crimsoning, struggled with words. "Does the captain know?" he finally blurted.

At least they knew and respected Iain, owed him a tremendous debt. "I don't want him to." She wished she could tell them that he'd offered to marry her should this befall, but it would sound like daft boasting, something she'd dreamed herself into believing. "I'm afraid that if he knew, he'd want to take the child away, have it fostered on the mainland."

"Mainland indeed!" Morag's eyes flashed. "We'll do far better here for the bairn! Though 'twill be hard getting the babe christened."

"We'll worry about that later," said Andrew. By then Mairi was weeping, embraced by her brother and sister and Sheila. Rising from Fearchar's chair, Andrew enfolded them all in his great arms. "Don't fash yourself, lass. Your baby will have all us older folk for parents and grandparents and Seana and Alai for brother and sister."

"I'd be proud to stand as father." They turned to stare at Gavin who colored but went doggedly on, "If you'll wed me, Mairi, I'll be the best man to you that I can. I'd care for the child as if it were mine."

Touched but appalled—how could she bear to have any husband but the man she loved?—Mairi tried to refuse gracefully. "I thank you, Gavin. But you must find a woman who'll love you and my heart is already taken."

"You'd do well to marry Gavin," began Morag, but Andrew

shushed her. "Mairi will have her bairn and rear it with our help and love. That's all that need be said."

The new houses were roofed with timbers from the broch which now stood open to the sky, peat-blackened walls calling up memories of that winter when its shelter had brought together strangers and made them like kin. Barry pried up the hearthstone and carried it to its new place in the center of the MacLeods' dwelling.

"There's magic to this one," he said. "Och, but we'll still be gathering around it of an evening."

Cridhe stood draped in her plaid, so the place was immediately home though after living with thirteen people and two babies, the cottage seemed very quiet to Mairi. It was lovely, though, to share a bed only with Eileen. Tam had his closeted nook as a divider between hearthroom and sleeping chamber where Gran had the other box-bed. The byre adjoined the hearthroom, opening on one end to the barn and on the other to the *fasgalan*, a small entry that held the quern and bench with milk vessels. When doors of barn, byre, and fasgalen were all opened, they created a draft for winnowing grain. All this, snugged into the slope, was enclosed in walls thick as a tall man and roofed with thatch secured by nets weighted with stones.

Within a week, the peats were carried home and each house had a neat oval mound beside it, enough well-dried blocks to last till summer. Delving up the potatoes was the last autumn chore. The others had urged Mairi not to dig and lift, but though she was almost five months pregnant, she was still light on her feet and the rounding of her belly didn't show because of her full skirts. Mairi was carrying a load to the potato corner in the barn when she spied a man striding from the north, a man in a dark kilt and red jacket.

"Calum!"

Dropping the creel, she sped to meet him, but Eileen and Tam reached him first. Hugging, laughing, weeping, brothers and sisters embraced in a tangle of arms and kisses, then drew back to gaze at each other.

"Can it be little Eileen?" Calum marveled. "I wouldn't know you but for that moon bright hair! Tam, lad, you're nigh tall as me though you've some filling out to do. And Mairi, you— you're a woman!"

He soon must know how true that was. But for this moment, how wonderful to touch muscle and flesh of him, gaze into his warm hazel eyes, caress his face, leaner and more weathered, the always strong jaw more prominent. He'd gone away a lad and come back a man, Mairi thought with mingled pride and regret. The bloom and innocence were scoured off him, just as with Iain.

"Hurry!" Mairi tugged him along as Andrew, Barry and Sheila took their turn at greetings. "You've got to see Gran!"

"And our baby!" laughed Sheila. She and Barry had married the week before Calum went away.

Calum squinted toward the Gunns and Mackinnons. "Who're the folk lifting 'taties?"

Briefly explaining, Mairi said, "You'll meet them later. But look! Gran's heard the racket and here she comes!"

Calum admired his wee cousin Seana and Alai, met the Gunns and MacKinnons, gave reassuring news of Lucas and Paul, and devoured bannocks and crowdie and barley broth as he told them something of the army and the distant lands where he'd fought for the English queen. Only when he went with Mairi to fetch water from the burn did they have a chance for a private word.

"So there was a letter from Catriona?"

"Gran has it safe."

"Caty's happy there, over the sea?"

"She sounded so. And as Gran told you, love, she says you'd better come before she flits with some Texas Ranger or other lonesome bachelor." Mairi dropped the teasing and faced him. "Will you go, Calum?"

He rubbed his ear, just as he had in childhood when handed a puzzle. "It rankles me that she just went off and I can follow willy-nilly or lose her. But you've men enough for work and I've never fancied any other lass." That hard jaw clenched. "I've a debt to settle first."

Mairi's heart froze. "Calum! Fearchar wouldn't want you to hang or be transported!"

"It's not Fearchar I'm suiting, lass. It's myself."

She caught his hand, a hand that used weapons and certainly had killed—killed men with whom he had no quarrel. How could he be expected to spare the man who'd caused the death of one he had greatly loved, burned his home and driven away his family? "Please, lad!" Mairi entreated. "Don't leave us to mourn you, too!"

"Hugh Sinclair lied to me out of his black beard, and to Paul and Lucas," Calum's voice held cold rage. "Said, he did, if we went for soldiers, our folk could bide safe in our crofts. And even with us gone, didn't he wait till the men were at the fishing to come with constables and torches? I won't forgive him that."

"You don't have to forgive him!" Though she had hoped against hope that her brother would stay at Clanna, Mairi said now, "Calum, if you're going to America, what does Sinclair matter?"

Calum didn't answer but she knew she hadn't changed his mind. Should she tell him about the baby? Maybe he'd think it his duty to kill Iain, too. Shivering inwardly at the thought, she decided it was better for her brother not to know. She'd warn the others not to mention it to him. If he left for America soon, he wouldn't hear about it for a long time.

As days passed and Calum seemed in no hurry to find Sinclair, Mairi began to hope that maybe her urging had some effect. He went fishing with the men and helped break the new croplands with the cas-chrom, wearing Barry's clothes till Mairi and Gran could make him some that would fit. Except for his erect carriage and brisk step, he looked like any young crofter.

And then, the second week of November, he dressed in his

new clothes with the jersey Gran had knitted his name into so if he were drowned, the body could be identified. Stuffing his few belongings in a pack, he said he was going to Stornoway and find a ship there or on the mainland to carry him over the ocean.

"But—you haven't given us any warning!" Mairi protested. "Oh, Calum, at least stay the night and make a proper farewell!"

He smiled but the shake of his curly brown head was determined. "It's bad enough being cried over for ten minutes. I can't bide an evening of it, Mairi. Washes strength from a man, do women's tears." She was crying and, awkwardly, he patted her cheek. "Come, lass! We've had a good visit. I know you're well-settled and can manage without me. So I must be on my way."

"But Calum—"

He pressed a finger to her lips. "Wheesht, lass! What if I came late to Texas and found Cat wedded? Or carried off by those red Indians?"

Mairi threw her arms around him. "Please, Calum, will you come back and see us some day, you and Cat? Maybe bring your children?"

"To be sure we will," he soothed, roughly smoothing her hair. "And maybe you'll bring your children to visit us. We'll be one family, one clanna, even with the ocean between us."

Ah, but their children would be strangers, and his would grow up far from the Island. With an effort, she smiled through a blur of tears. "Ever and forever, lad." She lowered her voice. "You won't be looking for trouble?"

"Would I do that?" His tone was bland but a smoldering in his eyes filled her with dread.

As soon shout into a gale as argue with him. As for asking Andrew and Barry to reason with him, they, or at least Barry, might feel honor-bound to take a hand. That would make things even worse.

Perhaps Calum couldn't find Sinclair. Sir James had brought in a new factor. It was possible Sinclair had gone back to the Lowlands. But if he hadn't—

Mairi made a quick decision. "We need some indigo and other things," she said. "I'll walk along with you, brother, and have that much more of your company."

"You can't tramp back alone in the night."

"No need," she returned airily. "Annie Gordon's said I may spend the night with her whenever I'm in the town."

He gave her a look of mingled vexation and amusement. "Hurry up with you then. It's a long trudge to Stornoway, even for a soldier."

In half an hour, they were on their way, darting glances back and forth, till finally he threw back his head and laughed. "Mairi, Mairi, you've an eye on me like an eagle on a mouse! Or a color sergeant on a malingerer! Give over, love. Let's be happy these last hours together."

"Gladly if you'll give your word not to hunt for Sinclair."

Calum sighed. "I won't lie to you. But it's far and far to Stornoway. Tell me more about Catriona."

"What?"

"Anything. It gives me happiness just to hear her name."

"Then I should think you'd let nothing get in your way to her."

He didn't answer.

18

At the lodge, Mrs. Fraser made much of Calum, and gave them raisin scones and steaming tea. When they wouldn't stay the night, she packed a meal for them. "No use spending money on that rotten stuff they'd feed you in the town," she said briskly.

On the way to Stornoway, Mairi told Calum in more detail about her desperate walk this way almost a year ago and how Magnus had rescued Tam. "Eileen had a fancy for Liam Fraser till she saw Magnus," Mairi finished with a laugh. "And now she's set her heart on Magnus waiting for her."

"And from all he hear, he's set his heart on you."

"He's a sailor," Mairi shrugged. "No doubt he's courted a dozen women since he was with us."

It was Calum's turn to shrug. "I walked with lasses these past years when I had a chance but they were for the time and place. 'Twas always Catriona in my heart and dreams."

Mairi made a face at him. "And how would you like it if Catriona walked out with some lads?"

"That's different!" At Mairi's snort, her brother grinned sheepishly. "Maybe, when I catch up with my lassie, we won't be asking questions."

"That would be the canny way."

"When the captain was wounded," Calum said in a sudden turn of conversation and with a searching glance at her, "it was said in his fever he called on a Mairi. Of course that's a common name."

"The commonest."

"But he asked her to play her harp."

"Perhaps he thought on Mairi of the Isles, Mairi nighean Alasdair Ruaidh."

"That Mairi MacLeod is dead near two centuries."

"Her songs live on."

"True enough," said Calum drily. "But I doubt Captain MacDonald was having dreams of her."

Mairi said nothing. Calum persisted. "It's said he had a rosy purple coverlet that he held to as if it were a Christian."

"We gave him that. 'Twas little enough."

"He did not, it seems, think it a trifle."

Weary of sparring, Mairi turned on her brother. "If it solaced him, I'm grateful. And yes, I loved him, and I do, and yes, I will for always."

"He's gentry, lass."

"I know that. Don't fret, Calum, my lad. He'll come no more to the island."

"You won't grieve after him all your days?"

"Indeed, I won't. Didn't I promise Fearchar on his bier that I'd be happy and keep a high heart?"

Calum sighed. "I'd breathe easier if you'd wed this Magnus. He sounds a proper man."

"He is that. I like him well. But I met Iain first."

"Iain, is it?"

"Why not? Stir your spurtle in your own porridge, my lad."

His look of affront passed quickly. "Lass, sorry I am I was away when all this trouble came upon you. The captain helped finely, I won't deny it, but without you, Aosda would be utterly scattered. I have no place to stand when I would question you. But Mairi, whatever else you are, you're still my little sister."

With a sobbing laugh, she threw her arms around him. "And you're my big brother! Don't worry, love. All will be well with us. I wish you might stay but I can understand why you follow

Caty. If ever you and she want to come back, you'll have a hundred welcomes."

"Myself, I'd be glad of them. But Catriona—"

"Is a Viking. New lands for her! It was always in her blood." To ease him, Mairi added, "After all, not everyone can stay. That leads to three families scratching where scarce one could live. Why, in a few years, you'll be used to burning wood and own lands greater than the Black Moor with hundreds of cattle munching themselves fat on grass. Think of it, Calum! Catriona says that cows there stay out all winter!"

" 'Tis all a wonder to me." Calum glanced from the glimmering sea to the darkening winter's sky. "But, och, Mairi! It's sad I am to leave you and the island."

"To be sure. But when you meet with Catriona, how glad you'll be!"

It was dark when they stopped at Annie Gordon's. She welcomed them in and said at once that Calum could sleep in the shop. "No need to spend coin for the stinking hay of a sailor's mattress." Putting another peat on the fire, she set the kettle on and smiled at Calum who gave her a shy but appreciatively male grin that brought a glow to her brown eyes.

Nothing would do but for her to heat up the mutton broth she'd had for supper, and they produced Mrs. Fraser's mealie pudding, tatie scones and spiced treacle cakes. "Mairi would have been glad of you this time last year when Tam was stolen by that carnaptious Captain Tarbert," Annie reminisced. "A good thing Magnus Ericsson was handy."

Calum looked grim. "I was gone when my family needed me most. For sure I owe some debts. One is to Magnus though unless he comes to America, I doubt I can ever pay it." A smile relaxed Calum's face. Mairi had a flash of seeing him not as her brother, but as an attractive young man who had been out in the world. "At least I can thank you, Mistress Ann, for being kind to Tam and Mairi and paying a good price for the weaving."

"No thanks to me for that. I've sold at a profit and it's fine work. You could thank Magnus, though, if you'd wait in town a while. A friend of his was in my shop last week and said he'd seen Magnus at Castlebay down on Barra. He's been trading between there and Glasgow but was starting back to Orkney and will put in at Stornoway. Said there was a lass he had to see." She laughed at Mairi's blush. "I wish 'twere me he spoke of but it wasn't."

"He'd best take care," said Mairi, trying to laugh away her confusion. "Our little sister worships him. She didn't take it for a tease when he promised to wait for her."

"I wish I could meet him," said Calum. "Especially if one road or another he's going to be my brother-in-law. But my lass is meeting Texas Rangers and who knows what so I must take the first ship I can."

"If you decide to wait for Magnus," said Annie, "you're welcome to bide here. But you must be worn out, the both of you. Go on to sleep Mairi, do, while I make up Calum's pallet."

Mairi was asleep before her hostess came to bed, and when she woke in the darkness of a November morning, Calum had already gone out. "He'll be at the harbor to see about his passage," Annie said and gave Mairi a frank smile. "I could wish he'd have to wait a week or two. Wheesht, lass! No need to go all rosy-red. He's a fine, strong lad and I'm a lonely woman. I have a sweetheart on the mainland but he won't move here and so far I haven't been able to decide to sell my shop and go to him. Meanwhile, well—"

If it could have been as simple as that with Iain—but then it wouldn't have meant more than a good meal or comfortable bed. Annie made porridge and set out a pot of fresh butter to stir into it. "Must you go home today, lass?"

"I should." Mairi frowned. "But I'd like to see Calum on his ship first. If he happens into Hugh Sinclair—"

"Well, you can pick out what you need from the shop. Maybe Calum will be back by then." She winked. "Should your brother have to wait for a ship, I'll try to keep his mind off Sinclair." She opened the door to the shop and drew her shawl closer at the rush of cold air. "You need indigo?"

Mairi made her purchases, including Gran's favored toffees, Jeddart snails, and was deciding on black strippit balls and sour plum candies to treat the rest, when a stout little woman burst into the shop. "Annie, Annie, what a moil! Hugh Sinclair's roof burned around his ears, and him trounced within an inch of his life! A lad did it who's been off to the wars and came back to find his folk burned out! He was caught and dragged to gaol. Hanging for him—or at best, hard labor in Australia." The woman stared as Mairi cried out. As the room whirled, Mairi swayed and leaned against the door frame.

"She's the lad's sister," said Annie.

"Och, I'm sorry, to be sure! Had I kenned—"

"Leave us, Peggy, for now." As the woman withdrew with a pitying look, Annie put her arm around Mairi. " 'Tis an ill thing, love. But likely the judge will be merciful since your grandfather died from the burning, and Calum's got a chestful of medals for his soldiering."

"Why did he do it?" Mairi wailed. "More grief it is to the rest of us, and if he hangs—" She sobbed on Annie's firm shoulder till the worst shock passed and her mind began to work. "I've met the laird. I'll beg him to do something."

"The laird's in England," Annie said with tears in her eyes.

Mairi groaned, thought desperately. "Do you know the gaoler, Annie? Is he a drinking man?"

"Mother's milk to him the whiskey is." Hope flared in Annie's face before it faded. "Och, lass, if you got Calum out of gaol, what use? Ships will be warned not to take him aboard. He can't hide long on this bare island."

"If we could get home, the men might take him across to Skye in our boat."

"A fishing boat cross the Minch at this time of year?" Annie demanded. "The Minch that is ever hungry for men? Didn't it steal my strong young husband? I doubt your brother would let the others risk themselves. Besides, there's nowhere to hide on the Black Moor. The constables would come up with you long before you reached home. Then you'd be in the hot gruel, too."

"I have to do something!"

Annie considered. "Let's go to the harbor. If there's a captain or mate I'm friends with, maybe I can fix it for them to be off with Calum before the hue and cry is raised."

"You mustn't make woe for yourself, Annie."

Annie gave her a straight look. "I'm not so light with whom I frolic that I can blithely see such a lad bound for the gallows. Wrap up warm, lass. Let's be stepping."

The overcast sky threatened rain. Gray clouds merged with gray sea, obscuring the lurking Beasts of Holm, but the wind, though chill, wasn't blowing hard. On a site overlooking the inner harbor, dozens of workers toiled on the walls of what must be Sir James Matheson's castle. More men labored on the road; still others were building long wooden platforms protruding out into the harbor, quays that would make loading and unloading much easier.

"Sir James is making a difference," said Annie. "He's already started to drain bogs and build schools. It's a new thing for a laird to pour money into his holdings rather than squeeze his tenants for money to dice and drink away on the mainland." Scanning the ships riding at anchor, she let out a glad cry. "Mairi! The *Selchie's* in! And who's this rowing to shore but the lad himself!"

It was Magnus bending to his oar, Magnus who leaped to the sand and ran toward Mairi, fair hair an aureole around his tanned face, while his companions hauled the boat ashore. He was wearing the blue-gray jersey Sheila and Gran had made for him. Catching Mairi up in his arms, he kissed her cheeks and then her mouth.

"Am I dreaming, lass? Are you the first one that I see?"

"I'm here, too." Annie's tone was dry.

"Och, Annie!" Magnus encircled her in one great arm, kissing her soundly, but he held Mairi fast in the other. "Talk of a king with two crowns!" Looking more closely at Mairi, he asked quickly, "Why, lass, have you been crying?"

She told him, Annie filling in when Mairi's voice broke. His eyes, blue with that haze of gray, darkened like night. He called over his shoulder to his crewmen, "Have your fun, lads, but stay sober enough to sail!"

Drawing the women along with him, he said, "Don't fash yourselves, lassies. We'll have Calum out of gaol and away on the *Selchie* but that'll have to wait for dark. Let's go to your place now, Annie. I'd be glad of tea and a bannock while we plan what's to be done."

Laughing, he swept them along with him, so big and strong and buoyant that Mairi took heart. He made himself so at home in Annie's private quarters that Mairi was sure he'd been there often. He and Annie were banteringly affectionate with each other, but without possessiveness. They seemed comrades more than lovers. Mairi was both aghast and envious. She desired Iain in every way, longed for his dear body, but only because her heart and spirit needed him.

She had to make it clear to Magnus that though she would be forever grateful if he helped Calum escape, she couldn't reward him with herself. If necessary, she'd tell him she was carrying Iain's child. She shrank at the thought because she valued Magnus, didn't think she could bear to watch the delight and worship in his eyes turn to disgust. But she would, she'd bear anything to get her brother free.

While Annie attended to a customer, Magnus poured Mairi some tea and made her sit in the one chair by the fire while he pulled up a stool. "Well, lass, it's a rare tangle, but I can't blame your brother for settling scores."

"Much good Hugh Sinclair's burned house and cracked bones are to the family if Calum gets himself hanged!"

Quietly, Magnus said, "I have heard that you yourself put a curse on the factor."

Long ago that seemed—the blazing roofs, Fearchar dead by his harp. But indeed and indeed she had cursed Hugh Sinclair. Bowing her head, she muttered, "A minister might say Calum

217

carried out my curse. All the more reason I have to get him loose."

"We will. If the gaoler doesn't drink himself senseless, I'll tap him on the head." Magnus laughed. "Never fear, sweeting. I've broke my crewmen out of better gaols than this." He placed her hand on his, laughed at the difference in size. In spite of rough work that kept her fingernails short and broken, Mairi's hands were shapely. Magnus brought the one he had captured to his cheek. "I'll find my men and send them back to the ship to tell the rest of the crew that if the tide allows, we'll slip out of the harbor as soon as we can see in the morning. They'll have to wait for Glasgow to enjoy themselves. I was coming to see you. Now that'll have to wait so I must use this little time we have."

She tried to withdraw her hand. "Magnus—"

He set his hands on the back of the chair on either side of her but she was trapped more by his gaze than his arms. Her heart tripped heavily. "Well, lass?"

"Well?"

"Will you?"

"Will I what?"

"Wed me."

"You know why I can't."

"I can hope you've had an attack of good sense and realize what a grand husband I'll make when you straighten out a few wrinkles in me."

Still not touching her with his hands, he kissed her long and deliberately, his mouth warm and hard with the taste of the sea on it, but Iain's child now grew within her body. A year ago Magnus's kiss could rouse her. She was sealed to him now. He drew back, frowning.

"I've had warmer kisses from a stone, but last year, girl, had I wooed you with care and wile, I could have had you. You were ripe for it, ready to a skillful hand." His eyes widened before they narrowed. He gripped her wrists, hurting her. "Is that it, Mairi? Did that man you love seduce you?"

"Seduce me he did not! But—" She took a breath and plunged. "I will have his bairn."

Magnus let go of her as if her flesh seared him. He turned from her, bleached yellow head bent as if he had sustained a deadly hurt. At last he said in a tone squeezed carefully dry of feeling, "Will he help you?"

"He doesn't know. I don't want him to. He'll come no more to the island." Mairi sat with her head bowed for she was sorry to lose Magnus's respect.

After what seemed a very long time, he turned and lifted her from the chair to his lap. "You need a husband, Mairi, and a father to your bairn." He cradled her as if she were herself a child. "Wed me. The tyke will never know by any look or word of mine that it wasn't got in our marriage bed."

She buried her face against his massive shoulder and sobbed until she was exhausted. He smoothed her hair, whispered tender, loving words. When she quieted, he tilted back her chin and smiled into her eyes, traced with his finger her mouth and nose and forehead.

"Let's talk with the minister this day, lass. After I've landed Calum safe where he can find a ship for America, I'll come back. We'll marry, with a great feast. Proud I am to have you, and the world shall know it."

Resting in his arms gave her a wonderful feeling of being cherished and protected. He would love her child. It was not in Magnus to be harsh to any small, weak creature. Iain intended never to see her again; he wouldn't even know about the baby.

Every reason to wed Magnus against the single truth of her heart; it was Iain that she loved. She moved her head in sad negation. "Magnus, in the whole world, you're my dearest friend. But—" Again she shook her head.

He gripped her by the shoulders, giving her a shake. "You'll make a bastard of your child to keep some sort of useless faith with a man you'll never see again?"

"I still am his."

"You're daft, Mairi MacLeod!" Magnus's fingers bit into her flesh. "Wicked, too, to set such a load on your wee bairn."

Stung, she cried, "The Clanna know. I offered to go away but all of them, even Morag, bid me stay. They have sworn to be family to my child."

"Well they might," he said bitterly, "since where would they be without you? Of course they couldn't tell you to be off!"

"They knew I wouldn't be starving on the rocks." Wresting free, she stood erect. "The laird himself asked me to live at his castle. He wants a harper."

Magnus's square jaw dropped. "A harper?" He gave a scornful laugh. "Och, aye, if you believe that!"

"I do believe it for we had plain speaking. But it boots not since my people are ready to welcome my babe."

Drily, Magnus said, "Everyone is, it would seem, saving the father." He got to his feet, head almost touching the low rafters. "But think, lass. Grant that your child is nurtured in your township, has a place there. Supposing the bairn craves a different life? Or loves someone who'll abuse or reject him or her because of bastardy?"

Each word stabbed into the part of her where the baby grew, warmly hidden and protected now as it could not be in life. "A person who'd act like that wouldn't be a good wife or husband any road," she said. "Magnus, I thank you with all my heart. But I—I cannot do it."

"Then there's naught more to say." He swung toward the door. "I'll warn my men. And meanwhile you and Annie think upon the best way to get your brother out."

19

Darkness and fog pressed so thickly that Mairi could scarcely breathe as she moved with Annie through the narrow streets leading to the gaol. Annie had a jug of good whiskey under her shawl and Mairi carried a cruit, sort of a lute that Annie had borrowed from an ancient neighbor. An afternoon's practice on its six strings couldn't turn Mairi into an accomplished player, of course, but she could pick out a few pleasing tunes.

"Mind now," cautioned Annie. "We've come to visit Calum and give him a cheering dram. It's up to you to sing and play so sweet that Angus Roy, the gaoler, will sit with us and tip the jug till he's snoring. Magnus will wait for us at the net-loft on the harbor."

"But won't you be blamed if you come in the gaol with me?"

"Och, no! To save his face, Angus will have to say two or three stout rascals overpowered him. And he won't want trouble with me for it's often I've let him have food on credit for his wife and bairns when he'd drunk up his wages."

Sure enough, Angus, a wizened sharp-faced man with red hair, opened to them gladly and made no difficulty about pulling them a bench into the passageway leading to a few musty cells. He fetched a cruisie that cast yellow light on Calum's face as he came to the small barred window. Mairi gasped at the bloody weal across his cheek and a bruised swelling at one temple but he chuckled and said, "If you think I look tousled, lassies, you should have a peek at Hugh Sinclair."

"Oh, Calum!" Mairi breathed. "Why did you not just flit to America?"

"So was my intention. But by bad luck, someone saw the fire and fetched constables whilst I was in rearranging yon factor's ugly face." He added regretfully, "He'll not die of his whipping but maybe after this he'll be less eager at thatch-burning."

"Under the new laird there'll be no evictions," Mairi pointed out. "Calum, laddie, would you had left Sinclair to God!"

"Too slow," said Calum unrepentantly. "I could by no means sail to America with that canting, lying, black-bearded chiel not a whisker worse for what he did to my folk."

Angus Roy nodded. "Those sorry about what you did to Sinclair will only rue that he wasn't killed entirely. If that be a jug beneath your plaid, Mrs. Gordon, I could relish a drop."

"To be sure, Angus." Producing several small cups, Annie poured out drams for Calum, the gaoler and herself. *"Slainte!"* she toasted. "Health to your bones! 'Tis a shame you don't like the good uisge-beatha, lass, but surely you'll give us a tune?"

"I'll try, though it was only this afternoon I met this cruit." Mairi teased her brother by singing "Beloved Calum is my Sweetheart," and then plucked the strings as she sang her longing for Iain. That was the best thing about songs; there was one to say anything your heart cried so you could have the relief of voicing your feelings without betraying them.

> "I would go, I would go with you across the Irish Sea, Where high billows rise, where whales, dolphins and monsters follow the white-sailed ships . . ."

"Ye play fine, lass." Angus wagged his head and held out his cup which Annie filled to the brim. "Would ye ken the ballad about the selchie of Sule Skerry?"

She sang that and a dozen more, marveling that Angus could drink as much as he did and still be sitting up. Maybe he wasn't going to get drunk. Maybe he could lounge there all night, swilling cup after cup, moving his dingy red head in time with the music. Maybe—

Her nerves had reached the breaking point when the gaoler rose with a sigh and unlocked the door of Calum's cell with a great iron key. "I could listen to ye all night, lass, and drink your good whiskey, Mrs. Gordon," he said with a roguish wink. "But ye must be off with the lad before prying eyes can see."

As the women stared at him, his shoulders shook with mirth. " 'Twas a canny notion, to wile me with music and get me drunk, but God bless you, 'tis a long time yet you'd be waiting. Take that rope there and tie me up, do, so that 'twill be seen in the morning that I could not prevent this lad from 'scaping."

As they tied him hand and foot, Angus said hopefully, "Another dram, Mrs. Gordon? To help me sleep sound on these plaguey stones?" He drank as thirstily as if it were his first drop. "I'd have ye crack me on the head, but that would hurt. Just muss my hair a bit—best gag me, too, so there'll be no wondering why I didn't screech."

"You're kind, Master Angus," Mairi said. "It's not as if my brother were a right criminal."

"I've no love for Sinclair." He cocked a ruddy eyebrow at Calum. "Wasn't I a soldier meself and came home to find me aged mother turfed out of her house? The devil fly off with factors, I say, and with landlords, saving Sir James!"

Annie knelt to gag him with a strip torn from the coarse sheet that covered the straw in the corner. "One last drop?" he wheedled. He got it, and a quick kiss, before Annie secured the gag and they slipped out into the fog and murk.

Magnus loomed as they approached the net-loft, having stopped at Annie's for Calum's pack. The men shook hands in the darkness. "We'll get acquainted between here and Glasgow," Magnus said. "Is the gaoler well-foxed?" He laughed at their explanation and took advantage of the rough footing to slip an arm around both women as they made their way down to the small boat they'd row to the *Selchie.*

Mairi hugged her brother tight, relief at his freedom mixed with sorrow at losing him. "Calum, you'll come back to see us?"

"Aye, and with all our brats, so that you'll be glad when Caty and I take ourselves back to Texas!" Gently disengaging her hands, he gave Annie a hearty buss, thanked her again, and rolled up his trousers so he could help push the boat into the sea.

Magnus was a solid blackness in the shadows. Silence thickened between him and Mairi. "You're sure, lass, that you won't need anything from Glasgow?"

"A thousand thanks but all I need is at Clanna."

He brought her so close that even through their heavy clothes she felt the hardness of his bones and muscle. "I'd wed you after the bairn comes," he whispered. "I'll wed you, Mairi, any day you'll have me."

Releasing her so abruptly that she stumbled, he joined Calum. The men softly called farewells out of the darkness. Then there was only the plashing of the oars.

Weary though she was, Mairi drowsed fitfully that night. At the first hint of dawn, she got quietly out of the big bed where Annie slept with her head tucked into her arm. Dressing, Mairi wrapped her shawl around her and stole through the shop and into the street, grateful that the fog had lessened.

Down at the harbor, anchored ships bulked as slightly darker shapes against an iron sky. Thank heaven, the wind was right to fill the sails. An experienced captain like Magnus, who knew this harbor well, could maneuver out of it even in this dimness.

As she watched, the shadowy form of the *Selchie* began to move. Like a sable wraith, it glided against the horizon, gathering speed as the sails filled. Mairi waved though no one could see, called farewells though they could not hear.

"God keep you, Calum. And you, Magnus! Travel swift and safe and come to good harbor!" Tears blinded her as the ship merged with dark ocean and sky, but her grief at Calum's departure was lightened with gratitude that he wouldn't hang or be exiled as a convict. Still, as she walked back to the shop, she couldn't see where she was going and stumbled frequently.

"Hot porridge will set you right. We can breathe easy, now you've seen the ship sail." Annie was up now, briskly stirring oats into water. "Did you have good potatoes this year?"

"Grand ones, fine and fair and firm." Mairi thought Annie was making conversation to divert her till the older woman frowned and said, "The word is the crop is lost in Ireland, rotted in the earth. And the Irish live on 'taties even more than we."

"Poor folk," said Mairi. "When potatoes fail, winter's too close to plant again."

"This will make a hungry winter in many parts. The crop was lost in Belgium, Denmark and Sweden and they do say in Canada."

"I was only eight when the blight ruined the potatoes in '35," said Mairi. "But well I remember gathering dulse and shellfish for that was all we had to eat."

"The chief of the Clanranald MacDonalds that brought potatoes to the Highlands and Islands a century ago thought he did his folk a service since no great crops of grain can grow here," sighed Annie. "But the devil was in it for folk depend now on them—don't plant other crops. It's reckoned two-thirds of Highlanders live mainly on potatoes nine months out of the year. When the crop fails, it's starving time."

"Maybe the blight will die with the winter."

"Let's pray so. But the weather's freaky this autumn. In September a strange white powdery dust fell on the Orkneys. Awful storms along the Caithness coast have wrecked boats and thrown fishermen out of work. It's stayed warm much too long. I do not like it, Mairi."

A chill fingered Mairi's spine. "We have more land for grain next year, but it's still potatoes that must fill us. All we can do is plant them and hope."

"Aye," nodded Annie. "A bad thing it is to depend on one crop. If it drowns or withers or blights, where are you? But no use to fash about what may not happen. Another cup of tea, lass? She looked at her with a keen, kind eye. "Is there anything else you need help with?"

Annie knew. She had guessed what most people couldn't detect yet. Mairi blushed. "How did you—"

"It's the glow to your skin more than anything, love. The hard work you do keeps your muscles tight and holds in the bairn." Anbnie hesitated. "You wish to have it?"

"Oh, yes! And my folk know and will help."

"Will the father?"

"He mustn't know. We cannot wed and this would grieve him."

"Och, aye!" sniffed Annie. "He must not know what his pleasure brought but you'll be saddled with his bairn while you should be finding a husband." She gnawed at a fingernail. "Magnus—"

"Magnus deserves better than a woman who loves somebody else. Don't fret, Annie. The babe and I will do fine."

"Well, that's up to you," shrugged Annie. "But it gets lonely unwedded. If my best sweetheart didn't live on the plaguey mainland, I think I'd marry him—and I may anyway, though I'd be sorry to give up my business."

"We would sore miss you, Annie."

"And I'd miss you. But if I'm to have a bairn, I can't wait too much longer." She grinned. "I'll admit I had hopes of Magnus—till he met you. But we're probably too much alike to do well in wedlock. My mainland sweetheart can keep me steady. We were bairns together but I stayed here and married my captain while Arthur Mitchell went to Inverness and made his fortune. He's been at me to wed ever since my poor husband drowned six years ago. Maybe it's time I did."

Marveling at Annie's casual matter-of-factness, Mairi savored the strong, bracing tea. The *Selchie* should be safely out of the harbor and skimming southward. Now that Magnus had saved her other brother, she could never repay him, nor could she thank Annie, but Mairi did her best. Stowing her purchases in the creel, Mairi embraced her hostess and was off before the town was properly waking or any alarm sounded from the gaol.

*   *   *

Before they left for the winter fishing that started in January, 1846, the men prepared the potato beds, and on good days fished from the boat for cod, ling, white fish, skate and turbot. Mairi hated baiting the lines, thrusting limpets or sand-eels on hooks that dangled by horsehair snoods from the lines. These had to be arranged carefully on a basket so that the end of a line could be fastened to an anchored float and the rest played out so there would be no tangling of the hooks. These expeditions yielded fresh fish in plenty and quantities to be salted or smoked for later use.

"If we had a way of getting our catch to market!" said Barry, who hated to leave Sheila and Seana to fish out of Stornoway.

The township had an agreement to supply the lodge folk with cured fish but there was no other local sizable demand. "When Lucas and Paul come home," mused Andrew, "maybe they'll find wives with brothers who'd join in our fishing. Then we'd have two boats. That might make it worth some captain's trouble to call in here." He glanced at Mairi. "Think you Magnus would?"

She'd told the clanna how Magnus had spirited Calum away but not that he'd asked again to marry her. "If he won't, some captain might."

Tam looked up from twisting heather rope. His chapped wristbones showed inches below his sleeves and his elbows poked out. Time to knit new sleeves into that jersey! He seemed to sprout taller each time Mairi looked at him and was now at eye-level with her.

"I'll have a ship someday," he said with a toss of his fair head. "I'll take our fish to market."

"Hoots!" scoffed Eileen. "How will you be getting a ship? Don't we call it a grand thing to have our own boat?"

"I'll sail with Magnus when I'm not needed to make up our crew." Unruffled, he grinned at the others. "It's up to the rest of you to weave and knit and catch fish enough to pay for a ship once I've learned the knack of handling it."

This was greeted by howls of laughter. Their tiny community

227

own a real ship? But Murdo narrowed his gray eyes. "It may be, lad," he said thoughtfully. "Gavin, old Meggie and I were harried from our home less than a year ago, but here we are in better case than ever I remember, saving of course that Gavin's poor lass is gone."

"Aye," said Donald, with a fond look at Katie who was rocking Alai to sleep. "Never will I say the folk of Clanna can't do what we purpose."

A heady goal, but why not try? Mairi felt a tug of guilt; if she had taken Magnus, Clanna would have use of his ship—might anyway if she asked. But she couldn't seek more favors from a man who had already done so much for her family.

While the men were away at the fishing grounds, the women started planting potatoes. Mairi, heavy now in her seventh month, prayed there would be a bountiful yield. Those poor folk in Ireland! Sometimes she wondered if even America could hold the starving thousands from the Highlands and Ireland and other beleaguered lands.

After much inner debate, Mairi had told the others about the potato blight. She hated to worry them, but it was a threat she couldn't bear alone. The soil of the lazybeds was so fertile, though, and the seed potatoes so healthy, that she thought surely the plague wouldn't reach here. The surrounding seas shut the island off from many good things but were also a barrier to disease.

Back from the fishing, well pleased with their earnings, the men took their cas-chroms to plough the croplands. If only the blight didn't reach them, this should be a prosperous year.

The spring of 1846 was unseasonably early which roused fears that the potato plague might spread. Then Ewan Fraser brought the fearful news that when potato pits were opened on the mainland, most held nothing but rotting, stinking slime. Every time Mairi got potatoes from their corner in the barn, she rummaged deep to see if they were sound and sniffed for any suspicious odor. They remained wholesome but she watched the planted beds intently. What if the seed potatoes spoiled in the ground? What if her folk lost their main food for the winter?

The wheatears were just back from the south, warbling from hillocks or as they flitted in search of insects, when Mairi woke on the twentieth of March with cramping pains. *Iain! I wish you were with me now—that you, not my young sister, lay in this bed beside me.* Wherever he was, she hoped he was thinking of her, that he still loved her, now as she fought to bring his child into the world.

She met the pangs as a swimmer the waves, trying not to be swept under, not so much frightened as amazed. In spite of the swelling of her body, the increase of her breasts, even the quickening of the babe and its restless moving, she could not quite believe she would bear a child.

Now she did. There was a separating, cleaving quality to the contractions. For the first time she realized how profoundly her life would change, would center around the unknown little being glowing in her darkness, bright seed of her lover, who racked her now in urgent striving to come out into the sun.

Little blind one, I'd gladly help you but I'm new to this myself. Hoping the bairn would sense her love, she stroked the mound of her belly, then caught in her breath at a pain that gripped her and clutched deep, relentlessly. When the spasm eased, remembering Sheila's delivery, and that walking had helped, Mairi got out of bed, wrapping her shawl over her shift, and built up the fire. Gran was instantly with her.

"The babe?"

Mairi nodded. Gran attached the water kettle to the hook. "Best not eat anything, lassie. We'll brew you tea from these tormentil roots and just you walk around the hearth. You'll do better to stay on your feet or squat as long as you can. Keeps the bairn swimming in the right direction. Shall I fetch Katie and Sheila to you?"

"Let them have their sleep out. It's still quite a time between pains."

"When the next pain takes hold, wait till it eases and start singing a waulking song, lass, one that only takes five minutes. By the time you scarce finish one song before the next cramp starts, we'll have in the other women."

The fist again knotted inside Mairi. She breathed deep to absorb it, and as the contraction passed, she sang softly so as not to awaken Eileen and Tam, finding a song for Iain. *"A pity I am not with my black-haired lad in the side of the hill out of the rainstorms, in a hollow of the wilds, some secret place . . ."*

Three songs before the pain coiled again. Mairi walked and sang and drank the hot draughts Gran gave her. Tam came out, yawning, blinked and stammered, "I—is it the bairn?"

"Aye." Gran handed him a bannock. "Have your porridge and on your way to the field, tell the other women not to start anything they can't leave. Eileen will come for them when the time's nearer."

He ate so hastily that Mairi laughed. "No need to gulp your bannock whole, Tam. I'm thinking you'll sow a lot of barley before I have the babe."

"I don't like to see you hurting," he blurted.

"Ochone, my lad," said Gran severely, " 'Tis the only way of getting born. Every body you meet walking the earth came with a woman's pain. Remember this side of it when you start to dally with the lasses."

He blushed and escaped as Eileen crept in, eyes wide and frightened. "Can you bear it, Mairi?"

"I have to, love." Mairi tried to smile. "What a good thing you can look after Seana and Alai while we get this one born!"

Eileen was soon sent for Katie and Sheila, not so far past their own birth-giving. They walked with their arms around Mairi, encouraging her, while that great, gripping hand tugged at her muscles and flesh, clenched tighter and tighter till she could no longer force back her cries and panted heavily between seizures.

"Scream all you want, dear," Sheila urged, wiping Mairi's sweating face. "It helps, it does."

Getting her to bed, they gave her their hands to squeeze. This couldn't be natural! She was being riven apart. She would die, the babe with her, and Iain would never know.

Screams tore from her throat. Oh, she was breaking! "Push, lass!" Gran's voice from far away. Sheila and Katie saying, "Push! Come, Mairi, push! That's it, that's our brave lass!"

She tried to gasp that she couldn't. Pain hurled her into fiery blackness, pain that had no ending, that accomplished nothing. After an eternity, she heard Gran's voice—from a long way off—from another world. "Her bones are too narrow. I fear she must die, and the babe in her—"

Not Iain's child! Tearing herself from the darkness, summoning strength from some power beyond her, Mairi crushed her friends' hands, bore down with all her will. "Iain!" she called.

On his name, rending agony was followed by a last clutching of that giant hand. It loosed. She thought she had died and then she heard a thin wail and Gran exulting. "Och, 'tis a fine lad with the black hair of his da'."

Mairi lay panting, unable to believe it was over. "He's—he's all right?" she demanded when she could speak. It had been her nightmare, that the child would be punished for their sin, be born deformed or ill-favored.

"See for yourself." Old eyes glowing, Gran finished washing the babe, swaddled him in a soft linen towel and placed him in Mairi's arms. "Look at him, nuzzling for his dinner! A bonnie, bold lad for sure."

Indeed, he rooted like a blind little animal, groping with his tiny perfect fingers. Damp from being washed, his black ringlets were beginning to fluff. Though his nose was stubbed down and his eyelids flattened, he bore a clear resemblance to Iain, especially in black brows that furrowed imperiously as he howled protest against this strange new universe. Mairi nudged him to her breast. His yowl stopped as he clamped strong little gums around the nipple and began to suckle.

"You'll have no milk for a few days," said Gran, patting his rump. "But that clear syrup is mightily good for babes and his sucking will help bring your innards back to normal. Don't let him pull too long at first, lassie. 'Twill make your breasts sore. Change him from one t'other and in between rub in this plantain ointment. We'll clean you up now and you can sleep." Bending, Gran kissed her. "Your work's well done for this day."

20

Now her wee lad was in her arms, Mairi could scarce remember how it had been without him. She never tired of marveling at the perfection of his skin, gazing into his thickly-lashed smoke-colored eyes or watching him fall asleep at her breast, every now and then giving a lazy little tug that dimpled his cheeks. Seana had been scarlet at birth, her face splotched, and head bent out of shape but David—Mairi would have him christened Michael David after Fearchar—had been white as her breast from the start, with no bruises or birthmarks. In spite of the difficulty of his birth, his head was beautifully molded.

If only Iain could see him! Her son so filled her heart that she wondered how she could still miss Iain so much and love him even more. David was a constant reminder of him, of course, but now she needed Iain to father their child, not only as her man.

This expanded, overflowing awareness affected her body as well as her heart. Breasts that had so sweetly and briefly thrilled to Iain's caressing hands and lips now were ravished with feelings as sensual but totally different. David's whole instinctual little being was absorbed in drawing nourishment from her. The sensation of feeding him from her body, of being all he needed was indescribably sweet.

Along with this knowledge that she was her son's world came a great longing for the mother she remembered only with a child's vision, the mother from whom she had nothing but the black wedding dress folded at the bottom of a chest. There were many to hold David, yet almost as keenly and bitterly as she missed Iain, she now wanted her mother to hold and love and praise her child, wanted it so much that she sometimes wept.

" 'Tis natural to feel weepy after a baby," Gran consoled. "After all, it's a great change you've had." So in a mysterious yet freeing manner, while she gloried in her child, Mairi also mourned her mother and felt at last that she had communed in spirit with the woman who'd given her birth.

All this went on while Mairi regained her strength. David was worth losing her figure for but she was mightily pleased that her limp, flaccid belly was beginning to firm. The small, serried pink lines on breasts and thighs came from stretching, Gran said, and were honorable scars.

As she grew stronger, Mairi could no longer put off the hateful necessity of approaching the Reverend Marcus Guinne, minister of the kirk where Seana had been christened, and asking him to perform that rite for David.

Not only would he take her to task for not trudging eight miles to service every Sunday and the same walk back, but he would certainly belabor her for conceiving out of wedlock. Still, if she wanted her baby baptized a Christian soul and given his name, she would have to accept whatever reviling came with it.

When she voiced her fear to the younger women, Katie patted her cheek and said bracingly, "No doubt he'll grumble and grouch but it's his duty to baptize. He cannot refuse, love, and we'll walk along with you, all of us."

"We will," promised Sheila. "And the lodge folk say Reverend Guinne is hot for religion these days but it wasn't so in his youth."

In the end, Sheila and Morag went with Mairi who carried David for he would have to be fed four or five times during the all day journey. Morag, the only person from Clanna that attended kirk, might have some credit with the minister.

She did, enough for him to pity her ties to a parcel of godless heathen. Standing on the threshold of the parsonage that stood near the kirk in the small village, the Reverend Marcus Guinne ranted at Mairi till he ran out of breath. When she said nothing of regret or excuse, his florid heavy-jowled face went even redder. He was soft-fleshed, a thing seldom seen on the island, had straw-colored hair, and a small puckering mouth. Eyes the shade of dried seaweed and as lusterless, lingered on Mairi's bare throat like an obscene touch.

"Do you not understand, woman? You have played the harlot—"

"Bless you, sir, she did not!" Sheila, usually so gentle, confronted the minister with eyes ablaze. "She loved one man."

"A vile lust of the body! Do not think, Mistress MacLeod, that there's not been shrewd guessing over who gave you your bastard."

Mairi had come steeled to endure whatever he might say but for him to say such a thing of the innocent child at her bosom! "You will not call my child that!"

"Why not? 'Twas you made him so."

"No! Men like you make bastards by naming children that!"

He glared at her and then composed himself. "Och, yes, it's about his naming that you've come." He studied for a moment. "Well, the child must not go unbaptized because of your haughty and rebellious spirit. He may have his christening on Sunday."

"Thank you, Reverend Guinne."

Mairi turned to go. Guinne's voice stopped her. "Before the naming," he said, rolling each word on his tongue, "You will stand bareheaded before the kirk while decent folk come in. You will not answer whatever they say to you for your soul's sake, for you be mightily in need of mortification and must bear all in a spirit of humility."

Mairi recoiled. Even Morag looked aghast. Sheila stared in speechless shock, but Mairi turned her shawl to protect her baby's face from the wind. "I can do that for my bairn."

"See you are here early." Without offering them a drink of

water or a crumb, he turned on his high heel that was all the fashion for gentlemen and shut the door in their faces.

"Now I pray I never need have another babe christened by yon cruel man!" Sheila breathed.

"He was over hard," admitted Morag though loath to speak against clergy.

"David will have his name as a Christian," Mairi said, cuddling him as they set off across the moor. "That's all that matters."

When the rest of Clanna heard her penance, Tam knotted up his fists. "I'll give that mealy-mouthed parson a drubbing!"

"That won't get the lad christened," growled Andrew. He, too, had reddened and veins stood out in his temples.

Ducking his face into Alai's dusky curls, Donald said in a husky voice, "I cannot bear seeing Mairi shamed when she saved our lives!"

"Nor we," said Murdo and Gavin at once.

"It will only be for an hour or so," Mairi said, though the thought of it, of the prying eyes and sneers, the dirtying of her love, made her stomach churn and weakened her legs. "I will stand there a short while and my laddie will have his name for all his life."

Gran came over and put her arm around her. Gran had shrunk this past year; her head now barely reached Mairi's shoulder, but her voice was clear and resonant. "I'll go, lass, and stand with you."

Katie clapped her hands together. "That's it, we all will!" As the others stared at her, she said, "Those mean enough to jeer at a lone lassie may not find it so easy to gibe at strong men."

"You've hit on it." Andrew chuckled in relief. "Now won't that give that sleekit minister a fit? 'Tis a grand notion, Katie. Eileen and Meggie can tend the wee ones while the rest of us go."

"It may anger Reverend Guinne till he won't baptize David," Mairi protested.

"And that will show fine in him, won't it, to punish a babe? All we're doing is letting the world know that the township of Clanna stands by its own." Rising, Andrew gathered Mairi and David into his arms. "Don't be sore-hearted, love. 'Tis sad wee Davie's father cannot be looking after you, but you have here five men to take your part—nay, six, there's Tam! All we can do, we will."

"And we women, too," said Katie.

Undone by their courage and kindness, Mairi turned, still shielded by Andrew's arm, and held out her free hand. Katie took it, drawing Donald and Alai along. Sheila came next with Barry, Gran and Seana. Then Morag moved into the circle with Eileen, Tam, Gavin and Murdo, all embracing, all united.

"We'll have a christening feast," Gran decided. "Bid all the lodge folk saving Madam Hen's-arse and send word to Annie Gordon, too."

"That's too much," Mairi demurred but Andrew rumbled, "Our township will have weddings and funerals and other christenings, but, Mairi, lass, it's good our first feasting will be for your bairn who is in a way the child of all of us."

With that, Mairi could not argue.

On Sunday, in her mother's black wedding dress, Mairi stood in the kirkyard with David in her arms but she was not alone. Her friends and kinfolk, dressed in their best, were scattered around, not in a close knot, but two in one spot, three in another, moving as if by accident to place themselves between Mairi and those passing into the kirk.

These shot curious or scornful glances at her though none of them paused till one much-wattled long-nosed woman gave a fleering laugh and said to her husband, "That's Captain Mac-Donald's hussy and his by-blow."

Barry stepped in front of the woman. "That's Mairi MacLeod of Clanna," he said, and gave the woman such a grim look that she gripped her scrawny husband by the arm and hurried into the kirk.

Ewan and Mrs. Fraser appeared with Lachlann MacKenzie,

whose brawny smith's shoulders strained his Sunday coat. Yellow-haired Simon and Fergus were with him, but Liam, to Mairi's relief, wasn't along. There had never been a fond word between them, but he had often watched her with his young heart in his eyes. She didn't want to see the hurt or contempt that would be there now.

Ewan stopped to talk with Andrew. Mrs. Fraser spoke to Gran and was introduced to the MacKinnons and Gunns, but neither she nor her husband moved on, nor did the three MacKenzies who also met the newer members of Clanna.

As the hour of the service neared, Reverend Guinne came out of the parsonage, a so-called "white house" because of its mortared stones, and stopped in his tracks. Scanning the little crowd around Mairi, he almost hurtled toward Ewan and Lachlann.

"Go your ways in! Go in to the service, Mr. Fraser, Mr. MacKenzie."

The rangy, crinkly-haired gamekeeper smiled blandly. "Och, is it that time, Reverend Guinne? Come along then, Mairi lass, and sit you by my wife on the women's side."

"No!" cried Guinne. "She shall not go in."

"Wheesht, parson!" Andrew boomed, looming over the smaller man, his leathery skin and big hands with rope-corded muscles a marked contrast to the pink-faced minister with his hands softer and less-used than any woman's there. "My cousin has done your bidding—stood outside the kirk while your righteous folk shanked in."

"She was not alone!" cried the minister. "Your whole ilk stood with her—even these folk from the lodge!"

"Aye," cut in Barry, blue eyes aflame. "You'd have no doubt liked it better had folk thrown rocks and spit at her! Well, heark you, sir, such will never happen to one of our township while any of us breathe!"

Guinne took a gasping breath. "Is this true? Is this true indeed?"

"Aye." The voice of all the people of Clanna mixed with Andrew's thunder.

"Have you thought on the hour of your death?" The minister turned to Katie and Sheila. "You are of an age to bear more children. Think you I will christen the offspring of such rebellious folk?"

"We'll seek a minister who will," said Katie. "Much good baptism or the kirk did our Alai when we were driven from our homes and starving."

"You think of your bellies when you should quake for your wicked, wayward souls!"

"It does not help over much to quake, parson," said Murdo drily. "We are preached fire and brimstone and told precious few will squeegle into heaven no matter how we twist and cower. As well stand upright while we can and trust the God who made us has some whit more of justice than you preachers say He does."

The minister glared from one person to another. "Will you go in now?" His voice shook. "Will you go into the kirk and leave this sinful woman here?"

No one moved. Guinne hunched his neck into his shoulders, then thought of something that jerked up his head. Fleshy lips engorged, he stared at Mairi.

"I will tell you how it is, Mairi MacLeod. You have puffed up the hearts of these people. You have made idle music that filled their minds with heathen pride. I will christen your child only when you bring me that harp I have heard of from my friend, Reverend Campbell, that harp for which your vaunting old grandsire went into earthly flames and earlier than need be into those of hell."

Mairi shot Gran a frightened look but she seemed not to hear. "What would you want with the harp?" Mairi asked.

"You will burn it here, before the kirk, as should be done with all pipes and fiddles and such that encourage folk to light-mindedness."

Though she knew many harps and musical instruments had been burned throughout the Highlands and Islands at the ministers' urging, Mairi could scarcely believe her ears. She would put

239

herself in the fire before she would yield up Cridhe who carried the music of their line, Cridhe, for whom Fearchar had perished.

But for her son not to have his name? When Gran's mother was a girl, people believed fairies might steal an unbaptized child and uneasiness still lingered till the rite was performed. Did an unbaptized soul, even a baby, burn in everlasting flames?

Mairi held David closer at that horrible thought. Her knees turned to water. Everything spun about her so that all she could see was Guinne's face, exulting now, sure of his victory. What could she do? Burning Cridhe was unthinkable but so was condemning her child to hell.

Suddenly, she felt the presence of those spirits of the hearth that Gran invoked each night, that had followed from Aosda. They were real, they were love and protection, older than the kirk, older than Christian ways. A vision of the Stones rose before Mairi, where David was begotten, and she thought of the ancient, often-blessed hearth.

She would carry David to the Stones and show him there. She would give him his name that night when Gran smoored the fire. Turning from the minister, she settled David against her shoulder.

Guinne shouted, "You'll bring the harp?"

"I will not."

He trotted along beside her. "Don't think another minister will grant what I refuse till you rid yourself of that devil's plaything! I shall send word of your wickedness through Lewis, yes, and Harris, too—through all the Long Island."

Mairi stopped and looked at him. What an ugly, mouthing creature he was to be sure! What kind of blessing could come from his twisted heart? She thought better of God than that He would punish a baby, or that He willed all music should cease save chanting of plainsong in the kirk. Without music, without their songs, how could people live with kindliness or joy? What else could give them hope and pride in these hard times?

"Don't fret yourself, Reverend Guinne. I will not be asking any of your sort to give my bairn his name."

"Will the devil do it, then?"

"Brigid will and she was sure Christ's foster-mother."

His jaw dropped. "You prate papist idolatry!"

"It is past time for service, sir."

He took a furious breath. "Aye, and I shall give it to those worthy to hear! But you, you shall not enter my kirk till that harp is burned before it."

"Then I will never enter."

"Woman," he cried in a trembling voice, "with every word, you damn yourself! I leave you with your folly!"

He flung away. Mairi turned to her friends, trembling now that it was over. "Go to service or back home. I will come soon but first there is a place where I must take small David."

Gran's face widened in quick understanding. "A good notion, lass. I'll come with you."

"I will go to kirk," said Morag, pale and distressed. "Och, Mairi, child, I'll pray for you! A fearful thing it is, not to have a Christian name to the babe." In a frenzy of dread, she caught Mairi's shoulders. "Lass, lass, can you not give the harp over? What is a thing of wood beside an immortal soul?"

"Cridhe has a soul," said Mairi, but she was moved by Morag's concern, touched that the pious woman had stayed beside her in the kirkyard. "Morag, it comes to me strongly that a prayer at our hearth will bless my son."

Morag groaned. "Lassie! Those are tricks of the evil one!"

"I believe it the goodness of God."

"I will pray," Morag cried despairingly, and made for the kirk where she went in with the MacKenzies and Frasers.

Andrew laid his hand on David's cheek. Through all the commotion and broil, the baby had slept, but he yawned now and gave a squirming stretch. "Shall we walk with you?" Andrew asked.

"Go along and make ready for the feast," Gran counseled. "We'll strike across the moor here, but it will be late ere we come home."

The others started homeward. Mairi didn't have her strength

back fully. Little and dear as her burden was, her arms and back were already weary. "Let me have Davie aways," Gran said. "Och, what a bonnie lad he is! My great-grandson! I doubt I will hold another."

"Of course you will." Mairi flexed her cramped muscles and made a joke. "You'll get to rock Eileen's and Magnus's bairn if she stays loving of him and he keeps his promise."

"I would be blithe of that," smiled Gran, "for Magnus puts me much in mind of my Michael. When he comes, how proud he'll be of our laddie."

"Aye." Mairi felt the twinge that always came when Gran spoke so of Fearchar. In a short time, David began to whimper. Mairi sat on a rock near a thicket of whortleberries in profuse pink bloom and nursed him till he was satisfied. Rested, they journeyed on.

For days now, the skies had been patterned by whooper swans and greylag and white-fronted geese flying north to their summer breeding grounds while kittiwakes, terns, guillemots and puffins flocked to sea cliffs where shags and cormorants had braved the winter. As Mairi and Gran knelt to drink at a burn, a returning greenshank stalked the bog and speared downward with its long gray-blue bill, while above them, a short-eared owl circled upwards, crying, "Boo-boo-boooo!" before suddenly dropping, and clapping its wings below its body.

At last the Stones reared against the dark sea. This brisk April day there was no mist. The waiting pillars with their irregular shapes seemed more than ever a gathering of archaic beings, cloaked and hooded, some graceful women, some gaunt patriarchs, others chunky giant dwarves. Random sun struck jeweled glints from the crystals in the stones, especially from the large nodule in the central megalith. It glowed like a celestial eye.

Gran beside her, Mairi walked down the aisle and stood in the center at a place that emanated power. It might have been on this exact spot that she and Iain had embraced, where their loving had created the child in her arms. She uncovered him as if showing him to a group of revered kinfolk.

This child was got here on Midsummer morn, she told the Mystery long worshiped in this place and surely still existing. I give him the name of David Michael. Accept him. Bless him.

Gran took David then. Crooning soft words Mairi couldn't distinguish, she walked three times sunwise around the great stone. A golden eagle soared upward, tips of its great wings splayed, and as it burst through streaked clouds, light rayed on the ancient circle, gave an incandescent luminance to David's flesh so that to his awed mother, he seemed a being of sun and air.

Gran put him back in Mairi's arms. "He will be a great man of our people. Let us hurry now, or we'll come late to his naming feast."

The dim yellow glimmering from Clanna's rooflights and windows guided them the last stretch over the moor. They were welcomed to a company already merry with Gran's heather ale, whiskey brought by the lodge people, and French claret. This was the gift of Annie Gordon, who sat laughing amongst Simon and Fergus and Liam who vied in filling her cup and fetching her dainties from the waulking table which had been set up on one side of the hearth. It was a relief to see Liam frolicking; his heart wasn't too afflicted.

As Mairi and Gran came in, Sheila and Katie hurried to pour them tea and bring them bowls of barley broth. Mairi, with her tea, retired to the bedroom to feed David. When she emerged and started to put him in the cradle he'd inherited from Seana and Alai, she exclaimed at the presents filling it.

"We brought the cup," said Ewan Fraser. It was silver, much like the one Iain had given Seana. "The spoon's from me," called Annie, "and the bit jersey." Lachlann MacKenzie had made the porringer bound with finely-wrought iron bands. "It has a false bottom with a few dried peas between," he chuckled, demonstrating the rattle. "That way, the laddie can let you know when he craves a second helping."

Mairi hoped she would always have it to give but pushed

away forebodings and praised these gifts, the small wicker chair from Barry, an array of animals carved from driftwood by Murdo and Gavin, warm knit garments from Clanna's women and the real feather pillow from Peggy, the maid at the lodge who had been kind to them. She and Gavin had discovered each other, and in a quieter way were enjoying themselves as much as Annie and her boisterous lads.

The guests had contributed to the gala meal. Besides barley broth, there was cock-o'-leekie soup, finnan haddie, savory bannocks filled with cod livers, potato scones, crowdie, raisin and spice scones, treacle tart, frothed milk, carrageen pudding with raisins, and a basket of sweeties, another gift from Annie.

When David was tucked in his cradle, Mairi tuned Cridhe and played a song Fearchar had composed to his harp.

> "Your voice is sweeter than those of fairy women,
> Healing wounds, luring birds from their nestlings.
> You are waves of the mystic sea, flashing of blades,
> Smile of a mother; dweller among the race of Conn,
> Our homes are roofed with your music, filled with your
> melody . . ."

The harp responded joyfully as if knowing Mairi had refused to yield it to the burning. When Mairi tired, Tam played his pipes, inspiring Murdo to dance a fling on a space no bigger than two peats, pointing his toes and arching feet with great dexterity while the rest cheered him.

Nothing would do then but to clear away the table and dance foursomes to pipe and harp. "On your feet, my pretty little love, on your feet, my darling . . ." Saving Mairi, Morag and Meggie, everyone, including Gran and Eileen, danced at least once but the neat-stepping foursomes were usually Peggy, Gavin, Annie and one of her three young admirers. It was almost dawn when the visitors spread out to sleep through houses and barns and Mairi and Gran were at last alone by the fire.

Gran banked the ashes and arranged the peats in the name of

the God of Life, the God of Peace and the God of Grace while Mairi brought David, still sleeping, to the hearth.

"Thou Sacred Three," prayed Gran. "Save, shield, protect this babe, bless him as David Michael MacLeod in this life, and after death, receive his soul."

Dipping her finger in the ash, Gran touched it to his forehead and then she kissed him. Mairi, finding her way to bed for what was left of the night, thought her son well-christened. If his father had been there, she would have lacked for nothing.

21

Though it seemed she had scarce laid head to pillow, Mairi was up early to milk the cows now grazing on moorland leased from Sir James. Sholma, so long as she had her favorite song, would stand patiently, but Rigga, like the cows Sheila and Katie were milking, needed the plaited hair fetter secured around her hind-legs. Clanna had traded smoked fish to the lodge for grain and fodder, so the animals had come from the byres on their own legs and were starting to gain flesh. Three would calve in July, and six ewes would lamb in June.

Starting toward the row of houses sheltered by the slope and guarded by the broch, Mairi felt as if the humiliation of yester-day was an evil dream. She was glad David had his christening at the Stones and from Gran beside the hearth rather than by Reverend Guinne, that wicked man, who would destroy her people's music and pride.

The men had already made a start on houses for the MacKin-nons and Barry and Sheila who now happily revealed that she was expecting a baby. As soon as the barley was sowed, the men went off to the fishing.

The women joined in the spring washing. That was what Mairi had been doing a year ago when Iain came riding up. Was his limp gone? Had his scars faded? Swept with a surge of longing, an overwhelming hunger of heart and body, she shut her eyes, calling the image of him up behind her eyelids.

Oh, Iain, Iain! Will I really never see you again? Will you never hold our bairn? She glanced toward David, slumbering in a basket while Seana and Alai played on a blanket spread on the heather. Mairi swallowed hard and brushed her tears away. David would grow up the child of Clanna with no one in the township roughening his life. But what a loss that he and Iain would miss the joy each could have given the other.

The kale, seeded in planticrues last spring, was now large enough to transplant to the kale yard, walled to keep out animals. The cabbage-like plant would be a welcome addition in any case but should the potatoes fail—

Mairi glanced toward the lazybeds where some green was already sprouting and felt frighteningly helpless for there was no way to tell if the hopeful infant plants carried the blight, and nothing to be done anyway.

Worry wouldn't help. She concentrated on tamping the soil firmly around each kale stalk, admiring the veins in the crinkly leaves with their finely-toothed edges. Would Catriona have kale and potatoes in Texas? Was Calum there yet? Oh, if only it weren't so far!

The sound of shod hooves penetrated her reverie. Straightening, she saw a rider approaching on a mettlesome chestnut. There was something about him—something familiar—Her heart stopped. No, it wasn't Iain. There was just a likeness in build, in the proud carriage of head and shoulders. She'd never seen this man before.

Someone from the lodge, perhaps, or one of the other leased holdings. As he neared, Mairi was filled with misgiving. This man could almost be a model of Iain in thirty years. The craggy face was weathered brown which gave the light gray eyes an icier hue. Black hair was streaked with white and the mouth was a grim line.

"I would speak," he said in a deep voice, "to a certain Mairi MacLeod."

"You have your wish, sir."

Cold eyes probed her. He said in his excellent Gaelic, "I've heard you have a son."

What concern of his was that? Apprehension filled Mairi. "I do have a son, sir."

"I wish to see him."

Mairi stiffened. He wasn't Sir James, laird of the island! Gentry this stranger was for sure, but he'd no right to make such a demand. "The baby's sleeping, sir."

Dark brows joined over a hawk nose but there was a glint of amusement in the chill gaze. "Would it make a difference if you knew I am Roderick MacDonald, uncle to the Captain Mac-Donald with whom, I believe, you are well acquainted?"

Mairi would have given anything to sink into the ground, and failing that, to run, run far out of sight. If she had to see any of Iain's kin, why must it be when she was smudged and muddy, hair blown wild, bare feet mucky? Why couldn't she be neat and tidy at her loom or spinning wheel?

Roderick MacDonald gave a harsh laugh. "Where's the vaunted Island hospitality? Will you not invite me into your house?"

Mairi fought an inner struggle. Hospitality, the offer of the best one had to anyone who happened by, was a rule so deeply engrained it was second nature but she didn't want this man to see David.

"You are welcome, sir, for the captain's sake," she said at last, glad that everyone except Meggie was busy outside. Washing her muddy hands at the burn, she led the way to the house. "If you're thirsty, I'll fetch you some milk." She paused at the threshold, deeply reluctant to let him see her son. "There's crowdie and cold bannocks."

"Never mind, I've claret in my flask." He glanced impatiently beyond her. "Are you ashamed of this child? Is he deformed, an idiot?"

"Indeed not!" Mairi stepped in and went swiftly to the cradle. David slept with his face nestled against one chubby arm, dark hair clustering on neck and forehead.

He was not a rosy child, but ivory-skinned. Mairi worried, in fact, if he might not be too finely made for the work of a croft. But surely he'd outgrow his look of fragility. There was nothing weak about Iain and David was his image.

"No doubting the father." Was it a trick of light or had the chill eyes softened? "Iain had that very look when I went out to India. By the time I returned, of course, he was grown, and a hard-bitten officer, but I remember how he looked in my sister's arms." Shrugging off the memory, Roderick MacDonald stared at Mairi across the sleeping child. "Since this babe is of my nephew's getting, I'm prepared to take him—pay for his fostering in some worthy home."

When Mairi stood speechless, MacDonald said, "You must see that would be an advantage to you both."

The nape of Mairi's neck stiffened. Wasn't this like the old tales about an evil fairy come to curse a child or steal it away? "I cannot think it an advantage to either of us."

"Come now! How can you hope to find a husband with a bastard at your knee?"

"I could have had two good husbands already," Mairi retorted. "Both would have been kind fathers." What would this haughty gentleman say if he knew Iain had wanted to marry her should there be a child?

"Then why didn't you—?" MacDonald broke off, eyes slitting. "You plan to use him on Iain?"

So outraged that she clenched her hands to keep from slapping those scornful lips, Mairi kept her voice low in order not to wake David. "I could have told the captain about my bairn before he left last autumn. I didn't. I never will."

The disbelieving gaze probed her. "Why? You don't seem so prosperous as to spurn a settlement."

"We've enough."

"What if your potatoes rot as they have in Ireland?"

Wincing even to hear that disaster named, Mairi lifted her chin. "We'd manage."

"You'd starve your child?"

"It's for me to feed my son."

For what seemed eternity, their eyes locked. "You are not what I expected," said MacDonald slowly. "I believe that you love my nephew and it's clear you love your son. Wouldn't you like for him to be brought up a gentleman and educated to the level of his abilities?" His hand swept disdainfully past the view from the window, houses built into the slope with their scatter of lazybeds and the kaleyard to the dark moor and the peat bank. "Don't you want something better for him than this—endless grubbing to barely scratch a living?"

"It can be a good life," defended Mairi. "We have our boat and cropland."

"And when the oats and barley are beat to the ground by storms? Or if the potatoes rot?" He made an impatient gesture. "Even if you feed yourselves, what life is it for Iain's son? You don't seem stupid. It's likely the boy will be intelligent. With proper upbringing, he could become a factor, perhaps even a lawyer."

"A factor? To squeeze rents and bully the poor? I'd rather see him dead."

"You speak foolishly."

" 'Tis only truth. Will you kindly be on your way, sir? I must get back to work."

"You wouldn't need to work if you'd give me the child." MacDonald had the grace to color at her astounded gasp. Quickly, he soothed, "Iain wanted you provided for, young woman. That's how I learned of you."

"He—he didn't tell you—?"

"No. He told his solicitor—who is also mine—to send you the better part of the allowance I've made him. Naturally, Galbraith thought he'd better tell me." With a crooked smile, MacDonald said, "I'm willing now to let Galbraith send the money. To salve your pride, you can know that it's from Iain."

So Iain had taken care for her! Even in this tense moment, that filled Mairi with joy. Still, she set herself between her son and Iain's uncle. "Once for all, you cannot have my bairn."

"Though you couldn't even have him christened?" taunted the man. "What you call love is a marvel of selfishness, Mairi MacLeod."

There was an inch of truth in that. Mairi winced but barred David from his great-uncle's view. Strange to think that this frightening gentleman was indeed blood kin to her son. For a long time, their eyes battled.

She didn't look away, terrified as she was. He was rich, powerful. Was there some way he could forcibly take David? "Think on it," he said at last. "Think of the lad's future. I'll be at the lodge the rest of the week. After that, should you see reason, Sir James's agent knows how to reach me."

He turned, a tall wiry man, just starting to bend a trifle at the shoulders. Mairi hated to ask anything of him, but the words burst from her lips. "Please, sir! Is Iain well?"

"The last I heard. Garrison duty in India with a little skirmishing now and then with hill bandits." He looked at her curiously. "You don't hear from him, then?"

"It's better not."

"I'm glad you've the sense to see that, at least. Good day then, Mairi MacLeod. I shall hope you decide to put the boy above your selfishness."

Ducking his arrogant head, he went out. Mairi tucked the coverings closer around her son. Her fingers shook and she had a hollow feeling in her middle, but it was a blessing to know Iain was all right and that he'd tried to provide for her even when he hadn't known about David.

Roderick MacDonald would never tell him, that was sure. In fact, now she thought it over, she suspected that his main interest in getting David away from her was so she wouldn't have that hold on Iain. Now he was assured that she wasn't in contact with his nephew and had no wish to tell him about David, she thought it likely that the elder MacDonald would leave her in peace.

When Mairi told Gran and the others about her visitor, Gran swore like a sailor—"Thinks he can buy our laddie?" and no one hinted that it might have been wise to turn David over even though they were haunted by fear of what would happen if the potatoes failed.

The men came home long enough to cut peats for five hearth-stones. When the blocks were lifted from the bank and drying, the men sailed off in *Clanna*. Though Roderick MacDonald had troubled her no more and had surely left the island, Mairi couldn't rid herself of uneasiness. It was like walking in the dark while expecting an ambush, the same sort of helpless anxiety she felt while daily scanning the potatoes. During the first of the two June hoeings, the women worked with special care. The plants were so green and luxuriant that Mairi thought the tuber beneath must be sound, too, but how could one be sure?

The ewes had lambed and the little creatures were skipping on the slopes and butting fleecy heads together. A throwback to the ancient Highland sheep, a year-old ewe named Cailan stood out among the other sheep with her short, perky tail and four horns. Mairi hoped when she was old enough to lamb that she'd produce more of her kind. One ewe had died that season, wandering far down the coast to have her first lamb. Eileen found her dying with the lamb's head protruding, tongue swollen and purple. It was sad, but every bit of both animals was utilized, flesh to the salt barrels, hides for shoes, fleece added to that shorn from the living flock.

In spite of heavy storms that set the women praying for their men and all poor folks at sea, the potatoes thrived through the second hoeing and the cows calved safely, adding three heifers and a little dun bull-calf so gentle and affectionate that it was decided to keep him for breeding.

Home again, the men laid up the walls of the new houses. Their tidings from Stornoway filled Mairi with a sense of loss though she wished Annie well. A mainland investor had offered Annie such a good price for her business that she'd sold it and gone off to marry her old sweetheart, Arthur Mitchell, who had an import business in Inverness. She'd left a message for Mairi, wishing her all good fortune and giving her own address in Inverness. The new owner of her business had put a tight-fisted Aberdeen man in charge of her shop.

" 'No credit,' he says, in a nasty, squint-eyed way," Andrew growled disgustedly. "He has more goods than Annie did but it's no joy to trade with him."

"Did you ask if he'll buy our woolens and knit things for what Annie paid?"

"I did not for I was not wishing to talk with him longer than need be." Andrew scowled. "Annie made money at that price so why should he change it?"

"Best to make sure," Mairi said.

That fear of something veiled and waiting roused in her again, but she tried to convince herself it came from regret that Annie had departed without a farewell visit. Probably she'd had a chance to sail quickly with the likelihood of a long wait if she delayed. Mairi hoped Annie would find this marriage so happy that she'd never long for her single independence.

August came with butterflies shimmering green and blue over ling and heather and bees humming as they plundered harebells and marsh gentian. Mairi stepped out one morning and, as had become her habit, glanced first toward the lazybeds.

The plants drooped, looked withered. How could that be? Only yesterday they had been so green and flourishing that she'd believed the blight would surely miss them. Panic rising in her, she smothered a cry and ran to examine the crop.

God, oh God! The plants were blackening, shriveling, as if scorched by invisible fire. She saw not a single healthy bright leaf, not one. She walked the length of each of the five lazybeds, bending to search desperately among the greener foliage.

It seemed to wilt and spoil at her touch. Groaning, Mairi closed her eyes, tried to think. Perhaps under the soil, the

253

potatoes were good. Maybe only the leaves were ruined. Falling to her knees, she dug into the soil so tediously, painstakingly created on the rocks. Her fingers struck slime. A putrid smell sent her retching.

Frantically trying another plant, she exposed small potatoes that oozed stinking fluid. So did another; and another. Mairi buried her face in her hands, not bothering to wipe off the loathsome mess.

Better than two-thirds of their food for the year! After all their work and careful tending! *Oh, Iain!* she wailed inwardly, not to beseech his help, but because she needed to weep in his arms, sob out her fear and disappointment. Even as she sat there, numbed and despairing, she knew she must hold herself together before the others, somehow encourage them through this terrible curse.

Fearchar! Help me! Cridhe's songs would be sorely needed and she, somehow, must find the strength to play them. A tiny edge of hope stirred. Though all the leaves were stricken, maybe some potatoes had escaped. Small as they would be, better to lift them now than chance rot. Oh, please, please! Let there at least be enough for next year's seed.

"What is it, Mairi?" cried Sheila from her door.

At once, Katie appeared in hers and Morag and Gran and Eileen hurried out. Only Meggie remained within, and who was to say on such an evil morning that, isolated in her strange private world, she wasn't the luckiest?

Mairi didn't have to phrase the deadly words. The others ran to the plants and stood dazed. "Och!" wailed Morag, dropping to her knees. "Oh, God of Wrath and Justice, how have we offended Thee? Have we been too prideful, trusting in the fruit of our labor? Have we grown proud-spirited now we have houses and fields again? We are but worms before you, burrowing in the dust—"

"Wheesht!" Gran cut in before Morag could get to what was probably most on her conscience, that the township had harbored Mairi and defied the minister so that the youngest soul in

Clanna was not even a baptzied Christian. "If 'twere for our sins the 'taties failed, why is it some years instead of others? Will you say the folk in Ireland and Belgium sin more than the English, Germans and French? Don't be a daftie!"

Katie ran wildly along the beds, pausing every few steps to peer down the blasted rows for any untouched plant. Sheila clutched her arms against herself, rocking back and forth as if to deny what she saw.

"Will we starve then, Mairi?" Eileen had crept close and watched her big sister with imploring eyes.

Jolted out of her incredulous horror, the hope that it was a bad dream, that it couldn't really be true, Mairi's thoughts raced. It *was* true. They must face it, do what they could to lessen the disaster. But what?

Managing a smile, Mairi drew Eileen close in a reassuring hug. "We won't starve, darling. Don't we have kale and barley and oats growing finely? There's fish in the sea and shellfish and dulse for the gathering, eggs from the hens and milk from our cows. Indeed, we're lucky we have so much else."

Only in starvation would they slaughter the cattle and sheep that supplied them with wool, cheese, butter and milk. Even had they not known each animal by name and cared for them with affection, it would have been wasteful to kill a creature for flesh that, living, could give much more value.

"Aye," nodded Morag. "For that we must praise God."

Forbearing to say that their own efforts had something to do with it, Mairi turned to Gran. "I was only eight when the first blight ruined the potatoes but didn't we find a few good ones? Enough for seed the next year?"

"We did," said Gran and Morag.

Without another word, they all set to work.

22

Digging wide and deep in every hill of putrefying sludge, the women rescued enough small, sound potatoes to plant a fair crop next spring, but there were none for eating. They washed the potatoes carefully, making sure that no fleck of decaying ooze was left on them, dried them, and spread them in straw in the scrubbed potato corner of the granary. Every day, they were checked for any hint of spoiling so that a tainted one could be got rid of before it contaminated others.

"We must be digging silverweed," said Gran. "And drying dulse and laver and carrageen. Praise God, the barley and oats promise finely, as does the kale."

No one said what chilled them—that if any of the other crops failed, it would be a hungry winter, perhaps of near starvation. Trying for cheer, Mairi said, "We're lucky to have the spinning wheels. With them, we can do enough woolen goods to trade for grain and what we're lacking."

They would have to find another buyer, though, one who'd advance them wool. When the men returned with the fearful news that indeed the potato crop had failed throughout the Highlands and Islands, Andrew scowled to remember his encounter with Angus MacBride, the Lowlander who'd bought Annie's shop.

"Says to me, did yon nippety little man, that he'd only pay half what Annie did! Says he can get cheaper goods from the Glasgow factories, dyed with bright colors, not the soft ones Rosanna makes out of God's own heather and other plants! Our wool is old-fashioned, says our little man—not wanted by any but crofters who can't afford to buy it."

The room swam around Mairi. Fear twisted her entrails. She reached out blindly to steady herself against the door. Half what Annie paid would scarce buy wool. Looking at the other women's stricken faces, Mairi thought how they had all counted on selling woolens to tide them through the potato blight.

"Merciful God!" Morag wailed.

"There, lass, 'tis not all bad news." Andrew enfolded her in his great arms and beamed at the rest of them. "We got enough for our fish to buy all the grain we could carry home, and we've good coin left. There's fish in the sea for us to eat fresh or salt for later. Thanks to our boat, we can win more of our living from the sea when the land fails us—and that moolie Lowlander with his cheap dyes and factory weaving!"

For sure, owning their boat was the saving of them this season, especially if their knitted and woven goods no longer had a reasonable market. Mairi wasn't ready to accept this Angus MacBride's opinion, however. How could he, a Lowlander, be so sure of what would sell?

"Andrew, you didn't ask any of the other shopkeepers if they'd buy our things?"

His jaw dropped. He rubbed it sheepishly. "Nay. Belike I should have but I was so flummoxed by wee MacBride that I had no thought but to fill our creels with grain and get home. Any road, Mairi, I've no tongue for the haggling."

"You do not," agreed Murdo. "If I hadn't vowed we'd take our catch to another curer after the next fishing, this one would have charged near double what was agreed on for salt and barrels."

Andrew nodded mournfully. "It's no head I have for twisty-tongued figures and arguments. 'Twas a good thing you spoke up, Murdo. From now on, you'll take charge of our dealings with curers and such.''

"If it suits everyone," said Murdo. "But Andrew, you're our skipper. No one can match you knowing the sea and where we'll find the fish."

Cheered, Andrew smiled. "It's good I have my uses. Perhaps, Mairi, we should send Murdo back to hunt a market for the woolies."

"I'll go myself," Mairi said. "Since I help make the goods, I can talk better with the shopfolk—find out if there's something different we could be making. Or there might be a captain who'd find us a buyer on the mainland and carry our goods there for a share of the profit."

"It's Magnus you mean," said Eileen with a sniff. "Oh, no doubting if you smiled at him, he'd take our wool to America!"

"It would be grand if we had enough fish to make it worth his while to stop here." Barry sighed. "If the 'taties hadn't failed and the winter fishing went well, we'd been talking of building us another boat—letting a crew use it on shares of their catch. But now—Best be glad we can eat!"

Mairi started to nod agreement, then stopped. This was exactly the time to have another boat, with things desperate on the land. If there were a way to borrow— But with Annie gone, they'd do well to market their woolens for any kind of profit.

Still, during harvest, following the scythers as she bound grain or stooked it, the bold idea nagged at her. Another boat would benefit not only Clanna but employ the men of six other families. There were plenty of people around Stornoway who were hard-pressed. Another boat would rescue only a handful of the destitute folk of the island but at least it would save that many. If the township was to do more than live on the barest level during hard times, Clanna needed the means to earn more than subsistence. If she couldn't give little David a better life than that, wouldn't she be selfish to keep him by her rather than allowing his great-uncle to take over his rearing? She'd do that before she'd see David starve, but she had to find a better way.

When harvest was over, along with fishing, a house was started for Sheila and Barry. It would be finished well before their new baby was born. Sound driftwood had been saved for roof timbers and Barry had brought three small precious panes of glass from Stornoway. Stone and thatch cost nothing but labor, thank goodness.

With Tam for company and to help carry home the wool she hoped to get, Mairi set out for town. Reluctantly, she left David. Gran and Meggie would give him milk from a cup, a bit of gruel, and much loving, but she hated to part with him even for two days. How could she bear to give him over to Roderick Mac-Donald?

At the lodge, Mrs. Fraser gave them news over steaming tea and buttered scones. The Queen's government was too involved in financing far-off wars to spare money to relieve the starving Highlanders but it had encouraged local authorities to spend funds allocated for drainage and road building—hire those in the worst need. A few lairds were digging into their own pockets to feed their tenants. Sir James was buying grain and employing men to drain bogs, build roads and improve the Stornoway harbor. They also worked at building his castle and planting thousands of trees on the grounds.

"This island is lucky to be owned by a laird who's rich as well as caring for the folk," said Mrs. Fraser. "For money must be poured into Lewis with not a patch of it coming back. Ewan frets sometimes that we don't have our own bit of land but he's not spoken of that at all since the potatoes failed."

"Crofters be ever at the mercy of weather and blight," said Mairi. "It's cruel to be also at the mercy of lairds." She slipped on her creel, laden with jerseys and fine weaving. As she walked on to town, she saw sheep grazing where people had once lived, passed a huge tract set aside for a deer park.

Even under the comparative benevolence of Sir James, there'd never again be enough cropland and moor grazing for crofters to survive on that alone. They must fish, and for any margin of comfort, they must be able to make and sell something. Woolens were the obvious thing but if indeed there was no market for Gran's beautiful, muted colors—

Besides MacBride's, three shops handled woolens. They sang the same tune as the Lowlander. The mills of Glasgow and other cities turned out cloth dyed with Prussian Blue and other bright colors, cloth that could be bought and sold far cheaper than hand-loomed goods. The spinning wheels that were the pride of Clanna couldn't compete with the speed of machines. It was the same for knitting. Two shopkeepers offered her a little more than half of Annie's payment but after buying wool, the Clanna women would get almost nothing for their labor. There was nothing for it but to search the docks for a captain who'd either buy what Mairi and Tam had brought or sell it on the mainland and bring back part of the money—and what a gamble that would be! Even if she found an honest captain, a ship might sink or the mainland market be as poor as it was here.

Work was still going on at the harbor and castle. Tam glanced at men who were draining a bog in a distant field. "Maybe some of us men can get work from Sir James," he said.

Sir James! Mairi stopped in mid-stride. He would know the fashions in the great cities—know if there was a market elsewhere for Clanna woolens. It was surely to his advantage to have his tenants self-sufficient. If he had money for harbors and roads and drainage and a grand castle, he might be willing to finance another boat for the township.

"Mairi!" cried Tam as she turned abruptly toward the castle. "Where are you going?"

"To see the laird." Her step faltered for a moment. Then she thought of David, of Gran and the others, and flashed Tam a smile. "We're going to make him a proposition, lad."

Mairi knew they shouldn't approach the grand front entrance but she feared that if they went around to the back, servants would never let them see the laird. As it was, they were being roundly berated by a paunchy uniformed servant who opened the door when Sir James himself came down the hall.

"Bring these young folk some refreshment, Talbot," he bade the red-faced man. "We'll be in my study." Smiling at Mairi, the dark-skinned, shrewd-faced owner of Lewis lifted an eyebrow at the creels. "No harp? When I saw you coming, lass, I thought perhaps you'd decided to become my musician. Leave the creels and come rest yourselves while you tell me why you're here."

"Please, sir, I want to show you what's in the creels," said Mairi.

"Woolens? You want to sell some to my wife?"

"Why—that would be grand, sir, though I doubt she'd have use for the jerseys, but I have a matter of business to put before you."

"Do you, indeed?" Mairi didn't care for his amused tone, but at least he seemed disposed to listen. In a few words, gripping her hands behind her to conceal their trembling, she presented her arguments while Tam stared at her as if she'd suddenly changed into someone he didn't know.

Sir James heard her out with inscrutable patience. Then she wondered if he *had* heard for he said, "How is your son?"

"Well, sir." Her breasts, full with milk, ached for the tug of those rosy lips. "He crawls at a gallop and we have to be careful every minute that he's not under our feet."

"According to my old friend, Roderick MacDonald, the child has the look of his father."

Alarmed that the men had discussed David, Mairi said, "That may be. But, Sir James—"

He raised his hand. "Sir Roderick asked me to let him know if you fell into straits that would dispose you to see that the boy would be better off under his care. If you will send the lad to him, I am entrusted with advancing you £500. That is on condition, of course, that you swear to entirely give him up and never

261

make any claims of kinship or trouble Sir Roderick in any fashion."

"I'd think his conscience would trouble him!" Mairi burst out. "Sell my bairn? I'd let his great-uncle take him if he would starve otherwise, and that is all!"

"If you love the child, don't you want him to have an education and rise in the world?"

That stabbed. After a moment, Mairi said slowly, "David is my son, too, sir. Love of our island and sea is in his blood. If he can make his living here, I think he'll be happier than wearing the Queen's uniform or casting up accounts in some crowded city. Our life is a good life."

"When you're not starving."

Mairi flushed. "I'm not begging, Sir James. That's the finest weaving and knitting in our creels. Surely it's to your advantage to help us find a market—surely it's cheaper to lend money for another boat than feed the six men who'd crew it along with their families."

A girl in a ruffled white apron and cap brought in a tray heavy with raisin scones, shortbread, ginger cakes and a steaming porcelain tea pot. With a puzzled glance at Tam and Mairi, she curtsied and withdrew.

"Will you pour, Mistress Mairi?" asked the laird. "I'll have a drop of the hot milk in the smaller pitcher and two spoonsful of sugar."

The tea pot was heavy. Holding it steadied her nervous hand but when she added sugar, her fingers visibly trembled. She knew Matheson noticed. She hoped he'd pick up his cup but he waited. Nothing for it but to hand it to him with her chapped hands, painfully conscious of ragged fingernails and torn cuticles. He thanked her and waited till she'd fixed Tam's cup and hers before inviting them to sit down.

"My wife is a friend of Lady Dunmore, who has, since her husband bought the Island of Harris, encouraged the weavers there and found markets for their tweeds," said Matheson. Tam ate as if he feared the delicious treats might vanish but hungry as she was and toothsome as the ginger cake was, Mairi found it difficult to chew and swallow, intent as she was on what the laird was saying. "I think it likely Lady Matheson would take an interest in promoting your township's products. But before you show her your goods, tell me more about this fishing enterprise."

At least he was hearing her out. As well hang for a sheep as a hare. "Sir James, you're giving employment to many to keep them from starving. If you'd lend the township enough for barrels and salt as well as another boat, we should be able to get a captain to stop for our fish."

"You have not overmuch cropland as it is. Where will these six new families live?"

"We can build more lazybeds. If they have beasts, perhaps you, sir, would grant them moor grazing. If your wife will help us sell our woolens, the women of the new families could join us in weaving and knitting."

"You mean that you would share with them—after you've borrowed the means from me. God knows this island needs no more landless folk. That's the trouble now—too many people."

Mairi felt a hot tide rush to her face. "Ah, but not too many deer in your parks, sir, or too many sheep on the land taken from crofter folk—the best lands on the island!—and leased to sheep farmers! Nor were there too many folk when the lairds needed swords at their call, or when kelp brought in fortunes—" Horrified at her temerity, she strangled the bitter words. Whatever hope there'd been, she'd dashed it now.

"I led no clan to Culloden," returned Sir James equably. "I made not a shilling from kelp. In truth, lass, this island bids fair to cost me tenfold its rents, including those from deer parks and sheep farmers. I shall continue to urge emigration and pay the way of those who're sensible enough to prefer owning their own large farms in Canada or America to scrabbling here on a few rented acres." The shadow of a smile lit his somber eyes. "But you aren't sensible, are you?"

"I will never leave the island—nor will my grandfather's harp."

263

"And you would liefer play that harp in a peat-smoked black house than in my castle."

"The songs belong to my folk, Sir James, and I belong with them."

"You ask for much, Mairi MacLeod. It seems hard that the laird of Lewis should have to beg for a song."

"Indeed, sir, I will gladly play for you and your lady—but afterwards I must ever go home to Clanna."

"I have your word you'll entertain my guests when I send for you?"

"I cannot promise they'll be entertained, especially if they don't have the Gaelic, but I will come, Sir James, so long as I'm not in the middle of work I cannot leave."

"So my music must wait on harvest or planting or who knows what?"

"You will find music with us whenever you come, sir, for there are songs for planting and reaping, churning and grinding, weaving and waulking—music with all we do." She thought hard, trying to make him understand. "Songs are woven into our lives like part of the warp and weft. And our lives are woven into the web of this island."

His mouth bent down. "As mine is not, though I've bought it?"

"Lewis has changed lairds many times, Sir James, but my folk raised the Stones at Callanish. Time out of mind, our bodies have turned into Lewis earth. We are rock and soil of this island." She would make a song of this, a song for her people— and him and his guests, too, if he sent for her.

Her heart thudded sickeningly in her ears. Had she been too bold? She went limp with relief when at last he smiled. "I'll instruct my factor that he's to advance to your township the sum needed for another boat and salt and barrels. You'll need lumber to build a quay and curing shed. Interest on these funds will be 3% and the township has three years to pay. Also, the six new crewmen may each have four acres of arable land—if they can find it along the coast—and graze on the moor two cows or their equal in sheep, lambs or calves. They will pay the same rent as the rest of Clanna. And you need wool for weaving and knitting."

Mairi's head whirled at the enormity of the undertaking and the strange words. Interest! Percents! But any road, Clanna would be well free of the curers who often managed to keep fishermen in debt to them so that they were never able to own their boats or find a better market for their catch. Matheson must have seen her apprehension. "No gain without risk, lass. Do you want to lay the matter before your men?"

That would make her feel better but it would take more time. There was none to be wasted if the men were to build another boat in time for the winter fishing. Feeling as if she took a heavy load on her shoulders, she said, "The folk of Clanna are willing to leave business to me."

"You'll sign an agreement?"

She nodded, terrified. "But—what if the fishing's poor? Or a boat wrecks as my grandfather's did? What if we can't pay?"

"You can lay hands on £500 any time you choose to."

Mairi recoiled. "Only to save his life would I let David go!"

"You have something else I'd accept as collateral." When she frowned her puzzlement, he said, "Collateral is something of value that secures a loan. It's forfeit if the loan isn't repaid."

"You'd take our beasts and furnishings? Or the boats?"

"No. Your harp is very old. I've a taste for antiquities. Should your township default on the loan, I'd count the harp full payment."

Risk Cridhe! The pride of ancient forebears, the harp Fearchar had died to rescue? It was almost as unthinkable as using David for surety. Looking straight into Matheson's dark eyes, Mairi spoke through a tight throat. "Were you the devil, sir, and we struck a bargain, I'd liefer stake my soul than my harp."

He smiled. "Oh, you could keep your harp—if you came to play it in my castle."

She groped for words. "It is being with my people that gives Cridhe her soul. If she leaves us, she will be only wood and strings."

"Nevertheless, will you agree that the harp secure your loan?"

Cridhe, Fearchar, forgive me. For myself I never would. This is for our people, that they may live on the island. "If we cannot pay you, the harp is yours," Mairi said.

Sir James nodded and pulled a bell rope. "The agreement will be prepared while you show Lady Matheson your woolens."

Lady Matheson, a small dark-haired woman with a plain, kindly face, admired the weaving and exclaimed over the soft colors. "I'm sure my friends in Edinburgh and London would buy all the cloth you can make as long as it is of this quality," she said through the Gaelic-speaking maid who'd brought the Mac-Leods to an exquisitely furnished room where the laird's wife was engaged in some kind of fine needlework. "You say your grandmother concocts the dyes from heather, lily roots, lichens and other such substances? That will appeal to those who like the unusual. As for the jerseys, my husband's agent can sell them to mainland shops our estate patronizes."

"You are kind, my lady," Mairi said, her joy overcast by fear that Clanna would have to wait for payment till the goods sold in far-off cities.

For all her wealth and rank, there was a common-sense air about Lady Matheson. Through the maid, she said that Sir James's factor would pay now the best price Mairi had ever received for comparable work. There would almost certainly be additional money from cloth sold to society friends.

"I would far rather encourage self-sufficiency than give money to parish relief, though I do that, too," ended Lady Matheson. With a smile, she resumed her chair and needlework.

The maid led them down the stairs and through halls to the first room they'd entered. Sir James looked up from a book, nodded with satisfaction at the maid's report, and instructed her to unload the creels. A thin bespectacled young man with flaming red hair brought in a paper which he presented to Sir James with a bow. At a word from the laird, he bowed again and disappeared.

Rising, Sir James moved to a polished table where a silver pen lay by a silver inkstand. "Our contract is written in Gaelic," he said. "Read it before you sign—a good rule always, lass."

Some of the words were unfamiliar but the meaning was clear. Mairi's heart stopped, then beat sledgingly when she saw the words pledging Cridhe should the township fail to repay the loan by three years from this date. Apart from rare letters to Catriona, Mairi had no occasion to twist her fingers to writing. Though she took great care, her name sprawled across the whole lower half of the page and she smudged ink on the paper and her hand.

It was done. She felt she had wagered her soul. But when she and Tam left the castle, the silver fetched by the red-haired man made a soft, lovely chinking in her creel, and it was not borrowed, but earned.

23

Rather than spend any of that precious coin on an inn, after buying wool and other necessaries, Mairi and Tam started home. As she walked, she knitted on a sleeve of Tam's new jersey. When night settled deep and thick, they found a protected slope and made a nest of the wool that filled their creels. Tam chortled as they munched on bannocks and cheese.

"Wasn't it grand, the way that muckle-mouthed shopkeeper looked at our coin when we stepped in to buy? Fair flummoxed he was that Lady Matheson herself had bought our woolies!" He hugged himself. "Och aye, he was ready enough to pay a good price then!"

Mairi laughed, too, but her joy at Lady Matheson's patronage dimmed when she remembered that pledge she had signed, then flooded back with such wonder and pride that she felt like weeping or shouting. There would be a second boat—a living for six more families—barrels and salt so that Clanna would be free of the cheating Stornoway curers. Surely between woolens and fishing, the loan could be repaid within three years.

Thinking of David, she let herself dream. A harbor below the broch—half a dozen good boats with her son the skipper of one of them, bringing in fish to Clanna's own curing station. On the moor, Sholma and Rigga's progeny and dainty, four-horned sheep like Cailan among heavier black-faced ones. Fields of ripening barley and oats, ample kaleyards, big patches of carrots and peas so there'd be food if potatoes failed.

Nestled against her, Tam said sleepily, "Someday I'll have a ship, Mairi. We'll carry our own fish to market, and bring back things to sell."

Her instinctive wish to shield him from disappointment, from dreaming what couldn't be attained, made her start to caution him, but she swallowed the dampening words. If he dreamed, he'd try. If he tried, he might succeed. After all, who could have guessed two years ago that a huddle of crofters burned out of their homes would now be a thriving township with a boat and the women earning, too? Clanna folk would eat a lot of fish and seaweed that winter but they could sustain not only themselves but the families of a second boat crew.

Still, there was a dark undercurrent beneath the sparkling flow of Mairi's exhilaration. Should a time come when she couldn't provide decently for David, she'd have no choice but to send him to his great-uncle. How could she bear that, to lose her son as well as Iain? And if the loan couldn't be repaid, how would she live without Cridhe? What was that word James Matheson had used? Collateral. The true collateral for the loan was her heart and her soul.

Two extra men were working on Barry and Sheila's house. Someone from the lodge? Mairi gave a glad cry as the men dropped thatching and ran lightly to meet her. "Lucas! Paul!" Embracing them, she sobbed and laughed at once. "Look at you, brown as those hill tribesmen Calum told us about!" She gazed at her two sturdy, broad-shouldered cousins, Barry's younger brothers. "You're not lads anymore! Full-grown you are!"

"I should hope so. We've a-plenty of the Queen's medals though not so much of her coin." Lucas had rust-brown hair and hazel eyes. At twenty-three a year older than fair, blue-eyed Paul, he was also heavier. "Men we had better be for we've brought home wives."

Andrew, hurrying up behind his sons, looked an anxious

question. Mairi beamed at him and the others gathering round. They needn't know what she had pledged—only that there'd be money. "You've come at a good time, lads. For the laird will lend us money for a boat you can help crew—and there'll be money for salt and barrels, Andrew! Even for a quay and curing shed!"

By then, everyone had assembled, swarming from wherever they'd been working. Proudly, Lucas and Paul brought their wives forward. Sisters they were, Paul's small dark-haired Rose looking no more than sixteen while Lucas's Barbara was about Mairi's age. Both girls had tawny eyes that put Mairi, with a pang, in mind of Catriona, but Barbara had yellow hair and was nearly as tall as her husband. Orphaned three years ago after their family was evicted from their Sutherland croft, they'd been working in a Glasgow factory when Lucas and Paul rescued them from the insults of some drunken soldiers when the sisters were on their way home to the one-room hovel they shared with a dozen former neighbors.

"Lucas feared I wouldn't want to leave Glasgow for a croft," said Barbara with a merry laugh. "When it was near time he was mustered out, I had to ask him if he wouldn't like to marry."

"I knew Aosda was lost," said Lucas defensively. "And though Captain MacDonald told us you were making a brave new start, how could we guess there'd be a proper township with moor grazing and croplands as well as a boat?"

"Is Captain MacDonald well?" Mairi tried to keep her voice steady but it treacherously faltered.

"It's Major MacDonald now," said Paul. A shadowing of his blue eyes told her he knew who David's father was but his gaze was sympathetic. "A good officer—more careful of his men than himself. He sent his greetings."

Greetings! It was almost worse than no message at all. Did he no longer care, or did he think it dangerous to send a kind word? Stabbed deep, Mairi flinched but quickly forced herself to kiss Rose and Barbara and tell them how welcome they were before she gave the good news about Lady Matheson's interest in Clanna woolens.

"We can weave and knit." Barbara glanced happily at Lucas. "I'm glad we can earn a bit and not just be eating our heads off."

Rose nodded, with an adoring look at Paul. "We saved our pay," he said with a teasing grin at his older brother. "Mostly, that is. Outside of what we need to set up housekeeping, all we've saved can go toward the boat."

"Aye," said Lucas. "And we know where to find the rest of our crew." Laughter faded from his hazel eyes and he gazed across the moor toward Aosda. "Truth is, we could man a fleet with lads who went for soldiers because that was supposed to keep their folk safe in their crofts. Plenty of them went home to burned thatch—found their families gone over the waters or slaving in Glasgow. Neil MacAskill got himself wounded dragging me off the battlefield. His township's been cleared on South Uist. When he heard it, I told him he must come to us after he'd found his family. That was taking a lot on myself but I reckoned if there was no room for him here, there was none for me."

Andrew dropped a great hand on each returned son's shoulder. "Praised be the good God, there's not only room for him. He's needed, along with three more men. Now we'd better hurry with Barry and Sheila's house! We have a boat to build before the winter fishing!"

An Clanna made several runs to Stornoway to fetch seasoned wood for the boat. On the last trip, *The Selchie* followed the small craft like a whale with a calf, anchored as close as was prudent, and offloaded barrels, salt and window panes—enough for Barry and Sheila's house and the one that would shelter some of the expected newcomers. Lucas and Barbara would live with Andrew and Morag, Paul and Rose with Barry and Sheila. There was time to raise one more roof and already peats enough to warm its hearth that winter.

The last barrel was stowed out of the weather in the broch

passageway till a shed could be built nearer the harbor. As Mairi came from milking Sholma, Magnus loomed between her and the house. Taking the foaming bucket, he gave her a long look from those mist blue eyes.

"So, Mairi. Here you are, Mother of Clanna, and the township growing in spite of famine." His voice hardened. "What surety did you give Sir James for all of this? I mind he had a fancy to your harp—and you."

Did he think her a whore because she'd borne Iain's child? Icily, Mairi said, "That's none of your concern, Magnus Ericsson." Then she was forced to remember all he'd done for them—rescued both her brothers, and she flushed. "I'm sorry for that word, Magnus. You've a right to know, good friend that you are."

His mouth twisted as he heard the details. "I like it not, your being so beholden to Matheson. Let me raise the money to pay him, lass, along with his pesky three percent."

It was tempting. Magnus would never evict them. That was the trouble. "We can't let you go in debt on our account," Mairi screwed up courage to speak straight and honest as he deserved. "Magnus, if you haven't forgot me—"

"Forgot?" He stared out at *The Selchie*, rising and falling gently with the foam-topped waves. "Would I be here, Mairi MacLeod, were you not grown into my heart?"

"I'm sorry—"

"I won't beg you." He slanted her a glance that made her keenly aware of him. How good it would be to rest in his arms, surrounded by his loving strength. She knew Magnus's softness for small beings. A kind father he'd be to David. But, oh, Iain! And even if she could respond as a wife to Magnus, he deserved better, deserved the best.

She tried to say something of this but he hushed her with a motion. "It would seem I must bide for Eileen."

"That wouldn't be fair—to her or you."

"I'll worry for myself. As for Eileen—she is blood of your blood, Mairi. I will love you in her so well that she'll have no

272

cause, ever, to envy another woman." At Mairi's frown, he said, "Rest easy, lass. I'm no ogre to trouble little girls or bind them in their foolishness. No word of this she'll hear from me till she's sixteen and not then if she's taken with some laddie near her age."

"Magnus—"

He tilted his head jauntily. "Well, *ceann cinnidh*, head of the clan, let us strike a bargain, since it'll be to my advantage to have well-to-do kindred."

"What bargain?"

He laughed at her wariness. "Like a cat you are, Mairi, looking every which way as you come to a door, acting as if you expect to be murdered!" He set down the bucket by the bench that held the milk things and watched as she strained it into pans where Sholma's thick golden cream would rise. "I want to see crofters stay on their land. Already I have agreements with several crews that own their boats. For a percentage of what I sell their catch for, I'll carry the fish to the mainland. Maybe some will do well enough to buy barrels and salt next time. It's safe to reckon I can get you twice what the curers pay. How does a one-third share for me sound to you?"

It sounded wonderful after years of usually winding up in debt to the curer. "This is a matter for the crews," Mairi said. She spoke soberly but couldn't resist giving the empty bucket a gleeful flourish. "Come in and sup with us, Magnus. I think you have more partners!"

Andrew was dumbstruck but Lucas cast a keen eye up and down the length and breadth of the Orkney captain. "How will we know you're keeping only a third?"

He subsided under indignant shushes and a litany of what Magnus had done for them. "Give over," he said at last, chuckling and pretending to shield his rusty head. "I see I'd better have accused St. Columba!" He held out his hand to Magnus. "I'm fresh from the army, man. You won't grudge that I was trying to look after my folk."

Andrew cleared his throat. "We will hear ayes for those favoring Magnus's offer."

The walls gave back the glad chorus. They settled down to barley soup and kale, scarce missing the potatoes. After they had eaten, Magnus asked for a tune since he must leave in the morning. Lucas got his fiddle, Tam his pipes, and Mairi led the songs with Cridhe, truly her people's heart.

Barry and Sheila—and Paul and Rose—had scarcely warmed the hearth of their new house when Sheila's baby was born on the dawning of a day as fair as the child, unusually fine weather for a late November day. The infant's hair was bright silver and her eyes were that deep fathomless newborn color between brown and blue. She came into the world with as little trouble and pain to her mother as possible and seldom cried. Two-year old Seana and Alai were entranced with her and vied to croon at or rock her if she started to fret though they didn't abandon David who, at eight months, was pulling himself up. He still fell every time he tried to take an unsupported step but he got lots of wobbly-legged practice as Seana or Alai held his hands and encouraged him till he collapsed with a merry gurgle.

Grand playmates the children would be, four of them with only two years between oldest and youngest. Growing up with cousins and other Clanna children, David would never feel a need of brothers and sisters. Or a father; all the men treated him like their own. It was Mairi who ached when she saw Iain's face in her son's, who would have given years off her life for them to have known each other.

Not for a flash had she regretted having David. He was the wonder conceived at the Stones in a covenant more binding than words in a church. He was the mingling of souls, hearts and bodies. She could have no other man, ever, but she prayed that David would never come to grief because of this, that he would be happy in the life of sea and moor and not hanker after far places where his birth could shame him. When his tiny fingers kneaded at her breast and his cheeks dimpled to draw in her milk, Mairi felt as if the essence of her flowed with it. She melted with the sweetness of nourishing him, of providing for this short, magic time, all he needed to thrive, of being for him the most important person in the world. This couldn't last long. She knew she must take care not to let the invisible cord between them become a strangling snare for him.

He was the joy of her life, her perfect song. Beside that, what did it matter that folk beyond Clanna chattered about her, or that she couldn't go to Caitlyn's christening? This did cause her pangs—was David, named at the Stones, safely Christian? But the God she saw on the moors, in waves, sun and wind, had nothing to do with Reverend Guinne and his small chapel. That God, the Shining One of the Stones, would surely protect the child got in that ancient circle.

If only there was a way to hear now and again that Iain was alive and well—only that. Mairi was sometimes tempted to appeal to Sir Roderick to send her that word through his factor, but she was afraid to remind him of her existence. If he set his mind to it, who knew what a wealthy, influential man could do, especially since he was a friend of James Matheson.

Murdo, who'd been elected skipper of the new boat, painted *Brighde* or Brigid on the graceful prow of the finished craft, and that same day the hearthstone was tamped in place in the new house set snugly into the slope beneath the broch. One small window squinted from beneath the thatch toward the harbor and the other faced the moor.

"A proper township we're getting to be," said Barry, smiling at Sheila who cuddled tiny Caitlyn while Seana laughed from her father's shoulder. "Five houses! By the time each couple has a home, Clanna will be bigger than Aosda—"

His voice trailed off. Aosda had been home to Fearchar, Gran, Catriona, Adam and Kirsty, the twins. Calum, too. But to children born at Clanna—Seana, Alai, Caitlyn, David and the rest who'd spring from young parents—to them, Clanna would be home and Aosda only one of Cridhe's songs. It made Mairi feel very old, though she would only turn twenty that April of 1847.

A few days later the new house was filled and room was shared out in the other homes, for Lucas and Paul's friends, the MacAskills, arrived with others evicted from their village, all their belongings in the creels on their backs.

Thinking of mouths to be fed, Mairi watched the straggling procession with a kind of horror till the burdened shapes turned into people and then she thought, *Of course we can feed them. Their men will make up the crews. The women will weave and knit. There's dulse and fish and we'll buy the grain we need.* She hastily put more kale in the barley soup, set water on for tea and hurried out to meet them.

The MacAskill brothers, in their thirties, were small, wiry black-haired men with gray eyes. Neil's wife, little son, and aged parents had all died of exposure after they were forced from their croft. Gerald's wife, yellow-haired Marta, was knitting as she trudged toward Clanna but thrust her work into her creel to embrace Rose and Barbara who were the first to reach their kin and former neighbors. Molly, about twelve, and Noreen, perhaps ten, had their father's dark hair and their mother's clear blue eyes.

Malcolm Fergusson had dark hair salted gray and piercing black eyes. His wife, hazel-eyed Flora, who'd also been knitting as she walked, was as willowy as her gypsy-looking daughter, Margaret, whose green eyes slanted upwards in a heart-shaped face. Margaret must have been sixteen but there was something about her silvery laughter that made her seem even younger than the MacAskill sisters.

"Margaret's simple," Rose whispered to Mairi. "Flora says she was the cleverest little girl that ever was till she nearly died with fever. Sweet and biddable she is, but any man who'd marry her must be ready to treat her as the oldest of his children."

From the way Gavin watched the girl, Mairi reckoned that man would not be hard to find. Flora's brother, the final crew member, Allan Bailey, was a broad-shouldered tall lad of about Mairi's age. He watched her with shy brown eyes in a way that made her feel old enough to be his mother and a little sad that this was so. The newcomers were welcomed in and fed. Weary though she was, Flora, after a bowl of soup, went to build a fire on the hearth of her new home, for it was quickly agreed that the Fergussons would share that house with Neil and Murdo. Gerald, Marta and their daughters would share the Gunns' house and Gavin and Meggie would move in with Andrew, Morag, Lucas and Barbara. All of them were used to crowded quarters and so grateful for shelter that not even Morag complained.

After what Barry laughingly dubbed "the Clanna fleet" was off fishing, the women tended the cows in the byres, brought in the sheep in the worst weather, and slowly, steadily added to the many-hued store of knitted and woven goods piled at the foot and back of Gran's big box-bed. Spinning wheels hummed, shuttles flew, and needles flashed, the new-come women happy in knowing that far from being a burden, they were producing cloth and clothing that would sell for a good price. Now that Eileen had girls near her own age, Molly and Noreen, for company and competition, she strove to improve her skills and old Meggie was teaching them how to weave the tiny checks and overchecks.

Thirteen womenfolk now instead of six, they cared for the children, sang at their work, and got to know each other while they waited for the boats to pull up at the fine new quay and unload their catch in the shed. Only Margaret was dubious help apart from keeping the wee ones entertained. She could weave and knit passably but quickly tired of any monotonous task and often escaped outside to roam the moor or run along the beach.

"Sometimes I think the fairies changed her when she had the fever," Flora said. "Never till then was she wild like this. What's to become of her only the good God knows for a man might as well marry the breeze in the heather." She shook her neat brown head. "My brother Allan's a good lad. I just have to pray that when Malcolm and I are gone, he'll give Margaret hearthroom."

Mairi glanced protectively at David. It was hard to imagine

life without him. Yet wouldn't it be tragic to watch him grow in body while his mind remained a child's? She hoped the look Gavin bent on Margaret at first meeting meant what it had hinted. He was old enough to cherish a child-wife—and if they had children, why, there was all of Clanna to help just as they had with David. That was one of the best things about what amounted to one large family; you shared each other's joys and burdens. Mairi knew she was depended on for crucial decisions but she also knew that her strength sprang from her folk and all that bound them together. A sad thing and lonely it must be to fare alone as some did, even if you were rich and at no one's mercy.

"Don't fret over Margaret," she told Flora. "She'll have a home here."

Flora gazed at Mairi. A sigh escaped her. She relaxed and smiled. "Och, I believe that."

When the laden boats came into harbor, old Meggie and Gran looked after the children while the other women and girls hurried down to take charge of the fish, silver-gray mounds of cod and ling. All of them had gutted fish, but Barbara and Rose had worked at a curer's and showed how to pack the washed, cleaned fish, graded according to size, in barrels between layers of salt. Next day the fish had settled enough to have more added, and after ten days, each barrel was filled again and sealed, ready to be taken to the mainland.

Buffeted and chilled by the wind, though the shed at the end of the quay was open on only one side and sheltered from the worst of it, the women kept a fire going under a kettle of tea so they could warm themselves when their fingers were too numb to use a knife. Their hands chapped and split but the salt that stung these cracks also kept them from festering. Every barrel they packed was money for Clanna, though, and they kept plenty for cooking fresh and drying in the peat smoke of the houses.

Mairi rubbed Gran's ointment into her sore hands after a stint of packing, but they were still so fissured and rough that she hated to touch David with them, and it was several days before she could weave, knit or spin without continually snagging the yarn on crusting edges of skin.

"Our fingers will be as cured as the fish," said Eileen, grimacing as she rubbed in the ointment which had a sting of its own. "I hate being thirteen! Everyone treats me like a little girl—until it's time for work. Then I'm a woman!"

"You'll grow up soon enough," Mairi said dryly.

"Magnus is already grown! I—I'll just die if he marries someone before I'm old enough for courting."

"There are other young men."

"That doesn't seem to count with you," Eileen said with a pert wrinkle of her nose. "You wouldn't have Gavin. Now Allan Bailey moons after you the way Liam Fraser used to, but you sail by him with no more of a smile than you give anyone. Will you be an old maid, Mairi?"

"That'll give me more time to rock your babies," Mairi teased though it smarted to be lectured by her young sister. Was that what everybody said behind her back?

She went out to cut kale to go in the pot with fish. A horseman was approaching, wraithlike in the overcast, misty day, sitting tall on a big black horse. Something about the set of the head and shoulders— She drew in a breath that pierced her like a blade.

Iain? Catching up her skirts, she ran past the kaleyards toward the moor, faltering when she saw that though the rider's posture was near Iain's, it was different. She halted, peering through the rainy mist and her heart plunged and twisted like a fish trying to escape the hook.

It was Roderick MacDonald. There was no way, none at all, that his coming here could bode well.

24

The gray eyes, so like Iain's but without that inner light, gazed somberly at Mairi from the long, weathered, hard-jawed face. "Iain's son is well?"

"Very well, sir." Sir Roderick looked—sad. Cold of another sort than that of the bitter day penetrated to Mairi's vitals. Wrapping the shawl tighter to hide her shivering, she spoke through wooden lips, "The captain—I mean—the major?"

"Missing in action. Presumed dead." The words were dry flakes, all feeling gone, as if the aging man had probed and studied them till they were worn thin.

An involuntary cry ripped from Mairi's throat, quivered between them like an exposed part of her body. For the first time, MacDonald seemed to really look at her. "I'm sorry to distress you, young woman, but it's best you know."

He hadn't come on her account but in the black swirling that tried to suck her beneath it, Mairi raised the image of David and clung to it till the world stopped rocking and she could make out Sir Roderick's face. "Yes, sir. I'd rather know. Where—where did it happen?"

"Afghanistan. A skirmish with hill tribesmen. His body wasn't found. There were no survivors but his horse was dead and there was blood on the saddle. One hopes the Afghan women didn't get to him." The strained voice trailed off.

Calum had said what the women did to wounded enemies. The blackness swirled again. Struggling against it, Mairi whispered, "Will you come in, sir, and have some tea or soup to warm you?"

"Last time," he said with a bleak smile, "You didn't want me under your roof."

Let her not cry in front of him. "You're cold now."

Mairi set off for the houses nestled in the slope beneath the broch. The lazybeds of which she was so proud, stone edgings curved to follow every bit of soil, or laid out in narrow oblongs, suddenly looked to her like graves. But Iain couldn't be dead! She would have felt it, known it in her bones. Only perhaps it was different when someone died so far away; that soul might not find the low road home, the underground path traveled by spirits. She desperately needed to weep and lament but she must keep from that till Iain's uncle was gone.

Gran was next door brewing a soothing syrup for Seana who had a cough. Eileen had taken David to play with Alai while she, Molly and Noreen giggled over their knitting. MacDonald tethered his horse out of the wind between the houses and bent his white-streaked hair to follow Mairi inside.

"Where's the child?" he asked as she stirred up the fire and put the kettle on.

She didn't want the man to see David yet under the circumstances how could she refuse? "I'll fetch him, sir."

Annoyed at being caught up from the sheepskin where Alai was marching a toy calf after a cow, David stiffened his sturdy little legs against her in protest and his lower lip began to tremble. "I—I'll tell you all about it later," she apologized to Katie and Marta.

Quieting David with nonsense, holding him warm inside her shawl, Mairi hurried back. He wore a long wool gown over his linen one and she was glad they were clean and smelled of the lady's bedstraw she kept in the chest with his things. Hushing at the sight of the big strange man, David stared at him.

Sir Roderick proffered a finger. David struck at it and buried

281

his face against Mairi's neck. "He's cross because I took him from his play," Mairi said.

"A boy needs a temper." MacDonald sounded more pleased than discomfited as he sat down cautiously in Gran's wicker chair. "He's the picture of Iain at that age."

Settling David on her hip, Mairi poured boiling water over the tea in the crockery pot and put out mugs. "There's crowdie, sir, if you're hungered, and barley broth."

"Thank you, lass, I have not much appetite."

Nor did she but the hot tea melted the edges of the deep, still cold within her, quelled the nausea writhing in the pit of her stomach. He drank the brew so quickly that she marveled that he didn't scald his throat. She poured for him again and sat on a bench. Head on her breast which was full of milk for him, David watched his great-uncle suspiciously from the corner of his eye. Mairi longed to feed him, comfort herself with meeting his need, but she couldn't in front of this gentleman. She had heard, though it seemed incredible, that ladies didn't suckle their babies, but turned them over to wet-nurses.

"Your township has grown," Sir Roderick said. "But you seem to be eating in spite of the potato blight."

"We have another boat. And Lady Matheson is sure she can find markets for our woolens."

He nodded. "Yes. And you owe for that boat and quay lumber, and salt and barrels."

It made her feel vulnerable that he knew their private business. Why wouldn't he be gone? She needed to weep for her lover and feel their son's lusty tugging at her breast. "Indeed, sir, you seem to know our affairs."

He had dropped his cloak on the chair but from his coat he brought a piece of paper, held it for her to see. Before it blurred, she saw her signature at the bottom. The agreement with Sir James.

"I will burn this in the fire," said MacDonald, "if you will let me bring up Iain's son." He raised his hand. "Hear me out. I will adopt the boy, make him my heir. And you may stay with him, as his nurse, till he's of an age for school."

Gentry! They thought they could buy anything—and the pity was, in famine times they almost could. Mairi wanted to rage at him but she thought of Iain and subdued her wrath before she trusted herself to speak.

"I hoped we could treat each other with charity since we both loved your nephew, sir. I thought I was plain before but I'll say it again. I will not sell my son."

"That's not how to think of it, girl." MacDonald leaned forward. "Can you think I'd offer to adopt any crofter woman's son, blood of mine though he might be? You love the child. Do you love him enough to open the great world to him?" His voice dropped. "Do you want to see him hunch over the *cas-chrom*, root like a hog to find a few sound potatoes in the rotting ones? Will you knit his name in his jersey so you'll know his body when it washes up on shore—if it's found at all?"

Was she wronging David? Should she let him go? For a moment, she wavered. Then Iain's face rose before her. She remembered how he had spoken of his uncle's world—how he had enjoyed helping with thatch and lifting peats, how he found peace at their hearthstone.

"David will grow up with all Clanna to love and teach him. He'll belong here, not float like a chip on the ocean." She bit her lip but couldn't hold back the words. "It was ill-done of Sir James to let you have our agreement."

MacDonald got to his feet, head nearly touching the soot-blackened inner thatch. "He reckoned, as any sane person must, that you'd be glad to see your son inherit his father's place." As if he still could not believe her refusal, Sir Roderick spoke very slowly. "I am not offering only an education and better opportunities. Your son would possess my lands and wealth."

Mairi said nothing. MacDonald stared at her. "You're mad." She didn't answer, with all her might willing him to go.

The eager, almost pleading look vanished as if it had never

been. With a closed, haughty face, he rolled the paper, dropped it on the smoldering peats. "That's all *your* son will ever have from me. Not that this loving family you prize so highly won't be deep in debt again long before the boy's old enough to understand, if you'd tell him, what you threw away when he was too young to choose."

Cold wind rushed in as he went out, fanning the crumpled paper into a short, small blaze. Stunned, Mairi watched it fade into ash.

They didn't owe for the boat, barrels and salt? No one could take away the shed and quay? Was a wisp of smoke all that remained of a debt they'd have done well to pay with three year's fishing and weaving?

There was relief in it for Mairi, but no joy. It was as if fate, in an unholy bargain in which she'd had no voice, had given Clanna this grace in return for Iain's life. She cuddled David to her breast. Only when he was falling asleep, replete and satisfied, did she put him in his cradle and run out on the moor where she could weep and keen and call Iain's name.

The thought of David brought her home at last. Gran was making bannocks while Eileen tried to give a fretful David milk from a cup. He stretched out his arms to Mairi, greeting her with almost words.

As she fed him, she gave Sir Roderick's tidings as briefly as possible. When David was contented, she drew off Cridhe's plaid. Her anguish poured through her fingers to the strings in the Salute to the Chief and the Lament for a Chief. She played Iain's favorites, then, remembering him with his pipes, remembering him at their hearthstone. Oh God, where was he now, where was his body? And he had never even known he had a son. She played all this, she played till her fingers bled, and though she still could not eat, she could sleep.

When the men knew they owned *Brighde* outright, they came to Mairi with a daring proposal. *If* the winter fishing, after Magnus's share, made a profit above what was needed to live should

284

potatoes fail again, would the women, *if* Lady Matheson paid well for their woolens, consent to pool funds in order to build a larger boat for the summer herring fishing? Then the herring could be followed to the North Sea in July and fished till September. *An Clanna* and *Brighde* could fish coastal waters, crewed by a few Clanna men and others recruited from perpetual debt to the Stornoway curers.

"But we can see, lass," said Andrew, "that this is Davie's fortune. 'Twould be only fair to put aside for him what would otherwise go to Sir James."

Mairi was still too grieved for Iain to thrill to the boldness of a small township vying not only with the great fishing fleets of Scotland but with those of Germany and Holland. All the same, she wished Fearchar could know. He'd told her how for two centuries the Dutch had ruled the North Sea herring trade with their "Dutch secret."

"Which was naught," he'd chuckled, "but knowing fish kept longer if gutted before going into the salt barrels. Brought their curers on board with them, did the Dutch, but all secrets leak out in time and it's been called the 'Scotch cure' for years now."

"If Clanna fares well, so will David," Mairi said. "You have given him love and a place to belong." She hadn't told anyone of how Sir Roderick had wanted to adopt her son. "Let's ask all the women."

In a meeting like the one where Clanna folk vowed to treat David as their own, the women agreed to add their earnings to fishing profits beyond what was needed to sustain the township in case of crop failure.

"And the wool we'll have to buy," added Gran. "Build your fine boat, lads, but next time we're buying as many good sheep as we're allowed on the moor grazing so the clip will furnish all the fleece we can use."

"We should try to have a cow for each family," said Morag. "The children need milk and crowdie and curds are good, especially if there's no 'taties."

It was agreed to buy a cow if there was coin left after supplies were bought, and the makings of the North Sea boat.

That was what they named it—*The North Sea*—lean and graceful as the Viking ships of their ancestors. It was a proud day for Clanna when *The North Sea* sailed after the herring on a bright morning in mid May of 1847.

In order to have her ready, Donald and the best builders had worked on the boat instead of going after the early herrings but their places on the small craft were filled by men from Stornoway, glad of having a share in the catch rather than slaving to pay off an ever-growing debt to the curers.

Winter rains were always so heavy and constant that the fragile soil couldn't be worked till spring. Then, in the few weeks before herring fishing started, every able-bodied person of Clanna worked at preparing and planting the fields and lazy-beds. Into the starved earth, men with their cas-chroms worked in smoke-permeated thatch, dung from the byres, and seaweed.

"Plant early and a bitter April or May will kill plants," sighed Andrew. "Plant too late, and crops won't ripen at all." Still, spring brought the birds and brighter weather, a greening of the moor, and everyone sang at their work—prayed, too, when they planted the hoarded seed potatoes, taking heart that only a few had spoiled and that in the normal way, not oozing slime.

Magnus had got a good price for the barrelled winter catch and Lady Matheson said she could dispose of double the output of wool goods. Mairi felt a little guilty that all was going well for Clanna when famine stalked the Highlands and Islands. The Mathesons' benevolence and employing men on public works kept the worst misery from Lewis but in spite of desperate appeals, the Queen's government was doing nothing though her chaplain was making pleas for private donations. With money from the Lowlands, England, Canada, Australia and South Africa, Destitution Boards were organized in January of 1847 in Glasgow and Edinburgh. They apportioned food in return for work, granted meager rations to those unable to toil, and tried to set up industries to employ the homeless.

"Doubtless the Boards keep many from starving," Magnus grudged. "But a body has to be destitute before they'll help. That means a crofter must sell or eat his cattle and sheep—yes, even devour his seed potatoes—before he can get his pound-and-a-half of meal for eight hours' labor on roads or drains on his landlord's property."

"What of his family?" asked Mairi, appalled. Once bereft of their livestock and means of farming, how could a crofter household ever be independent again?

"A worker gets a half-pound of meal for every child too young for employment," Magnus said. "The wife can spin for her three-quarters pound, or if she has many children and the minister speaks for her, a good-hearted relief officer may allow her food just for taking care of her family. A rare job that must be in the alleys of Glasgow slums!"

"Well, they can emigrate if they're deemed worthy prospects by The Society for Assisting Emigration from the Highlands and Islands of Scotland," said Murdo bitterly. "I do hear the Lord Mayor of London and the Governor of the Bank of England are on the committee of management, and the Prince Consort—German Albert, who's got himself a kilt and tartan and loves to stalk game in the Highlands—he's the Patron. Gave the Society £100, he did, and the Queen gave £300."

Magnus grinned. "The Bishop of Argyll and the Isles sent ten shillings—but he did preach a sermon that coaxed £36 from his congregation. Highland soldiers have donated a day's pay and settlers who went over the ocean have contributed. And to be sure, many landlords have."

" 'Tis said the Duke of Sutherland is spending thousands of pounds to feed his tenants," said Andrew.

"No more than he should after his mother shipped off most of them," gritted Murdo.

"Lord MacDonald's beggaring himself to feed his folk," put

in Barry. " 'Tis said he's feeding eight thousand people—not just his tenants but many from neighboring estates." The young man shook his fair head in wonder. "Costing him between £225 and to £300 pounds a month, it is! Can you imagine it?"

"Beggary for the Fourth Baron of the Isles is something different from beggary for the likes of us," Gerald MacAskill snorted. "What happens when his creditors take over his affairs?"

Through the summer, Mairi and the women cleaned and packed the fish the small boats brought in and kept weeds hoed out of the crops. When they went to milk in the mornings, they paused to scan the potato plants, breathing easily only after they saw that the leaves were green and healthy.

One morning in August, the plants looked shriveled. By noon, blackened vines sprawled over the lazybeds. Frantic digging rescued a handful of small potatoes, not enough for seed. They were cooked for the children who'd never tasted a potato and that was the last of months of planting, tending and hoping.

"We're lucky," Mairi said to hearten the others. "We're eating good carrots and peas and there'll be lots to store. And the kale does finely and the barley and oats."

"There's fish," said Gran. "Milk and crowdie."

"And lovely cloth to take to Lady Matheson." Sheila tried to smile as she straightened, flaxen-haired little Caitlyn in her arms.

But what of the others? Mairi thought. *What of those who'll have nothing if their crop rots, who somehow managed to hold out till now but can never endure another famished winter?* Nature was joining with landlords to force remnants of crofters off their holdings, folk who'd dug into precarious footholds that must crumble now.

Cridhe wailed for them that night, the cry of the bard Ian MacCodrum for the poor folk of Uist a lifetime ago—a lifetime that had seen such woe over all the Highlands and Islands, a lifetime that had seen village after ancient village burned to make room for sheep and deer parks. "*See the gentry with no pity, with no kindness for their kin. They do not think, my people, that you belong to the land . . ."*

But singing was not enough. What of those who had no songs?

Next morning Mairi kissed David, who at seventeen months was almost weaned, and with a creel of woolens, set off for Stornoway Castle.

"I must borrow against my harp all that you will lend me," she blurted to Sir James. Not at all the careful, logical speech she had rehearsed but those words had fled her mind.

He frowned, looking weary. Not an easy time for landlords, those who had hearts. "The potatoes are failing again, my factor says. But surely from cured fish and weaving, your township will have coin to buy grain."

"We will. But, sir, many will not."

His dark eyes flickered. "Lassie," he said as to one daft. "You cannot provide for others. Even I cannot, with thousands of pounds laid out. There are too many people. I'll forgive the back rent of any who'll go to Canada, and pay their way there but to let them starve along is doing them no favor."

If you gave them some land from your deer parks, Mairi wanted to cry. *If you let their sheep and cows feed on the moor instead of the beasts of Lowland farmers—* But angering Sir James would ruin any chance of gaining his help. Besides, he had done more than any laird to aid his tenants even though he wasn't bound to them by ties of blood and tradition.

"Those who'll go over the ocean, God speed them," she said softly. "Many like my cousin and brother crave a new land, a fresh beginning. But what of those, sir, who feel they'll die if they're torn away? What of those who are part of the rock and earth and sea?"

He passed a hand over his forehead. "You have a bard's tongue, Mairi MacLeod, but I can't let it magic me into what would be cruel mercy in the long run. Those who can't win a living on this island will have to go where they can do that."

"If they had a chance—as Clanna did—"

"Clanna had you."

"I have Cridhe and Fearchar's songs."

He shrugged. "Without you, there would be no Clanna—no boats, no sale of woolens. If there were one of you in each township, it would be a different matter—though thank heaven there isn't or you'd take over the island. Look you, Mairi MacLeod: apart from employing men to improve the harbor, build roads and drain bogs, I've put in a brickworks and a paraffin works and tried to start fisheries. I'm hiring men to cut away the peat from the Stones of Callanish—"

"The Stones?" Mairi gasped, forgetting her manners. Gran had not been up to the trudge that Midsummer, but Mairi and Eileen had gone, Mairi's exaltation at dawning mixed with fresh grief for Iain as she remembered how they'd loved each other in that changing rosy mist. "The Stones will look the way they did when the Old Ones raised them?"

"Much more than now, at any rate. I daresay they will attract lovers of antiquity from all over the world." Sir James, looking gratified at her interest, continued with his tally of improvements. "Lady Matheson and I have built and endowed the female seminary in Stornoway to educate poor girls and prepare them for a trade. In spite of all of this, thousands would be starving except for our charity. Now the potatoes have failed again. Surely you see people must support themselves or emigrate."

An idea had come to Mairi, so bold that it frightened her. "You want to start fisheries, sir. Our Donald Gunn is a fine boat-builder. He didn't go north for the herring but is fishing from one of our small boats. He and his best carpenters could help the men of townships to build boats. Gran could teach the women about dyestuffs and we could show them the kind of patterns Lady Matheson says sell handily. We can get them to planting carrots, peas and kale instead of depending on potatoes." She looked him squarely in the eye. "And where there's no music, there must be pipes or a fiddle or harp, even an accordion. I'll teach them the songs if no one remembers. Folk have to have the songs."

"Oh, Mairi, Mairi! A boat, kale, weaving and music! That's your remedy for the islands? Your dour Free Kirk won't like the music. Didn't the ministers hound people into burning their fiddles and pipes?"

"They did, but instead of cheering folk and lifting their hearts, they grind them down and say that our sins have earned our woes but no deed of ours can merit the slightest grace. Pain now and hell hereafter, that's their gospel." Thinking of Reverend Campbell who'd wanted to rant at Fearchar's funeral and Reverend Guinne who'd refused David baptism unless she gave him Cridhe for burning, Mairi threw back her head. "My grandfather had naught to do with the kirk and neither will I until it does something for people other than preach despair."

"I fear you're a heathen, lass, but I agree it's sad that the kirk has silenced music and with it so much ancient Gaelic tradition. In spite of its—originality—your plan makes more sense than the doings of the Destitution Boards which only aid those so broken they cannot help themselves. Crofters are a stubborn lot, God knows. Likely they'd heed you before advice from my factor. Have you asked your people if they're willing to spend their time helping others instead of earning for themselves in this year that may well be harder than the last one?"

She thought of Donald and his family rescued from the snow, of the others who'd found a haven at Clanna. "I'll have to ask them, of course, Sir James, but I can't think any would refuse to make our broth a little thinner so that others will have something to cook in their pots."

She held her breath. He turned to the window and gazed out over the harbor to the Beasts of Holm where Fearchar had lost his boat. For Matheson, the jagged rocks were a problem for shipping; for Mairi, they were age-old threats that had changed her township's life. Her heart beat painfully as Matheson faced about.

"I'll spend the money on meal, lass. As well give you a

chance. For townships able and willing to build and crew a boat, I'll supply the lumber. My factor will get seeds for planting. Strange as it will look on my accounts, I'll buy such musical instruments as you deem necessary. The expense will be charged to each township and repaid within five years—with interest. Through the winter, until your scheme can have results, my factor will employ the men on drainage and roads, perhaps improving natural harbors." He raised a hand to stop her thanks. "But before you make your rounds, my factor will visit the crofters. With the potatoes blighted, I think many can be persuaded to go to Canada."

"If they can be persuaded, they should go."

He studied her with shrewd dark eyes. His hard mouth softened. "I was sorry to hear that Iain MacDonald is probably dead."

The words pierced to her center. She dealt with her grief by praying that somehow, somewhere, Iain was alive. "I cannot think it was well done of you, sir, to give over our agreement to Sir Roderick."

"You're daft," he said good-naturedly. "When did ever a crofter lad have such a chance? It's lost now. Though he often told me he'd never marry, your refusing him an heir drove Sir Roderick to wed. He writes gloatingly that his bonnie young bride is with child." Shaking his head, Matheson laughed ruefully. "Yet you almost convince me that the boy is better off with you. Go along home with you, lass, before you have me dwelling in a black house and squeaking on the pipes."

"Do you want the pledge of Cridhe?"

His hand made a dismissive gesture before he checked it. "You could be a dangerous woman, Mairi. That harp is your soul. Yes. I will have a pledge. Are you willing to forfeit the harp if any township you encourage defaults on its loan—or if you exceed your authority?"

It was one thing to borrow money against Cridhe that she herself was responsible for. How could she risk her harp on the efforts of people she didn't even know? Yet Sir James had taken her challenge and offered to do far more than she could have dreamed.

"I will sign your pledge," she said.

25

To protect Cridhe from salt air and water, Donald fashioned a strong case which Mairi lined with MacLeod tartan. Late that August and into the autumn, *An Clanna* sailed the coast, crewed by Donald, Murdo and Tam while Gran and Mairi held to Cridhe.

From the sea, they saw deserted huts and byres. Once they spied people trudging from a village with laden creels and such furnishings as they could carry, wailing like lost souls. Mairi was sorely tempted to go ashore there and urge them to stay, but she had promised Sir James that she would only visit those who had resolutely turned their backs on emigration.

The women of Clanna and the men who were left had lamented the ruin of the potatoes but they whole-heartedly supported Mairi's plan. "There's enough of us to carry on while you're doing this grand thing," said Katie, violet eyes shining as she cuddled Alai and David at the same time. Her skin was unusually rosy and smooth for she would have a baby early in the new year.

Donald smiled proudly at his wife. "If we can help others stay on their land, it will be a glad thing. Och, Mairi, you've a silver tongue to wheedle the laird into this!"

"He's spending the money anyway," Mairi pointed out.

"This way he has a chance of getting it back and having tenants who can live—and pay their rent—when potatoes fail."

Clanna folk had eaten much silverweed, nettles, seaweed and shellfish that summer but these were varied with kale, tender new peas and carrots, crowdie and milk, and purchased barley and oats. The fields promised a harvest that should supply the township's grain all winter. Strings of smoked fish hung in the granaries and storerooms and barrels of cured fish were stored not only in each house but within covered passages of the broch. Peats enough for every household had been cut and were drying. One great advantage of a larger township was that while the men at the North Sea fishing would share their cash earnings, they would find the work of their crofts caught up and would know that if they were late at the fishing, the harvest would be got in and peats brought home and stacked by their dwellings.

So with the women. A few could care for the children while the others were packing fish or tending crops. Waulking the cloth went faster with so many hands and they gathered in each others' homes to weave, knit, and spin, some continuing their tasks while others looked to the children or prepared meals.

And Mairi and Gran could fare out on *An Clanna*. In townships where people groaned over rotting potatoes and wandered the coast in search of shellfish and dulse, Mairi and Gran promised wool for the looms, and where the secrets had been lost, showed how to gather and make soft, natural dyes for the plaids and tweeds Lady Matheson had found most popular. Mairi also showed them how to set out tiny kale plants and grow carrots and peas from the seeds she left for planting next spring.

None of these townships had boats, which meant the men could fish only from the rocks. They were joyous at the prospect of a craft that would let them sail out in search of fish that would go a long way toward feeding their families, though many didn't believe the lumber and cordage would be sent till Sir James's wagons rolled up or a boat brought the materials. The factor explained the five-year loans and the elder men of each village made their marks or signed their names.

Tam played his pipes at the ceilidhs and Cridhe sang of Conn of the Hundred Battles, of Viking forefathers and mighty heroes. Mairi sang the songs of her namesake, Mairi nighean Alasdair Ruaidh, who made songs on the threshold when she was forbidden to make her songs of freedom inside or outside the house. She sang Fearchar's songs and ones she had made herself—her lament for him, her conviction that the folk of the island were an indestructible part of it, that they would remain here so long as they kept their spirits strong with the songs and pride of their ancient roots.

In a few villages, an old man brought out a squeaky fiddle or a grizzled soldier produced well-worn pipes and joined in the music. Several taught Mairi and Tam tunes they didn't know. In townships where there was no instrument, Mairi watched those who listened most intently, who seemed to be trying to capture the music in their heads. Always, one would say wistfully how fine it would be to have such tunes all the time. Then Mairi asked if they'd learn the pipes or fiddle and if the township was willing to add the charge for it to the amount owed Sir James. Several of the larger townships undertook debt for both fiddle and pipes in spite of objections from a few disapproving kirk people. Later, Tam and Lucas would make their way through the villages to teach the pipes and fiddle where there was none who knew how to play.

While Donald and Murdo stayed in a village to help build its boat, two of the villagers crewed *An Clanna* on its way. In this fashion, returning often to Clanna to see David and help with the harvest and bringing home the peats, Mairi, Gran and Tam fared up and down the coast from the Butt of Lewis to the hills of Harris. Their mission was over by mid-November. By Christmas, a score of villages had new boats so the men could fare out to the winter fishing, and they had new hope, and their own music.

A miracle it seemed, yet only many times multiplied what had worked for Clanna. *The North Star* was home after turning over the bountiful packed catch to Magnus to sell in an English port.

The rents were paid, a supply of wool was laid in for weaving through the long winter, there was ample fodder for the cows and sheep, and after additional grain was bought, there was still a mellow clink of silver in each family's place for keeping what had up till now been precious few coins.

Added to the trove in Gran's sugar bowl were three United States gold pieces sent by Calum and Catriona in a letter that was even more treasured. They had heard of the second failed potato crop, sent the money to help if it was needed and for luxuries if it wasn't. Also would Mairi, if possible, repay Captain MacDonald for Catriona's passage? They owned an expanse of fertile land along the Brazos River. This supplied all their food but Calum made their cash money by catching and gentling wild horses which he sold to the army. Their daughter, Mairi, was just starting to walk and they hoped the child Catriona now carried would make her a brother. Adam and Kirsty owned land adjoining. The twins could ride like red Indians and usually rope whatever they whirled their lariats after. "It's a grand country," Calum wrote. "If only you would come, it would be perfect. Don't be proud if you change your mind. There's a thousand welcomes for you here." "Ever and *forever!*" Catriona had scrawled.

Each time Mairi read the letter, her eyes blurred and she winced at the mention of Iain, but she was glad the far land had been kind. If Calum and Catriona prospered, surely one day they'd at least return for a visit—and who knew? One of their children might feel the call of the sea and broad moor and come back to live. Then she thought of Iain who wouldn't return even if he could. Pain and loss welled up in her as if she had just learned he was missing and her only solace lay in holding David so close he wriggled and in singing her grief to Cridhe, her longing and her love.

For the third summer, the potatoes failed in 1848. Though the townships *An Clanna* had visited survived and the relief plans of Sir James saved Lewis from starvation, Clanna's fishing crews off the shores of Harris, Uist and smaller islands saw people scouring the rocks and beaches for seaweed and shellfish. Often the boats landed and distributed their catch among the famished.

"Tugs at your heart," said Donald, hoisting his brown-haired baby girl to his shoulders while Alai, a bit jealous, begged to be swept up, too. "Some we've talked to can't get meal from the Destitution Boards till they get rid of everything they have, even their cas-chroms, their foot-plows. How will they put in crops then? They're trying to hold out so they can work their crofts and not be paupers. If we could do something—"

"Aye," nodded Murdo, bristling gray eyebrows meeting above his wedge of a nose.

"I gave my bannock to a woman who was carrying a baby in her shawl." Tam's thin brown face was somber. "She tried to give the tyke a little. It was dead."

Sheila glanced at wee Seana who was helping a gleefully squealing even wee-er Brigid walk. "I would give my share of weaving money to buy grain for those poor souls."

"And I," said Katie. Morag and Flora nodded, and so did Rose and Barbara. The sisters were both big with child so Lucas and Paul hadn't gone with *The North Sea* that summer but fished from the smaller craft nearer home.

"I'll give my pennies," Margaret offered. An eternal child, the beautiful girl had no patience with spinning or weaving and her knitting was full of lumps and bumps though Gavin, who had married her, fondly wore the misshapen jersey she'd made for him. Margaret loved to help Gran gather dyestuffs, though, and merrily joined in the waulking, so she was always given a share of the woolen profits.

Eileen tugged at Mairi's arm. Her hair had darkened to rich honey but her eyes were the same deep cornflower blue. Allan Bailey had given her a gilt brooch for her fourteenth birthday that spring but though she enjoyed dazzling him into confusion with a smile or word, she made no secret that she was waiting for Magnus. As for Magnus, the last time he'd called in for their fish, he'd stared at her and shaken his bleached yellow head. "You're near grown, lassie! How did that happen so fast?"

"Magnus! It's taken ages!" she'd protested.

They both laughed then, but there was confusion in it, and since, he'd acted ill at ease with her. Though she felt for her young sister, Mairi found grim amusement in this. He'd thought he could marry an echo of her in Eileen but now he was seeing that the younger sister was a different person, completely herself—and no longer a child he could tease and banter with.

Now Eileen said, "Mairi, there's still the American gold! That would buy a lot of grain, surely."

The result was that next day, *An Clanna* put in at Stornoway. Lucas and Paul helped Mairi carry the latest store of woolens to the accountant's office at the rear of the castle. The gawky red-haired young man, Bruce MacNeil, had authority to buy all Clanna goods. Having learned that Mairi turned a deaf ear to his attempts at gallantry, MacNeil was swift and businesslike in their transactions which suited her well.

Today, however, as he counted out pennies, shillings and pounds—what wealth! Mairi could still scarce believe it—he said, "The townships you heartened last year, Mistress Mac-Leod, paid their rents this year with woolens. They say that with fish and vegetables, they'll live in spite of the potato failure." He smiled and that made him a bonnie lad in spite of his freckles. "Several townships even paid a bit on their loans."

"That makes glad hearing. But I hope they saved enough coin for meal."

"They did that, you may be sure. But they're determined you won't lose your harp because of them."

Mairi stared. "I never told them about the pledge and I asked Tam and the others not to, either. They've burden enough without worrying over that."

"Sir James thought they should know," shrugged MacNeil. "The factor told them when they signed for their loans. Owing a rich landlord is one thing but causing you to forfeit that harp with which you sang to them, that is something else indeed. Now how much fleece will you be needing?"

"Not so much this year. Our clip is almost enough to keep us busy." She handed back money for a tight-packed creelful and was on her way to the storehouse where rents paid in kind were kept when Sir James overtook her.

"Well, Mistress Mairi, as prosperous as Clanna is, I keep expecting to see a gold brooch on your shawl or shoes made by someone other than your township cobbler."

Mairi flushed. "Andrew's shoes serve well." Twenty-one years old and the mother of a son, she'd no reason to gaud herself up like a young lass at a fair but the teasing words stung a little. "Everyone in Clanna has all needful—and to have more in these days seems near a crime."

He glanced sharply at her. Realizing her words could be taken as a reproach, Mairi flushed more deeply. "I didn't speak of gentry, sir. You've been a generous laird, the best in the Highlands and Islands. It's different for crofter folk who know what it is to hunger and be without a roof."

That only made matters worse. She floundered to a halt at his ironic smile. "I was just down in the town," he said. "Your kinsmen are buying a great lot of meal and grain. Can it be you intend to speculate? Sell it at a profit when winter starving begins?"

She gazed at him, astonished. He had the grace to redden. "I know it is not that, lass. But what do you purpose? None of my tenants are going hungry, nor will they, though more than ever I am urging them to emigrate."

"Most lairds are not like you, sir. Along the coasts of Harris and Uist, folk scavenge for shellfish and seaweed. It won't take winter to kill them. They're so weakened they go ill and die, especially babies and old ones."

His breath caught in. "You mean to take them food? Though they're not of your island?"

"They're my people," she said defiantly though she went cold inside from fear. "Even if they were not, they are starving. Every grown person of Clanna wishes to send food so we can eat our bannocks without them sticking in our throats."

His dark eyes probed hers, seemed to pierce into her soul. "It didn't occur to you that this is—what does it say in our contract—exceeding your authority?"

"I never thought of authority. If people are hungry and you can feed them, you do it." When he looked at her even more strangely, she blurted, "Is that not Scripture, sir?"

He made a dismissing gesture. "It sounds like something Jesus might say but I do not think it a text often preached. I've small use for sermons, Mairi. You won't catch me that way."

She stood in silence, waiting. His scowl deepened but she didn't avert her eyes. At last he said, "So long as you pay your rents and support yourselves, I suppose what your township does with its little hoard is no concern of mine. But heed this, Mairi. Do not interfere with evictions or the legal rights of my fellow landlords. If you do, you will lose your harp."

Interfere with evictions? How could she do that? There were always constables as there had been at Aosda, or sometimes even soldiers—Highlanders forced to herd their own kind away from their huts. "I hear you, sir," was all she said but he gave her another searching look before he nodded and started away.

"Mairi." He turned back suddenly. "I'm having guests the end of the month. It would pleasure me if you would play your harp for them."

How could she refuse him? But it went against the grain to entertain gentry, some of whose tenants were probably roaming those wind-scourged beaches in search of the food their land could not grow. "I doubt they will understand the Gaelic, sir."

"They can still appreciate the music. All have heard the pipes but it's surprising how few have heard a harp."

"Not so surprising, sir. When pipes took the place of the harp in battle, they took over at other times, too. And then came the ministers to threaten musicians with hell and burn such harps as were left." She couldn't keep bitterness from her voice. "If it weren't for using pipes in the Sassenach queen's army, we'd have lost them, too, their music great and small."

"Your playing could well inspire some of my guests to try to bring back the harp and the old songs. Several of the ladies play the pianoforte most charmingly."

A hot rush of anger flooded through Mairi. Ladies genteely amusing themselves while their tenants starved? When she could speak, she said, "It'll do no good to have the songs without the people, sir, just as the people must have their songs."

"Ah, Mairi, a fine warrior queen you would have made—leading your troops with a harp, not a sword. Shall I send a carriage for you?"

"It would sink to its hubs. Let me know when you want me, sir, and I will bring Cridhe in one of our boats."

"Lord Dunmore, the owner of Harris, will be here with his lady who has encouraged the weaving of tweed," said Sir James. "And so will Lord MacDonald, the proprietor of Skye and North Uist. He is near £200,000 in debt, mostly from feeding his tenants these past hard years. For him, at least, Mairi, you should not mind singing."

"I promised to sing when you wished it but my tunes will not be merry with this famine in the land and folk driven from their homes."

He sighed heavily. "Mairi, the long and short of it is that most of them must fare across the seas where there's good land a-plenty—not bog or rocks like this."

"While Lowland sheep feed on the good *machair* meadows and deer browse among the ruined villages?"

"Make me no laments, Mairi! I am doing all I can."

"For that I thank you, sir. I will come when you send for me."

He strode away, anger in the set of his shoulders, and Mairi went into the storehouse for the fleece.

On the coast of Harris, where blue-green sea lapped on white shell sand from which marram grass flowed back, rippling like a mermaid's hair, *An Clanna* found a few families of crofters sheltering among the rocks, living on seabirds, shellfish, seaweed and such fish as could be caught from the shore. The 78th Highlanders had been called on to help the civil authorities evict the people. At the name of Iain's old regiment, Mairi's heart felt such crushing pain that she couldn't breathe for a moment, and then it hurt. Had he lived, would he have carried out that order? If he did, she would have wished him dead.

"I am almost ninety," quavered one old man. "Seventy rents have I paid faithfully to the laird. Never did I think to flit except into my grave. And now where will that be?"

"The laird was paying us two pounds, twelve shillings and six pence for a ton of kelp," said a blond young woman with a pallid baby in her arms. "It fetched only two pounds, ten shillings in Liverpool. No wonder he thinks Cheviots more profitable—but God's curse on him all the same!"

"The factor said we could fish for a living," said a black-haired handsome lad. "But how can we fish without a boat?"

"My son will come in a week or two and help you build a boat," said Murdo. "For now, we can leave you oats and barley."

"Must we sell our tools first, and our cow?"

Lucas shook his fiery head. "No. We be folk like you, not from the Destitution Board."

Perched on a rock, Mairi played Cridhe. By the time the grain was unloaded, the old man, with one of the children nestled in his lap, was teaching her a song of his youth.

"You'll not be forgetting that boat?" the dark lad panted as he ran along to help launch *An Clanna.*

"We'll not forget," vowed Murdo.

On North Uist, the next large island southwest of Harris, Lord MacDonald was employing and feeding his tenants though so deep in debt that it was only a question of time till his creditors would insist he manage his lands in a profitable way. But nothing anywhere had prepared Mairi and the Clanna men for what they found on South Uist. It had been bought in 1840 by Colonel Gordon of Cluny who had been disappointed in his hope of reviving the kelp industry, and disappointed in his scheme to sell Barra, a neighboring island, to the government for a penal colony.

Unlike the rocky coasts of Lewis and most of Harris, South Uist's sandy western beaches stretched for miles, though Murdo said that its eastern side, facing Skye, was wild moor and bogs. On this Atlantic shore, broad strips of coarse, tough-rooted marram grass bound the sand and kept dunes from encroaching on the *machair*, rich, dense undulating billows of clovers, buttercups and daisies. In some places it was grazed so close that it was a smooth carpet, but in other stretches, clover scent carried to the boat and patches of yellow and white spangled the brilliant green. In spite of the waves of the vast ocean, this seemed a gentle, hospitable coast with meadows to support the livestock of many crofts.

Instead, they heard shrieks and wailing even before they saw smoke curling yellow and thick from a cluster of houses on the edge of the machair. Men and women fled uniformed constables who wielded truncheons, knocking their quarry to the ground, dragging them toward wagons.

"Can it be?" cried Lucas. "Is it dogs they've set on those poor folk?"

It was. Beasts that led their masters to fugitives hiding in some ditch or thicket. Paul swore, starting to turn *An Clanna* toward shore. Murdo caught his arm. "We can do naught, lad," he said in a choked voice. "Save for the dogs and wagons, 'twas so they cleared my township. They must purpose to cart these poor folk to a transport ship, likely harbored over at Lochboisdale. Och, Gordon of Cluny! May you roast in hell forever with the cries of your tenants in your ears!"

Blackness engulfed Mairi. The burning thatch was that of Aosda, the wailing that of her kinfolk. Fearchar, ablaze, stumbled from his hut with Cridhe in his arms. This time he didn't fall. He burned but he did not die, and in that brilliant flame, he sang to his harp. The words etched themselves in Mairi as she fell into swirling darkness.

She roused to Lucas's shaking her. "Mairi! Shall we put in to try and rescue that couple? Look, they're running with their babe, as if they mean to plunge into the sea before they're taken! 'Twill break your pledge to Sir James but—"

Waves swept over the feet of the fair-haired man and woman, surged back, tugging her skirts. She held an infant to her breast. Constables stumbled through the marram grass; hounds bayed.

"Put in for them," said Mairi.

26

In a frantic yet controlled scramble, Mairi took the infant and helped the woman—a girl, really—into *An Clanna* while Murdo held the boat and Lucas and Paul fought off the constables and hounds with their oars. Murdo pushed into deeper water and the brothers retreated, fending off cursing pursuers. Splashing through thigh-high waves, they piled gasping into the boat and were still gulping air when they started plying their oars.

An officer of the constables shook his fist. "We mark you well—the name of your craft! Your laird will hear of this!"

"Let him hear!" yelled Lucas. The sun turned his hair to an aureole of dazzling fire gold. To Mairi, he looked like an ancient hero, Cuchulain or Conn of the Hundred Battles. "Damnation to you for your hard hearts, treating your own kind like cattle bound for slaughter!"

"Aye!" shouted Murdo. "Damn ye all! May ye see the thatch burnt over your own heads and be glad of a bit of seaweed to eat!"

Rowing away, Paul said, "Now there be men I could kill with a better will than ever I had in firing on poor heathen for the Sassenach queen!"

The woman was shaking, doubtless from terror and the chill of her wet garments. Mairi wrapped her own plaid around mother and child while Lucas gave his jersey to the man, who, like the woman, scarcely seemed to realize what had happened.

"Will your families fear for you?" Mairi asked.

"Families?" The woman's gray eyes seemed really to see for the first time. She glanced dazedly around her, but when the baby whimpered, she put it to her breast. Color flowed to her cheeks. Bonnie she looked now with her black-lashed eyes and red lips, even with face smudged and hair blown wild. "My close kin have mostly died of sickness worsened by hunger. One brother I have left, cousins, an uncle and aunt. All left for Canada last month."

"The same for me," said her husband, a thin but strong-muscled man of perhaps Lucas's age. "Save I had only two sisters left to go with their men on the ship. I served four years in the army to protect our lease." He spat in the waves. "This is what came of it." Looking from face to face, he drew a long breath. "I am Marcus MacFarlane, my wife is Una, our laddie is Angus, and whatever happens now, we are in your debt. Belike you can set us down somewhere along the shore." Incredibly, he managed a wry smile. "By choice, where there's shellfish and seaweed."

Mairi gave their own names and said, "Why don't you live at our township for a while? There's fishing for you, Marcus, and spinning or weaving for Una, if she likes."

Hope brightened the MacFarlanes' faces but then Marcus frowned. "Your township, didn't you lose your 'taties?"

"Yes, but we have other crops, plenty of fish, and cows on the moor."

"But your laird? That's one of their great complaints, you ken—that their tenants take in homeless kin and other folk till none can win a living."

"All have a living at Clanna," Mairi assured him. "There's room for you. So long as we pay our rents and are no charge on him, I doubt Sir James worries overmuch about how many we are. In better times, perhaps you can come back to your home place, but till then at least you'll be in the islands."

"But if the constables report you —"

"Since they were for sending you to Canada, we saved them trouble," returned Lucas cheerfully. Then, stricken, he glanced at Mairi. "But lass, your Cridhe!"

Cridhe was forfeit. Mairi's heart was wrung for that but she didn't think Fearchar—or any of her line of MacLeod harpers—would blame her. Her vision of Fearchar, the words of his song, filled her like a battle cry.

"Sir James wants me to harp for his fine guests," she said. "Lucas, Paul—and you also, Marcus—having been soldiers, you know English. You will help me make such a song that those lairds who hear it will never forget. Such a song that if Cridhe never sings again, this song will sound and resound through the isles so long as there is one Gael left."

When *An Clanna* sailed into the harbor, Mairi noticed a tall stranger was among those who hurried down to the jetty. A black-haired man, taller than the other men who were in from the fishing . . . and . . . and wasn't that David on his shoulder? Her heart leaped. She put her hand over it as if to quiet it, hold it in her body. It couldn't be! Yet there was that slight limp and now she could make out the face that was often and often in her dreams though she tried not to let it rise before her in the day.

The sky spun into the sea; everything whirled around her. Through her dizziness, she heard the MacFarlanes welcomed in the same breath that Murdo called, "Major MacDonald, is it you indeed, sir?"

"What's left of me, Murdo." Strong hands lifted her almost bodily from the boat, supported her on the planks or she would have fallen. "Mairi!" A wealed scar ran from left eyebrow to right temple but his eyes glowed from within like sun rays radiating through dark clouds. "If you hadn't sailed home tonight, we were going in search of you tomorrow."

"Iain! You—you're alive! Your uncle told me—"

"Truth as far as he knew it. I crawled into some rocks so the women missed me with their butcher knives. Oddly, it was an Afghan woman who found and hid and nursed me. It was months before I could get back to the regiment and send word to my uncle."

"He might have let me know! *You* might have!"

"He never told me he'd been to see you—never told me we have a son. And I still thought it best for you to have no contact with me."

He caught a long breath and smiled up at David who hugged him gleefully and crooned, "Da! My Da!"

The Clanna folk, knowing the lovers had much to say, were moving toward the houses, the MacFarlanes in their welcoming midst. Moving back to hold her at armslength, Iain said grimly, "Why, Mairi? Why didn't you send me word of our laddie? I told you to let my agent know if you needed anything."

"Would I do that?" she cried, suddenly overwhelmed by the pain, humiliation and grief of the past years—standing in the kirkyard while people called David a bastard, fending off Sir Roderick, mourning Iain as dead. "Your agent—didn't he tell your uncle you'd tried to provide for me so that here comes Sir Roderick, trying to buy David—and trying twice as hard when he thought you dead?" Choking, fighting now the strength of his hands, she whispered, "Why are you here, Major MacDonald?"

The sternness vanished. He looked into her eyes. Her body, so long sealed from love, quickened as if frozen blood began to warm, painful, restoring feeling to nerves and flesh where there had been numbness.

"I've come to beg you to have me, Mairi."

Disbelieving her ears, she shook her head. "You said it yourself. We are of different worlds. Never could I leave my island."

"You don't have to, love. I'll live here, with you and our son. Sir James has promised to give me a lifetime lease on the land between Clanna and the lodge."

Too much to take in. "But—the army—"

"I resigned my commission. When the 78th was ordered to help evict crofters on Harris this summer, it was too much to stomach." He brought her close to him again. This time he kissed her long and sweetly. "Nor am I fettered by being my

309

uncle's heir. He has a healthy son and another child on the way. Having at last decided he must produce his own line, he's gone at it with a whole heart and actually dotes on his young, pretty wife and the baby. Since I plan to raise horses, he's given me the choice of his stables, but that's all I'll have from him." Iain traced her face from brow to chin, rested his fingers on her throat. "So you see, Mairi mine, I'm a broken down, scarred, half-pay retired officer—no great catch for a woman of your resources. Sir James tells me you'd be close to rich had you built for yourself on what you've earned instead of trying to succor the whole Western Hebrides. However, Rosanna and Eileen let me hope you might still have some tenderness for me."

"Some tenderness! Oh, Iain, Iain! I have dreamed of you but never, ever, did I dare dream this—"

Setting David down, he kissed her thoroughly. Wakened and roused, she answered his hunger with her own. She was no girl now, but a woman reunited with her man, her only man. They were both trembling when David wriggled between them and tugged at his father's coat and his mother's skirts.

"Da! Carry me!"

Still with an arm around Mairi, Iain laughed and swung the squealing boy to his shoulder. "Laddie, you'll have to learn there are times you should run and play but we've three years to make up so I suppose we can spoil you a little."

They walked toward the village in the last rays of sunlight. Then everything Iain's return had pushed from her mind rushed back with sickening force. Iain was still gentry, a friend of Sir James. When he knew what she intended to do—

She would lose him. Him and Cridhe both. That was too cruel! Too much! Surely God meant them to be together or it wouldn't have worked out this way. Look at David, proud of his father, adoring. She'd continue to help the scattered crofters. Surely that was more useful than insulting Sir James's guests. But again she saw the MacFarlanes' village burning, saw them hunted like beasts to the shore. Again she saw Fearchar blazing with Cridhe in his arms, again she heard his song.

310

The joy that had blazed in her was quenched in sorrow. "Sir James wanted to hold our wedding," Iain was saying. "I told him, though, that I was sure you'd rather it was held at Clanna. We'll invite him and his lady, of course, and my uncle, too."

"Iain." Each word wrenched Mairi's heart and lungs. "We have to talk. As soon as David's tucked in bed."

Iain's male side-glance and pressure on her hand told her why he thought she wanted privacy. That brought a crueler pang. Well, they could sup together. David would have this one evening with his father home. After that—perhaps he could visit Iain sometimes, not entirely lose him. She felt as if she were bleeding inwardly and almost wished the flow were real and mortal so she wouldn't have to tell her lover what she must.

The MacFarlanes would stay for the time being with Morag, Lucas and Barbara. After supper, Lucas brought them to the MacLeod house. Una's bright hair was braided and coiled behind her ears. They had washed off the cinder smears and made themselves neat as possible.

"We won't stay," said Marcus, holding their little son. "But Una didn't think we'd thanked you properly. So we thank you now, Mairi MacLeod. We will thank you and pray for you every day of our lives."

"I'm glad we were in time to help." Mairi smiled at them honestly in spite of the weight on her heart while Gran made them sit down and bustled to fetch heather ale for everyone save Una to whom she said, "What you need, lass, is a beaker of broken milk." Beating oatmeal and creamy milk till they frothed, Gran handed the drink to the young woman and indeed that or the fire or both together brought a glow to Una's fine-boned face.

Evidently resigning himself to a host's manners, Iain said, "Rosanna, your ale is better than the Pictish king's, but we need some music with it. It's a long time, Mairi, since I've heard your harp excepting in my dreams."

"Get your pipes, lad," entreated Gran. "Eileen, run tell the others that we're having a ceilidh! Lucas, go get your fiddle!"

311

Bittersweet it was, calling up the celebration on the eve of Catriona and the MacNeils' departure for America, those nights when they'd been making that first shelter in the broch, Iain's last visit when he'd helped build this house. How deep he'd grown into her life even before there was David with his smile and eyes and hair! Iain had returned to her from the dead. He was willing to give up his place in the outside world for her. How could she persist in a course that would ruin all that?

The MacFarlanes sat warm and safe but what of those poor folk, bound like criminals, thrown in a ship to be sent over the ocean? What of all those famished, homeless wanderers who must live on the mercy of rocks and sea since there was none in their lairds?

Watching Iain while his grace notes wove in and out of her music, Mairi had never loved him more than in this time when she knew she must sing for her people though that would surely drive him away. It was still early when Gran yawned ostentatiously and said it was time they were all abed. The company took their leave. Eileen had already carried off a slumbering David. Gran blessed the hearth and kissed Iain on the cheek before she went to her box-bed in the other room.

Mairi and Iain were left alone in the soft glimmer of the banked peats. Iain rose. Mairi raised her hand. If he held her, if he wooed her, she would be undone.

"Iain, I have broken my pledge to Sir James. Cridhe is forfeit—but before I yield her up, she will sing such a song to Sir James's guests that they'll never forget it. You must hear that song."

Puzzled, he sat down. As she sang, she saw not Iain, but Fearchar. When she finished, even in the near dark, she could see that Iain's face was set like stone. Even though she had nerved herself for his anger, the defiance of the song curdled in her, turning her weak and shaken.

"So this is your thanks to James Matheson?" Iain demanded.

"The song is not against him. It's for Colonel Gordon who sets hounds on his tenants, the Staffords who burned out thousands in Sutherland, the Clanranalds who have time and again cleared their clansman who once paid those chieftains' debts with kelp and black cattle, the Dunmores who—as well you know—called in the army to clear villages in Harris, and their ilk."

"If you insult Matheson's guests in his very castle, you won't be a good argument for aiding one's tenants, Mairi. And that last part of your song could be taken as a threat."

"It's a prophecy! Iain! You were there when Sinclair burned Aosda, when my grandfather died! What are manners and courtesy when such things can happen—are happening every day through the Highlands and Islands?"

He got to his feet, head almost touching the rafters. "If it would do any good, Mairi, I could understand. But you'll gain nothing. You'll only anger the lairds and perhaps frighten them for indeed some fear their tenants may grow violent and resist evictions."

What he said was true. And she was tired, so tired—She wanted to run into his arms, weep, and be comforted and soothed. "If you can't play for the gentry—and I know perhaps you can't, let me make your excuses to Matheson. It may even be that I can persuade him to let you keep your harp." Iain came as close, she knew, as he ever would to pleading, although he did not touch her. "Let me do that for you, Mairi."

But Fearchar blazed between them.

"This song was sent to me, Iain." She could barely force the words through her aching, tightened throat. "It was given for Cridhe's last singing in the hands of a MacLeod. Some lairds may not know how their folk are evicted. And perhaps if they hear it in a song they know will be sung for generations, they may pause to think if this is how they want to be famed, if this is how they want their names remembered."

"Most won't understand the Gaelic." Iain looked a bit relieved.

"Lucas, Paul and Marcus MacFarlane will help me put it into English."

313

Iain stared at her, his eyes reflecting the smoldering light of the peats. "You will do this?"

"I must." She spoke through lips so stiff she could scarcely move them.

He turned his back. "In some part, Mairi, are you punishing me? Because David, as Rosanna told me, was baptized at the Stones instead of by the parson? Because you mourned me for dead?"

"If you can think that—"

"I do think it." He turned to confront her. His voice rasped but he kept it low. Oh, their sleeping child, who little dreamed how his parents were wounding each other! "I think, Mairi, that you can't forgive me for being gentry. That would always be coming between us."

"And I think you don't want me to embarrass you before your kind!" she hurled.

He winced as if she'd struck him. After an endless time in which she longed to throw herself into his arms, embrace and caress him, say only their love mattered, he said heavily, "One thing is sure, Mairi. You would always place your people ahead of me—ahead of our son, even. Perhaps you don't know it, but Matheson says you're renowned as a bard. They call you Mairi of the Isles. Here at Clanna, there's no doubt you're ceann-cinnidh. I could deal with that, I hope. I could even help you. But I cannot live with a wife more avenging fury than woman, who scorns my advice and thinks any mad idea she has comes straight from God and her ancestors."

"That is for you to say." She would not weep. Not till he was gone.

"There's David."

"Yes." Her pride broke. "You—you will see him sometimes?"

Iain drew a deep breath. "I want to do more than that. If you're not afraid I'll contaminate him, I want to father my son."

She blinked at the rush of tears to her eyes. "How—"

He gripped her shoulders. "We owe it to our lad to marry

314

though it seems we must live apart. If Matheson will honor my lease, I'll still live on the island. David can live with you part of the time, part of the time with me."

A surge of joyful hope soured in her. "And you'll have a pony for him, bought playthings and fine food, servants to spoil him. 'Twould be a marvel if soon he didn't want to stay with you entirely."

"My half-pay will stretch to a cook-housekeeper, gardener and stable-lad. Not much spoiling there."

"You'll want to send him off to school."

"I'll tutor him till he's old enough to decide whether he wants to go to a university. Who knows? He may want to be a sailor or take over breeding horses."

"You'd not argue that?"

"If you won't argue should he decide he wants to be a doctor or lawyer or the like."

Mairi pondered this unheard-of solution. "But Iain, surely if we don't—well, if we don't live together, you'll want a real wife. You'll want more children."

"I'd rather have David than a dozen like my uncle's fat-cheeked get," he shrugged. "I do not want another wife. I can find the only ease another woman can give me when I visit the mainland now and then."

That didn't please her. But for David to have his father—oh, it was more than she'd dared hope for. Awkwardly, she said, "Shall I make a pallet for you?"

He shook his head. "There's moon enough for me to make my way back to the lodge. Tell David that his Da will come to see him soon."

Did he, like she, feel hollow and twisted in his loins? Why shouldn't they, at least this once, love again in their bodies? But he moved swiftly past her and she stepped well out of his way. Loving him would melt her and she must be a sword.

315

27

Iain was gone next morning before anyone was up saving lap-wings and pee-whits. "Your Da will be back," Mairi assured a sobbing David. "Indeed he will be and you'll see him often."

"What talk is this, often?" Gran's blue eyes drilled into Mairi. "Your lad told me he wanted a wedding."

"There may be a wedding, but—I can't talk about it now, Gran. I'll tell you later."

"Hmph! Indeed you don't float two feet off the floor as you did last evening. Don't stand on your pride, lass, and make woes for both of you and wee Davie."

"It's not my pride, Gran, but something I must do and Iain cannot bide it."

"Mickle foolishment it sounds to me, after all you two have gone through," the old woman grumbled. At the tears in Mairi's eyes, she patted her cheek and said briskly, "With such a love as you bear each other, and your little son to bind you, God willing it may turn out well. There, child, don't cry. I'll pry no more." Gran sighed and then gave a small chuckle. "A good thing I made a lot of heather ale this summer. And a grand feast we'll have, whatever nonsense you and that black-haired laddie have set betwixt you!"

Sir James came himself to tell Mairi that his guests were assembling in four days. Sipping the fresh milk Mairi brought him, the laird smiled like a man at last winning a wager. "So Mairi, if you keep your word, for one night at least, you'll be my harper."

"I'll keep my word on more than that, sir." Why, when she knew it must be, was it so hard to say? "If you haven't had complaints from the constabulary or Colonel Gordon, you doubtless will. On South Uist, the officers were coursing people with hounds, dragging them off like felons. Our boat put in to rescue a family that was trapped between the constables and the waves. So I have forfeited my harp."

Matheson stared at her. At last, he grimaced. "The harp without the harper is not such a trophy, lass. It would take a stony heart to leave anyone in such a plight. When you're married to Iain, he won't let you go searching for woe."

Pleading and promises, she was sure, would ransom Cridhe. Before she could weaken, Mairi said, "Major MacDonald and I may wed for our son's sake but we will not be sharing a roof, so don't count on that, Sir James, to change my tunes."

"What nonsense is this?" Matheson's dark eyes narrowed. "For you, he's giving up position and place! And I know you have loved him only. Though you bore a child out of wedlock, my factor says the few men who've slurred the chastity of Mairi of the Isles have got drubbings that cured them. What's gone amiss?"

Although her knees were weak, Mairi returned Matheson's gaze unflinchingly. "There's a song I must sing for your guests if I sing at all and Iain does not like it."

That sardonic face became a mask. "I must suppose then that I won't like it, either."

"You will not, sir."

He colored. "I am not renowned for patience, Mairi. What's to prevent my serving all your folk at Clanna with eviction notices come next rent day?"

"You are just," said Mairi quietly though her heart skipped a beat before it hammered in her ears. "I cannot think you will cast out what you've called your best tenants because of me."

Her throat was suddenly so dry that she had to swallow before she could go on. "I will flit if you ask it, but I beseech you to leave my brother and sister in peace with our grandmother."

"Let's strike a bargain. Entertain my guests in seemly fashion and you may keep your harp."

"Sir, I will fetch Cridhe to you now if you wish it—but if I play in your castle, I must sing the song my grandfather brought me in the flames of a South Uist village."

His face was still impassive but heat flickered in his black eyes like flame in peats. "So long as your folk pay their rents, I will not punish them on your account. You are another matter. You will play for me, Mairi MacLeod. What you sing is of your choosing. But if you persist in folly, your harp is indeed forfeit— and since without you it is only scarred willow wood and brass strings, it may go to the fire since that's where your cursed song came from." He set down the beaker and strode to his horse. "In four days, Mairi."

He didn't look back.

Morag loaned Mairi her good black dress, the one she'd been married in and wore only to church. Gran artfully draped the dark green and black MacLeod plaid with its blocks of lighter green and lines of red and blue over one arm and under the other, pinning it at the shoulder with the gilt brooch Fearchar had given her in their courting days.

"Pretty mother!" David patted the brooch as Mairi knelt to kiss him good-bye, carefully traced Sheila's combs that swept the waving hair back from Mairi's face and gathered it in a mass at the crown. "Will you bring back my Da?"

"He'll come again soon, David, and give you another ride on his horse."

Rising, she reflected bitterly on Iain's single visit since their reunion. He hadn't come to see her where she was down packing fish, but had taken David on a jaunt to the lodge where Mrs. Fraser gave them raisin scones with their tea. A fine marriage theirs promised to be! What lad wouldn't rather prance about on a horse than gather seaweed or spread peats to dry? Her only hope of David's remaining part of Clanna was that he'd inherit Tam and Fearchar's passion for the sea.

It wasn't that she especially wanted David to hunch over a cas-chrom but she dreaded that he might leave the island, that he might not love it as she did. Well, that would be as it would be.

Tam and Eileen should have children who'd remain on the land—what time the men weren't on the seas. Kissing David a last time before Gran took his hand, Mairi passed Cridhe's case to Lucas and climbed into *An Clanna*. Her cousins, Murdo and Donald, were taking her to Stornoway and would buy necessities while she sang in the castle.

Holding to Cridhe, so carefully protected by tartan and case, Mairi felt as if she were taking an unknowing friend into a battle from which she might not return. But surely Sir James, with his esteem for harp music, wouldn't give Cridhe to the fire no matter how angry he was with Mairi—or would he?

Many a harp song had been composed on a battlefield, had spurred clansmen on to triumph. In olden days, no slave could touch a harp; it had been the pride of kings as different as Brian Boru and James I to play well. Bards held an honored place in chieftains' halls. *If I can get Cridhe to sing sweet enough, if I can charm the gentry before I play Fearchar's last song—if I can do that, Sir James may spare Cridhe whatever he does to me.*

Brigid, God of Life, help me this day!

A high-nosed English footman took the harp from Mairi while a maid led her to a small sitting room warmed by a brisk fire and brought tea and a tray of tempting food. Mairi was too nervous to eat more than a few spoonsful of crannachan but the hot tea took the sea chill from her bones and warmth from the fire melted stiffness from her fingers.

The maid, a yellow-haired lass with great blue eyes, smiled shyly at Mairi. "My grandfather had a harp but the minister wouldn't let him in the kirk till he gave it to burn along with my uncle's fiddle and my father's pipes. I remember the music, though. Most folk in service here in the castle hope to stand in the hall and hear you play."

"I'll think of you when I'm playing then," said Mairi, losing some of the fear that had turned her palms clammy. She smiled at the young woman who looked near her own age. "I'd liefer sing for island folk than for the gentry."

She'd almost said she'd play for the servants later in the kitchen if they'd like that, but with slashing pain, she remembered that Cridhe would no longer be hers after this afternoon—indeed, might not even exist. To destroy a harp as ancient as Cridhe seemed in a way worse than murder. Mairi prayed that at the crucial moment, Sir James's fondness for harp music would be stronger than wrath. If Cridhe perished, though, it would be a warrior's death, one to be remembered, honored, and lamented so long as there were Gaels on the islands.

When the haughty Sassenach footman came to escort her to what proved to be a large and elegant drawing room, Mairi held her head high and tried to move like the head of a clan, dignified and gracious, though she was dazzled by the glittering of the ladies' jewels, the plunging necks of their gowns, and the rustle of skirts so flounced and wide that the wearers couldn't get near each other. Several of the men wore kilt, plaid and Highland bonnet and gems flashed from the *skean dubh* or dirks stuck in their hose.

Lady Matheson greeted her kindly. This led Mairi to suspect that the mistress of the castle had not been warned by Sir James of Mairi's intentions. He welcomed Mairi with aloof courtesy that was vastly different from his usual pleasant manner.

"Will you have a chair, Mairi, or will that bench by the window serve better?"

"The bench, sir." By sitting with her side turned to the gathering, she could rest Cridhe on the bench without an indecent display of ankle. As she settled herself, taking the harp from the footman, Sir James spoke to his guests in English.

One of the kilted lairds laughed roughly, said something in a scornful voice, and shrugged, crossing his arms. A younger lady twisted a flashing ring on her finger. "I've told them you're a bard, Mairi, not a paid entertainer, and they should, as Highland gentry, remember that bards have ever been like Old Testament prophets, full of lamentations and accusations." Sir James paused, hard black eyes piercing her. "But mind you well: it's your choice whether your harp leaves here in your arms or as smoke up the chimney."

"I had thought, Sir James, that only parsons burned harps."

"I begin to think they did well, though for wrong reasons." He stepped back to sit in a large chair by his wife. "Play till you're weary or our guests start to fidget."

Mairi tuned the harp, using the ancient brass key and strummed, summoning Cridhe's memories, the spirits of all the harpers who had ever brought music from her strings. Like the bard who'd fashioned Cridhe from Irish black willow, Mairi sang of Cuchulain and Ossian, war songs to rouse valor, laments for fallen comrades, peace songs played after victory. There was the haunting song of the seals and a merry one composed of lilting bird calls which so excited Lady Matheson's white cat that it crouched by the harp as if waiting for lapwings and larks to fly out. Next came the swan's mournful tune; songs made by the Skye bard, Mairi nighean Alasdair Ruaidh; music of that Lewis man, Rory Dall, who'd taught his songs to Fearchar's grandfather; and a few fine melodies by that other blind Rory, the Irishman O'Caithain, who came to Scotland to vie with Highland harpers and who was not the least flattered when James VI of Scotland—England's James I—placed an approving hand on his shoulder, but said a far greater man, the O'Neill chieftain, had laid his hand on him. There was the lament for beheaded Charles Stuart, a medley of waulking tunes, David's lullaby, songs for the harvest and planting, and Fearchar's own poems.

Mairi sang to Cridhe more than to the gathering, pouring out her heart, for this was the last time she would hold her beloved harp, and unless Sir James relented, the last time, ever, Cridhe would sing. Cridhe seemed to know it. Her notes had never been more sweet and resonant; her strings responded, it seemed, almost before Mairi plucked them. *"Cruit mo cridhe . . ."* Harp of my heart.

Though she sang in Gaelic, there was no shuffle of feet, coughs or clearing of throats. These folk must admit the tenants they considered profitless encumbrances came from a world of music, of legends, of tales going back to the heroes. And now it was time.

Mairi slipped the plectrum into her plaid and rippled the strings in the old way with her fingernails, though her fingers were sore and cramped. This last time to play Cridhe, she wanted nothing between her hands and her harp.

Closing her eyes, Mairi invoked the spirits of the hearth, the Old Ones of the Stones, Brigid, Fearchar, and the God of Life, before words she had not planned sprang to her mouth. "Oh harp!" she cried in Gaelic. "In your last singing, tell your own story! Tell of your centuries and those who played you—for no one ever owned you!" The answering ran through Mairi's fingers to her lips.

I was made by the bard of Conn of the Hundred Battles;
Many a battle have I led; many a bright queen I have
praised; I have made glad many a royal feasting.
I have lamented heroes.

A Druid bore me to war against Julius Caesar.
I was at the court of Niall of the Nine Hostages
and with his great-grandson, St. Columba, when he
brought to Pictland the ever-living, ever-dying God.
Prizing me not when he meditated on a white book,
the saint gave me as a peace-gift to King Brude.
The Pict played me in his fortress, Craig Phadrig.
I dwelled with kings till I became the treasure
of Bjorn Cripplehand, bard to Norway's Magnus.
Dying, the Viking gave me to Leod, first Lord of Lewis.

Since then, I have sung only on this island,
only for Leod's children.

Figures of a great host vanished from beneath Mairi's eyelids,
visions of the harp inspiring warriors, delighting kings, attend-
ing coronations, funerals, christenings, and weddings. Drawing
in a long breath, Mairi began Cridhe's last song.

Oh Mary Mother, of the Black Sorrows!
I have seen townships swept, thatch pulled away,
picks stuck into walls, foundations pried up,
couple-trees split by axes, so that in a moment,
roof, rafters and walls crashed over the scattered
hearthfires. I have seen strong men bound like cattle
and their children wailing.

Once this island belonged to the clanna.
The chief was our father, our ceann-cinnidh;
he lived among us and was of us, our elder brother,
wisest, kindest, strongest to lead in battle and peace.
His rent was swords. The land belonged to all.
Cattle and sheep grazed at the shielings
And there was grain for all.

But now our chiefs have sold us, sold the land that was
their kinsmen's. They have sold us to strangers.
Sheep have scattered the warriors and destroyed their
homes. Lowlanders' sheep devour the land of our love.
Our fields lie untilled under bracken and heather;
I see our folk departing on the white-sailed ships.

Had we been roes, deer, sheep or bullocks, the lairds
would give us a value. Men are worth nothing. They
cannot be shot at like hares, blackcocks or grouse, nor
hunted for game, nor fished, nor clipped like fat
Cheviots.

But when wars begin, Highlanders will be wanted;
The empty glens will answer, "Let deer defend you,
and your hornless sheep!"

Yet some will endure between the rocks and the sea.
If you would be rid of us, you must break the stones,
you must sink the islands below the ocean.

One day will come justice. Isle men will take deer
from parks made of their fathers' fields; their sheep
and cattle will graze on the moorland and on the
flowery machair. Folk will bide safe in their homes.
There will be no one with power to cast them out.

This is the last song of Michael MacLeod,
the last singing of his harp.

There was silence. Drained, trembling, Mairi bowed her head
to her harp. In a moment, she must rise, give Cridhe into Sir
James's hands, and what would be, would be. But it had been a
brave song, a true song, and even after Cridhe burned, the words
would be sung through the islands. So long as Gaels had
tongues, they would keep their songs in spite of kirk and lairds.

She must be dreaming! That was pipe music! Rising above
angry or derisive English words, the pipes were playing the
MacLeod Salute to the Chief. She had only heard one piper who
could so weave in the grace notes.

Looking up, Mairi stared at Iain. He wore the MacDonald
tartan, and beside him was David. Iain finished the Salute and
bowed gravely to her before he turned to the gaping company.
He spoke in English. In the amazement that followed whatever
he'd said, he came to Mairi and raised her to her feet.

"I told them they could boast to their grandchildren of having
heard Mairi of the Isles. And I told them you will be my wife."

Mairi's head swam. He'd come to protect her. In spite of his
hurt and anger, he had placed himself between her and these
gentry. Sir James approached and grasped Iain's hand. "That

324

was rare piping, Major MacDonald—and I am glad that after all you accepted my invitation."

Iain shrugged. "At the last, I couldn't keep away," he said with a rueful smile at Mairi.

The laird turned to her. "I must felicitate with you on your marriage, but there is still the matter of your forfeit. Give me the harp, Mairi MacLeod."

Numbly, she lifted Cridhe, held her to her breast in a futile protective impulse, and then put the harp into Matheson's grasp. The fire was blazing. Even tough black willow wood would burn swiftly when it was far more than a thousand years old.

Sir James didn't stride toward the fireplace. Instead, he placed the harp in Iain's hands. "This is a wedding gift, my friend. I hope I may be invited to the feast. The two of you should beget a line of notable harpers and pipers. And now it is time we had some refreshment."

Iain had ridden with David in front of him, leading a horse for Mairi. They journeyed home together while David and a securely wrapped Cridhe traveled on *An Clanna*. Only Colonel Gordon had angrily left the room before savories and wine were served. Lady Dunmore, with Iain translating, emphasized that she had fostered the making of fine tweeds on Harris, and her husband said it was not his fault that kelp prices had fallen so low. Lord MacDonald, fourth Baron of the Isles, a troubled, handsome man, praised Mairi's singing and drank her to her health and happy marriage.

"I have fed my tenants till I am fair bankrupt, Mistress Mairi," he said in Gaelic. "When you hear of what my creditors will do on my lands when I can no longer fend them off, I pray that you will feel for me as well as for my people."

"I do feel for you, my lord. Almost alone, you have been a true ceann-cinnidh. But you will not starve nor lack a roof to your head."

His broad shoulders hunched. "That would almost be easier, I think, than not being able to protect my folk."

Now, as she rode along with Iain, holding to the saddle, for she was unaccustomed to horses, Mairi cast side-glances at Iain but dared not speak till his eyes intercepted hers. "I am obliged to you, Iain. I think if you had not been there with your pipes, Cridhe would be ashes."

He gave her a grim smile. "I doubt it. Sir James confided to me that it would be a blasphemous soul indeed who would destroy a harp with such a lineage."

"You are still angry with me."

He let out an exasperated breath. "What man wouldn't be, to see his beloved so risk herself, he knowing full well that she will always be first for her people and only then, for him?" He took her horse's reins and drew close alongside, circling her with his free arm, finding her mouth. "I meant only to protect you today. But when you played Cridhe's story and the lament—I knew, Mairi, that you and your songs cannot, should not, be ruled by any man. If you will live with me in love, I will count myself the luckiest of men."

She clung to him. And then he tethered the horses and spread his cloak on the heather.

Annie and her husband were invited from Inverness for the wedding. Arthur Mitchell was a dark, quiet, frank-faced man with a twinkle in his brown eyes and a glow of prideful love whenever he looked at Annie. The *North Star* crew was back from the fishing in time for the wedding and when Magnus stopped for their catch, he stayed on for the ceremony. He was glad to wish Annie happy in her marriage and he and Arthur took to each other. The way Magnus smiled at Eileen, it was clear that he saw through new eyes that she was fifteen and very beautiful with hair that had never darkened, but shimmered like the moon. Sir James had fetched his own chaplain who did not balk at holding the service in the open air for there was not room for the assembly in any of the houses.

So it was under the sky with birds calling and the distant crash of the waves in their ears that Iain and Mairi stood before the company and their little son, pledging themselves forever. When Iain put his mother's ring on Mairi's finger and bent to kiss her, there was a stifled sound from Gran.

She was the first to embrace and bless them. While Iain was surrounded, she drew Mairi aside. "Did you see him, love?"

"Who?"

"Fearchar. My Michael."

"Oh, Gran—"

Rosanna MacLeod lifted her hand. "Hush, lassie, don't fear. He came to see you wedded, he was at my side, and joyful. But I remembered then that he died when our hut burned." Tears glistened in the bright blue eyes but Gran was smiling. "Fearchar let me think he was at the fishing till I could bear the truth—and this day I can do that, Mairi. Now go to your feast and know you have your grandfather's blessing."

As if nothing had happened save a happy wedding, Gran served around her heather ale while nipping herself at the aged whiskey Iain supplied along with delicacies that made this the grandest feast in memory. After the banquet, served from waulking tables covered with linen sheets, Tam played his pipes and Lucas his fiddle while Iain led Mairi in the old Lewis Bridal Dance while the others lustily sang.

> Red her lips as rowans are, bright her eyes as any star,
> Fairest of them all by far is our darling Mairi . . .

Iain smiled down at her. "Now how do you suppose whoever made up that song a long time ago could know enough to use your name?"

"It's a common name in the Islands."

He held her closer. "It may be common, but you, my love, are not!"

"Indeed, no," she teased, laughing. "For do I not have you for my husband?"

They danced with other partners then, and Mairi, when stopping to rest, sounded her joy on Cridhe. She could feel her grandfather's presence and knew he rejoiced with her.

By the time Sir James danced nimbly between his sword crossed with Iain's, it was growing dark. People dispersed to their houses, some needing a supporting arm. Even Morag had caught up her skirts and danced a fast jig with Andrew. When Sir James reluctantly started home, carrying with him Gran's last jug of ale, Eileen strolled off with Magnus while Tam swung David to his shoulders, grinned a good night, and went to Andrew and Morag's house.

Gran knelt to smoor the fire as she had done so many times. "The Sacred Three to save, to shield, surround the hearth . . ."

When she finished, she kissed both Iain and Mairi, drank to them with a final draught of whiskey, and left them together. Only Cridhe, wrapped in her plaid, saw them go into each other's arms and find their marriage bed.

Afterword

What came after:

When the lairds tried to raise regiments for the Crimean War, people baaed at them like sheep and told them to let sheep wear red coats and fight for them. The Clearances caused such bitterness that island folk no longer respected their lairds or the churchmen and authorities who supported them. When those who were children during the Clearances came of age, they began to demand back the lands taken from their forebears to be turned into sheepwalks and deer parks.

In 1887, the famous Park Deer Raid took place on Lewis where protesters killed two hundred deer and held a barbecue (with a stately old man saying grace over the meat). Several journalists were invited. Though the ringleaders were arrested, there was such popular support that they were let off.

On Skye, dispossessed tenants turned their animals into the landlord's pastures and fought the constables at The Battle of the Braes. There was such public outcry that the rioters were only fined, and several of their supporters were elected to Parliament. The government, after a hundred years of atrocities in the Highlands and Islands, was compelled to investigate.

The result was Lord Napier's report and the Crofter's Act of 1886, remarkable legislation for its day, that set an independent body to assess rents, gave tenure to crofters so long as their rent was paid, and did away with the worst inequities. There was still not land enough and anger smoldered against the landlords who maintained huge, vastly profitable deer parks while their tenants were not even allowed to prevent the deer from devouring their crops, or keep a dog to run them off.

The final assault on the Island of Harris came with Lord Leverhulme's well-meant plans to turn the crofters into productive fisherfolk and processors employed by him. Buying the island from Matheson's widow, he struggled with returned soldiers from World War I who felt they had a right to a croft and didn't want to give up that diversified if inefficient life for much better pay and a regimented existence.

Leverhulme, after a few years, turned much of Lewis back to the people and took himself to Harris in the hope that folk there were more progressive. He was a good man but failed to understand the Hebridean nature and the tremendous love and need of the people for a bit of land. When he died in 1925, the Long Island of Lewis-Harris was sold off to several proprietors, though the crofters, of course, now had secure tenure.

The islands remain sparsely populated and comparatively uninvaded by tourists though a bus load of day-trippers from the mainland may pull up at Callanish or a van of bird-watchers park above a beach. Few crofters make their whole living from their lands; many do some fishing or have other jobs. Men more often than women run the looms that create the renowned Harris tweeds. The islanders have survived, and so have their songs and deepest ways of life.

Glossary

Athole Brose. *Mix half a pound of oatmeal with half a pound of honey and enough water to make a thick paste. Then slowly add two pints of whiskey and stir briskly till mixture foams. Bottle and cork tightly.*

Bannock. *A flat bread cooked on a griddle.*

Beasts of Holm. *The treacherous rocks guarding Stornoway Harbor; caused many shipwrecks.*

Beltane. *May 1, the ancient Celtic festival that marked the coming of summer. Hearth fires were extinguished. Sacred fires were built to honor Bel, the sun god, and cattle were driven between them to protect them from disease. Hearth fires were then relit from this purifying flame.*

Brian Boru (941–1014). *The king of Munster who united Ireland and made it so safe that a beautiful young woman, richly bejeweled, could travel without harm from one end to the other. In Boru's old age, the Norse in Ireland rose against him. He defeated them at Clontarf near Dublin but was killed shortly after in his tent.*

Brigid, Brigit, Brid, Brighde. *The ancient Celtic mother goddess who was patroness of learning, art, and poetry. Each year on February 1 she restored life to the dead winter and dipped her hand in the sea to warm it. Transformed into Saint Brigid and the nurse of Jesus, she was especially revered in Ireland and Scotland where mothers besought her help during childbirth.*

Broch. *Defensive towers found throughout the Hebrides, built by Picts or earlier folk. People took shelter in brochs from raids but did not live within them on a regular basis.*

Callanish. *Bronze Age stones ranking with Stonehenge and Avebury in interest. A circle of flattened megaliths that has the tallest stone in the center; from the center, four aisles lead to the outer boundaries of the circle. Sir James Matheson had the peat cleared away from much of the site.*

Carnaptious. *Capricious, touchy.*

Cas-chrom. *"Crooked foot," a foot-plow. The six-foot shaft of oak or ash had a bent lower end, or head, about two-and-a-half feet long with a six-inch metal tip. A wooden peg was fixed on the right side of the head. The ploughman set his foot on the peg and drove the head into the ground with two jerks. The cas-chrom could turn up boulders weighing two hundred pounds. Twelve men could dig an acre in a day. Because of the rocky soil, this implement worked better than a regular plow.*

Ceann-cinnidh. *The head of the clan.*

Ceilidh. *An informal party when neighbors gathered for an evening of music, stories, riddles, and dancing.*

Cheviot. *A breed of sheep that could withstand the Island and Highland winters.*

Chiel. *A youth.*

Clanna. *Children; an extended family or clan.*

Cogg. *A wooden bucket.*

Conn of the Hundred Battles. *The semi-legendary High King of Ulster who ruled from Tara circa* A.D. *125; ancestor of the Mac-Donalds.*

Crannachan. *A dessert of toasted oatmeal, honey, and whipped cream.*

Croft, crofter. *A small individual holding of land, seldom more than seven acres, and the person who rents or owns it. Pasture was usually shared by a township.*

Crotal. *A lichen that yields a rust-brown dye; not used for fishermen's clothing since it was believed crotal came from the rocks and would try to return to them.*

Croman. *A hoe.*

Crowdie. *A soft white cheese.*

Cuchulain. *The greatest of the Celtic heroes whose feats were celebrated in bardic poems called the Ulster Cycle.*

Culloden. *A battle in 1746 when Bonnie Prince Charlie, who, as a Stewart, had a claim to the English throne as well as that of Scotland, was defeated by the English. Many harsh laws were enacted to break the clans and insure that there would be no more uprisings against England.*

Dotterel. *A plover, a shorebird with white eyestripes, chestnut lower breast and black belly; chief call is a sweet trill, wit-a-wee, wit-a-wee, wit-a-wee.*

Drystone. *Stone walls laid up without mortar.*

Dulse. *Seaweed with flat brown leaves; nutritious but must be simmered for five hours.*

Carrageen. *Seaweed that when dried and powdered makes good pudding, especially tasty made with milk and dried fruit.*

Eelgrass. *Used for bedding.*

Excise man. *A tax collector; much hated by distillers and smugglers of whiskey.*

Fasgalan. *An entryway to a hut that holds the quern and a bench with milking vessels.*

Fash. *To worry, fret.*

Finnan Haddie. *Haddock smoked over a peat fire.*

Gille. *A follower or manservant.*

Gormless. *Brainless, lacking in initiative.*

Greenshank. *A long-legged wading bird of moors and bogs that has slightly upcurved bill and olive-green legs.*

Gruamach. *Grouchy.*

Guillemot. *A short-necked, short-tailed diving seabird. The most common of the auks, breeds in colonies in inaccessible cliff ledges.*

Kittiwake. *A white gull with gray wings tipped with black. Graceful, buoyant flight. At breeding time, cries kitt-ee-wayke.*

Lazybeds. *Planting beds from three to eight feet wide, often built on rocks or steep hillsides. Soil may be dug to heap on the rocks, or, where there is no soil, sand is carried from the beach and layered with seaweed. Where necessary, rock walls hold the planting mixture in place.*

Lochan. *A little lake.*

Long Isle. *The Outer Hebrides, consisting of Lewis and Harris, North and South Uist, and Barra. These islands form an almost continuous chain; Lewis and Harris are actually the same land mass.*

James I of England, James VI of Scotland. *The son of Mary Stewart, the ill-fated Queen of Scots who was beheaded at the order of Queen Elizabeth I. Ironically, James inherited the English throne since Elizabeth had no closer heirs.*

Kelp. *Seaweed that could be dried and used for fertilizer; brought a brief prosperity to the Islands.*

Kelpie. *A water horse, a supernatural creature that would carry off and drown the unwary.*

M'eudail. *My darling.*

Machair. *A flowery meadow on soil enriched with fine-ground shells; stretching between the beach and other land on the west side of some islands, it is rich pasture.*

Mairi nighean Alasdair Ruaidh. *Mairi of the Isles; a seventeenth-century bard who composed poems in the ancient manner. Because she sang of freedom, she was forbidden by the authorities to make her songs within or without the threshold. She therefore composed her poems while standing on the threshold.*

Marram grass. *Coarse, deep green grass that binds the sand and shields the machair from the seawind.*

Mickle. *Much.*

Minch. *The body of water between the Long Island, or Outer Hebrides, and the mainland and Inner Hebrides.*

335

Muckle-mouth. *Big mouth.*

Niall of the Nine Hostages. *The Irish king of about* A.D. *358 who invaded Wales and was killed on a raid into Gaul. He was the ancestor of the O'Neill kings of Ireland. During the reign of Niall's son, St. Patrick came to convert Ireland.*

Papish. *Catholic.*

Peat. *A fuel of partially carbonized plants that decayed under water; still the common fuel of Ireland and the Hebrides.*

Peerie. *Pict or fairy. Picts were mysterious folk who inhabited and ruled the Highlands and Islands, successfully repelling the Romans. When the Scots crossed from Ireland, after some fighting they married into the royal house of the Picts and the Picts were absorbed.*

Planticrue. *A round stone-walled planting bed for kale; filled with sand and decaying seaweed.*

Quern. *A grinding stone.*

Rowan. *A tree of the rose family with small bright red berries.*

Retting. *Soaking flax plants until the stem and stalks rot and can be separated from the fiber, which is then spun into linen thread.*

Saint Columba. *The Irish missionary who, in* A.D. *560, came to the Hebridean island of Iona where he founded a monastery. From this former Druid stronghold, he launched his efforts to convert the Picts and Scots (Irish) on the mainland. The monastery has been restored, and most of the island is now administered by the National Trust for Scotland. Many Scottish, Irish, and Norwegian kings were buried here, including the Duncan slain by Macbeth.*

Samhain. *November 1, when burial mounds opened and spirits roamed; marked the beginning of winter and was the Celtish New Year.*

Sea campion. *A low-growing, white-petaled flower that grows in patches along the Island coast.*

Selkie. *A seal. Some Island families claim descent from seals.*

Shag. *A large, dark diving sea bird; a type of cormorant with a stout, yellow hooked bill. Breeds in colonies on rocky cliffs.*

Shielings. *The huts in summer pastures where cattle and sheep were taken in the spring. On Lewis, the huts were stone, shaped like beehives. Young women often had charge of the herds, the milking, and the making of cheese and butter.*

Silverweed. *A yellow-flowered plant with an edible root.*

Skerry. *An island.*

Slainte! *A toast: To your health! Here's to you!*

Smoor. *To prepare the hearth for the night, covering the coals with ashes and removing large peats to save for the next day.*

Stook. *A stack. Also, to stack sheaves, usually eight of them, in a conical stack.*

Taraisgear. *An iron tool for cutting peat.*

Tormentil. *A low-growing flower with yellow petals; from the roots and leaves a brew was made that helped women to give birth with less pain.*

Torquil the Viking. *The first of the MacLeod chieftains of Lewis and the son of Leod, or Liotolf, a mid–twelfth century chief.*

Uisge-beatha. *Water of life; whiskey.*

Waulk. *The process of cleansing woven wool fabric of oil and thickening it. The washed, wet material was stretched across a ribbed board or a frame of wattles which could be set on a table or outside on the grass. Indoors, working in rhythm with their songs, four to fourteen women rubbed, pushed and stretched the web back and forth across the board. Outside, they sat on straw bundles and worked the cloth with their bare feet. There were many waulking songs.*

Wheatear. *A thrush-like bird of the moors with black wings, white rump and a pale brown breast.*

Whin. *A spiny, evergreen shrub with yellow flowers.*